a novel by
BARNEY LEASON

With consummate insight and shocking candor, Barney Leason weaves yet another scandalous tale of sexual obsession and the shameless pleasures of those who live only to indulge their insatiable passions.

Veteran reporter Barney Leason is no newcomer to the elite society of the Beautiful People who have been brilliantly portrayed in his previous Pinnacle bestsellers, Rodeo Drive and Scandals. As a writer, roving correspondent in Europe, and West Coast bureau chief for Look magazine, Leason has seen, heard, and once again, tells it all.

"Barney Leason knows the fashion business from the inside . . . with all its glamorous and cunning characters. He also knows the fashion press. Best of all, he knows how to weave a yarn about the Beautiful People, their wiles and their wickedness."

> —James Brady
> former publisher of *Women's Wear Daily*
> and author of *The Press Lord.*

"Barney Leason has succeeded in bundling the boudoir aerobics he so graphically described in *Rodeo Drive* with the not so haute couture behavior behind the scenes of legendary Paris fashion houses into a tidy package for *Passions.*"

> —Vidal Sassoon

"Barney Leason has the ability to make us forget everyone we ever knew and take on his people and their lives as part of our own . . ."

> —Mr. Blackwell.

Other Pinnacle Titles by Barney Leason:

RODEO DRIVE
SCANDALS

Passions

BARNEY LEASON

PINNACLE BOOKS **NEW YORK**

PASSIONS

An original Pinnacle Books edition, published for the first time anywhere.

First printing, September 1982

ISBN: 0-523-41207-X

Cover Photo by Cosimo

Location: Russian Tea Room

Gown by Criscione

Fur by Ben Kahn

Printed in the United States of America

PINNACLE BOOKS, INC.
1430 Broadway
New York, New York 10018

To Jay Allen,
who read this book first.

CHAPTER

ONE

The skies were clouding over and as Kelly entered the back door of the Ritz Hotel he heard a rumble of thunder from the northeast. The first rain, big drops of it, splattered on the sidewalk.

Inside, the bar was empty, André, gloomiest of bartenders, stood behind his polished wood, arms folded, staring at nothing. When he saw Kelly he came slowly to life.

"Ah, good evening, Monsieur Kelly."

"Not evening yet, André." He ordered a beer. André served it with a flourish. Kelly tasted, then drained the glass. "Thirsty," he explained. "Better give me another, please."

Kelly took off his trench coat and put it on a nearby chair, then propped himself comfortably on the bar. He lit a Gauloise cigarette and sipped the second beer. He sighed.

"André, have you ever considered that there is a great deal of truth in a simple glass of beer?"

André shrugged and stared past Kelly toward the windows. "All beer is true, Monsieur Kelly."

"André, did you ever know Hemingway? They say when he was in Paris he used to hang out here in the back bar of the Ritz."

"No, monsieur." André was not interested. "Who is it?"

1

"An American. A man with a mustache, sometimes a beard. He used to write books, fight bulls, go to wars. He had balls—*cajones*, they call them in Spanish."

"No, in truth, I never knew this man."

Kelly smiled. Clever André. But why should André be familiar with Hemingway? André was not a member of the French Academy after all. It didn't matter. The back bar at the Ritz was Kelly's favorite place and conveniently close to the offices of his newspaper, the *Retailers Apparel Guide*, known as the *RAG* in most circles within and outside the fashion industry. People who came to the Ritz to drink needed nothing, nobody, only the brass rail and the wood. Generations of expatriates had given the joint its reputation and they had all been self-sufficient people, tough, cynical, and the world never took them by surprise.

"But Monsieur Kelly," André observed, as if to soothe him, "you too are a writer."

"Yes. But a journalist, André. I don't write books. There's a difference."

"Words, words," André said.

"There's a big difference, André."

It was five-thirty now and outside it had begun to rain in earnest. Steam rose from the sidewalk. Kelly ordered another beer.

"Just you and me, André," he remarked.

"*Oui. Très romantique*," André drawled. "Still, monsieur, the rain will break up the heat."

Tomorrow would be August first, the beginning of the cruelest month.

"Have you seen Perex lately?" Kelly asked.

André shook his head and began humming to himself.

Kelly had first met Rafael Trujillo Perex about six months before in Geneva at the Polish Bridge Club, a dusty and nondescript gathering place of refugees, journalists, and spies not far from the main railroad station. Sometimes, people actually did play bridge there. Now, whenever Perex was in Paris on business he always looked for Kelly at the Ritz.

"Monsieur Kelly," André asked, "is it true that Monsieur Perex was married to the daughter of your president?"

"Yep. They got divorced about three years ago."

"She is a very good-looking woman, Monsieur Kelly. A blond."

"Yeah. She's beautiful, André, except she's a fruit-cake, according to Perex. And he couldn't stand the president. That's when he moved to Switzerland and started up the Mount Vernon Trust, that investment thing of his. But don't worry about Perex, André—he's got dames coming out of the walls."

André's eyes lit up appreciatively. "He is what you call a . . ."

"A big cocksman, that's what we call it."

Perex, being unmarried now, did much better in that field than Kelly. There could be no doubt a whole branch of the female species would consider the Cuban misfit an elegant smoothie. Although Kelly did not nec-essarily believe it, Perex claimed he had to have a woman every day or he became nervous and irritable. He owned a house in Geneva which he said had once belonged or been lent to Voltaire and it was plentifully stocked with "gash," as Perex fondly referred to his female houseguests.

"One thing, André, I wouldn't leave my daughter alone with him, if I had a daughter."

André smiled, but he did not know Perex's full story.

In a manner of speaking, Perex seemed to be taking his revenge on womankind for his treatment at the hands of Westerley Washburn Perex. She was a spoiled and wanton only child, Perex said, whose favorite joke had been to describe Perex to her friends, and in his hearing, as her Cuban heel, and she made a mockery of his native Spanish. She was also, Perex hinted, a woman of unusual desires. Perex had never gotten along with her father, President George Washburn, a thick-skinned and insensitive political animal who resented Westerley's marriage from the first. Washburn was harder on Perex than his daughter—to Washburn the "Cuban heel" was a "greasy spic" of absolutely no political use since most of the Cubans in the country didn't have the right to vote.

"And Monsieur Kelly," André asked next, "how is the wonderful old lady, Madame Zouzou Mordaunt?"

Kelly smiled. "Ah, there's a question. I'm going over to the Maison Mordaunt tonight. Zouzou invited me, as usual—she and Victor are putting the finishing touches on their fall-winter collection. Mordaunt shows tomorrow morning." He groaned lightly. "André, it's been nonstop. Thank God we're at the end of Couture Week."

Yes, at lunchtime Saturday it would be all over—until next time.

"And then?"

"Then I want to take some time off. It's been a rough one, André. You know I have to write a story on every goddamn fashion collection in Paris. Then the parties, the late nights. Jesus. Anyway, I've got to wait for my secretary to get back. She left today for the mountains."

"You and Madame Maryjane will travel to the Riviera?"

"Maybe me," Kelly said shortly. That was another good question. "Not Madame Maryjane. She's already left."

"Ah?" André's eyebrows lifted. "Madame Maryjane will meet you there?"

"Possibly, possibly."

The truth was Kelly had seen little of her in the past week and sometime yesterday she had packed and left town. That was the bold truth of it. Should he worry? No. This was by no means the first time it had happened. When Maryjane grew restive, when the urge to hit the road struck her, she traveled far and fast. Money was of no consequence. Her father, the redoubtable cowpoke and now oil millionaire, Claud "C.T." Trout, shipped money to Paris on a regular basis and Maryjane always kept a bundle of foreign currencies at the ready.

She had paused long enough to write him a note, as was her habit, but gave only the barest clue as to her intentions. "Jack," she had scribbled on a piece of her monogrammed notepaper, "this is really it. I've had it with you and the *RAG* and that fucking old bag. I'm going somewhere for a quickie."

Old bag? Obviously, she meant Zouzou Mordaunt. Quickie? Was she referring to divorce? She had never threatened that before. The problem was Maryjane didn't understand—she couldn't comprehend the pressure of his daily deadline, especially during fashion week, or the continual hard work that went into making the *RAG* such a powerful force in international fashion—how much stroking, for example, was required to keep a friend like Zouzou Mordaunt, leading couturière, sweet and happy.

Should he worry? No, he should not worry.

By 6:00 P.M., rain-soaked patrons began to hustle into the bar, and André was drawn away from their conversation. It was a few moments before Kelly could catch his attention again.

"One more, André. I'll be right back. Going for a leak." He glanced through the revolving door. Rain was beating on the sidewalk. "Christ, I'll be here for the duration."

"You will dine in the restaurant, Monsieur Kelly? Will I make a reservation for you?"

"Not on your life, André. It's too goddamn expensive."

"Perhaps Mr. Perex will arrive and be your host." André snickered slyly. It was an unkind cut. Andre knew that when Rafe Perex was in town he picked up all the tabs. His expense account was limitless, and he seemed to have a special directive to shower as much of it as possible on Jack Kelly of the *RAG*.

Perex was standing in front of the mirror in the men's room combing his slick black hair. When he saw Kelly, his eyes jumped and he smiled broadly. Perex's face was round and tanned. His white teeth flashed like white rice in a bowl of brown refried beans.

"Caramba! Jack, my dear, this rain is a bitch. I have gotten my trousers wet."

"Rafe—we were just talking about you."

"We?"

"André and me."

"You discuss *me* with a bartender?" Perex cried haughtily. "Jack . . ."

"Nothing specific, Rafe." He knew better than to be concerned by Perex's snobbery. "So you're back in Paris?"

"Where else, Monsieur Reporter?" Perex winked teasingly. "Come, shake the dew off your lily and let us have a drink, my dear."

Perex looked splendid, as if he had just stepped out of an exclusive men's-store window. His suit was chalk-striped gray and with it he was wearing a stiff white shirt and a figured black silk tie. Kelly felt almost grimy beside him as Perex put his brown felt hat, a trilby, down on the bar and folded his hands expectantly before him. He wore a gold signet ring on the little finger of his left hand. A heavy gold Rolex watch hung off his wrist.

"André"—Perex announced himself airily—"for me a scotch and soda. Another beer for my friend." André shot him a surly smile. "Fag?" Perex asked, opening his gold Tiffany cigarette case.

Automatically, Kelly quipped, "No, are you?"

This was a sort of joke they had. Absentmindedly, but also sometimes pointedly to remind people of his Oxford education, Perex often slipped into English slang expressions. Nonetheless, he frowned, took a Benson & Hedges out of the case and lit it with a small gold lighter. He snapped the lighter again for Kelly's Gauloise, the strong French cigarette that Perex detested.

"And how is your beautiful Texan, Jack?"

Kelly shrugged. "She's off—on another trip."

Perex's eyebrows waggled. His eyes became more inquisitive than André's.

"So soon? I thought she was away only last month. Well, dear boy, so you're batching it again, are you?" He put his hand on Kelly's forearm. "Shall we go out after a bit of fluff, dear boy? No, no. I know better than to ask. So pure, Jack, so faithful." Kelly nodded absently and Perex joggled the arm. "You're missing her, aren't you?"

"She only left yesterday. What's this you say about fluff?"

Perex gasped exagerratedly. "Heavens to Betsy!" He

shook his head violently. "Never, my dear, I would not take the responsibility. I respect your Texan too much. Besides, Jack, you are not an adventurer like me."

"I'm not so sure, Rafe. Maybe I should be. I don't think *she* gives a good shit for me. She takes off at the drop of a hat. Wouldn't that make you wonder?"

"Tut, tut, dear boy," Perex admonished him carelessly, "better than being married to a nymphomaniac."

"Westerley?" He hadn't heard that dimension of the Washburn story.

"Of course," Perex said acidly. "The whole family is corrupt."

Yet Perex was still associated with the Washburn family interests. He had his investment firm, of course, the Mount Vernon Trust, but it was obvious to Kelly that Perex also served in a shadowy role as European watchdog for Amalgamated Freight Inc., a conglomerate upon which the Washburn fortune was based. It was due to this vague role that Kelly had met Perex in the first place, and within hours of his first visit to Amalgamated Freight's European headquarters—he'd traveled to Geneva in search of background and facts relevant to his investigation of his blockbuster story COSMETICS LOVENEST MURDER SHOCKER. Such a lurid piece as the headline indicated might have seemed out of place in a daily fashion newspaper, but cosmetics, that vital ingredient of the fashion industry, was the link. The question was, as he put it to Perex that very night at the Polish Bridge Club, whether a certain Hans Igl, found stabbed and garroted in Paris, had or had not been employed by AmFreight's European cosmetics subsidiary. Perex said no.

Washburn's political enemies had often laid a charge of corruption at the door of his administration. But the whole family? And even if Westerley Washburn was a nymphomaniac, which he doubted, given Perex's talent for exaggeration, it didn't signify that she was also corrupt. "I'm surprised to hear you say that, Rafe."

"Perhaps, my dear," Perex said bitterly. "You know,

when my family firm was merged with AmFreight in Florida, I received only a small slice of equity."

"Yes, I remember you telling me that."

The Perex family had fled Cuba in the late fifties, bringing their business with them—a firm called Castro Oils, a manufacturer of suntan products. It seemed a slightly ironic name, in the light of political events, but Perex had pointed out huffily that Castro was a very common name. In any event, Castro Oils had disappeared into the maze of AmFreight's brand names some six years before.

"So Washburn *is* as big a crook as everybody says?"

"I used to believe the man was the soul of honesty, Jack."

"That's what you told me in Geneva," Kelly growled. "Remember: Cosmetics Lovenest Murder . . ."

Perex scowled. "Could I forget? That fucking story gave me a lot of trouble, Jack. It still does. But you could never confirm anything, could you?" There was some satisfaction in his voice.

"Thanks to you, buddy boy," Kelly said. "It all hinged on Igl. He made the cosmetics connection—without that, it wasn't any story for us."

"And you couldn't make the connection."

"That's right and I got my ass burned. That's when they shot the story down in New York."

Perex nodded gloomily, as if to say Kelly's story was the least of his concerns. "I curse the day I met Westerley Washburn," he mused. "It was at a pool party in Palm Beach. We were drawn together by ultraviolet block. Westerley is very fair-skinned. She thought at first I was a black, but it was merely the work of Castro Oil. We fell in love. But it was a completely sexual love, you see. The point is, my dear, that it was on Westerley's say-so that AmFreight bought my family business. Thusly was I drawn into the Washburn web and now they are cheating me out of everything. You realize Washburn never gave me any kind of a golden handshake for agreeing to the divorce?"

Kelly nodded hesitantly. "But isn't that all water under the bridge now, Rafe?"

"Sometimes I think they will have me killed."

"Killed for what?" Often Perex could not be taken very seriously.

"Merely for being. That is why I carry a pistol now." Perex patted his chest, then exclaimed, "Shit! I have forgotten it."

André was listening in, smiling sadly. Kelly winked at him.

"Is it so dangerous, marrying a president's daughter, Rafe?"

"It could be, if you know too much. But I am a brave man, my dear. We Cubans are outstandingly brave." Perex raised his head proudly, staring at Kelly. He smoothed his black hair and straightened his tie.

André nodded agreement. "Fidel Castro is a very brave man, Monsieur Perex."

Perex seemed to jump several inches off the floor. His eyes glittered angrily. "So they say, *mon vieux*," he drawled insultingly. "André, you are dismissed. Go to the other end of the bar. *Là!*" He pointed and Andre morosely slid away. Perex then very deliberately lit another cigarette and whispered, "You are familiar with this drug—Grovival—*mon cher*?"

"Familiar with it? For Christ's sake, I wrote about it, didn't I? That's what the whole story was all about. Don't you remember? I can quote it verbatim: Hans Igl reportedly was clutching in his dead hand a gummy pill called Grovival, identified by Parisian authorities as a newly discovered youth elixir. . . . Does this signify that Igl's employer, AmFreight, controlled by the Washburn family, is engaged in a head-on confrontation with French cosmetics interests in a battle of the international conglomerates? And so on. Shit!"

Perex waved his hand. "Jack, that was six months ago. We want Grovival and we want it very badly."

Kelly's irritation increased. "Who's we?"

"AmFreight, naturally."

"Who you *don't* work for—remember?"

"Correct," Perex said slyly, "for whom I do not work." He pursed his full lips. "The problem now seems to be that the French want Grovival too, and they feel they have some sort of mandate over that pismire country of its origin, Mangrovia, and simply because Mangrovia was once upon a time a French colony." Perex paused, smiling enigmatically. "Your dear friend, Madame Mordaunt, is mad to gain control of Grovival."

Kelly smiled too. "Zouzou's already got it. She claims she uses it every day and that it makes her young."

"Silly old cow," Perex jeered and spat. "In what form, do you know? Pills or injections? She could be risking her life. An old peasant woman in Switzerland broke out in giant warts. . . . She was a guinea pig, I'm told."

Kelly snorted. "You amaze me. If that's so, why is it such a hot item? What do you want with it?"

Perex slowly lifted his scotch and soda, then drew thoughtfully on his cigarette. Leaning toward Kelly, he whispered, "Jack, *mon ami,* not *me.* They! They want it because it has properties which are evidently quite astonishing. It is said that Grovival not only rejuvenates but that the stout men of Mangrovia have the longest dollywhackers in all of Africa, if not the world. Do you see the implications? You see why Madame Mordaunt is so eager to have it as a cosmetics product?"

Kelly nodded reluctantly. There was a certain logic to it. Mordaunt perfume, lotions, cologne, body balms—numbered One, Two, Three, and Four—were crucial money-makers for the House of Mordaunt. Fashion was important, true, for it popularized the name on which Mordaunt One to Four were sold, but it had often been said that without the ancillary perfumes and so on, even the most brilliant of Parisian couture houses would go bust.

Craftily, Kelly chuckled, for in Perex's words he could foresee the resurrection of his Lovenest Murder blockbuster—and his vindication. He kept his elation at bay. "This whole Grovival thing is even more fucked-up than I thought. . . . Maybe they were right to kill it. Who's going to believe such a load of bullshit?"

Perex drew back, glaring. "Really? Think about it. Mangrovia is the only known source for the vegetable root, i.e., Grovival. You cannot see a struggle developing between Washington and Paris over African spheres of influence?"

"Bullshit, Rafe," Kelly scoffed. "A country covered in giant warts?"

"Bloody hell, Jack! Not invariably. Warts may be merely a side effect, or a one-in-a-million chance. I tell you it has been established—the milk of the root is used in puberty rites in Mangrovia. It has to be very carefully refined and those crazy natives know how to do it."

"And what effect, may I ask, does it have on women?"

Perex smirked. "It stimulates incredible sexual appetite. Don't you see, if carefully used, in small measurements, for salves and such, it could be a powerful aphrodisiac, a genital stimulant? It would stretch the pleasure principle. And," he crowed, unmindful now of nosy André, "it is damned good for the skin, my dear!"

"Maybe. But it sounds like quackery to me."

"Think what you like," Perex cried. "You do not see the forest for the trees. People would come from all over the world to visit Grovival clinics. It could be a major, very major cosmetics development."

"Have you tried it?"

Perex nodded shyly. "A little."

"Did it work?"

"Not yet. But that's beside the point, Jack. He who wants Grovival must control the West African state of Mangrovia, a leftist, Marxist-oriented swamp of a country. Here we clash with French interests."

"But," Kelly pointed out, "the population *is* French. Convicts inbred with blacks."

"Also British convicts, Jack," Perex said calmly. "Some did not make it all the way to Australia, you know."

"All the worse. A mishmash country."

"With no racial hostility, *mon cher.*"

"Murderers, pirates, slave traders . . ."

"Not all of them, Jack," Perex said severely.

Kelly allowed his annoyance to show. "Why do you keep telling me things I already know? You screwed my story—and now you're telling me I was on the button. I'm really pissed off. AmFreight raised hell in New York. . . ."

Perex nodded, smiling complacently. "And your father raised hell with you. No, my dear, it is not easy being the boss's son."

"The publisher's son—that's even worse."

"I can tell you it was that rascal, President Washburn himself, who gave the order for your boss to come down on you. Isn't that nice to know?"

"Very flattering, Rafe," he said dryly. "I can say it again—you certainly seem to know a hell of a lot for somebody who doesn't even work for AmFreight."

Perex acknowledged the point by nodding lazily. "I carry AmFreight in my portfolios. What is good for AmFreight is good for Mount Vernon Trust, and vice versa."

"All right. Fine. Then let me ask you: what about Igl?"

"He was murdered."

"I know that! He was found dead in AmFreight's hospitality suite in the Plaza Athénée Hotel." Almost snarling, he added, "If it weren't for the murder of Igl, the whole goddamn story would be too comical for words."

"Possibly," Perex said. "I told you at the time that Igl no longer worked for AmFreight. When he left Geneva they should have made him give up his key to the suite. . . . A slipup. At the time of his murder, Igl was trying to make a deal on his own with the Mangrovians." He shrugged coldly. "His employment, shall we say, was terminated with the utmost prejudice." He giggled breathlessly. "An old CIA term."

"Who terminated him then?" Kelly demanded.

Again, Perex moved his shoulders negligently. "I don't know. Perhaps the Mangrovians, perhaps the French. Perhaps . . ."

"Perhaps the Americans," Kelly taunted. "A hit squad from AmFreight headquarters. Shit, maybe the chinks. Rafe, I can see why you've taken to carrying a gun—if you hadn't left it home."

Perex's hand trembled on his glass. "I advise you not to make fun, my dear. This is a deadly serious business."

"And dangerous . . . Oh, *Heavens to Betsy!*" Kelly mocked. Perex's face went slack. "Thank God you Cubans are such brave guys."

Perex almost sobbed. "Caramba! Shit! What can I say to a man like this? Oh my, oh my."

"Okay," Kelly said, "what are you getting at?"

Perex perked up. "You are very close to Madame Mordaunt, no?"

Kelly nodded. This was true. He was very close to Zouzou Mordaunt. "She's a good friend and a good source too."

Caustically, Perex said, "I have no doubt she was a very good source on Igl—never mind. She is very powerful and through her we could know exactly what is in the mind of the French government. Her relationship with—"

"Aristide de Bis." Kelly supplied the name of the minister-without-portfolio, a member of the French coalition government.

Perex's liquid eyes flitted furtively from his cigarette, held gracefully upright between thumb and forefinger, to his glass, to Kelly's face.

"Dear boy," he said jovially, as if to disclaim what he was about to say, "would you consider it a terrible blunder, a major faux pas, if we were to open a small Mount Vernon portfolio for you?" His voice rushed on. "Say with ten thousand in it for starters? Jack, don't say anything now," he concluded hastily, aware Kelly had jerked back.

Kelly put his hands lightly on the bar. Balancing on the balls of his feet, he cocked his jaw at Perex. "Listen, let's make believe you never said that, Rafe."

With a miserable, punished look on his face, Perex

whined, "I knew it would be a mistake. Jack, my dear, forgive me, please. Please forgive me."

Kelly slowly nodded. "Rafe," he muttered, "I see things very clearly now. Tell me, *'mon cher,'* how many of Europe's leading statesmen carry ten thousand dollars' worth, or more, of Mount Vernon Trust certificates?"

Perex's shoulders shook, as well they should, Kelly thought, for he had possibly given it away, the vehicle used for Washburn's payoffs across the Continent. Perex wept quietly, his face turned to the wall so André could not see him. Nevertheless, the bartender was sensitive enough to the drama of his bar to know something was wrong. In his eyes there was malicious concern.

"It was not my idea, Jack," Perex murmured huskily, "and you should not conclude anything."

"Shit, who do you work for anyway?"

The dirty bastards, he told himself, now they had tried to bribe him. Payoffs had been offered to him before but never on a governmental level. Coat-and-suit manufacturers, on the lookout for favorable headlines, had tried to slip him money or favors, but never an agent of . . . whom?

"Dear boy," Perex whispered, so softly Kelly could barely hear him, "sometimes it is very difficult to escape one's past."

Kelly had to admit this was so. Obviously, Perex's background, the Cuban business, his connection with the Washburn family, made him a hostage—the poor, manipulated bastard. Suddenly, he felt sorry for Perex, his friend. Perex had been put on him by God-knows-who and now their relationship was undermined by his assignment.

Perex turned and looked him in the eye, annoyed that Kelly had embarrassed him.

"No one is simon-pure," he said spitefully. "Please to remember one thing. Your father-in-law, the great one, Claud Trout, is one of Washburn's closest cronies. He is one of the conservators who manage the Washburn interests while George is in high office. As you spout your pieties to me, kindly remember that this Texas in-law of yours is pulling the strings.''

Kelly flushed. "You mean C.T. told you to buy me? You no-good . . .''

"Do not say heel, *mon ami*.''

Kelly turned away gruffly, gulping his beer. "All right, goddamn it, Rafe, let's just forget the whole thing.''

"Yes,'' Perex agreed quickly. "Numero Uno is we remain friends.''

"Let's hope we can.''

Perex's expression turned as swiftly sunny as it had been stormy.

"Thanks be. Thanks be. But, *mon ami*, you will promise not to reveal anything of what we have discussed?''

Kelly was not willing to be completely squelched. "I'll file it, Rafe, in the back of my mind. You never know . . .''

CHAPTER

TWO

It was August, the season of the doldrums. Paris was musty and humid. The city smelled of sweaty clothes and feet, of garbage in the alleys. Heat wave held the streets in clammy hands again, after the rain, invading the shade and infiltrating even the smartest hotels.

Supposedly, once upon a time, the gay-nineties pile on rue Rimbaud, that museum of Parisian haute couture, or high fashion—Maison Mordaunt—had been air-conditioned. What this meant in practice was that Madame

Zouzou Mordaunt forbade any windows to be opened, even during the cruelest month, and even though the stifling second-floor salon was packed with fashion faithful come to see the last of the Couture Week collections.

Kelly yawned behind his hand and groaned. It was too damned hot and definitely not the place to be at ten-thirty on the morning of August first. Yet, they were all here, the Fashion International of buyers, press representatives, photographers, good friends, and devotees of Zouzou Mordaunt, all worshiping at the shrine of Paris *chic*.

He and Rafe had made a night of it; then at midnight Kelly had come along to watch Zouzou and Victor put the last buttons and braid on dresses, suits, sophisticated playwear, evening dresses of the same collection that was now passing before his burning eyes. Hangover danced on his forehead and tangoed through his gut. Ordinarily, hangover was not a disaster, scarcely an inconvenience for a seasoned foreign correspondent. Simple hangovers were simply treated with a few extra hours of sleep, then a leisurely cabdrive to the shabby Right Bank offices of *Retailers Apparel Guide*. Kelly would have had a few words with his secretary, Olga Blastorov, and read the overnight cables. There was always a confusion of these; from his editor, Frank Court; sometimes directly from his father, Harry Kelly, president, chairman, chief operating officer, and general supremo of Kelly Communications. Then, still hung over but not guilt-ridden, and as soon as it was decently possible, he would have strolled around the block and up to the Ritz to bridge the hours until late afternoon— late afternoon in Paris but still only lunchtime in New York, with plenty of time to answer the cables or shoot off another blockbuster.

But not this morning. This morning he had been bound to rise early and make his ritual appearance at Maison Mordaunt, even though he had already seen all the clothes and knew, almost to the last adjective, what he would write: Smasheroo Collection from Zouzou, Fashion Eternal.

*   *   *

Imagine, if you can, the palaces of Babylon, gambling halls of old San Francisco, the red velvet bordellos of prewar Bucharest, marble-lined pissoirs of Grand Central Station, other marvels of stone and gilt and gold, the odor of stale cigarette butts, perfume gone rancid, fermenting sweat and urine, brandy boiling out of all Kelly's pores. This was the Maison Mordaunt, the House of Mordaunt, a crossroads of fashion for the past thirty, forty, fifty years.

Fortunately, he had been placed in the *RAG*'s usual place of honor, smack in the front row; for Zouzou, besides being a friend, feared and respected the *RAG* for what it could do for her. Those behind him were crammed together, like pins in a box. As Zouzou was so fond of saying, "*Merde,* they are merely journalists, *mon cher.*"

Kelly pulled a red bandanna handkerchief from his breast pocket and wiped his face. Was it too early for a cigarette? Did he dare? His hand trembled as he scribbled notes on his program: Number 52, a tweed suit with braided trim, the ditto of Number 51. *Merde.*

Number 53 emerged from the double archway at the rear of the salon as if shot from a sling. The listless mob of fashion stalwarts applauded weakly. The noise disturbed him; it was another twist at the scrawny neck of the morning.

Hell, he would chance it. A cigarette could not possibly make him feel any worse. He hooked an ashtray away from the heavy ankle of his neighbor, Shirley Bigfellow. Shirley was an important buyer from Palm Beach, whose decrepit population lived out their lives in Paris couture clothes. Shirley hated Kelly. She claimed he had once misquoted her in the *RAG* and thus cost her a year-end bonus. Not so. But it was true that Shirley, like her name, was big and heavy, and she was perspiring profusely into her hairy upper lip.

Kelly placed a Gauloise in his parched lips and lit it. Shirley performed a half turn in her seat and frowned. Instantly, he realized he had made a mistake. His head spinning, he reached down and desperately snubbed out the fuming cigarette. Across the way, the *Womens Wear Daily* contingent snickered at his discomfort. Those pricks.

By eleven o'clock, even the fresh flowers had begun to droop. From behind his dark glasses, Kelly's eyes groped around the room. He was not the only tired soul. Everyone looked exhausted from this week of nonstop fashion. As powerful *RAG*'s Paris bureau chief, Kelly's presence was required at all the key social affairs. He could afford to be discriminating to a point. When Pierre Cardin's party was announced, Kelly dutifully attended. If St. Laurent summoned, Kelly accepted. He might safely refuse an invitation to a clambake or buffet at Maison Billy but there was no way of dodging a cocktail party at Chanel. Most correspondence from the Maison Cuir he could toss in the wastepaper basket, but the same was not true for Lanvin. And so on. But that was not all. More often than not, the evenings during the fashion spectacular ended in the small hours at one or another of the season's "in" boîtes, leaving him time for no more than a catnap before the first collection of the morning. Then came lunch with his best American buyer-sources. And somehow, in the late afternoon, weary, feet dragging and gut upset, he made time to write his daily report for the *RAG*'s next morning edition in New York. No, it was not an easy time and it was not much fun. This was what Maryjane had never appreciated, never really tried to understand. *Merde* . . . He was not up to brooding about her this morning. She was gone. That was it, simply. She was gone . . .

Determinedly, promising himself that it would soon be over, Kelly concentrated on the show. He listened intently to the recorded background music, a lugubrious medley of Paris street songs, à la Piaf. But the tape was fuzzy and out of sync with the machine. Zouzou was too cheap to have anything fixed properly, or replaced. The audience was not paying attention anyway. They were in constant movement, trying like himself to find some posture of tolerable comfort on the tiny gilt chairs, these

built for children or rigidly dieting women—small cheeks,
he thought of small cheeks. The gilt chairs were one of
the paramount curses of Couture Week. He wondered
how big-assed Shirley Bigfellow managed. Each time
she moved, her chair creaked in protest. With any luck,
it would give up and land her on the floor.

The Fashion International came together in Paris twice
a year for the collections—this one, the fall-winter, and
then in the early new year for the spring-summer show-
ings. Fall-winter was bigger and more important. Buyers
and press people arrived in hordes from all over the
world, from Europe but also from North America, New
York, Los Angeles, Montreal, Toronto. Swarthy Latin
Americans were also members of the International and
so were the Orientals. Rich Japanese blandly watched
the proceedings, chattering among themselves and grinning, and there were the Europe-domiciled Arabs, wily
and not easily sold, and a smattering of Indians who
smelled of curry and were forever pulling at their crotches
and scratching. All the women tried to be smartly dressed
but it was not easy in such heat. Others were much less
elegant and Kelly had always considered that a special
award for drabness should be reserved for women fashion writers, often as tackily dressed as the clothes they
wrote about were sleek and beautiful. They were a
tough lot, having in common a desire to compensate for
something undefinable but more obvious than that Indian
itch. They crossed and recrossed their legs, fiddled with
buttons and pulled at the tight elastic of brassieres and
pantyhose, exposing yards of haunch and thigh.

And, oblivious of thermometer or barometer, the models did come and go, gliding in and out of the archway
with perfect cool, prancing with that singularly icy contempt models have for all others. For they were the
handmaidens of fashion, dedicated to the deity of couture which, after all, is itself devoted to nothing more or
less than the efficient worship of sex. But the models
were sexless and cold, frightening. They might have
come out of the dressing rooms stark naked and the
sensual impact would have been the same.

Crotches, crotches, scads of crotches, he thought, wilting. But nothing there: no moles, no holes.

Not quite. Zouzou's star model, Simone, her leading edge a jutting pelvis, slid onto the floor in a silk sheath so formfitting it might have been not second skin but skin itself. Simone's blond hair was cut gamine-short and coiffed severely close to her pin-head. Those flaring nostrils and that wide unsmiling mouth distracted him. Kelly knew on intimate authority—his own—that Simone's only body hair was that slicked down on her head. Her armpits and pubic area were kept religiously shaved. She swept past him, casting him such a distant glance that no one could ever have assumed that he was anything but a total stranger. A disdainful flutter of almost nonexistent eyelashes faintly acknowledged that, yes, she might possibly have seen him somewhere before. Kelly remembered her rubbery mouth and was instantly smothered in a new dimension of heat, that of the morning-after erection, surely the most lustful erection of all.

God! He hugged his quivering stomach and forced up the risky solace of a tiny burp, tasting remorsefully of brandy.

Shirley Bigfellow turned again, this time openly scowling.

"So sorry," Kelly murmured. "Something to do with my metabolism."

"Your breath stinks," she informed him.

She *did* hate his guts. But didn't they all. Because of his special relationship with Zouzou Mordaunt? He was Zouzou's champion. In the pages of the *RAG,* she *was* the Fashion Eternal and forever, in her genius, at the lead of the Parisian couture pack. Zouzou had been quoted often enough in Kelly's behalf. Kelly, she told anyone who would listen, was the best American writer to grace the fashion *arrondissement.* And God knows he had written enough about Zouzou and her rotund colleague, *le grand* Victor. But God must also know, and this was a worrying thought, that *les créations Mordaunt* hardly ever changed these days.

There was a lesson in this, Kelly realized. The more things changed, the more, as the French liked to say, they remained the same. Come sunny skies or catastrophe, civic serenity or urban guerrilla warfare, prosperity or depression, war or peace, certain institutions prevailed. And this one, of high fashion, possessed more stamina than even church or faltering state.

The Couture Week, therefore, was fashion's high holy week, fashion's celebration of itself and at the same time its bacchanal. It was a week of fashion, fashion all day long and the merriment of the Fashion International all through the night. It was a continuous feast for the dedicated and each of the couture maisons had an offering for the banquet. And somehow, magically, the themes were set which would define the look of women's clothes in the sophisticated capitals through the coming winter.

The other maisons had all performed by now: Cardin, Dior, Laroche, Chanel, Givenchy, St. Laurent. And the lesser houses: Cuir, Chevaux, Maritimes, Versailles, the Arabistes, and naturally, Maison Billy, which took its name from the Brooklyn-born maître, Billy Bostwick. Kelly covered still other minor designers but only perfunctorily, and they hated him for his inattention. Yet he could not be everywhere and they were apt to forget that it was also his duty to pass judgment on the purveyors of the raw materials without whom Paris could never have perpetuated itself as the fashion capital of the world: the makers of buttons, buckles, braid, belts . . . zippers, thread, linings . . . leather . . . costume jewelry, and most important of all, the fabric merchants of Lyons.

It was not only appropriate but a well-deserved honor that Zouzou Mordaunt should close this Olympiad of Fashion. For it was Zouzou who had preserved and showered personality on the art form through both the darkest and brightest days.

But her very grandeur was a problem. What about the immortality that Kelly had bestowed on Zouzou in the *RAG*? She had been making clothes for ages, for perhaps too long a time if the truth be known. In the back of his mind, there was always the worry that Madame Mordaunt would abruptly go gaga and make a fool of him. For all he knew, she was just around the corner from oblivion. Zouzou had already retired twice and each time triumphantly returned. As far as he could judge, Zouzou reigned as powerfully now as she had fifty years ago. But was this merely on the sufferance of her fashion peers? It was abundantly clear they respected her age, not that anybody knew how old she was. Whatever the years, she carried them lightly. She was quick on her feet, she possessed energy seemingly to overflowing. Her hearing was good and she ate and drank with care. She claimed for herself the line usually attributed to the duchess of Windsor—a woman can't be too rich or too thin.

And now, Kelly thought mournfully, she had discovered Grovival. She had assured him the elixir was the greatest thing since Pernod, and to hear her describe it, one would conclude it was as powerful as rocket juice.

Kelly was forcefully reminded of Grovival and of the disputed state of Mangrovia by the sight of Aristide de Bis, Monsieur le Ministre who, he suddenly realized, was sitting on the other side of the steamy salon, a few seats behind *Womens Wear Daily*. Aristide, one of Madame Mordaunt's oldest friends, was the proud bearer of an ancient name and also, handily, of one of the easiest French names to pronounce. It slid off the tongue as a simple "B". De Bis was the leader of the most nationalistic of the right-wing splinter parties in the ruling coalition and he looked the part. There was a close resemblance between de Bis and the late Charles de Gaulle. Like the deceased president of the republic, Aristide was tall, pear-shaped, and disdainful, in profile as hawk-nosed as any Napoleonic eagle.

Aristide de Bis was also violently anti-American. If Rafael Perex was right about a burgeoning Franco-American struggle for influence in West Africa, then this minister-without-portfolio would have cause to hate Washington and President George Washburn all the more.

Aristide's hooded Gallic eyes flicked toward Kelly, aware of his recognition. A studied sneer passed across the long and petulant face. Aristide and Kelly occasionally met in Zouzou's penthouse atop the rue Rimbaud establishment, but Aristide never had more words for him than a curt *Bonjour* or *Bonsoir*. Perhaps there would not be even that much for Kelly now, for Zouzou had hinted that Aristide was not overjoyed by Kelly's snooping into the shocking Cosmetics Lovenest scandal.

On the other hand, Aristide de Bis was not all-powerful. Rumor had it that the parties of the center, the moderates and conservatives, kept de Bis in the coalition merely as a means to defuse his political wrecking activities in the countryside, where his support came from estate owners and small peasants alike. De Bis, like many American politicians, was a crusader against "big government" and his pet fiscal scheme was to abolish the income tax altogether; thereby, he preached, to stimulate industrial investment and create jobs. His demagogic tactics, in particular the pledge to do away with taxation, had built a following among extremists of every party, including, it was said, the Communists.

Politics aside, Kelly had always considered Aristide to be a fascinating man, a true Frenchman, and almost lovable in his predictable anti-Americanism and yearning to restore, yet again, *la gloire* to France. If encouraged, Zouzou could go on for hours about Aristide de Bis. He had been immensely important to her business. After the Liberation and despite his shady politics even then, Aristide had been able to assure Zouzou of vital supplies of scarce fabrics. He had eased the way for her with the customs authorities; he had helped her with her tax problems and, Kelly had no doubt, in the tricky business of hiding money in Switzerland.

Such were the facts of life in Europe. Power, influence, wealth: all these radiated from the center and Aristide de Bis was at the center.

This morning, Aristide was with his wife, surely an unusual event, for it was said he by far preferred the company of his young mistress, the Countess Beatrice de Beaupeau. Countess Beaupeau, Kelly knew, was an outstanding woman in her late twenties and one of striking beauty. She was long-legged, slim, and quite tall for a Frenchwoman, a being of whose pearl-toned skin one might easily dream on sultry nights.

The affair of Aristide and Beatrice—surely at least thirty years younger—had been so long-lasting and was so widely known that Zouzou had assured Kelly that there was nothing in it for his gossip columns. Indeed, the alliance, Zouzou warned, was something that, in his own interest, it would be best not to report. For, along with her adoration of the man, Zouzou was deathly afraid to do anything that might offend Aristide—and she was a woman who professed to worry about nothing.

Kelly smiled wanly in Aristide's direction, but the minister took no further notice of him. He sat motionlessly, without expression, watching the models intently, his heavy body as straight and inflexible as his face. He was, indeed, very much like de Gaulle, or General MacArthur, both men who had never been known to sweat.

Now, Kelly noticed someone else for the first time. Behind Aristide sat the most tantalizing woman in the salon, models included. She was a youngish vamp with heavy black hair, a pale face, and vivid dark eyes. Taking his halting smile at Aristide to be meant for her, she stared sharply at him. What with the black hair, the pallor of her face, and the smoldering eyes, she could have been a much younger version of Zouzou. God, he sighed to himself, a woman and a half.

Kelly was surprised by an eruption of applause. The show was over! Damn! He had planned to beat the mob to the stairway but, daydreaming, he had not only missed Victor's final dress but the chance to get to the exit before it was blocked by a noisy gaggle of embracing women. Worse yet, Victor was already hurrying down the steps from the third floor and heading toward him. Kelly began to feel very sick again. An exquisite in his own right, Victor was wearing a fresh white linen suit, a peach-colored tie, and between the thumb and forefinger of his right hand he was carrying a single red rose.

The rose was one of his trademarks. Like Zouzou, he was of indeterminate age, heavily jowled, and lightly lipsticked. His large head was sparsely covered with rust-colored hair. There were smudges on his jacket collar where the dye had run. Victor paused to peck cheeks and squeeze tender parts of female bodies but his course was set determinedly for Kelly.

Kelly disliked Victor more than ever this morning—for one thing because he looked so cool and relaxed. Naturally, he cursed, since Victor, along with Zouzou and her goddamned monkey Charles, had been watching the show from the comparative comfort of the top step of the third-floor staircase.

"Jack Kelly!" Victor hailed him happily, his face creased in a giant smirk, like an oily beach ball in need of kicking. "*Mon ami*, what do you say? *Fantastique? Superbe? Magnifique?*"

Kelly could only mutter in response and point at his stomach. Would Victor get the message that he was in critical condition?

No. "Madame is above. She asks for you to come to have champagne with us and tell us what you think of the Maison Mordaunt on this marvelous day in August. . . . And where is charming Madame Maryjane?"

Kelly ignored the last question. Victor should have known by now that Maryjane was not interested in haute couture. "Champagne! Victor, please," he excused himself. "One glass of champagne and it's rigor mortis."

"Jack, come, come."

"Victor, please tell Zouzou I'll drop back later."

Kelly would normally have been effusive in his comments on the most important collection of the year. He would have slapped Victor on the back and, if necessary to make his point, kissed him on both cheeks. What they were hungry to know, of course, was what he would write. His report in the *RAG* could make all the difference to sales. If the *RAG* said Mordaunt was a smasheroo, all the store bosses would be on the phone telling their people to buy more.

But he badly wanted a pissoir. That was uppermost in

his mind. He needed more time to adjust to the morning. He tried to edge past Victor. He was perspiring heavily now and a nasty pressure was building up between his legs.

"Jack, you have not said . . ."

"Victor, the Mordaunt Collection is always tops, you know that. What more can I say?"

"Say you will come upstairs and have some champagne."

"Victor, I'm dying . . . I can't . . . I'm feeling sick."

Victor's eyes shadowed with displeasure, then suspicion. "You do not wish to tell us?"

Aristide de Bis and his wife were moving in their direction. Good—the minister would divert Victor.

"Madame will be disappointed," Victor pressed. "And Charles . . ."

"Fuck Charles."

Victor smiled thinly for he too despised the monkey. But this did not mean he would not tell Zouzou what Kelly had said.

"Jack . . ."

"Victor, I'm not kidding, I've got to get out of here. Did I say the collection was tops? I mean superb . . . great . . ."

"Yes, yes, and my dresses?"

Victor waited eagerly for Kelly's verdict but Kelly could not tell him the dresses had passed him by in a bilious blur. He spoke with an effort. "Victor, I can't talk anymore. I'm speechless. Please . . . I've got to go."

Victor grabbed his arm and shook it roughly. "What means this?"

"Victor, please stop that."

"Jack!" Hysteria shook Victor's heavy chest.

Heads turned as Kelly felt his control waning. It was at this point, fortunately, that Aristide de Bis and his wife reached them.

"*Bonjour,* Monsieur Victor," Aristide said harshly. "Et Monsieur Kelly."

"*Bonjour,* Monsieur le Ministre," Victor exclaimed pitifully. "Madame, what of my poor dresses?"

Madame de Bis began to speak but Aristide laid a hand on her arm, cutting her off. He glanced scornfully at Victor. "Monsieur Victor—the spectacle was much too long," he stated.

Victor emitted a tiny shriek. His fingers bit into Kelly's arm.

"Please let go of me, Victor." Finally, desperately, he wrenched his arm away.

Victor turned on him ferociously. But why? It was Aristide who was being unpleasant.

"*Cochon!*" Victor exclaimed.

Then, it was too much to be believed.

WHAP!

Victor slapped Kelly. The sound of perspiring hand hitting sweaty face resounded like a body hitting the pavement from ten stories.

"What the hell is wrong with you? Why did you hit me? Jesus Christ!" Madame de Bis's face puckered in distaste. "All right, Victor," Kelly cried wildly, "you want to know? Your goddamn dresses are worse than Brooklyn Billy's. Now? *Now* can I go?"

He began to pull away, aware of undeserved humiliation. But it was too late and what made for a rotten memory was that the shock of the slap triggered him off. Sickness surged from his lower depths. He spewed a jet of wine, aged and soured overnight in the tun of his belly, all over Victor's shirtfront and tie.

"Aagh, *merde*," Aristide de Bis cried disgustedly.

Victor shrieked again as Kelly grimaced an apology. There was nothing to be said and no time in which to say it. Drool oozed from the corners of Madame de Bis's mouth and she began to make choking sounds.

"Mathilde!" Aristide raged.

It was too much for Victor. He gasped once and his eyes rolled up in his head. He sagged. Kelly caught him before he hit the floor and eased him back to the staircase.

"Mathilde!" Madame de Bis started being sick.

Kelly did not pause. The time had definitely come for escape.

A volley of obscenities poured down from above, which shocked the startled fashion pack even more. Kelly anxiously glanced upward. Zouzou, her eyes popping and sizzling, was in full rant, as only she in a runaway rage could rant.

Kelly pushed through the crowd. The fat was in the fire. He ran down the steps and outside into the rue Rimbaud.

CHAPTER

THREE

Over the weekend, the city had emptied. *Tout Paris* had broken for its traditional August holiday, hopefully to regain equilibrium in the mountains or by the sea. For it had not been a splendid year so far. It was a disastrous time of uncontrolled inflation, and party turmoil and international bickering which old-timers said reminded them of the tumultuous days of the prewar thirties.

Olga Blastorov had chosen the mountains for a week and had gone there with her father, Count Boris Blastorov.

Kelly was alone in the office, halfheartedly finishing his final roundup on overall business and fashion aspects of the week of haute couture. Even four days later, he was embarrassed about what had happened Saturday at the Maison Mordaunt and more than a little worried about the venomous story he'd shot off for the Monday issue of the *RAG*. With self-loathing, he remembered that morning—he had been unfairly used by Victor and, horribly, Aristide de Bis had been witness to his shame.

His Mordaunt report had been unreasonably harsh, a complete reversal of his usual coverage. But he had been in such a foul mood that Zouzou could not blame him. Still, he knew there would be terrible repercussions. He thought of telephoning Zouzou but she was not in Paris. Her intention had been to spend a few days with Beatrice de Beaupeau at the Château de Beaupeau in the Burgundy region.

He would just have to bite the bullet. In fact, considering it, he was not really sorry he had written so wrathfully of Victor. Never mind about Saturday—Victor had always grated on the smooth surface of Kelly's Americanism, and if there had been a convenient way of doing so, he would, long since, have taken Victor over the high jump. The problem had always been one of torpedoing Victor without damaging his own fruitful relationship with Zouzou Mordaunt.

It was an unlikely alliance Kelly and Zouzou enjoyed, she the aged and still aging empress of French fashion; and he the brash young reporter. The eternal Zouzou and puckish Jack Kelly, as they described him when they were being kind. He stood, at six feet, like a tower over her. People said he looked like his father: the same crinkly eyes and the Irish smile. When they were being unkind, critics accused him of being vindictive, even vicious, and then they called him "that prick Kelly at the *RAG*."

Fortunately, fashion was not Kelly's only assignment in Paris. Harry Kelly had once told a luncheon meeting of New York financial analysts that the editorial beat of the *RAG* was nothing less than the "heartbeat of Western civilization." Frank Court had enlarged on this when Kelly junior was sent to Paris: "I want screwing, scandal, perversion, and subversion, bauchery and debauchery, mayhem and murder, larceny big and petty." That was Court's idea of Western civilization.

In the five years he had been in Paris, Kelly had advanced in age from twenty-eight to thirty-three, and he believed he had fulfilled all but the most ambitious of the *RAG*'s expectations. He had titillated Seventh Avenue, the grimy home of the American fashion trade. He had dredged for sin. He had insulted, pilloried, and dumped dirty laundry. He had made himself hated and feared; but respected too. He had been snubbed at the Lido, reviled at Régine's and socked at Maxim's. He had been offered sex, money, and attractive new jobs. All this came with the territory, as they said, for next to making clothes, generating gossip was the preoccupation of the fashion industry. Vis-à-vis gossip, the strength and the weakness of the journalistic trade was that no one really wished to keep their private affairs private. There was no woman unprepared to rat on her friends and no man reluctant to dump on his closest chums in his search for advancement. Any story could be ferreted out with the astute use of these levers.

Zouzou Mordaunt was Kelly's golden key—to the boudoir, the cabinet, and the boardroom, into the secluded estates and the town houses. Zouzou was linked to every nerve end in Paris. She knew everybody and everything, and it was she who conducted Kelly to that shadowy place where fashion met decadence.

But Victor was another story. In the thirties, as a mere youth, he had already become the darling of Paris. Then, surprisingly, just before the war, he retired, proclaiming that his future lay in his rose garden. He disappeared into the south of France, the perfumed regions of Grasse, from time to time wafting back to the capital for a visit to his bank, the opera, a drink at his favorite café, a cheap dump near the Invalides. Then, again, he would drop out of sight. Detractors said that even in the thirties Victor had been playing footsy with the Nazis. Others claimed, more tolerantly, that he had suffered a nervous breakdown. Whatever, Victor remained a mysterious figure: his refusal to grant an interview became the interview; his escape from the photographer, the picture. The Mediterranean sun burned him a Grecian brown and lit his veins as well, it was said, with all the vices of ancient Greece. The war came. One story placed Victor in the underground. Another said he had fled to North Africa to live out the bloodbath in the Algerian casbah. But the most devastating theory was that Victor had slunk to Berlin, to stay for a time with Hitler and Eva Braun and, monsieur, everyone knew how *très kinky* those two individuals were. Time elapsed. Memories faded quickly, as they did in Europe, and eventually, under the aegis of the House of Mordaunt, Victor returned to Paris. Forget the past, Zouzou philosophized; it was altogether proper that Victor should come to the Maison Mordaunt where, as a pimply adolescent, he had begun sewing buttons for the haute couture.

It was about three in the afternoon when the Associated Press called.

Was it true, as *Womens Wear Daily* reported, that Jack Kelly had been party to a shocking incident at the Maison Mordaunt and that editorially speaking he had misfired by calling the Mordaunt Collection a "bomb"?

The question, a reminder, made him feel almost as ill as he'd been Saturday morning. He had not seen the item, he stuttered, and anyway it was all an accident and he had never called the Mordaunt Collection a bomb. What he had written was that the Maison Mordaunt was not up to its usual standards.

The voice speculated gleefully. "How long's it been since a reporter barfed all over a faggot dress designer?"

"Uh . . ."

"*WWD* says you're going on a long vacation."

"I'll talk to you," Kelly said weakly and hung up.

Vacation? What the hell was that supposed to mean? He and Maryjane had been talking about a trip to Normandy but that seemed to be off.

Shaken, Kelly tried to return to his story. Vacation? Christ, for all he knew Maryjane had been eaten by a Mangrovian snake by now. She was as likely to be there as anywhere else. She'd heard from him about Grovival. She was a sucker for fads and at some point in her travels she'd acquired an avid interest in maintaining youth and vigor through herbal medicine, glandular manipulation, and contemplation.

Damn her anyway. He had not realized she'd been revving up her motor for another flit. One might have assumed she had everthing at home a woman could desire: life in the City of Light, friends, good restaurants, museums that wouldn't stop, and plenty of money. Clearly this was not enough. Maryjane rose, like one of C.T.'s gushers, to a high pitch of pressurized boredom, and before Kelly could be aware of it she'd blown town again.

But what had they to talk about? Money? Yes. Food, wine, or taking a trip somewhere, perhaps to the gigantic Trout spread in east Texas? Yes. Her addiction to antiques, which she knew little about and bought recklessly? Sure, he sneered to himself. Or the health of her sturgeon, sole occupant of a fish tank that took up practically one whole wall of the apartment? Maryjane believed the goddamn thing would lay eggs—caviar, that is—not being willing to accept that getting at a sturgeon's caviar was a very painful process for the sturgeon. Their months—years—together in Paris had not improved their rapport. They had a failure of communication.

So, yes, he thought, two-to-one Maryjane was in Mangrovia right now.

Thoroughly discouraged, Kelly sat in limbo, one foot planted on the floor, the other stuck in his wastepaper basket, a posture Rafe Perex suggested was strongly appropriate to the kind of work he did.

The call from A.P. was very unnerving. His old man and Court would see the WWD item too and would be raising all kinds of hell. It could be only a matter of minutes before the bell on the Telex machine would start clanging: RAG PARIS KELLY.

Harry Kelly was tough, as he would have to be as the son of the founder of the empire, Terrence Kelly. The RAG had been born in the late 1900's as a daily broadsheet supplying vital textile information: quotes on cotton and wool futures, rudimentary figures on retail volumes, and most vital, up to the minute bankruptcy reports as they affected the textile trade. In time, Terrence had expanded into broader publishing activities and then, things being what they were, into slot machines, burlesque houses, and it had been charged, bordellos. Terrence was of the breed of city boss. He supported Woodrow Wilson and it was his backing of temperance and *that* amendment that induced family and friends to suspect that he had dropped an oar. The next thing they knew Terrence was in the Hoover camp, but by then it was too late. He hung on for years, finally ending his days in a high-security nursing home in Rahway, New Jersey.

Son Harry divested the company of its holdings in all but publishing. But Harry too had his political failings. the *RAG*, by now the "Flagship" of the enterprise, turned on the Democrats and on F.D.R. in the early forties, and as part payment for this treachery, Harry came under intent IRS scrutiny. As soon as was decently possible he assigned himself as a correspondent in wartorn Europe and thus avoided what might have been a different kind of trip: to Lewisburg Pen. Harry survived the war and F.D.R. to reach the respectability and dignity of his middle sixties.

But he never lost his ambition to build and maintain the *RAG*'s broad base as a world fashion arbiter while also becoming a political force and a quotable source on every topic that touched even vaguely on fashion. Harry's theory was that fashion was invariably an expression of the times, whether lean and hungry or affluent and wasteful. Despite this, both boosters and critics of the *RAG* insisted on identifying the paper with fashion alone. Supporters said it was the voice of the "rag trade," as the apparel business was called, and thus aptly nicknamed. Detractors scoffed that the *RAG* was indeed a "crummy rag" in the journalistic sense, that it was trivial, foolish, superficial, and frivolous.

Hell, yes, the old man and Court were definitely going to be livid when they found out what had happened at the Maison Mordaunt. They hated being a laughingstock. Hell, yes, he wished they had killed his Mordaunt story as arbitrarily as they had deep-sixed Kelly's Cosmetics Lovenest scandal.

The only thing he could do now was to try and

convince Zouzou that the New York editors had committed grievous faults with his copy. But would she buy that?

No, he acknowledged, the situation was hopeless. Kelly punched his typewriter a few more times, then stood up. He had to get out of the office before that bell rang on the Telex machine. He paused at the door to study his trench coat. At that moment a moth flew out of the sleeve and he swatted it angrily. Son of a bitch, trench coats were supposed to be mothproof, proof against anything but a direct hit by atomic missile. He grabbed the coat. It was still cloyingly hot but not as bad as it had been over the weekend, and there was a feeling of new rain in the air. Slinging the coat over his shoulder, he snapped off the office light, slammed the door and clumped down the stairs.

The streets were deserted. Most shops were closed, paper notices stuck to their windows: FERMÉ POUR VACANCES, closed for vacation. Kelly wished he too were elsewhere, somewhere, sitting by the water, even hiking in the mountains with Olga and Count Boris. Olga was a juicy little thing, and he had often toyed with the idea of screwing her. But no, one of the first things he had learned was not to fool around with the help. Men had met disaster time and again that way. And Olga had never encouraged him, although he was well aware of her eyes; she had a disconcerting habit of staring at his crotch when he stood in front of her desk.

It was hot, hot, hot. Kelly walked slowly, trying to keep to the shade, but nonetheless he was sweating by the time he reached the Ritz.

Perex was alone in the bar with André, the brown trilby at his elbow. From their sullen silence, Kelly assumed they had been having a political discussion and had reached an impasse. Both were relieved when he came through the door.

"*Bon après-midi*, Monsieur Reporter," Perex said heartily. "*Comment ça va?*"

"Can the French, Rafe," he growled. "I'm not so good."

André scowled. Listening to two foolish men did not lighten his mood. "One beer?"

"Why do you always assume I want a beer, André?" Kelly demanded. "No, today I want a Pernod and water."

"We do not serve such strong drinks to children," André said.

"André, give him a Pernod," Perex commanded.

"No."

Kelly had to laugh. "Did you ever hear of a bartender like this guy?" A grin spread across André's face. "All right, goddamn it, André, then give me a beer."

André pulled a beer and placed it on the bar.

"Well, Monsieur Reporter," Perex drawled, "what have you done to your Madame Mordaunt? Bloody hell, Jack, I think you've destroyed her."

Kelly paled. Oh, Christ, by now the air-freight edition of the Monday paper had arrived in Paris. "What do you mean, destroyed her?" he muttered.

Perex pointed to a sodden copy of the *RAG* laying on the sink behind the bar. It was too much—did everybody have to read the *RAG*? Kelly knew the issue by heart. The Mordaunt story was in the right-hand column; at center left a new picture of Jackie Kennedy.

"My dear, it is bloody devastating," Perex said. "What do *you* say, André?"

"Madame Zouzou Mordaunt will not be pleased," André said gravely.

"So, who's asking you?" Kelly snapped. "Shit, just let me drink my beer, will you? The story's not that bad."

Perex chuckled darkly, caressed his hat, and smoothed his tie. Today he was in a dark blue suit of a light summer fabric, a thinly striped shirt, and British regimental tie. Without moving his head, Kelly could see the light reflected off his highly polished shoes.

Carefully studying the cuticles of his fingernails, Perex said loudly, "I have always found incomprehensible your worship of Madame Mordaunt."

"Worship? Listen, buddy boy, I'm not in *her* back pocket either. I guess that story proves it."

"Just as incomprehensible is why you should turn on her so violently."

"But you don't know what happened at the Maison Mordaunt Saturday."

André clucked smugly. "Monsieur Kelly, all Paris knows what happened Saturday. *Le grand* Victor struck you in the face and you . . ."

Angrily, Kelly said, "Yes, I puked all over his shirt."

Perex's eyes watered. He was doing his best not to laugh. "Do not be flexed with me, *mon ami,* but that is very very funny, you know." Then he did laugh, weakly holding on to the bar. "I am sorry, my friend."

Grimly, Kelly drank his beer. It was bad; he understood that now. Everyone knew what had happened. He wondered if Zouzou had the power to have him deported.

"Do not be angry with us, Jack," Perex said, breaking into his silence. "We are your friends. True, André?"

"Yes, Monsieur Kelly, we are your friends. You will need your friends."

Kelly did not look up again until three people came into the bar from the hotel side. One was a man with a remarkably red face, and unfortunately, he was Pete Fink, an American fashion buyer of vague acquaintance, a *RAG* source of secondary importance.

"Hey, Jack!"

"Pete . . ."

"Buy you guys a drink?" Fink offered.

He came toward them, his right hand outstretched but before Kelly could take it, Fink had clapped him heartily on the shoulder.

"Jesus, Jack, you're really something."

"Pete, I'd like you to meet Rafe Perex of the Mount Vernon Trust."

The two shook hands. Fink was a careful dresser but of a more flamboyant school than Perex. His suit was powder-blue and with it he was wearing a red shirt and white tie. The chains on the insteps of his Gucci shoes seemed to trail the floor.

"Mount Vernon Trust?" Fink exclaimed. "What the hell is that?"

"A mutual fund," Perex replied moodily. People like Fink put him off balance. There was such a thing as being too American.

"Oh, I get it." Fink grinned. "You can trust in Mount Vernon, as honest as George Washington. That'd be the pitch. Am I right?"

"Yes, that's right," Perex muttered.

But Fink would not let up. "I can see it," he sang, "if George Washington had invested five hundred out of his expense account back in 1776, he'd be worth about a trillion dollars today."

"That is it, roughly"—Perex glowered—"if he did not squander it on women and rum."

"And provided he was still alive." Fink chortled.

"Yes, that too."

Fink laughed, too enthusiastically. "If you two would like to take the weight off, come and join us. You're always good for my expense account, Jack."

Fink's companions sat down at a window table. The woman was a loosely made creature with a sharp nose. Kelly didn't know her name but he'd heard a marvelous story about her—seems she'd said good-bye to her husband, setting out from New York on a multiple-sclerosis fund-raising drive, come home pregnant, a couple of months later, then landed in the garment business. Actually, it wasn't such a marvelous story, more ironic than marvelous. At any rate, she and her paramour, Fink, worked for a chain of stores that specialized in cheap "knockoffs," fast copies of Paris couture models. Kelly had always considered that side of the business to be the pits, like turning out plastic cups. The other person with Fink was a man Kelly recognized as a fabric salesman from Lyons. That figured; even now they were putting their tacky package together.

Sitting around with people like Fink was not Kelly's idea of a great evening. He wasn't up to talking about

Mordaunt or debating again about what was newest or freshest from Paris.

"We're just about to go out to eat," he told Fink. "Thanks though."

"Okay." Fink slapped him on the shoulder again. "Wanna say, Jack, it's about time you gave that old broad the business. I didn't think you had it in you."

Kelly gulped nervously. "Jesus, Pete, it was meant to be a constructive piece."

Fink roared with laughter. "Constructive? Come on, baby, you buried the hatchet six inches in their heads. Beautiful hatchet job." He turned to join his friends. "Nice to see you, Jack. Nice to meet you, pal. Give our regards to George, okay?"

Perex smiled thinly as Fink retreated. "Who is that, love? Christ, he dresses like a bloody clown. Acts like one too."

Kelly lowered his head and murmured, "Pete Fink is one of the fucking army of buyers over here for the collections. A cretin."

Perex admonished him sardonically, "Jack, these are *your* people. You must be more respectful. André, give us a couple more of these little dollywhackers."

They stood silently again. God, Kelly brooded, Fink and his ilk. These American fashion people discounted his objectivity by much too wide a margin. Perex did too; and so did Maryjane. People evidently thought he lived only for the *RAG*, that his only role was to serve as the old man's Crown Prince of Trivia. In truth, Kelly had always felt insignificant and envious of the good gray men of the good gray *Times* of New York, London, Los Angeles, and wherever else.

"I'm really feeling rotten now," Kelly said. "Let's go over to Pierre et Pauline's for dinner."

Kelly was waving at Fink, saying good night to André, and Perex was carefully adjusting his trilby when their moment of departure was shattered by a rude burst of noise at the revolving door. *Le grand* Victor charged into the room, trailed by a gray-haired woman Kelly dimly realized was one of Maison Mordaunt seamstresses, pranced forward, and halted before Kelly. Then, for the second time within the week, he hit Kelly a stinging blow, this time, however, with a much-folded and stained copy of the *RAG*. Victor hurled the paper to the floor and made much of stomping and spitting upon it.

Under his churning feet, Kelly could see the fateful headline: DOG DAYS IN PARIS.

Victor's voice was shrill. "That is what I think of you and your filthy newspaper."

Kelly put a hand to his face. Fink and his companions gaped.

"Victor," Kelly said mildly, "what seems to be the trouble?"

"*Cochon!* Dog! Pig!"

Kelly stooped to pick up the paper but Victor knocked it out of his hand.

"Madame is distressed, unspeakably distressed. And I—I am mortally wounded, insulted, defiled. You! I despise you and I hate your swinish newspaper. *RAG! Merde!*" He spat again, too recklessly, thus splattering Perex's right shoe with spittle.

"I say," Perex exclaimed, "have a care, *mon ami*."

Victor ignored him, and the laughter from Fink's table. Sputtering furiously, he stormed, "Kelly, you have said Victor should shape up or ship out. Kelly, you have written that Victor comes from Nowhere's *ville* and should return there. What means these insults? I demand to know."

Kelly smiled gingerly. "They don't mean anything, Victor. All that stuff was added in New York. I'm ashamed of the way they mangled my story."

"A lie!"

"Victor," he said, trying for his calmest voice, "you'll just have to accept what I'm telling you. I'm sorry this happened."

Fink's voice shattered his argument. "Horseshit, Jack, you said it like it is."

Victor went wild. He pulled back to unleash another

blow. Kelly grabbed him around the waist and pushed him against the bar.

"Just cool it, Victor, for Christ's sake."

Struggling against him, Victor screeched, "I will have my satisfaction."

"Of course you will, of course you will."

Madame Seamstress chose this moment to swing her pocketbook at Kelly's head, knocking him off balance. Victor lifted a knee, trying for his crotch. He managed to twist out of the way.

Finally, André interceded, but only when Madame Seamstress whipped open her pocketbook and flashed a long pair of scissors. "Madame!"

She brandished the scissors, thrust them toward Kelly's face.

"Madame," Perex cried fearfully, "control yourself. . . ."

"Cecilia"—Victor panted—"*s'il vous plaît* . . ."

Quivering with hate, she dropped the scissors back in her bag.

Perex tried to take Victor's arm. "Monsieur Victor, please be calm. You are creating a spectacle. Jack will straighten out this terrible mess."

"Cowards of the press," Victor howled. "I *will* have my satisfaction."

Kelly understood. Victor's head was on the block. His very life at Maison Mordaunt was in jeopardy. Zouzou was taking it out on him, as she should, for it was all Victor's fault, everything that had happened.

"Poor Victor," he said soothingly. "What a pity."

CHAPTER

FOUR

At 6:00 A.M., the Bois de Boulogne is a peaceful place in the dead center of France, close by the capital but far enough by car to be out of the way of all but the hardiest, most solitary of *les joggers*. Even in August, the Bois is apt to be chilly enough for a trench coat and damp with morning dew. White mist obscured the moist green of the forest floor and the ancient trees seemed to float in timelessness, gathering in their topmost branches what remained of the dawn.

The forest was full of ghosts, Kelly thought, the spirits of those long-dead bravos who had been talked into fighting it out on the field of honor on just such mornings as this.

He huddled in his trench coat, shivering. "Listen," he said to Perex, "they've got to be kidding. Nobody fights duels anymore. Duels are against the law."

Perex shrugged and frowned. He was wearing a Burberry over a tweed jacket and gray flannels. An Irish fishing hat had replaced his trilby.

"Jack, what I'm worried about is . . . I don't want any trouble with the French."

"My *second*. You arranged this goddamn thing."

"Honestly, *cher*, I didn't realize what was happening. A man came to see me. By the time I understood what the fool was talking about, it was too late. *You* gave him my address."

41

"Jesus H. Jumping Christ," Kelly grumbled, applying one of Maryjane's favorite expressions. "I thought he wanted to buy a Mount Vernon. A comedy—or tragedy—of errors."

The Bois *was* eerie, very pretragedy, he told himself. The cold, the damp, seeped like doom itself up through the soles of his shoes.

Perex growled. "It is a cheap, fucking macho gesture. I understand these things, being a Latin. Victor must prove himself to Mordaunt. Still . . ." He laughed nervously. "Think of it this way. It'll be a bloody good story for you, Jack."

"Oh, yes? Brilliant. Suppose I get killed? Look—it's after six. Let's split."

"No, no, dear boy," Perex said, "better give it a few more minutes. If we leave too early, your reputation would be ruined."

"Image"—Kelly groaned—"always image."

"You must accept things as they are, dear friend. I, personally, never argue with the de facto situation."

"Rafe—whose goddamn side are you on?"

Perex considered the question for a moment. Then he said: "You would have no survivors?"

"Rafe, I have nothing. No possessions . . . no children. No wife."

"A wife you have, you lovable dummy," Perex cried spiritedly. "But I had been meaning to ask you—why no offspring?"

This was not the time to be talking of such matters. Curtly, Kelly replied, "It was a religious thing. Catholic and Baptist."

Perex put his arm around Kelly's shoulders. He had found another common bond.

"With me too—Catholic, and Westerley an infidel Protestant."

Kelly smiled wanly. "Yeah, Claud Trout screamed bloody murder. He called me a mackerel snatcher."

Perex giggled. "George Washburn called *me* a spic Papist . . . Jack, when this is over I think we will need some girls. Was Maryjane very . . . you know . . ."

"Horny?" He thought about it, even though it was really none of Perex's business. "Sometimes . . . a little. Hornier before marriage than she was afterwards."

Perex nodded slyly, fiddled with his gold cigarette case. "Yes, that is often so. Westerley was insatiable. But with her it was like eating bananas—eat one, throw the peel away. Then another banana: the same . . . And another." He shook his head somberly. "I want you to visit me in Geneva. I have all shapes and sizes."

"You feed them all Grovival?"

"No, no, they don't need it. I have a Monique—she will chase you through the house."

Curious, Kelly asked, "Do you really lay all those girls?"

Perex drew himself up. "Jack, a gentleman should not ask such questions."

"Well, you brought it up."

"But I did not invite you to be explicit." Perex kicked at the wet sod, the brim of his fishing hat shadowing his face. He threw down the butt of his half-smoked cigarette and stamped on it irritably.

Icily, Kelly said, "Rafe, if you don't want to be here—even though you arranged it—you can piss off right now."

"Bloody hell," Perex shouted angrily. "I am here as your friend and now you insult me. I *should* leave."

But he made no move to go. Sullenly he lit another cigarette and puffed silently. Perex and Kelly saw them at the same time: Victor and two companions emerging from behind a clump of trees.

"Oh, bloody shit," Perex muttered. "I'm going to talk to them. We must get you out of this scrape, Jack."

He floundered through the grass toward Victor. But as Perex spoke, Victor shook his head violently, then dropped a full-length black cloak to reveal a ruffled white shirt. Jesus, Kelly thought, the girls at Maison Mordaunt must have been up half the night whipping that little number together.

As Perex was to say later, it was a very sordid

happening—also comic. But that was later. Now, Kelly felt the hairy spider of fear crawling in his throat.

Perex returned, shaking his head. "Macho-ism, macho-ismus, the death of whole nations."

"I could just walk away."

"No, no, my dear, it is too late for that now. Running away would finish you in Paris. And"—he stared blankly at Kelly—"it would be very damaging for the country. I mean *our* country." Kelly must have looked startled for Perex went on intensely, "it would get around that you were yellow and that would be damaging to American credibility in Europe. Disastrous, at a time when my former father-in-law is coming over here for NATO meetings. The French would sneer and laugh. If Jack Kelly turned tail and ran, they would ask, how would the American *force de frappe* behave in case of Russian attack?"

Kelly trembled at the incoherence of the logic. "Jesus Christ," he snarled, "NATO has got nothing to do with me being yellow."

But Perex only shook his head.

Victor and his cohorts edged toward them. On Victor's right was a man of about the same height and girth. The third was a scrawny figure dressed entirely in black and wearing what looked like an undertaker's stovepipe hat.

It was the latter, macabre individual who was carrying a narrow leather box which could only contain a brace of dueling pistols.

Perex passed Kelly one of his cigarettes. Lighting it, he whispered, "I have a brilliant thought." Then he hollered, "A doctor? My man will not fight unless there is a doctor in attendance."

The short stranger replied, "I am a doctor, monsieur."

"Balls." Harshly, Kelly announced, "I'm not taking a shot at you, Victor."

Victor sneered and spat in their general direction. Perex was outraged at that. "Very pretty, Monsieur Victor, very pretty." He added, "My man is ready to apologize."

"Yes," Kelly said, trying to sound as if he were in some small control of himself. "I've told you already, Victor, that I am truly desolated at the way New York screwed up the story. Surely it's not something to fight a duel over, a small editorial matter."

Victor's reply was to throw himself across the few feet that now separated them. He grabbed at Kelly's trench coat and, unbelievably, tore off one of the buttons— buttons supposedly sewn on with thread strong enough to hold a man's weight.

"Swine!" Victor screamed. *"Cochon! Assassin!"*

Now, finally pushed to the end of patience, Kelly responded as he should have at the Ritz. Victor was an older man, so Kelly hit him a gentle blow to the solar plexus. Victor doubled over gasping and fell to his knees, as if he had suddenly acquired religion or, as Perex cynically remarked later, was taking up a classical position of his own.

The silent figure whom Kelly, so far, had hardly noticed, spoke up for the first time.

"Merde! Get up, fat one."

The hoarse, strident voice identified her immediately.

"Madame Mordaunt! What the hell are you doing here?" Kelly cried.

"I am officiating at this farce."

Her tightly curled black hair had been tucked up under the top hat, her spare features neutralized by the absence of any cosmetic covering. Her face, in such natural austerity, was almost masculine, certainly menacing and unforgiving in expression. She too was demanding a pound of Kelly's flesh.

"Madame Zouzou Mordaunt?" Perex croaked.

Her voice husky in the moisture-laden early-morning air, Zouzou turned on Perex, demanding of Kelly, "And who is this trash?"

Kelly stuttered, "My friend . . ." Yes, Rafe was his friend. "Rafael Perex."

"Well," Zouzou said, rasping with contempt, "your *friend* should know you have severely affronted Monsieur Victor." As Perex stared at her, she continued,

"Are you objecting to me? *Non?* Yes? Well, your objections are no more to me than pigeon *merde* on the statue of Lord Nelson. This, messieurs, is not the first time Madame Mordaunt has adjudicated an affair of honor. My services were first used in the Ardennes in 1914 and again at the Maginot Line in 1940. *You* could object to *me?*"

Perex cried out, "I am objecting to this duel, madame, not to you."

"Are you frightened, monsieur?"

She directed the question at both of them, but it was for Kelly to answer. He wavered between yes and no; and, goddamn it, despite himself he remembered what Perex had said about Washburn's bargaining position.

"*Alors,*" he murmured, "No, I am not frightened. Fear is foreign to the Kellys."

What a liar he was, but it sounded good. Perex, his voice choking, exclaimed, "Bravo, Jack, bravo."

Zouzou glared at Perex, then abruptly nodded. "Very well, so be it. Monsieur Victor demands satisfaction. . . ." She glanced toward Victor. "And since you, Jacques, will fight, please to take your positions, back to back. Monsieur Jacques, remove your coat."

Kelly began to unstrap the trench coat, then thought better of it. Even though he had begun to perspire heavily, the coat made him feel stronger and safer.

"No, I will wear my coat."

Zouzou shrugged and flipped open her leather box. She presented for their inspection two long-barreled dueling pistols.

"Caramba," Perex roared, "you mean to go through with this, madame?"

"Naturally, monsieur," Zouzou said coldly. "You may inspect the weapons if you wish. That is your prerogative as Monsieur Kelly's second."

"*Cajones* of the Emperor!" Perez squalled. "It is an insane project."

Victor carefully chose one of the pistols, and Kelly lifted the other from the case. He held it up and sighted along the barrel. It weighed heavily in his hand.

"I warn you, Victor, I'm a dead shot," he muttered.

"Silence," Madame Mordaunt commanded. "Honored antagonists, back to back."

Victor's plump buns nudged against him.

"Now," said the old lady, "you will take twenty paces from each other. I shall be counting them aloud. At twenty, you shall halt, and when I command it, you will turn to face each other. Then, and only then, are you at liberty to fire."

Kelly knew real fear then. He hoped Victor did not feel his ass trembling. As Zouzou gravely announced "One," Perex turned away covering his face with his hands.

Kelly put his left foot forward, and at the count of Two, his right foot. He, this noble American pitted against a waddly little frog.

Three . . . Four . . . Five . . . Six . . .

Christ, she was really counting. He could not believe it. The count was like the clock of his world screaming out a final twenty seconds. The grip of the pistol was wet in his hand. . . . Feverishly, he tried to plan a strategy: when she gave the order to turn, he would fling himself down in the grass and roll and roll. He would make no target for Victor. But would he fire back? No . . . no . . . he would shoot in the air and Victor couldn't hit a pig in the ass with a banjo anyhow. . . .

Zouzou had reached Thirteen . . . Fourteen . . . Fifteen . . .

But somewhere between the count of Fifteen and Sixteen, the world went off its tracks. Kelly was never sure of the sequence of the next few seconds. He heard an ungodly scream, and despite his commitment not to turn until Twenty, he did wheel in time to see Victor twisting toward the ground. Then Victor's gun arm jerked, and as he remembered it, there was a flash and the sensation of BOOM reached his ears, like a cannon shot from across the years. . . . Next, and most amazingly, Kelly was tripping over himself and falling slowly, slowly, toward the wet grass. His eyes closed and he was aware of a bright and searing burn.

Very faintly, at last, he heard Perex's wailing cry and Zouzou's curse, the one that always preceded her invocation of fury.

After that, he noted meticulously, in some serene part of his brain, he was sinking, down and down, toward the center of the earth. He was being drawn inward by an irresistible force, one which mortals, he mused comfortably, had come to describe as Death.

He understood everything now. But did he hear music, perhaps a symphony? No.

CHAPTER

FIVE

Fortunately, it was not as serious as outright death, although sometimes in the weeks that followed, it seemed to Kelly as if that solution might have been the easiest, and indeed the sensation of surrender had been pleasant.

Later, in an hour or so, he returned from the beautiful excursion. He had been dreaming fitfully of Maryjane, regressing as far as their first summer together in New York, she fresh out of Vassar and he a year free of Yale. It was just months before their marriage and uppermost in the dream was a steady, sullen ache in his groin, all that summer long, as he tried to get past the kissing and fondling and into her pants. Blue balls, they'd called the painful yearning in those days; and to Maryjane's shrieking glee, he'd come more often than once in his own pants.

Emerging from the nightmarish swamp, Kelly didn't

know at first where he was. Across an expanse of sterile white, a dark figure was silhouetted against a window. Mr. Death?

No, it was Rafael Trujillo Perex. Hearing Kelly stir, Perex turned.

"Hello there, hero," he said, his voice choked.

Kelly tasted unaccustomed bile, a backwash, the dregs of some sickening anesthetic. He realized where he was aching: in the groin, as in his dream.

"Victor?"

Perex produced a gasp, something between a moan and a sigh. "We will remember that for your biography, my dear. Is there some reason we should concern ourselves with Victor?"

"He screamed. Did I hit him?"

"Far from it. Yes, he screamed. So did I. Victor tripped in some gopher hole and he was so angry he shot at you out of spite. I can tell you Madame Mordaunt is just a mite upset."

"The gun went off in my face, Rafe," he murmured. "Rafe, I hurt. . . ."

"Yes, they had to sew you up a little bit, my friend."

Kelly gazed down the length of his body, arranged in funereal posture under the white sheet. A horrifying suspicion gathered force. Perex was closer now, squinting at him. His eyes glittered tearfully and he swallowed hard while nervously playing with the beard-shadowed cleft of his chin.

"Rafe? What happened?"

"I fainted."

"You fainted? I can't believe that."

"Yes, I hate the sight of blood, the sounds of violence."

Kelly turned his head away. "Blood? My blood? Some brave Cuban. Rafe?"

Perex started to sob. "I am sorry, bloody hell. Caramba! You and your bloody duel. Putting me through such agony. It is inhuman."

Kelly began to groan. If he'd had the strength he would have jumped out of the bed and beaten Perex to death.

"Goddamn it," he said as loudly as he could. "Forget *you*. What happened to me, for Christ's sake?"

Perex told him apologetically. "The bullet nicked the end of your dollywhacker and cut a gouge across your right thigh." Torment ripped from Kelly's throat and Perex quickly continued. "You will be *all right*, you will be *fine*. It seems a button on your trench coat deflected . . . Do you realize how close you came to . . . bloody shit, my friend . . ." Perex collapsed on his knees at the edge of the bed. "I hate to think about it."

Cold sweat broke out on Kelly's forehead. "Are you saying . . ."

"No, no, thanks be to God, you are all right, my dear." Perex grabbed Kelly's left hand off his chest and kissed it. He was crying freely now.

Relief sang its joyous song inside Kelly's bosom, a euphoric ballad of survival. The remnants of the drug lifted him higher. He could see it now: the distinguished man with a slight limp. He was shot once during a duel with a crazed French dress designer.

"Yes, yes," he said aloud, "that man there with the lived-in face and the disfigured joint . . ."

Perex responded to this flight with a wild giggle. He leaped to his feet. "Yes, and Victor is dishonored," he cried, twisting his hands. "He is fortunate to be alive. Madame Mordaunt went insane with rage."

"That old bitch," Kelly said bitterly.

"She meant only to teach you both a lesson. She intended to stop counting at eighteen or nineteen. She will never forgive herself."

"Oh yes, she will," Kelly said.

"Victor violated the code of chivalry, my dear."

"Doesn't help me much. I'm the one hurting. I do hope this helps your president at his NATO meeting."

Perex fumbled with his tie, uncharacteristically askew. "Do not hate me, my friend." He was very troubled. "Am I a coward for fainting? Will you say now that all Cubans are not brave men? Will you write that?"

* * *

The doctor kept Kelly in the hospital overnight. When Perex had finally gone, leaving behind a mess of apology and self-criticism, Kelly basked in his good fortune. He was a lucky man. His trench coat had served him well.

Again the next morning he reminded himself he was fortunate to be alive and more or less in one piece. Stiffly, moving carefully, he left the hospital, caught a cab outside, and went home.

The empty apartment smelled of dust, dirty ashtrays, and dirty dishes. He hated it, hated Maryjane for not being here when he needed her most. To compound the loneliness of the place, Maryjane's sturgeon glared hostility from behind its glass. The fish, Ivan, hated Kelly too and he was hungry. He seemed prepared to jump out of the tank and devour the first thing available: his master. Swearing at the ugly thing, Kelly dumped food in the water. For himself, he opened a can of *pâté* and the best bottle of Bordeaux he could find. Then, in the silent bedroom, he undressed, sliding his bloodstained clothes past the bulky bandages, his injured parts. The worst of it would be pissing. Erection was out of the question for a while, and he wondered mournfully if he would ever again achieve that.

Kelly ate the *pâté* with stale crackers and began the wine in front of the TV set and a typical night's French programming: news, a variety show, and finally a scientific report from the bottom of the sea. This put him to sleep on the couch and he remained there all night, dreaming again but now of starfish and great ugly sturgeon.

The next day he felt better, but there was more stiffness in the leg and a sympathetic throbbing in his genitals. After-shock was peaking but he managed to hobble downstairs for a carton of Gauloises, a bottle of Pernod, a ripe melon, sliced ham, and a half kilo of runny Brie. By noon, he had finished the newspapers, half the Pernod, and a pack of Gauloises. He napped.

The phone woke him and the next thing he heard was Court's churlish voice. Kelly put on a phony French accent.

"Monsieur Kelly, 'e no 'ere. *Non, non,* Monsieur Kelly, 'e gone Strasbourg. *Oui. Alors. C'est ça. Oui. Merci . . .*"

He clapped down the phone before Court could reply and to put the man out of his mind turned to one of the many recent biographies about that outstanding politician of the forties: Adolf Hitler. This one was called *Warped Walhalla.*

Perex disturbed him at 5:00 P.M. "Dear friend, it is Rafe here. How goes it?"

"Better."

"I am in Geneva, Jack. Do you need me?"

"No."

"I will see you in a few days."

"Not if I see you first."

"My dear, you will be feeling better."

"No, my brave Cuban."

Perex's voice broke. "I told you I was sorry. You should not talk to me like that. I too am trying to forget."

There was no way Kelly could avoid going back to the office the following Monday but he did so with pain in his leg and trepidation in his heart. Trouble was sure to be waiting for him. And there it was.

Newspapers were stacked in the hallway outside and there was a pile of mail behind the door as he opened it. Messages were backed up on the Telex machine. Heart pounding, he read them from top to bottom.

RAG PARIS KELLY WWD CLAIMS YOU MISREAD MOR-DAUNT COLLECTION MAKING US LOOK STUPID. WE DISMAYED. WWD REPORT YOUR OUTRAGEOUS BEHAV-IOR AT MAISON MORDAUNT. BOSS SAYS EXPLAIN SOON-EST. COURT NEWYORK

And the next:

RAG PARIS KELLY UNRECEIVED REPLY OUR QUERY RE MORDAUNT. UNRECEIVED COLLECTIONS ROUNDUP DUE YESTERDAY. EXPLAIN SOONEST. COURT NEWYORK

And the next:

RAG PARIS KELLY TRYING REACH YOU ALL DAY. WHAT
DOING IN STRASBOURG? REPLY SOONEST ALL QUE-
RIES. COURT NEWYORK

Kelly ripped the paper off the machine and stumbled
to his desk. Muttering bitterly, he searched the newspapers
for the offending issue of *Womens Wear Daily,* then
blushed brightly as he read the lines in the EYE.

NEW YORK *RAG* CORRESPONDENT JACK KELLY HIT
THE NAIL RIGHT ON HIS THUMB IN HIS CRITIQUE OF
THE MAISON MORDAUNT WINTER COLLECTION MON-
DAY. BLACK-HAIRED AND EXPANSIVELY DIMPLED KELLY,
SON OF *RAG* PUBLISHER HARRY KELLY AND CHIEF OF
RAG'S PARIS BUREAU IS A LONG-TIME FAVORITE OF
ZOUZOU MORDAUNT. FOLLOWING A BRIEF BUT INTENSE
TÊTE-À-TÊTE WITH ZOUZOU'S BELOVED DEPUTY VIC-
TOR AT THE RUE RIMBAUD SALON SATURDAY, KELLY
BLASTED THE LATEST MORDAUNT COLLECTION TO
SMITHEREENS. IRONICALLY, WHEN THE PIECES FELL
BACK TO EARTH, THEY LANDED IN THE EAGER HANDS
OF THE WAITING PARISIAN LOCO-MOTIVES, STARTING
WITH THE BIGGEST ENGINE OF THEM ALL, THE WIFE
OF THE PRESIDENT OF REPUBLIC. PUT OUT BY KELLY'S
OVERBLOWN CRITIQUE OF THE DARLING OF FRENCH
COUTURE, *TOUT PARIS* IS RALLYING TO HER SIDE. THIS
COULD MAKE IT MORDAUNT'S BIGGEST SEASON EVER.

Merde and *merde* again! Kelly wadded up the paper
and hurled it into his wastepaper basket. Those pricks!
He'd get back at them somehow, he promised himself.
Sure . . . But in the meantime, what was he going to
tell Court? It was enough to piss a man off. Why was
Court always so willing to take *WWD*'s word for every-
thing? Had he ever, ever, let down the *RAG*? And,
Christ, hadn't he been through the mill for the *RAG*?
Being Harry's son had made it tough to begin with.
What about his trainee period in New York? He had

been handed all the shitty assignments: the fur market, then shoes, industrial apparel, finally women's accessories. Court and his friends had lost no opportunity to humiliate him, and even now nothing gave Court more pleasure than whipping off nasty cables to RAG PARIS KELLY. And what about his breaking-in time in Paris? Working for that son of a bitch Don Battlen? Serving drinks to Battlen's long-time Paris cronies and even carrying Battlen's golf clubs around the course at Neuilly? Battlen had finally been forced to retire and was now parked in a villa in Spain, the bastard, after raping his expense account for thirty years. Kelly made a mental note to cancel Battlen's complimentary airmail subscription to the *RAG*. And Court would be well advised to take his retirement too before Jack Kelly returned to the "Flagship" in New York.

As he wallowed in comforting thoughts of future revenge, the present was recalled by the clanging bell of the Telex machine, this modern instrument of medieval torture. Jesus, he groaned, another bullet.

RAG PARIS KELLY UNBELIEVE YOU PARTICIPATED IN EARLY MORNING STUNT RUMORED AROUND TOWN. IF SO, INEXCUSABLE, UNFORGIVABLE, INCOMPREHENSIBLE BLUNDER ONLY COMPOUNDED BY YOUR DISGRACEFUL MAISON MORDAUNT EXPLOIT. BOSS DEMANDS NOT ASKS FULL EXPLANATION COURT NEWYORK

Kelly was near hysteria, wounds burning, fingers perspiring as he composed his reply. But he answered only the first of the messages. Like Kennedy at the time of the Cuban missile crisis and as J.F.K. was dealing with another maniac, Nikita Khrushchev, he would ignore the most threatening of the Court messages.

RAG NEWYORK COURT STANDING BY MY ASSESSMENT MORDAUNT COLLECTION. IT STANK LIKE YESTERDAYS FISH. KELLY PARIS

He shot this off to New York and then, more calmly, sat down again to sort out the mail. There would be plenty of time to institute the "row-back" procedure: that process by which during a twenty-four period one made use of long distance and time difference to adjust New York's conception of reality to one's own. For the next hour or so, the office was quiet. No, he told himself, there was nothing to worry about. He could dodge reality. Court was crazy enough to accept crazy explanations. Personally speaking, there was nothing to worry about either. He would be slightly scarred but so what? Zouzou Mordaunt would be on the defensive because of Victor's unchivalrous conduct. His old man would forget it and Court would button his lip. It would be all right.

Then the phone rang.

"Here is Veronika Zenf."

He knew this klutzy broad. She represented in Paris one of the more loathsome German-family picture magazines.

"Herr Kelly, what we do not have is one picture of you. I will come, yes, to your office with my photographer."

"No! Reporters don't take pictures of other reporters."

"Ah no?" She hesitated. "You are quite well now, Herr Kelly?"

"Of course I am. Why shouldn't I be?"

She began to giggle. Veronika giggled with a German accent. "Is it fine now when you *machen* peepee, Herr Kelly?" Yes, German bathroom humor would appeal to her; also bathing in that uniquely German luxury called *schadenfreude*, the unspeakable joy derived from the misfortunes of others.

"You kraut bitch," he snarled.

He slammed down the phone. But he knew what they would make of it, photo or not. There would be a montage of pictures, a shot of the Bois de Boulogne, a couple of hundred sensational words expanding on his contretemps with Victor, then a paragraph on well-known historical personages blown away in the forest.

Jesus, how had he managed to work himself into this

spot? Kelly had always been one to keep his distance from personal embarrassment, a step away from such idiocies as he'd experienced with Victor. But it was different now. He had dumped himself into a situation of high visibility.

The sound, again, of the Telex machine shattered his restored confidence and optimism. Fearfully, he edged toward the machine and watched the flying keys hammer out another message of distemper:

RAG PARIS KELLY YOUR MESSAGE IGNORES OUR QUERY RE INCIDENT IN BOIS DE BOLOGNA. WHAT GIVES QUERY BOSS SAYS YOUR DEFENSE MORDAUNT STORY NO EXPLANATION. STILL UNRECEIVED YOUR COLLECTION ROUNDUP STORY DUE WEDNESDAY. BOSS SUSPEND-ING YOU PENDING UPCLEARANCE THIS WHOLE UNBE-LIEVABLE MESS. YOU OFF PAYROLL UNTIL ACCEPTABLE EXPLANATION RECEIVED. BOSS PLENTY UPBURNED COURT NEWYORK

His old man was "upburned"? Well, he was pretty burned up too. He was off the payroll? This had to be a special punishment, reserved for the boss's son. Why didn't they simply fire him? Jesus Christ! Disaster. How could he explain what had happened? Didn't they understand he had nearly lost his life, or at least his balls, defending the honor of the *RAG*?

He had often heard the apocryphal stories about far-flung correspondents telling headquarters to stick job asswards. But that was not how he worded his own message.

RAG NEWYORK COURT YOUR APPRECIATION THIS SITUATION APPALLING. YOUR LACK SUPPORT DIS-GRACEFUL. IMPOSSIBLE REPRESENT RAG PARIS IN SUCH CIRCUMSTANCES. KELLY PARIS

It was not as though he had thrown down both gaunt-lets. He had not told them in so many words to shove the job. He had left room for negotiation and eventual surrender. It was Court's decision to read between the lines.

Monday afternoon, when he'd sent the message, then left the office, he was still a *RAG* employee, albeit suspended.

When he came in Tuesday morning, feeling physically much better, he found that Olga Blastorov had returned. She was sitting at her desk sobbing.

"Hello, toots," he said uneasily, "how was your *vacances*?"

"Do not ask," she wailed. "I am so worried. I am ordered to change the locks on the door."

A piece of Telex paper dangled from her hand.

"Let's see that."

"Oh, Monsieur Jack," Olga lowed, clutching at her chest. "Because of Madame Mordaunt and Victor? What does it mean, Monsieur Jack?"

The cable was clear enough. "What it means, honey," Kelly squalled, "is that I'm canned, shafted, axed. The fickle finger, whatever you Frenchies call that." But he was stunned. He had counted on Harry pulling back from a showdown.

"Oh . . . Is there nothing I can do, Monsieur Jack?"

"No, nothing," he faltered. "Don't cry. You'll make do. You've always been the mainstay of the office anyway. Just one thing—don't tell anybody right away. Okay?"

"Not a soul in the world," she promised.

Olga's anxious breasts strained with sincerity against the peasant blouse she'd brought back from the foothills of Mont Blanc. Blindly, she reached for his arm and pressed. Without thinking, Kelly bent and kissed her cupid lips. She returned the kiss with a hungry mouth. Kelly was startled. He realized he was violating the basic rule. But he was no longer Olga's boss. He pulled her to her feet and put his arms around her waist. Unresisting, she crushed against him, breasts full and round, nipples stiffened like two thumbs. A snort of passion blasted his cheek. She had been taken off guard. Her eyelids fluttered and she hiked her pelvis at him.

"Olga, have you been saving it?"

"Yes, of course," she said, not understanding the question.

Too late, he remembered his infirmity. A shock wave of pain looped across the stitches in his leg and fire lit the end of his dick.

"Monsieur Jack?"

"Hell, it hurts, Olga. Victor shot me there. You know about the duel, don't you?"

She nodded sorrowfully. "All Paris knows."

Shaking, sweating, he backed away, and flustered, red-faced, she sat down again. "Monsieur Jack, this is not something . . ."

"Olga . . ."

"No, it is not something I would wish to happen. My father, Count Boris . . ."

Count Boris Blastorov, Olga's father, was a fierce Russian emigré who had been making ends meet in Paris since the late thirties.

"Olga, it's just that I never thought . . ."

"Monsieur Jack, you are lonely and now you are hurt. You do not really care for me. Besides, you are married."

"Olga, I do care for you. Don't say that."

She shook her head nervously and quickly began clipping the newspapers he had marked, Kelly's way of assembling background information he might need to lift for one of his Paris datelined stories.

"You can forget about doing that, Olga. I'm cleaning out my desk and for all I care you can throw out all the goddamn files."

Her face stiffened. "*RAG* must go on, Monsieur Jack."

"Shit!"

Her body jerked eloquently. Olga did not like such words. Then the phone rang and she jumped again. She was certainly edgy. The call was for him and there was no need for the voice to identify itself.

"Jacques," Madame Mordaunt said brusquely. "I wish to inform you that Monsieur Victor wishes to pay the medical expenses arising from this farcical affair. It is, *alors,* his fondest wish. He also has immense regrets. Of that, Jacques, I can assure you."

Phone at his ear; he fiddled in his desk drawer. Nothing he really wanted there: a few calling cards, check stubs, cigarette lighters, a picture or two.

"Oh, how splendid," he responded sardonically.

He winked at Olga who was listening, white-faced.

"Jacques! I wish to tell you this is not the end of the world," Zouzou said harshly. "Your doctors assure me you will be well mended in a few days."

Zouzou had never been big on apologies. But Kelly could tell from the tone of her voice that she was uncomfortable with the knowledge that her scheme had miscarried. He was silent and in a moment she continued.

"It is a long life you have before you, Jacques, and not one you should waste recriminating the past." He sat silently, waiting her out. Wheedling, she asked, "Is not the small taste of vindication sweet smelling, Jacques?"

"Possibly."

"Will you please call upon me at the Maison Mordaunt?"

"Possibly," he repeated.

"Ah, *merde,*" Zouzou hawked impatiently and hung up.

Slowly, he put the phone down. "Olga, I'm leaving. No point sitting around here." It was a minor relief that he wouldn't ever finish his Couture Week roundup; even that was worth something. "You will let me in when I come back?"

Her brown eyes were woeful but cautious. She had suddenly become suspicious of his intentions. "Is there nothing I can do?"

"Nothing you'd want to do. Look, I'll see you around, honey," he said, holding himself firmly in control.

He could hear her sobs after he closed the door. He went downstairs and strolled sadly down the block to rue Cambon, up the street to the Madeleine. He stopped at a kiosk to buy a copy of the Paris *Trib,* and continued on to the Café de la Paix where he took a sidewalk table and ordered coffee. After the funnies, Kelly read a Don

Cook piece, an advance story on the upcoming Washburn trip to Europe. Putting the paper aside, he considered the weighty question of perfidy. Harry Kelly had always advised him to duck in plenty of time; he'd learned that during the war.

Perex had retrieved the spent slug from the shot Victor had fired at him. Kelly dug this out of his pocket and laid it on the table beside the coffee cup. It looked gigantic and he imagined what it might have done had it hit him squarely. He shivered, then remembered he had to get the trench coat repaired.

Monsieur Pleven, his doctor, had prescribed exercise to restore the suppleness of his muscles, and in the days that followed, Kelly walked until he was weary, stopping at out-of-the-way cafés, resting in dusty parks and cool churches. He prowled the museums and in the evenings he read and sometimes went to the movies. He cut down on the drinking and he was sleeping well. This was a period of recuperation from his wounds, physical and mental, and the time in which he also weaned himself away from daily duty at the *RAG*.

Kelly smarted over his job, however, and he wondered when, and if, the old man and Court would relent. There were no messages from New York. It was as if they'd wiped him off the face of the earth by the simple method of canning him. But, for Olga, he maintained a brave front.

"Hello, honey."

"Monsieur Jack, several calls. No, not from New York. Monsieur Perex is very angry with you. He wishes to see you."

But he had not gone back to the Ritz. "Fuck him, Olga," he said, appreciating her gasp. "Zouzou? No. My darling wife . . . No."

"Monsieur Jack, Madame Kelly is not yet home?"

"She's been gone a whole month, Olga. Ask me how it feels to be a free man?"

"How does it feel to be a free man, Monsieur Jack?"

"Wonderful, Olga. I'm seeing Paris as I've never seen it before."

"Oh, yes? I pray you do not acquire a social disease, Monsieur Jack."

He laughed heartily. "Olga, you shock me." She probably didn't know what she was saying.

He did not visit Zouzou Mordaunt. He brooded only infrequently about Victor. Victor was too used up to be a good hate object. In the evenings, he began to spend time at Pierre et Pauline's, known as Pipi's, an undistinguished bistro on the Île de la Cité, its walls decorated with blistered varnish, the floors rough, tables uneven, and boasting a raw house wine. His wish now was to be alone but it was during this period that Perex reentered his life one night at Pipi's.

This was the first time Kelly had ever actually seen Perex with one of his lovelies. She was a black-haired woman named Maggi Mont. Perex boasted that she was an intellectual from New York. They said hello. Her hand was warm and firm, the fingers stubby, and for a second, thrillingly, he imagined them playing over typewriter keys. There was something very sensual about strong feminine hands manipulating a typewriter.

"I've heard of you," she said, "and I think I saw you at the Maison Mordaunt."

"I remember—you were sitting near Aristide de Bis."

"Yes, but he didn't notice me," she said.

"You saw what happened afterwards?" he asked embarrassedly.

Maggi Mont did not waste words. She was forthright, like Pierre's wine, strong and uncut, an intense woman. She studied him frankly.

"Maggi writes books," Perex announced.

"Oh? What kind?"

"How-to books," she said.

Kelly played along, aloofly. "How to what?"

"How to fuck," she said.

Perex blushed and averted his face. "Maggi, Maggi . . ."

"Well, that's what they are," she said briskly.

Perex, in confusion, tried to explain. "Jack, my friend, Maggi is one of America's leading sexologists."

Her frank appraisal of him took on fresh meaning. Kelly felt intimidated. The nerves jangled in his most important scar. "Interesting," he muttered.

Perex changed the subject. "I see, my dear, that you have chosen the oblivion of Pierre et Pauline's. And you have been avoiding your closest friend, Rafael Trujillo Perex."

He did not disagree. "I needed peace and quiet, Rafe. You know, of course, that I've been fired from the *RAG*?"

Perex threw up his hands. "Yes, good heavens, *cher*! What will you do?"

"Nothing."

Perex stared at him, not believing it. "And Madame Mordaunt?"

"We're completely out of contact."

"Merde," Perex muttered, "that is not good." Then his teeth flashed in a stunning smile. "Do not worry, *cher*. I have a plan."

"Spare me your plan, Rafe."

Maggi Mont's face was wary. "What's this all about?"

"My dear Maggi," Perex murmured, giving her a visual caress. "It is nothing of importance."

CHAPTER

SIX

It was toward the end of August when Kelly saw Maggi Mont again. He was sitting at his usual table at Pipi's reading André Gide when she came in. They talked for a while and then she left, stomping into the darkness in her hard-heeled leather boots, an independent figure of a woman in tight black slacks and snug turtleneck sweater. She returned the next night; and by the time August turned to September one would have described them as inseparable.

It was not that Kelly pursued Maggi, not at all. Skillfully, for once, in this matter of women and the obtaining of them, Kelly played her with a polite indifference, a distant air of smoldering integrity. During the daytime, she took to going with him on his long walks, following him around Paris as she would have a tour guide, he silent, almost morose in his aloofness; she muttering and watching him, baffled. In no time at all, she had concluded that he was an enigma.

"A man so withdrawn," she mused, fixing coal-black eyes upon him, "I have to admit I'm intrigued by a man who doesn't throw you down and try to fuck you after the first handshake."

What he was doing, of course, was remaining rigidly away from physical contact. At the Louvre, they stood together staring at the Winged Victory, Kelly remarking on this and that but avoiding any reference to the voluptuous torso. Maggi's hand brushed against his leg, deliberately of course. He shifted away. He avoided her hands, averted his eyes from her striking cleavage or charming thighs when she slid in and out of tight café corners.

But God, she was beautiful and alive with sensuality. Her skin was luminous, exotic, and the perfume of her body moved with her like an aura. No man alive could resist this for long.

Monsieur Pleven had told Kelly most recently, when the time came to yank rotting stitches out of his thigh, that he was on the undoubted verge of recovery of his powers, the restoration, so to speak, of his royal household. But there had been no sign of that yet. Pleven, always the sly optimist, had pointed out to him that the slight residual bump on the end of his dick would be its own attraction. But, whatever Pleven said, the master switch did not turn over. Kelly was petrified to try, and fail.

Maggi had her story too, though she would not tell it. She refused to acknowledge the past. Had it been so lurid and bitter? It was as if she had not existed before the Real Time of the ticking clock. Memory, she told him wisely, was merely a cloud, already dissipating in time as it was being formed. Was she an existentialist? Whatever, she made it clear she was a liberated woman. She had come to Paris, she said, in quest of stimulation, experience, raw material for her study of human sexuality—in brief, she growled, for more than the stench of centuries-old wine and piss.

Everything in life has its time and place, she said, and after a week of solid walking, timid verbalizing on Kelly's part as he imagined himself rolling viscously about in her tender insides, the time came. He found himself one night in her one-room flat on the rue Anjou having that last drink which so often spelled commitment.

She was thirty-two, she was telling him, and she had always been kissed by good fortune.

"Jacko," she said, this being the name she had come to call him, "Jacko, you fascinate me. There's something, *je ne sais quoi*, about you that reeks of quiet desperation. I wish I could put my finger on it."

That was the crux of the problem. He hurried his drink and asked, "Where do you come from, Maggi?"

"From everywhere," she said solemnly, "from the mire of the human condition." She leaned back, arching her body against an array of not very well stuffed cushions which turned bed into couch in the waking hours and eyed him judiciously. "But never mind about that, Jacko. . . . Do we live lives of quiet desperation? Do we? Is that the way the world ends, not with a bang but a whimper?"

"I don't get you," he mumbled.

"I think you do, Jacko. I know you're not a virgin. You're married. Where is she?"

He shrugged. "Who knows?"

"It's not like I'm going to corrupt a pimply-faced little choirboy," she said, thus telegraphing her intentions.

Kelly began to tremble. But he managed to say, "I'm as pure as the driven snow."

He remembered: that was what Maryjane had said so often during that hot summer in New York whenever he'd gotten close to scoring.

"'Jesuschirist," Maggi vented disagreeably, running the Lord's name into a single, slurred epithet.

She was not prepared to let him escape. By the time he was two gulps into a second, warm vodka-vermouth and before no more than half of a fuzzy Stravinsky record had been gnawed away by a blunt needle, Maggi was upon him, strenuously exercising her female prerogative.

She kissed him violently, unbuttoning his shirt and pulling at his belt in one all-encompassing act of aggression. She ran her hands over his bare chest, pinched the small roll of fat at his waist and began moaning and panting, all this while impatiently kicking off her intellectual sandals, revealing the Parisian dust between her stubby toes, unclipping the earrings she'd bought in decadent North Africa, and squirming within her loose-fitting cotton muslin smock.

It was obviously too late to avoid arousing her. She had begun to rummage inside his trousers like a wild woman at a garage sale. No, he thought heatedly, perhaps the time *had* come to surrender. If worse came to worse he would find a way to give her satisfaction in some clinically accepted fashion.

Maggi was tearing at his fly, pulling his pants down off his hips.

"Easy, easy," he murmured.

Momentarily, she stopped the attack and put her eyes close to his face. "Jacko," she hissed, "if there's something wrong, tell me. I don't think I'm basically unattractive, do you?"

As he shook his head, she leaped off the bed and flung the smock over her head to reveal bare breasts crowned with immense red nipples. They were resoundingly firm. She pulled off her brief panties, then stood before him, presenting herself to him, patch of tangled black pubic hair a foot from his face. Her thighs glistened with slick evidence of her excitement and Kelly quivered at the visual impact of the half-concealed lips of her most secret place twitching as if in promised merriment.

"What do you think of that, Jacko?" she crowed.

"God—I am . . . impressed."

"You may touch."

Delicately, as if reaching to defang a rattler, he put the palm of his hand under the mons. Juices bathed his fingers. Uttering a cry, she rubbed his fingers against the smooth folds of the opening. Now moaning without restraint or delicacy, she fell on her knees before him and busied herself with his shorts.

Kelly bucked in alarm and she pulled back instantly, sternly challenging him.

"Jacko, goddamn it, if you're gay tell me right now. I won't mind—but I'm not about to roll a heavy stone uphill for nothing."

"God, Maggi, no . . . I'm not . . . but . . ."

"Are you afraid of being unfaithful, Jacko? Some guys are. . . . It turns them into dippy wicks."

She didn't wait for a reply. She pushed his hands aside and pulled his shorts down. She stared for a second, then recoiled.

"Jesuschirist," she yelped, "what's that awful scar? Not a scar, it looks like a scab. A scab? Son of a bitch! I was prepared to do intimate things with it. . . . It's spread . . . from your leg. Oh no! That's horrible. Ugh! Get out of my house."

She jumped to her feet, cursing.

"It's not what you think, Maggi, not at all what you think."

"Jesuschirist," she yelled furiously, "it's a good thing the lights are on."

Angrily, he puffed, "Shut up for a minute, will you? I'll explain."

"What's to explain? I've got two eyes, haven't I?"

"Dummy," he said evenly, "I got that in a duel. I was shot there. Didn't Perex tell you?"

"A duel?" She stared at him strangely. "Why should Perex tell me somebody shot your cock?"

"Perex was there. He fainted."

She began to chuckle slowly, then laughed. "He would." She breathed more easily. "Does it hurt? Jesus, Jacko, I've never known a man in a duel." She sat down beside him and lightly put her square hand across his scar-headed penis. "Is that better?"

"Yes, thank you."

Gently, she stroked him. "Rise, dear Lazarus."

Anxiously, he said, "I don't think it will. I think a nerve must have been hit. I think I'm impotent."

"Balderdash," Maggi scoffed. "That's what a lot of men say, trying to seduce dames. There's nothing wrong with it, you'll see. More like psychological damage, if anything. . . . I was wondering what the hell was wrong with you, Jacko. You're just afraid to try it." She laughed delightedly, saying, "This is a hell of a challenge for a sexologist and one who's practiced surrogate sex. I know you're not impotent. I'd recognize that in a flash, Jacko. Just remember: this is not mission impossible."

She hopped up on her knees beside him and bent to

brush a big nipple across the livid scar. She put her head down, hair falling loosely like a shielding waterfall and gathered the injured rosebud in her mouth. She tongued him, but lightly, took everything in her mouth, covering him in moist warmth.

It was as simple as that. He was aware of a swelling but also of rippling ragged discomfort. He muttered worriedly and she lifted her head.

"See that? Who is it gives Lazarus a rise? I must say though, we smell a little gamey from walking all day. . . . That bother you?"

"No . . . I'm just afraid it might bust open again."

Maggi shook her head. "Uh-uh, Jacko. That thing is infinitely flexible. I've had a lot of experience with guys in duels." She grinned at him. "I might make that a chapter in my newest tome. Don't worry: give it a second or two. It'll be all right again."

"If you say so."

Kelly laughed breathlessly as Maggi put her hands on his shoulders, forcing him backward. She kissed him, mouth dripping, and lustfully at last, he felt the quiver, the shaking of the monster emerging from its lair. Maggi's mouth opened widely and took what seemed his whole mouth and lower face between her lips. She rubbed the back of his head, his neck, loosening muscles, then fell down on him again. Relaxed, he ran his hand across her smooth buttocks, along the crease where hip met belly, between her legs, and caressed the soft lips of her vagina, found with his forefinger the tiny button, the core of her being, and gently pressed it. Maggi heaved and worked him the more vigorously with her mouth until protesting scar was overridden by desire. He became hard and blazingly erect. She pushed his head from her breast to her belly, shuddering, and shoved his face between her legs, forced his nose to that lush spot which jerked to meet his mouth. Knowing this was what he should do, he thrust his tongue into her. It was like a torch and she groaned as if from pain.

Without warning, she flopped to the side and pulled him between her legs. She tugged him into her and forward until it seemed he had reached the edge of a cliff. He struggled against her mound, his entire being, microscopic pore by pore, drawn within her and held in a terrifying grip. Her muscles contracted, relaxed, expanded, sucked him more deeply and demandingly until, mad from her gyrations, he could hold out no longer.

He climaxed in full flood.

"Don't stop, don't stop," she cried excitedly, continuing to writhe under him as he jabbed less effectively, and then came herself with a shriek of pleasure. "Leave it there. Leave it there, Jacko!"

Depleted, he lay on her, felt himself go flaccid. Her breasts rolled under his chest and her legs were twined around him, locked at the ankles over his hips. Her internal muscles continued to work and she held him there, a prisoner. He felt the scar burning but there was no way he could escape. The muscular socket tightened on him with the progressive withering of his determination, as if threaded and each of its parts individually controlled, gripping as confidently as a ten-fingered hand. Slowly, he passed the barrier and began to harden again, not surprising after such a long drought. Alert to his signals, Maggi rocked her hips under him, reaching for him again.

Her face was pure passion, her eyes tightly closed and a smug smile flirting with her lips. She grabbed him by the hair and pulled his face down for another gaping kiss. Her teeth ground against his and her tongue reached for his voice box.

She muttered, "I got you, Jacko. Do it. Do it good, Jacko."

He stroked her, pulling back, then thrusting forward with all his might, the length of him, as long as a railroad car, reaching into her, exploring, searching for God knows what.

Maggi whistled between her teeth. "Don't spare the horsepower, Jocko. I can feel that scar, Jacko. Jesus, it is marvelous. It's going to make you famous. Women will go insane for it. They'll write songs about you. Wow-ee!" She whooped so raucously, he wondered about the neighbors. "Jacko, this is so good. . . . Is this good, or is this good, I ask you? Want to try it another way?"

Panting, he said, "Anyway you want, any way . . ."

"Shall I release you now? You know, Jacko, I've got the grip of steel. Uh . . . uh . . . They call it the Chinese Grip. Ah! Good-o!"

Her body shook with another, more minor, release. She held him a moment longer, tremblingly applying a final muscular caress. Then abruptly, her muscles went slack.

"Okay, I'm letting you go."

Cautiously, he withdrew, unsure of his freedom. "God—I've had it."

"I'll say you've had it"—she sighed—"from a master."

Afterwards, they had a tepid shower. Maggi scrubbed him lovingly, like a favorite toy, wriggling against him in the tiny stall.

"Scarface held out, I see," she observed. "Red but not dead. Would you say you've returned to the land of the living?"

"Thanks to you," he said happily.

She smiled and tenderly squeezed his parts. "We'll go to bed now. You don't have to leave. I'm relaxing my rules for you."

She threw the cover off the couch, dumped the cushions on the floor, and they lay down, side by side, under a single sheet. Her head comfortably on his shoulder, she absently fingered him as she talked.

"I do know plenty about sex, Jacko, and I've written scads about it too. But don't get the idea I'm some kind of easy lay. . . ." He shook his head, denying any such thought. "Like Perex said, I am a leading sexologist. I'm an expert in methodology, as you may have noticed. . . . For instance, my friend, the Chinese Grip, which you've experienced now, probably for the first time, is something I've worked to perfection. It's a very rare phenomenon—that little trick has been used by leading courtesans through the ages and it's made and broken kingdoms and empires. If you want, you can call it the Gift of the Maggi. Do you get the pun? Are you asleep, Jacko?"

"No, no, I get it."

"Good. One other thing I should ask you, Jacko, is: do you prefer the missionary position or other ones. Doggo? Sidesaddle? The twist?"

"I think I like them all, each and every one."

She held him lightly between her thumb and forefinger, gently massaging the large vein that runs down the center of the shaft, like the central thread through an expensive necktie.

Kelly knew it was perhaps out of place, and time, to ask the question but it was in the back of his mind: "What's your connection with Rafe Perex?"

"Oh, hell," she said drowsily, "I used to know his wife."

"Westerley Washburn?"

"Sure, we were in school together, me and that nut." She bit his left nipple, as if to recall him to more important things. "Tell me, Jacko, do I or do I not have lovely breasts?"

"They are exquisite, devastating."

"Do you think the nipples are too big?" He shook his head loosely. "Jesus, Jacko, they're as big as silver dollars."

"Right—the coin of the realm."

"Would you suspect that I've been siliconed, Jacko?"

"I don't know. It never occured to me. . . . I don't know much about that. But . . . I wouldn't suppose so."

He had said the right thing.

"Correct," Maggi said smugly. "These are all me."

Her cathedral chest fell away to a flat stomach, the navel basin a shallow, concave lagoon, smooth legs, the tawny loins and jungle at the Venusian delta.

She allowed him no respite. Cupping him in her hand and squeezing, she said, "Now tell me all about that duel, Jacko."

He did so briefly, reporting the salient points of the

sordid story and finally asking her whether she thought he should extract some sort of revenge from Victor.

"No." She touched the little bump on the end of his shaft. "You should thank him if you ask me." She kissed him, smelling of milky fertility. "I'm infatuated with your bod, Jacko."

He said, "Were you ever a dancer?"

"No, but I could have been, couldn't I? This body . . ." She ran her hands along her slim forearms, down her belly and between her thighs. "No, this body is geared to love, Jacko. And I like it. Don't get the idea though that I'm some kind of a nymphomaniac because I'm not. Love is my job, also a hobby. Rarely do people get to enjoy their work as much as I do. You know, Jacko, I'm really glad I've been able to help you, but from my side of the fence, you know, there's nothing like it, feeling that thing fill you up. That's how a woman feels about it, you know. It's the missing link—or joint, you might say."

She was spread diagonally across him, her breasts flattened on his ribs, her head in his armpit. Kelly trolled his fingers down her spine. The precise point of confluence of cheeks was supposed to be a very hot spot. It was. Maggi quivered.

"See," he said, "I know a little sexology myself."

"I want you again, Jacko," she whispered, "come hell or high water. I'm thinking—I want to go to Nice. Would you come to Nice with me? I know a small hotel and it would be nice to go to Nice with you. I'm working on a project—top secret."

"I'll go anywhere you want. You've got me in the Chinese Grip."

"Jacko, have you ever read my books or newspaper articles?"

He had to admit he had not. But she was not put out. Her work, she said, was fantastically scientific but it was also a service to people with sex hang-ups. She and her colleagues had done numerous laboratory experiments with human subjects, fitting the latter up with sensors and bits of wire stuck in the various orifices, then recording actual copulatory activity on sophisticated monitors, computers, and even sometimes observing through one-way glass windows.

"I can't tell you how interesting it is, Jacko," she murmured, "much more so than watching apes screwing and, naturally, a lot more revealing. Did you know, for example, that under ideal circumstances it takes the human female seven minutes to get it off—I mean if she doesn't have some kind of block."

He shook his head. "I wouldn't want anybody watching me."

"Au contraire," Maggie disagreed enthusiastically. "Some of our lab assistants get so hot watching they start humping right there in the middle of all the equipment."

"A kind of disciplinary problem, no?"

"Yes, and no. What we say to them is: if you're so horny, then let's just stick this wire up your coocoo and attach this sensor to your dingdong, and get going."

"And I studied liberal arts. . . . I must be crazy."

Maggi giggled cozily. "You know they nicknamed us the Fuckalot Wing of the Fordham Neurological Center. The Jesuit fathers didn't like it much. But, seriously, we've done work for the CIA, and I can tell you, off the record, my current project has to do with the sex drive of famous politicians, living and dead, leading anarchists, Marxists, all those kinds of people."

"For the CIA?"

"Sure. You know about the enemy's sex drive and you know how they'll respond in times of crisis. . . . Speaking of which, what's your view of anal intercourse?"

"I dunno," Kelly said. "You're getting a little deep for me there."

Christ, as far as he knew, that was still known as buggery in the courts of law and much frowned upon in most social circles. He realized sex was Maggi's business but was she really so experienced? A man liked to think his woman of the moment was relatively naive, that she had not seen and done absolutely everything.

"I'm not going to push you," Maggi said. "Right now we'll stick to the simple stuff."

She adjusted her body again so that her head rested on his thigh. Gazing up devilishly, she extended her tongue and licked his scar. Kelly slid his hand around her buttocks and compressed the lips of her vagina.

"Jacko," she said, "you're insatiable. Let me ask you: you are liberal, are you not?" Confidently, he nodded. "Well, the French call it *soixante-neuf*—because of the way the figures fall together. Does that alarm you?"

"No. Hell, we were doing it, weren't we?"

"Yes—I just want to make absolutely sure you know exactly what we're up to."

"Okay."

Her thick bush was at hand and he thought it his duty to reciprocate. He parted the hair and ran his tongue along the length of the ruffled lips, as crisp as steam-ironed lace. Voraciously, inspired, Maggi took him in her mouth, choking a little, he thought complacently.

"Boy," she said, "we're good and clean now, ain't we? We smell good."

The scent of her volcanic, unpredictable vulva was overpowering. She exuded a sweet odor, carried on a sticky moistness. She could not bear it—in a moment, she twisted, panting.

"Move over and stick it in. Then lie perfectly still. Yes. Now, think only of the coupling. Relax completely."

Kelly made himself quiet, unclenched his fists and the soles of his feet. Inside, her muscles were bubbling, although she was totally supine. He answered her with a pulse of tension.

"No, no, relax I tell you. Just *feel*. We're suspended in space. This is how the Indians do it—Indian Indians, not red Indians, although maybe they do it too. I must check that," she murmured languorously. "It's the highest form, Nirvana they call it. After you've perfected this method, you'll come without moving a muscle."

"You'd miss all that exercise. Good for you," Kelly reminded her.

He sensed a faint, faraway beating, yet forced himself

to concentrate on total inertia. Within moments, out of this studied lassitude, came the increasing tempo of his engorgement and a heightened vibration from Maggi's interior. He saw her eyes had dilated. She was breathing shallowly. A vein fluttered in her throat. He thought for a moment that she had passed into a trance but absorbed this only vaguely, for he too was far away. Faintly, the far reaches of her vagina began to quake. The swell of her clitoris bore down on him; from nothing, a pinhead, it grew to what seemed enormous size, with a life of its own, bulging like a Neolithic orchid. A musty, earth aroma, much like burnt coffee beans, rose between them. Was this the smell of sex undilute?

Their coupling achieved an existence of its own. Maggi's skin tightened and her breathing became more tortuous. Her heartbeat echoed into his chest cavity and her body, of its own accord, began to tremble, possessed by a motor reaction over which she had no control.

Finally, Kelly was conscious of a third heartbeat, that of the coupling itself. The beat became pronounced; it seemed to fill the room, rock the couch, pound against the walls. Blood charged through him, headed for the focus of their embrace.

There was nothing else now, only that.

By the time it ended, he was ready to cry out for mercy. Maggi climaxed in series, jabbering incoherently, ridden by muscle spasms. The contractions of her passage became fearful, insistent and entreating as she, at one and the same time, produced miniscule electrical shocks generated by the chemistry of the mating and extracted from him an entire reservoir of life-force. He came with a gushing finality and she climaxed one last time, bellowing weakly.

He collapsed on top of her, understanding dimly that he had been part of a rare happening, a sort of contained nuclear reaction. Exhaustedly, he rolled to the side and, still, even in his absence, her crotch bumped at the night. Languidly, she dropped her hand to his thigh.

"I couldn't," he muttered.

"Nor more could I, Jacko." Her voice was small and

feline. "Jacko, that was one for the books. If you ever need an endorsement. This goes in my book too. Is there anything else I can do for you?"

"No, no." He wanted no more just yet. "Do you think this is the highest form . . ."

"Of screwing?" She lifted her head to her elbow to peer gleefully at him. "It's definitely the highest form I've found, the unscrewing screw, Jacko. Do you have any idea how hard it is to reproduce this under lab conditions?"

CHAPTER

SEVEN

They stayed in a shabby but comfortable hotel two blocks from the seafront for ten whole days. Nice was quiet in the early autumn, almost ominously peaceful. At the end of the day, the sun set blood-red in the west over the water, as it had, said the old-timers, at dusk before the dawn of World War I.

Their ardor had not cooled. Kelly and Maggi made love in the morning, in the afternoon, before dinner, and after dinner. Their room smelled, Kelly often told her embarrassedly, like a sexual battlefield. Even the normally active cockroaches of southern France were numbed to a lethargy which made them easy targets for a rolled-up copy of *France-Soir*.

Kelly was not quite sure what had happened to him, or how long he would survive it. There had to be a point, he thought worriedly, at which such basic sexual madness would backfire.

But Maggi would hear none of that. At her urging, they ate large amounts of seafood.

"The month isn't right for oysters, Jacko, but have the *moules*," she would say. "Why here's swordfish on the menu—not to say there's anything wrong with your sword." Pinching him intimately, she would add, "I'm getting together a chapter sometime on the hormones of the sea, my little sea urchin."

They took a swim in the ocean every morning, ignoring at her urging the pollution level in this part of the Mediterranean, for Maggi was a firm believer in the power of saltwater. He began to understand that she was a sexual virtuoso with an infinite repertoire. Her instrument was capable of the most incredible flights. She understood the use of flattery, assuring him that he was a man of gargantuan appetite and insatiable lust. But, as depressing as it was for her, and try as they might, they were not able to repeat the crashing Nirvana of that first night.

"I dunno," Maggi brooded, "I don't understand it. I'm beginning to think that's something you get when love is completely fresh, maybe when the bodies are new to each other, like on the first night out."

"You'd think it'd be easier when the bodies came to be fine-tuned to each other," he observed. It didn't worry him as it did her. "Maybe it's the climate, or the mistral."

"A wind? What would that have to do with it? I thought the fish would help."

An amusing idea came to him. "Maybe we should have brought along some Grovival. Do you know about that stuff?"

She was disgusted. "I've read about it in the learned journals," she said. "Jack, things like that are no good. They're unnatural."

He was surprised that she didn't know the full Grovival story. Hadn't Perex tipped her off? Holding her fast in his arms, their bodies entwined in lazy mating on the sagging brass bed, he lightly said, "It's supposed to produce horniness in women and make men grow to great lengths. Not something we really need, I guess."

"I don't know. I could do with another inch or two." He strained into her. "Well, maybe a millimeter or two." She chuckled. "But who knows? If the stuff works like they say it does, it might be useful for treatment of some of the more extreme sex impasses."

"If you don't grow warts." He told her what Perex had reported about the Swiss experiments.

She sniffed. "Might know he'd be mixed up in it, that fiend. . . . But still it's interesting."

"Just professionally or for the sport?"

She bit his shoulder sharply. "Listen, Mr. Smart-Ass, I'm like a golf pro. Just because I teach, it doesn't mean I don't like to play the game for pleasure. . . . Don't get cocky, mister."

Whatever Maggi's professional preoccupations and personal pride she remained for him a garden of delight and he the agronomist who harvested her. Despite her worry about refining Nirvana and his concern that he would be turned into a slavering wreck of a man, he could not get enough of her. Each time was a revelation; her responses were as fresh and passionate as on Day One. Walking the beachfront, Kelly would suddenly become aware of that private, salty aroma Maggi gave off when she was coming into heat. A glance, a pressure of hands, and he would know for sure. Hurrying back to the hotel, they would throw off their clothes and hurl themselves into bed for another panting, heaving embrace.

"I don't give a damn about your professional credentials," Kelly would say. "I know you've never had anything like this."

"Pooh," Maggi would reply, but she did not deny it.

She did her writing in the morning, passion or no. While she worked, Kelly would sit by the window, resting and staring vacantly at dusty trees, a cobblestone street, and a row of small shops and cafés on the other side of the boulevard. What, he asked himself, would it take to get his creative juices, never mind about sexual juices, running again? He feared that the absence of deadline pressure had made him impotent for the writing game. He thought of the old *RAG* hacks: Cadissy, for instance, couldn't put fingers to typewriter with anything longer than a ten-minute deadline. The words had to tumble out; otherwise Cadissy sickened of his style, and of the story.

Kelly briefly considered digging up another Victor, some retired couturier rusticating on the Côte d'Azur but ripe and ready for a comeback. What, he wondered, had ever happened to Gilbert Fouchet? Dead, no doubt.

And another idea—an introspective piece on the dynamics of revenge. He dwelled vindictively on *le grand* Victor, rotund, depraved, and ruined; but the subject interested him little. Or, a low-down piece on sex—sweaty, numbing sex, as it applied to Maggi Mont's resplendent body, so perfectly formed and efficient in its own way, like a Stradivarius violin, the Mona Lisa, the continent of Africa.

"Maggi," he mused, breaking into her concentration, "I could write about you."

She sat, nude, at her portable. She didn't reply, merely gave him the finger across the keyboard and went on with her work.

"I'll call it 'The Venerable Mont.'"

But she did not hear and he thought about Victor again. He entertained the idea of assassinating him. But why? Kelly put his hand on the hard ridge of scar tissue across his thigh—one day that would have to be removed—and fingered his penis. Lucky Victor hadn't been using a shotgun: he'd have had to play it like a piccolo just to take a leak. Should he, perhaps, demand a rematch? No. Victor would probably be even more clumsy, and deadly, a second time around.

Maggi clicked her tongue against her teeth, swore gently, and shifted on the hard-bottomed chair. Kelly gazed wonderingly at the delicate ankle, the well-honed calf, the shank, and the uncreased buttock and belly, the rise of tit. No, what the hell: he would devote himself to love.

"Jack, when do mimosa bloom?"

"Around Christmastime."

"Shit . . ." She sat silently for a moment, staring at the paper in the typewriter. Then she lifted her eyes and said, "Jacko, I hope you realize that the physical side of love is not the be-all and end-all of it." He nodded, although he was not greatly impressed with the observation. "After all," she went on, "a climax is such a swift and instantaneous event that it's already in the past before you know it's happened."

He clucked insolently. "Beaver . . ."

"You swine. Don't peek." Her eyes turned soft with affection and she crossed her legs. "Don't think you'll get me back in the sack so easily."

"Well . . . I'm just sitting here on my ass, doing nothing."

"No," she cried, "you *are* doing something. You're recuperating from a lousy bullet wound and from that crappy newspaper. . . . And you're servicing me."

He ignored the last. "Crappy newspaper," he said, "but family."

She did not understand how much was at stake: property, position, power, membership in the University Club.

"Jacko," she remarked, "I'd just like to remind you that pounding a typewriter makes me very hot, that is sexually excitable, so don't take advantage. But"—she smiled, showing her white teeth—"at the same time, be prepared because at any moment of the day or night Miss Maggi Mont, famed fucker, will be all over you, like an avalanche of bosoms and beavers. . . . I have tricks of which you've not yet heard."

Kelly laughed mockingly and put his heels up on the windowsill.

"And I, Miss Maggi Mont, famed fucker, am not frightened. I know tricks as yet undisclosed in the pages of *Cosmopolitan* magazine."

Finally, when they had to leave and, on the exquisite Blue Train, headed for Paris, Kelly felt utterly a man of the world. He'd acquired a moderate tan and he felt clean and whole in gray flannels, a blue blazer, and open shirt with a foulard tucked in the collar. Maggi was wearing a pure white dress with a pleated skirt and V-neck top which showed the swell of her breasts. A handsome guy, a beautiful gal, on the way to Paris, France: who could ask for anything more?

He had been screwed to a fare-thee-well and was riding on the most elegant train in the world. They were sitting in the dining car: tablecloths gleamed as snowy white as bridal gowns, glasses shimmered under highly polished chandeliers, and the heavy, baronial silverware could have been used by Louis XIV at the Palais de Versailles.

The service was impeccable, the waiters attentive to the point of embarrassment.

They ate a crusty provincial *pâté* and washed it down with the local rosé.

"It's named after your street," he observed gently. "Rosé d'Anjou."

He watched lasciviously as Maggi introduced the wine to her mouth through her sweet lips and rolled it on her tongue.

A tried and true white Chablis came with salade-vinagrette. Maggi, her lips against her teeth, savored the flavor, the hardness and strength of the wine, and nodded. Her eyes grew moist with an unspoken thought, and Kelly knew what it was.

The train rocked through the night, lulling them. Maggi leaned indolently back in her chair and puffed her breasts at him.

"Is it merely rampant sex between us, Jacko?"

"Purely rampant."

The Blue Train throttled down in respect for a shaky section of rail. Outside, he knew, the peasants would be gawking at the passing splendor.

"Good sex is good sex, Jacko." Maggi said thoughtfully. "That's the body, nothing to do with the head. People who screw well together, do well togther. A certain respect . . . I hope we'll always be friends."

"Maggi . . ." He was shaken that she might think otherwise.

"You've been good for me," she continued. "You've got the knack of taking me right off my creative high horse. What I've been wondering is: have you ever discussed love and the making of it with Madame Mordaunt, your mentor?"

"Mentor?" There it was again, the veiled accusation that he was Zouzou's creature. "That old crow? Nobody's ever been able to figure out which way she bounces. . . ."

"You're trying to say she might be a lesbian, Jacko? Well, love is love, you know. . . . Of course, the physical attitudes are quite different than you get in your Pilgrim Father style of fucking."

"Naturally," he replied. "Would you know all about that too?"

"Well, don't you suppose I've had that experience? I'm a researcher, ninny. I suppose you've never experienced the other side of the emotional equation?"

"No, goddamn it," Kelly growled, "drink your wine, Maggi."

"You probably think it's un-American."

"And unnatural too, Maggi, of course," he said sarcastically.

She glared at him, eyes furious. "You know, you do get uptight."

"Come on, Maggi—shit, cut it out. Let's enjoy this."

The tempo of wheel against tracks increased as the Blue Train returned to full speed. But she was not finished with him yet.

"Hell, you never even asked me if I was on the pill. And you sure never took any precautions. What if I got pregnant?"

Speaking in a way he knew would infuriate her, he drawled, "You're supposed to be the expert."

"Shit! Spoken like a true male chauvinist pig bastard . . . The pill makes women's knockers big, you know."

"Can't be all bad then, can it?" He grinned.

She frowned petulantly and retreated to silence, staring at her wineglass. The dining car swayed gently, causing water and wine to wash in the glasses. He realized that somehow he had offended her.

"Well, anyway," Maggi murmured, "we had a good time, didn't we?" He nodded vigorously, wanting to please her. Flippantly, she said, "Shall we consider I'm your mistress now, Jacko?"

This was a disconcerting thought. Mistress? Christ, he was not a Frenchman. She must have seen the doubt in his face.

"What about it?" she demanded. "It's not as if we have to be in love. We just see each other when we get the chance, fuck ourselves blind and deaf for a few days, then return to our respective careers. You know, if we stay healthy, we could get in an awful lot of screwing on a three-day stint."

He shook his head. "I'm not so sure I like the word 'mistress.' Don't you think it smacks of that old chauvinist pig thing?"

She took the point. "Right. We couldn't call it that. We'll just say we're a couple of old buddies getting together for a good bang."

"I'll agree to that." He raised his glass to her.

She lifted a sceptical eyebrow. "Or are you feeling guilty about your loved one?"

He didn't think he was. "No, not that I'm aware of."

Maggi pursed her lips and tentatively suggested something that shook him. "Did it ever occur to you that your wife might be up in Geneva having it off with your pal Rafe Perex?"

He set his glass down slowly, feeling a tremor in his belly. "She is?"

"I didn't say *is*. I said *might be*. Rafe is a terrible ass-hound, as you know. They've met each other, haven't they?"

Kelly nodded. "Christ . . . that never occurred to me. Is it possible?"

Maggi chuckled with relish, enjoying his surprise, the emotion it set off.

"Anything is possible with Perex. But no—I have no reason to think it's so. I'm just testing you. Forget it."

"Forget it?" he cried. "You've planted a seed. . . ."

"Jealous? If you're jealous, then you're still in love with her. Only you know the answer to that."

Kelly nodded and fell silent. A vivid picture flashed through his mind. Maryjane, naked, long Texas legs flying, was being pursued around the Perex château, whooping and yelling, his friend Rafe hot on her heels, dressed in a pin-striped suit, his trilby set firmly in place. Goddamn it, he remembered, Perex had inquired none too subtly about Maryjane's degree of sexual demand. It *was* entirely possible, wasn't it? Rafe Perex had admitted he was a man who needed women on a daily basis.

The main course arrived, pressed pheasant, accompanied by the bottle of Bordeaux he had ordered. Their attentive waiter, moving like a ballet dancer through the dining car, put a knuckle of wine in Kelly's glass for approval. Perplexed and preoccupied now, he swished it around in his mouth and nodded.

Maggi, waiting for what he would say, toasted him. "Here's to you, Jacko. You're true-blue and you screw like a professional too. . . . May the rotten chancre of jealousy never soil your insides."

He smiled. "Why should I be jealous? I'm not jealous," he told her, "I'm not jealous per se. I can't say I really give a damn what she does. But if she's out fooling around, I'd rather it was with somebody I don't know. . . . Therefore, if I find out it did happen, I'll punch Perex in the mouth."

Maggi laughed gleefully. She filled her mouth with wine, allowing a trickle to escape from the corners, and then gathering it up with the tip of her tongue.

"Well said, Jacko, and for that I'm going to award you with a rip-roaring fellatio when we get back to the rue Anjou. . . . Head, that is."

"Please," Kelly said, "not quite so loud."

The Blue Train crashed through the tight funnel of a country railroad station, leaving a thunder of sound behind.

She leaned forward and whispered loudly, "Fast trains make me extremely horny, Jacko."

He put his hand on hers for a moment to quiet her, then deliberately picked up his knife and fork to cut into the bird and fresh asparagus. When he glanced up again, she was still staring at him. Didn't she understand it was impossible on the Blue Train?

Finally, she began to chew contemplatively. "Good. But nowhere as good as . . ."

"I know. What about some champagne?"

Kelly ordered a bottle of Louis Roederer Cristal and their waiter, delighted as only a French waiter could be to discover an American with even a modicum of taste, grandly carried the clear bottle of golden champagne to them in a gleaming bucket of ice.

To finish, they had big French pears, steeped in brandy and insidiously mellow. Maggi, of course, immediately had to make the physiological analogy: the pear—metaphor in most medical books ever written and secretively consulted by every puberty-ridden adolescent, for the female mons veneris. She was steadily becoming more possessed.

"This stuff makes it twitch, Jacko."

"Maggi, Maggi, we'll be there soon."

"If I had a bathtub, I'd fill it full of this champagne. I've heard the bubbles are very interesting."

"You've *heard*?"

"I did it once, in a hotel in London," she admitted.

"No," he said. "Now *that* makes me jealous."

She smiled. "It was nobody you know, and I promise I'll always do it best with you, Jacko."

They arrived in Paris at midnight. They were lucky outside the Gare du Sud and caught a cab almost immediately. Inside, Maggi flung herself into Kelly's arms and began kissing him madly. With no regard for the rearview mirror, she stuffed her hand between his legs and grabbed him. In seconds, both of them were panting.

But, passing through the Place de la Concorde, Kelly saw something that destroyed his erection. The taxi had slowed for the inevitable traffic jam, even late at night, and in front of the Hotel Crillon two figures were outlined in the stark blaze of the lighted entry.

One, he recognized instantly as his father-in-law, Claud "C.T." Trout. He would have known anywhere the bandy legs and huge Stetson. The other man was bullet-headed, a foot taller than C.T. and encased in a tight black raincoat. The two of them were dragging bags out of the back of a taxicab. If Kelly had doubted for a second that it was, indeed, Claud Trout, the doubt would have been as quickly dispelled by C.T.'s frantic waving of his arms and bellowing. Through the din of the traffic, he could hear the nasal Texas twang, although he couldn't understand what C.T. was yelling at the hotel porters.

"Jesus, Jacko, what's wrong?" Maggi demanded. "You look like you've seen a ghost."

"Not so loud," he whispered. "I have seen a ghost—and he might hear you."

CHAPTER

EIGHT

It was one of those wonderful days of early Paris autumn. Kelly knew that he was now well mended. The days with Maggi in Nice, exhausting but fulfilling, demanding but fabulously satisfying, had re-tuned him to the universe. His gait was light and springy. He was ready for the city again; he hoped the city was ready for him.

Even the knowledge that C.T. Trout was in Paris did not daunt him. What was Trout, after all? Merely a man. Maggi was going to be working at her typewriter all day, she said, so Kelly decided to make his rounds. One thing he definitely had to do was to pick up his trench coat at the tailor's: the button Victor had torn off had needed replacing and the bloodstains removed.

"I'm off then," he said. "You'll be all right? Dinner at Pipi's?"

"Perfect, Jacko, my sexually astute buddy. Jacko, I was thinking last night in the midst of luxurious rapture that if they had a fucking event at the Olympics, we could take the gold."

Maggi was happy too. He understood now that he had been too flippant with her on the train. He had underestimated her need for affection, not just sexually but spiritually. He kissed her warmly, tasting their morning café au lait, patted her through her silk kimono and departed.

His first stop was at the *RAG* office. He half expected to find his replacement already there, or C.T. staked out and waiting. But no. He interrupted a family scene. Olga was sitting with her father, Count Boris, and they were having a midmorning snack of Hungarian salami and yogurt—the latter, according to Count Boris, being the secret of Russian longevity.

Kelly had always considered eating at one's desk a disgusting habit; the combination of salami and yogurt seemed even more revolting.

Count Boris leaped to his feet. "Monsieur Jack," he exclaimed as his monocle fell out of his red-rimmed eye. "It is a feast for these eyes to see you again."

Boris Blastorov was a man of no discernible age. His face was as thin as parchment, and so wasted that his monocle seemed several sizes too small. But then, it had been fitted in Leningrad all those years before, presumably when he had been well fed on the protein of the steppes. Boris was nothing more or less than a hero. That was his profession; he was a hero. As to the title, Kelly had never been quite sure of that. He had often wondered if there was not some sort of Dun & Bradstreet for checking the legitimacy of claimants of European royalty. One never knew about these emigrés;

they had a habit of elevating themselves one order of nobility for each border they crossed en route to the English Channel.

Count Boris, to the embarrassment of Olga, got straight to the point. "Next time, Monsieur Jack, pray do me the honor of accompanying you to the field of combat."

Kelly nodded cautiously. "No next time, Count Boris."

Boris jammed the monocle back in place. "Victor, such a swine! I would have given him the *coup de grâce* on the very spot. Such a dishonored and cowardly rascal, you see."

Olga watched, her eyes teetering on the edge of tearfulness. She was wearing her treasured peasant blouse again and now, sexually acute as he was, Kelly stared frankly at the clear intimation of pouty breast. His eyes flustered her but Boris did not notice. He was still astride his white horse. He pulled himself up even more erectly, with such an exaggeration of military preparedness he might have snapped his spinal column.

"If you wish, Monsieur Jack, you have only to say the word."

"What do you mean?"

"Boris Blastorov would willingly repay the swine on your behalf."

There was no doubt what Boris was offering. "No, no," Kelly said quickly. Olga looked relieved. "Thank you, but don't think of it." He leaned on the desk, looking into Olga's eyes. "Anything for me?"

She blushed. She knew what he was hinting at but handed him a Telex message.

RAG PARIS PLS PASS TO KELLY. BOSS ASKS YOU PRE-
PARED APOLOGIZE QUERY EXPECT APOLOGY SOON-
EST IF YOU WANT RETURN TO RAG AT HALF PAY. I
UNRECOMMEND THIS BUT BOSS INSISTS. BOSS ASKS IF
SO WHETHER YOU PREPARED COVER WASHBURN TRIP
EUROPEWARDS. COURT NEWYORK

Holding the piece of paper in two fingers as if it were filth, Kelly dropped it in the wastepaper basket. This was not exactly what he had hoped for. But he was feeling too good to surrender so easily.

"You've read it, Olga. What do you think?"

Hesitantly, she said, "I hope you will reply in the right way."

Kelly paused weightily, then said, "Tell 'em to go to hell, Olga."

Count Boris's eyepiece dislodged itself again and he applauded noisily. "Bravo. Bravissimo, Monsieur Jack." But Olga burst into tears.

Kelly said sternly, "Olga, please . . . It's not the end of the world, for God's sake. Merely a *beau geste*. I can't do anything else. Count Boris understands that, you see."

"Yes, my daughter," Boris roared. "Please to shut up the crying and impolite wailing. Monsieur Jack is precisely proper."

Olga stifled her sobs, groping in her desk drawer for a handkerchief.

So that had been *their* throw of the dice and now he had thrown his. The next move was up to Harry Kelly and Frank Court. It was a sobering thought; he realized he had probably lost the game.

But Boris was very pleased with him. To a man like Boris, the beautiful gesture was everything. And he could not drop the subject of Victor.

"I would challenge him. I would kill him. It is simple, a matter of honor."

"Count Boris, I beg you," Kelly said, "put it out of your mind."

But Boris shook his head stubbornly. "I cannot. Any chivalrous gentleman is dishonored by the actions of a rascal. If I am to meet Monsieur Victor"—he pronounced the name with the poison he would have injected into a mention of Stalin— "if I meet him on the street, I will hit his face for the coward that he is. And that would lead—to the Bois."

Kelly sighed to himself. He wanted the Victor episode closed. "You wouldn't know Victor on the street and he wouldn't know you."

Boris nodded and exclaimed. "I know of him, and Monsieur Jack, when I see scum on the street, I recognize it. If not, I do nothing. Does that satisfy you?" He aimed his prominent nose in Kelly's direction and planted his hands on his swivel hips. After all, it was said that Boris had attended the Czar's cavalry school as a very young man, had been wounded in both arms and both legs, and had personally, if one believed what one heard, killed many Bolsheviki. "Be it understood," he proclaimed in his marching voice, "my services are always at your service."

Olga didn't care that he was a nut. Her eyes glowed. She was so proud of her father and her loyalty was boundless—but whether it extended equally to Kelly he was not sure, although she so obviously ached for his body. As soon as he left, he suspected, she would be on the phone to New York to tell Court that he was wavering.

Rafe Perex became the second person that day to offer help in the elimination of *le grand* Victor. Perex was in a state of high agitation when Kelly bumped into him at the Ritz. His eyes danced with delight and he pumped Kelly's hand excitedly.

"Jack, my dear friend, I so hoped you would come. Maggi told me this morning that you had returned from the south. I have news of the highest importance."

"Hello, Rafe," Kelly said coolly.

"Come with me for a moment to the door."

Perex led him back to the entrance and pointed at a black Citroen parked just down the street. "Jack, that man sitting behind the wheel? He is a sometimes employee of mine. . . . He is a killer of the greatest skill and cunning."

"So? Why tell me? Who is he?"

"He has no name."

Not much of the man was visible: a bowler hat, the side of a shrunken face and a long cigar. The "killer" sat staring straight ahead.

Perex's teeth flashed as he spoke and he nervously

stroked the lapels of his pin-striped suit. "My dear friend, I have been feeling so badly about my behavior."

Kelly told him to forget it. "Blood under the bridge, Rafe," he said cruelly.

Perex's face whitened. "Caramba"—he gasped—"you have a way with words. No, no, dear friend, now listen. I will deny I say this but there are ways of fixing Victor's wagon. Maybe you would like a broken arm, or something simple: a broken leg. That man outside; he is a hit man. An arm for fifty bucks, a kneecap—one hundred. He is very small. He uses a tinker toy for a getaway car."

Perex laughed wildly at his joke.

"Rafe, Victor isn't on my mind anymore. Forget it."

André was standing directly in front of them, staring vacantly out the window. But he was obviously listening and Perex suddenly became aware of him.

"André," he bleated, "you are eavesdropping again. Go! To the other end of the bar!"

The bartender was offended. "Monsieur, I merely wish to welcome Monsieur Kelly home from the wars."

"Thanks for nothing, André," Kelly said.

"Monsieur Kelly," Andre said sadly, "you have not been here for weeks. Why? There is no reason for you to be ashamed. Regard the situation like this: Victor was ever clumsy."

"André," Perex said sharply, "you are dismissed. If you are very lucky you may receive a gratuity."

André shuffled away. Perex hissed hatefully after him in Spanish, then put his hand confidentially to his mouth.

"Claud Trout is here. He is trying to locate you."

"I know. I saw him last night. Bad news—the little Texas fart."

"He is on a Washburn mission."

"Tell me about it," Kelly said sardonically. He ordered a Pernod and water.

Perex was trying to control himself but he was near convulsion. "It is so ironic, dear boy, that your father-in-law helps to increase the empire of my ex-father-in-law. Am I wrong or is that not very very ironic?"

Kelly could do no more than nod vaguely. He had another, more important question. "Tell me what I'm supposed to tell him about Maryjane, Rafe."

Perex's face lengthened. He stopped laughing. His eyes were serious. "Trout knows where Maryjane is. He told me this morning Maryjane is in Switzerland. . . ."

"Switzerland?" Kelly thundered. André whirled, alarmed, and dropped a glass. "In Geneva, I suppose, Rafe?"

He grabbed Perex by the arm and whipped him around. Perex stared, astounded.

"No, no, not Geneva, near Geneva . . . Good God, my dear, are you so worried about her? I didn't know. Trout says she is having treatments in a clinic which has . . . a certain association with AmFreight. Yes, yes," Perex cried, spraying saliva, "beauty treatments."

"You knew that? You better be very sure, buddy."

Perex commenced to stammer. "I did not know until Trout told me, Jack. Heavens to Betsy, my dear, what . . . . Are you suggesting? Oh, my dear. Could you have suspected . . ." Perex laughed shrilly, so forcefully his eyes began to tear. "Jack . . . Jack, oh no! My connection to everything is most tenuous. Oh, good heavens, you suspect me, your friend, of . . ." Perex's face turned sour and angry. "I am insulted. Insulted, do you hear?" He clapped the trilby on his head. "I will be going now."

Kelly shook his head. "You will like hell. One move and I'll knock you on your ass, Rafe. I'm warning you. I want to know—what kind of fucking treatments."

"I have told you: beauty treatments," Perex replied distantly. "Your gracious father-in-law told me she is having her . . . breasts . . . enlarged."

Kelly stared furiously. The next instant he was totally deflated. "Jesus Christ," he muttered disgustedly. He turned away from Perex. "Okay, so long then, I'll be seeing you, Rafe."

Perex whipped the hat off his head and slammed it down. "And now you are dismissing me—just like that. You are very rude, Mr. Kelly. I have something else to tell you." He glanced first down the bar at André whose back was turned stiffly to them. "Trout has a job for you. He has heard of your troubles here and with your father. He knows you were fired. He saw that in the *New York Times.*"

Not caring now, Kelly said, "I don't doubt it—that fucking Court would tell everybody, wouldn't he?"

"Whatever. You may not be aware but the Washburn interests own newspapers and Trout will offer you a job covering the president's trip for those newspapers."

"And fashion too, I suppose, to keep me in touch with Zouzou. . . ."

"Yes. But," Perex said proudly, "it was the best scheme I could design in your behalf. I have been thinking of you, you see."

"Forget it," Kelly said. "My old man would go absolutely insane if I went to work for Washburn. He hates Washburn. Jesus, *I'd* have to start carrying a gun."

"Not if my little friend outside were your companion," Perex said.

"You know that my old man and Trout had a fistfight once at the New York Athletic Club?"

Perex coolly said, "And what has that to do with the price of Cuban cigars?" Ruefully, he put his hand on Kelly's shoulder. "They are consumer papers, Jack, *normal* newspapers, the kind you've always wanted to work for."

"What's the name of the paper?" Kelly asked. It was beginning to dawn on him that this could be a way out, an opportunity, perhaps, to show the old man and Court that he was not without hope. He turned to Perex. "It would give them something to think about."

Perex looked disappointed. "You would not do it out of spite. . . ."

"Don't think Cubans are the only people who know about revenge."

Perex frowned petulantly. "Not all Cubans are emotionally unstable, Jack. I am not. I am an educated and restrained person." He stared at the aged bottles behind the bar.

Slowly, Kelly said, "All right, Rafe, I'm sorry. I didn't

mean to offend you. . . . I just got a fixation that you and Maryjane . . ."

Perex shrugged indifferently. "Don't be a child. I am your friend—or I thought I was."

"Sorry again—I've always thought you found Maryjane attractive. When you spring it on me she's in Switzerland . . . well."

Again, Perex began to fume. His body stiffened. "Spoken like a true American who does not understand friendship."

"All right, all right, goddamn it. This other thing, what's in it for Trout? Why should he do this for me?"

Perex frowned wearily. "You have already answered that question: Grovival."

"That shit again."

"Dear, poor, uninformed boy, how many times must I tell you that the international cosmetics firms would go to war over Grovival. Can't you get that through your Irish blockhead?"

"Rafe, you Latino asshole, none of it makes any sense anymore."

"Caramba, my dear, you hit where it hurts. One more remark like that and you and I will march to the Bois. Now, I will tell you this and this is the last time I will explain. AmFreight and its cosmetics subsidiaries want Grovival. To get Grovival they go one of two ways: either take Mangrovia out of French control or buy Maison Mordaunt out from under that old hag Zouzou, when she gains access to Grovival. Is that finally clear? It is horribly simple in its simplicity."

"Everything depends on Aristide de Bis," Kelly surmised.

"Aristide de Bis is a key figure," Perex admitted. "But you, dear boy, are an essential factor. You are a pipeline through Madame Mordaunt to the French government. Your interview with George Washburn, carefully conceived, will make it very clear to the French government that the United States is in earnest about Mangrovia. All else failing, it will be you who will convince Madame Mordaunt to sell out to AmFreight."

"To hell with that. I won't do it. Why should I get mixed up in AmFreight's dirty affairs?"

"It is not often a person gets the opportunity to do something important for his country, Jack. Are you frightened?"

"Rafe, you've heard it said that the last refuge of the scoundrel is patriotism. Don't appeal to mine again. The last time you said that I almost got my ass shot off. Besides, what the hell does patriotism have to do with AmFreight and Grovival?"

How could Perex claim Mangrovia was a matter of national concern? The only thing involved, in fact, was the plot of a multinational corporate conglomerate to steal somebody's national resources. Like copper in Latin America or oil in Arabia. He shook his head perplexedly and called André over. He ordered another Pernod and a scotch and soda for Perex.

"Rafe, I can't go along."

"Jack. All you would be doing essentially is working at your trade, the newspaper business. At that, you're a certified genius."

"No, I don't buy that."

"Remember, it will be an exclusive interview with Washburn." Perex began to relax; he had delivered his message. "No one else is going to get it. They'll pay you well too."

"There are more important things than money."

"Yes, my dear, then put it this way: pure low-down revenge."

He nodded. "Now, that I can understand. The old man would hate it, absolutely hate it. He'd kick Court's ass all over the second floor."

Perex was not so sure of that. "He might just cut you right out of the deck too, my friend. No," he said shrewdly, "I don't think I'd plan on making the *Appalachian Times* my life's work."

"That's it? That's the name of it? The *Appalachian Times*?"

"Yes," Perex said embarrassedly. "It used to be called

the *Mountaintop Observer* before the Washburn group bought it."

"Jesus." Kelly sighed. "I'd ask Washburn very tough questions, you know."

"As far as I care, you can ask him anything you want."

"I will. Another thing—who was that guy I saw with C.T. last night?"

"The ugly man?" Perex made a face. "His name is Maxwell Maxim. He's the new head of AmFreight's European Cosmetics Division."

"Ha!" Kelly laughed. "I'm learning fast. He takes Igl's place."

Perex nodded, grinning crookedly. "You have it."

"Listen, since you're being so free with the information today—is the CIA messed up in this?"

Perex answered the question with another question. "Isn't the CIA messed up in everything?"

"And what about you?"

"I'm overt, not covert."

"What the hell does that mean?"

"I'm overt in Europe. When it comes to Cuban matters, I'm covert. Do you see what I mean?" When Kelly shook his head, Perex said, "I refuse to discuss it any longer." He put his arm around Kelly's shoulder and smiled affectionately. "Ain't life bloody interesting?"

"The hell you say. I'm not convinced you're really a Cuban."

The remark caused Perex to resume his hurt expression. "You think perhaps I'm some kind of a fucking Costa Rican or Panamanian?"

"You could be Maltese or Lebanese."

"Yes." Perex frowned. "The man of a thousand faces, that's me."

"No, I guess you really are a Cuban," Kelly teased. "I can tell—"

"You're going to say 'by my heels.' Jack, I will fight you here in the Ritz. Jack, we get some girls so we can *fock* them, *sí*?"

"Okay."

"But, you like Maggi—*sí*?"

"A hell of a woman, Rafe. I'm glad you put me in touch with her."

"You got to touch her—*sí*?" Perex demanded, playing the fool.

"Gentlemen don't ask questions like that, Rafe. She went to school with your former—"

"Yes," Perex cried. "Did she tell you she used to work for the U.S. Chamber of Commerce?"

Kelly shook his head. "How does that fit in?"

Perex shrugged carelessly. "I ask you no more. . . . You ask me no more."

"The Mount Vernon Trust thing. That is a front, isn't it?"

Perex rolled his eyes and sought an answer. Evasively, he said, "Let's say it started as a front and now makes a lot of money. I didn't plan it that way. It is very ironic, this life. Did Maggi tell you about her laboratory experiments?" Kelly said she had. Perex chuckled bashfully, wiped his brow, shook his head. "Westerley and I . . . We . . ."

"Rafe, don't tell me. You—a wire stuck up your ass?"

Perex laughed wildly and lowered his head to rap it on the bar, shaking with merriment.

CHAPTER

NINE

Kelly's meeting with Claud "C.T." Trout at the Crillon was businesslike despite the fact the little Texas wrangler was half-drunk. They had not seen each other since the previous Christmas when C.T. had paid him and Maryjane a hasty visit, most of which he spent passed out in this same hotel.

After letting Kelly into the living room of the suite, Trout sat down in an easy chair and thrust his scrawny, misshapen legs and broken feet out in front of him. He was wearing underwear, long boxer shorts that reached nearly to his knees, and a T-shirt too big for his shrunken chest. Upon his head was the Stetson Kelly had spotted across the Place de la Concorde.

A bottle of bourbon, its level down to midlabel, a bucket of ice, and what passed for branch water in Paris were close at hand. Without asking, C.T. poured him a glassful of the mixture.

"Hear your old man fired your ass, J.K." Trout grinned, like a talking coyote.

His face was as battered as the rest of his body. He had been kicked and stepped on by many horses. The face looked as though it had been doctored by head-hunters: chin, mouth, teeth, and nose seemed to over-flow into the eyes. The latter were probably C.T.'s strong-est feature. They were cynical, crafty and, if they had not been so bloodshot, would have been penetratingly blue, long-distance eyes that could spot the brand on a cow's ass a mile away.

"He didn't fire me. I quit," Kelly said.

"Whatever happened, you're out, J.K."

"That's right, C.T.," Kelly said impatiently, "And if you're going to ask me where M.J. is, I don't know."

"Look-a-here, J.K., important thing is *I* know where she is. She's in Swizzerland in a hospital getting herself fixed up." Trout stared malevolently at him. "She's finished with you for sure, J.K." He lifted his glass in small sympathy. "Face it, boy, it was not meant to be. Romance? Ain't none. Love? Nothin' there, J.K. I ever tell you, J.K., Maryjane's meaner than bat shit?"

Already, Kelly felt himself slipping under. He had always been mesmerized by Trout's delivery. But he had to respond somehow.

"I don't know about M.J. But I had love. . . ."

C.T. hooted. "Bullshe-et. Maybe from your side, J.K., but from hers it was nothin' but polecat piss. Don't get me wrong, J.K. I love my daughter. I got a shitbird mare to home that I love too. But that don't mean she'll let me ride her. Do you take my point, J.K.?"

Kelly nodded and C.T. laughed sardonically. His small frame rustled against his cotton underwear and bourbon slopped from his glass.

"Maryjane was always very ambitious, J.K., and you know, boy, she had the hottest pants in Snakecrotch County. She was a ripper; it was a race against long odds to get her out of town and up to Vassar before she got knocked up. She musta gave her ass just about to every boy at the high school. She-et! J.K., I'm tellin' you she was somethin'. Why one time my friend George was down from Washington and goddamn if she didn't hump him too."

Kelly was struck dumb with astonishment. God! All those nights in New York—she, pushing him off when all the cocks in Texas had been on her and in her. "C.T., what are you saying? My God! Christ almighty."

Trout waved his words aside. He leaned back and tipped his big hat down over his eyes. "And what's she doin' up in Swizzerland? Tell you: doctor up there by name of Wolf-gang Errlizz, plastic surgeon type of man. M.J.'s gettin' her ass fixed and her titties bigger. She wants to go on the stage, be a singer, a stripper, somethin'. M.J. is takin' them injections," C.T. exclaimed. "Boy," he continued, eyes nailing Kelly to his chair, "you know about that new stuff?"

"I suppose you're talking about Grovival."

"That's it! We're gettin' that shit, J.K. You know what it does?"

"I've heard a few things."

"Then you know why we want it."

"But you don't know whether it works or not."

"It works all right!"

"I heard a farm woman in Switzerland developed big warts on her ass."

Trout exploded angrily, "You don't know that for a fact. You get warts from toads. Some toad bit that woman on the ass."

"Goddamn it, C.T., you don't know whether it's safe and you're letting your daughter take it?"

Shrewdness shone in Trout's multilayered eyes. "Don't that prove I got faith in it, J.K.? Couldn't stop her anyway . . ."

"It proves," Kelly said daringly, "that you're out of your mind."

Trout expelled an invisible plume of rage. "You little sonumumbitch, if we don't grab it, the goddamn Russkies'll get their paws on it. . . . Now, I'm asking you once and that's all—do you want to work for us, or not? Fired by your own father! Jesus, as much as a pain in the ass M.J. is, I never disowned her."

"Yes, I want to work for you," Kelly muttered. "But, C.T., you are a goddamn crackpot."

The insult passed C.T. by like so much buffalo wind. "That's more like it, J.K. Always liked you, never mind about you being a Catholic with that prideful sonumumbitch Harry Kelly for a father."

"Just leave my old man out of it, please."

"Okay . . . Cool your balls. Minute . . ." Trout jumped

spryly from his chair and hopped across the room to a beaten-up attaché case. He fumbled inside it, then came up with what he wanted. He tossed an envelope to Kelly. "Here's your cree-dentials, J.K. You're working now for the *Appalachian Times* and the *Times of Gulch City*. That's Texas. Some people call the place Gullshit, Texas, but that don't matter."

Kelly's name was inscribed on a plastic-coated card. The signature above the publisher imprint was that of Claud Trout.

"Okay," Kelly said, "very impressive."

"Pay is good," Trout said.

"What's my first assignment?"

"Washburn," C.T. barked. "One other thing, J.K., leave M.J. alone. She's doing her own thing. *Get'chasef* another piece of poontang and forget about M.J."

Kelly flushed. "Does that mean I'm being bought off?"

C.T. shook his head violently. "No sir-ee. We want you on our side. We're into important stuff, J.K. You're going to interview George Washburn—about NATO, Mangrovia, and all that kind of horseshit."

"*If* he wants an interview, that is."

Trout gazed at him benevolently. "J.K., lemme tell you somethin'. C.T. Trout says shit, President George Washburn goes into a quick squat."

The meaning of that was crystal clear. Washburn was in the pocket of the special interests—the ranchers, the conglomerates, unions, everybody. It was very big-time, and for a man like Trout who'd come up the hard way, a lot easier than broncobusting.

CHAPTER

TEN

It was by no means an unusual request Madame Mordaunt put to him as they sat, once again, in her penthouse atop Maison Mordaunt on the rue Rimbaud.

"Will you, *cher* Jacques, walk on your hands for me?"

They were drinking the specially bottled Mordaunt No. 10 vintage Brut champagne, initially made for Zouzou's private consumption and now sold in select restaurants and fine hotels across two continents.

Her question was part of their ritual dialogue. On cue, Kelly threw back his line: "It is not often, madame, that one tastes the marvel of fruit and nut combined in one fine champagne. A rare union, *n'est-ce pas?*"

And, as if reading from a script, Zouzou responded, "As rare as ours, *cher* Jacques . . . But come now, will you walk upon your hands while small Charles swings from the chandelier as in his circus days?"

Kelly was feeling extremely tired. He and Maggi had spent the day in bed, making love and talking. She had been impressed with his new job, particularly that he was to interview Washburn. He sighed wearily. But the jaded monkey, Charles, perked up.

"I don't know if I've got the strength, madame."

Few people knew of Kelly's gymnastic abilities. As a youth, he had been adept at standing on his head or springing up to a prancing inverted march of the hands.

He did not advertise what seemed a clownish accomplishment. But once, stupidly, in the early days, he'd performed for Madame Mordaunt and she had never forgotten.

"Please, Jacques. It is the least you can do for an old woman who has missed your company so much."

She had virtually melted, Charles beside her, into the soft brown suede-covered sofa that dominated the small drawing room of her lair. Zouzou loved all shades of brown, beige, tan, chocolate, whiskey, brandy . . . and Charles, of course, who was furred in the hue of horseshit. "I became," she had once related to him, "a lover of tweed in the year 1927, during a love affair with a young Scotsman. Maddening, you see, but there you are. I was young then and he was very handsome. He was killed in the Abyssinian War."

"Tragic . . . A Scotsman in the Abysinian War?"

"He was a fabric salesman, a purveyor of fine tweed. Emperor Haile Selassie was a client. Angus was in Addis Ababa when the Italians invaded. . . . Wops, one and all . . . Angus was shot through the lungs and died in a mud hole. . . ."

"Horrible, madame."

"He was bayoneted in the stomach. . . ."

"Awful, madame."

"His skull was ripped apart by shell fragments and his eyes gouged out. His arms were blown off in the pigsties."

"*Mon Dieu*, devastating."

"He was a hero, and I have never married."

The House of Mordaunt had featured tweed, stout cotton, and doughboy khaki in its collections ever since; and never anything but the finest, purest fabrics. "Those other rags," Zouzou would say, "the nylons, those polyesters, all reconstructed garbage, *merde, non?*"

Madame Mordaunt had reached the age where she was licensed to be as vulgar and rude as she wished. The dignity or demure gentility of old age she scorned in favor of a generous use of profanity, preferably English profanity, which she sputtered with pleasure and cunning.

She was a small and wiry woman. Her body, as

opposed to her language, was ample testimony to the grace possible in the declining years. She danced around her cutting rooms, hustled up and down the many flights of steps within the Maison Mordaunt. She was as quick as a bird in a tree. She had not been touched with arthritis because, she claimed, her forearms were loaded with crackling, tinkling, clanging bracelets of every material from cheap, lacquered wood to copper, silver, gold, and elephant hair wound in platinum coils. She wore them for their beauty, because she thought them therapeutic, and because she was intensely superstitious.

"I don't know if I can walk on my hands anymore, madame." Kelly resisted, knowing that eventually he would have to give in. "My wounds . . . But you have been such a big help, you and Monsieur Pleven."

"Ah, *merde*," she grumbled. "What are you saying?"

Sipping remorsefully on the Mordaunt No. 10, Kelly told her he was sorry about the story in the *RAG*. "It was New York. Those idiots, they took unforgivable liberties with my copy."

"I suspected as much," she said bitterly, holding out her glass for more champagne. "Ah, those American mother-fuckers, Jacques; they are so anti-French these days in that country of yours, *cher* Jacques. Anti-everything of beauty and sophistication. I think it is that president of yours, that fuck-ing Washburn, once one of our heroes, now our archenemy."

He reminded her gently of the episode in the Bois. "That was so terrible, madame. I was very frightened, you know. And Victor . . ."

She spat. "Victor is a pig and a pederast. And now, he is an errand boy. How I am making him suffer."

"But I'm very grateful to you," Kelly stressed, winningly.

"Ah, shit." She waved a gnarled brown hand from which bluish veins popped like violin strings. "For what, then, are friends. Here, Jacques . . ."

She rummaged in the pocketbook beside her on the couch. She carried it with her everywhere, even in her own house, as if she were the queen of England. She handed him a check.

"No, no." Kelly put up his hand. "I could never accept it. Not from you. Certainly not from Victor."

"*Merde!* You will not take it?"

"I cannot."

She didn't argue. She stuffed it back in the pocketbook.

"You see," Kelly said, with as much confidence as he could muster, "I have projects, madame. I am not in need of money." A lie. In fact, he had come close to asking Trout for an advance. The trip to Nice had dented his bankroll hugely. "You know, of course, I am no longer *RAG* correspondent. Simply," he said, making use of what had happened to best advantage, "because of that story. But I have a new post that is wonderful and full of opportunity."

"Ah, yes, and what might that be, Jacques?"

"I'll be working for an important East Coast paper—my first assignment is to interview George Washburn when he comes here for the NATO talks."

"Ah, horsepiss," Zouzou cried, "the man we call the Ultimate President. The Ultimate Crook? I hope you will expose him. . . . You know, Jacques, that during the war he was parachuted to France to aid in our Resistance? He was a hero then. Now he is a fuck-ing scoundrel."

"Madame," he protested gently.

"*Cher* Jacques. Perhaps one is not supposed to speak of another head of state in such a way. But I can say with a certainty that George Washburn is not a friend of France."

"Oh, madame, is that really so?"

"Think it or not," she said fiercely. "But it is so, Jacques. But no mind, no mind. I think your pressing problem now is relating to your virility, *n'est-ce pas?*"

He could do nothing but nod and agree. "But I think," he said carefully, "it's beginning to work out all right." The question bothered him. He wondered how much she knew, what with her spies and informants.

"I have spoken again with Monsieur Pleven and he assures me all will be well, *cher* Jacques." She started to laugh, her thin shoulders shaking. "Ah, that day of the

Mordaunt Collection, Jacques. It was what we say *très drôle*, you being sick all over Victor." She hacked with laughter and lit a heavy black Gitane cigarette. "But that is past. You must realize, that every man in his day has at one time or another been rendered impotent, even more, castrated, figuratively as well as literally."

"As usual, madame, you're dead right," he said.

However much he fought her domination, he was transfixed by this little old woman, so stuffed with intuition and perception. Nothing escaped her. He glanced at Charles; the little beast eyed him like an inquisitor.

Zouzou suddenly burst out, "You were a fool to write such a report on Maison Mordaunt."

He had not deceived her. "What must I do to express my regret?" he asked weakly. "I have my new paper now—I'll be writing much more about the Maison Mordaunt."

"No, no, Jacques. What haunts me yet . . ." She spoke tentatively. "I had hoped after you left the loathsome *RAG* that you might come to work here at the Maison Mordaunt. I had thought I could employ one such as you very usefully as my chief of what you Americans call public relations. But then—oh, shit—I see I am dreaming. You would not enjoy such work. . . . What is this place, *alors*? *Rien*. A dirty and disgusting business, you see, making good clothes for bad women."

"Madame, it never occurred to me that you—"

"What then? A partnership with Zouzou Mordaunt?" she demanded indignantly. "It never entered your mind? And why not? Would such an arrangement be so hateful?" He shook his head loosely, denying it. "Jacques, I am a realist. My next season will be superb, the Spring Collections, *magnifique*. But someone must be in position to write about it because we will want to bring these wealthy American tarts to *la belle France* to spend their money." She snapped her fingers, like castenets. "You ask, *peut-être*, what Zouzou Mordaunt thinks of fame and glory? To Zouzou, fame and glory are as nothing, *rien*, less than *rien*, nothing more than the unpurged bowels of the sewer rat."

Kelly winced. He would never grow accustomed to her sickening metaphors.

"But I *will* be writing about the new collection," he pointed out.

"*Merde!* Where then?"

"A newspaper in the east and one in Texas."

He realized these were a lame substitute for the *RAG*, for the *RAG* set the fashion tone of the whole country.

"Texas," she howled, "of what use is Texas to me?"

"Madame, there's more money in Texas than there is in New York."

Uncertainly, she pursed her lips. She looked at Charles, as if to discover what he thought.

"Texas women are crazy about French fashion, madame," he added.

Spitefully, Zouzou said, "Texas women are built like cows and they are all bowlegged. Yes . . . exactly like the wife who has deserted you. Yes, yes, don't bother to deny it. I know all about that." She did not give him a chance to disagree, even if he'd had a mind to. She waved her hands and commanded, "Come now, Jacques, up on your hands."

"Balance, madame, balance," he murmured.

"Jacques," she shrilled, "I never dreamt the fat fool would shoot you. Ah, *merde*, and now Victor has become such a burden to the Maison Mordaunt. . . . It is known across the world that he has violated the Marquis de Queensberry. . . . I wish he *would* return to the south of France, as you wrote."

"Madame," Kelly said quietly, "you are a very cynical person."

She was, and nothing pleased her more than being told so.

"Jacques," she said, her small black eyes twinkling, "to have reached the age of a . . . certain . . . maturity, and not to be cynical would be a sin against God. Naturally, therefore, I am a very cynical person. That is part of my realism. But, for you, Jacques, I will always retain a very soft couch in my heart."

Kelly was touched. He had come to her again with

the thought of being implacably reserved and cool. But he saw it was no use.

"Madame, I'm so happy to hear you say that. I really am. The old Kelly-Mordaunt alliance isn't finished, is it? I feel the same affection for you. Anything for you—you have only to ask."

Quickly, she put the question to him again: "You could not come to the Maison Mordaunt in partnership with me?"

"But, madame, I am a journalist. I couldn't help you here."

"That would be for me to say, Jacques. She waved the matter away. "Well, then, walk for me, Jacques, if that is all you can do for me. It amuses me above all else in life. . . . I have so missed that trick of yours—and *petit* Charles has been lonely in your absence."

Bored with the conversation, however, Charles had fallen asleep. Zouzou batted him across the head with her bracelets. Charles snarled disagreeably.

"Ah, *mon petit*," Zouzou apologized soothingly, "you grow old, and as we English or Scots say, crotchety and sour, like an old cunt. So rude, Charles, small *monstre, alors.*"

She smacked him again, more severely, and pushed him out of the way. Charles slid off the couch and out of the room.

Zouzou cried, "Next time I will kick your mangy ass, Charles. . . ." She nimbly got up to take a fresh bottle of Mordaunt No. 10 out of its cooler. She handed it to Kelly to open and mischievously scrambled his hair. "Ah, Jacques, what will be, will be."

Kelly wrestled with the cork and got it out of the neck of the bottle with no more than a whistle of escaping gas.

"Well done, Jacques." She patted his cheek with a leathery hand. Sitting on the arm of his wing chair, she said playfully, "Am I to understand, Jacques that you have, then, somewhat regained the use of . . . how should I say it? Your popularity?" Then, chucking him under the chin, she demanded harshly. "Can you make

love again? That is what I want to know. *Mon Dieu*
—why do I beat around the bush?"

Kelly flushed under her stare. "I'm coming around. . . ."

"What I mean, monsieur," she said, heavily sarcastic,
"is: are you able again to mount the plump saddle
between two trembling thighs and drive that long
instrument into the pear melba which man believes to
be his just dessert?"

He laughed shakily. She could not get much more
explicit than that.

"Jacques," she cautioned him firmly, "you must be
very frank with me. You must tell me exactly what you
mean to say. I am old enough to know all the words."
Zouzou swallowed half a glass of fresh champagne.
"Jacques, if I were ten years younger, even five years
younger, then I would cure you of all your trouble."
Kelly shifted uncomfortably, feeling her thin shoulder
against his. There was no doubt what she was talking
about and the thought of it made him feel queasy.
"Jacques, you have never seen my boudoir, have you?
Ah, what a delight, and I can tell you it has been a place
of much ecstasy. Some day, if you are a good *garçon*
you will see all. . . . Maybe me on my deathbed, *hein*?
You are thinking *that*?" she demanded. "And then it
would be *too* late, *non*? Unless you are fond of what is
called necrophilia. . . ."

Kelly groaned. "Please, madame . . ."

She ground out a sharp laugh. "Jacques, I can tell
you . . . for a woman of . . . uncertain years . . ."

"Madame! I've never thought of you as anything but
youthful. . . ."

"*Merde*! Do not mock me, Monsieur Jack Kelly."

For a second, she fixed her eyes on the bubbles
swirling from the bottom of the tulip glass, holding the
fragile stem of crystal between two fingers not much
larger or less stained than two burned joss sticks. Impatiently, she rose, put her glass down on the long coffee
table, and marched to the other side of the room to
open a gleaming Biedermeier cabinet. She took out an
unmarked tin box and carried it to him. Snapping it

open, she held under his nose an array of powdery white capsules.

"Grovival, monsieur," she announced proudly. "The very thing. Three a day keep the doctor away." She chuckled harshly, plucked one pill from the box and popped it in her mouth. She swallowed it with a gulp of Mordaunt No. 10. "Will you try one, Jacques?"

"No," he said, "no thanks . . ."

"You think Grovival untried and dangerous? I say to you, monsieur, what do I have to lose? I give them to Charles too. . . . But not for you, eh, Jacques?"

Again, he declined. He was not that foolish. There was something very sordid about Grovival.

"So far, Jacques, the effects have been only good. *Merde*! I know that I am old but I will tell you—in the last few months, Zouzou Mordaunt has been feeling new blood, fire, in her veins, a revival of juices long dormant and a new way—how shall I say?—of looking at the world."

Kelly carefully said, "Well, that's wonderful, madame, if—"

"You refer to side effects? No, nothing."

She nodded to herself smugly, closed the tin box, and sat down on the suede couch, crossing her legs under her.

She eyed him with amusement. "And the beautiful Maryjane? I know—still missing. But, tell me, what of your new friend, the American writer? Her name is Maggi Mont, *n'est-ce pas*?"

Kelly smiled, relieved he had avoided Grovival and that she seemed to have forgotten about making him walk on his hands.

"Madame," he said, flattering her again, "nothing escapes your eye, does it? You're right: Miss Mont is a friend."

Zouzou laughed insinuatingly. "Ah, and is she rich? Perhaps, as her name suggests, she has a mountain of gold. Let us hope so. But"—she sneered—"it is truly of no consequence, money. Money is the vomit of the

desert camel in oil-rich Arabia. Health is everything."
She emitted a thin chuckle. "Will *she* leave you too?"

Kelly shook his head evasively. "Madame, we're only
friends. . . . What makes you think . . . ?"

"*Merde!* This city is mine, Jacques. I know all." She
jerked her head up, in birdlike fashion. Then, with an
authority not to be denied, she said, "Now, we will wish
to see for ourselves, Jacques, that this wound of ours is
mending. Jacques, come! Do not hesitate."

He began to perspire. He told himself there was no
good reason why he should submit to her inspection.

"There's nothing to see—only a couple of scars," he
stuttered.

"Precisely," she said, "now, please to stand up and
do as I tell you, Jacques. . . ."

"Madame, really . . ." Nonetheless, he stood up.

"Yes, now, that is a good *garçon*. After all, I am old
enough to be your grandmother . . . mother. Unzip the
trousers, Jacques. Come closer. Ah, yes," she said
thoughtfully, leaning for a close look and tapping the
scar lightly with her forefinger. "It is fine, Jacques, as
Monsieur Pleven—"

She was interrupted by a sharp gasp from the doorway. Zouzou whirled, already beginning to rave.

Victor was standing there, his hand on the knob of the
door. His eyes bugged at what he was seeing and his
mouth fell open. He began to move backward, trying to
get the door closed.

"Pig," Zouzou shrieked.

Her champagne glass sailed through the air, bounced
off Victor's round head, and shattered in the hall behind
him.

"Madame . . ." Victor's voice was low, shocked,
apologetic.

"Son of a bitch," Kelly roared, as much in pain as
shock. For, in his haste to zip up his pants, he had
caught skin in the zipper teeth. He zipped down, shoved
his smarting dick back into his pants, and zipped up
again.

"Filthy spy!" Zouzou screamed. "How dare you not knock first, you fat fool?"

But Victor was gone.

Zouzou laughed unsteadily.

"Madame, did you arrange that deliberately?"

She glared at him. "Are you mad? How dare you suggest such a thing?"

"I caught myself in the zipper," he complained.

"So?" Her eyes hardened with disdain. "That was your doing, not mine. . . . Now, perhaps, you will understand why gentlemen prefer buttons. . . . Sit down, Jacques. As always, you overreact. What does it matter that Victor has seen your pecker?"

Kelly slowly sat down and breathed deeply. "I don't much care for the idea of Victor seeing—"

"Your pecker?" Zouzou hooted. "It is lucky he came in then, not a moment later. . . ."

Kelly nodded uncertainly. Was he to understand . . . yes, evidently. He groaned deeply within himself.

She was unrelenting. "Do you doubt, monsieur, that I would have kissed your pecker? You perhaps think Zouzou Mordaunt is too good to do a thing like that? *Non!*" she thundered. "Zouzou Mordaunt is a woman and women adore peckers, Monsieur Kelly."

He did not know what to say. He hung his head listlessly. Somehow, she had twisted it around: now he had insulted her.

Zouzou stared at him majestically, as she would at some stupid dolt from the countryside. She drummed her fingers on the suede. Finally, she softened enough to speak again.

"That small bump there . . . You are aware it will add pleasure for a woman? Yes? *Eh bien.*" She continued analytically, as if she were discussing a hemline. "That is why, Jacques, certain condoms, *les lettres françaises* they are called in Scotland, are often fitted with tassels, fringes or flanges, sometimes even with rivets and spikes for the more sophisticated, masochistic. *Mais, mon Dieu!* Why am I telling a young American such things? You will think me the very devil of a woman." She tweaked her nose and merrily laughed. "What I am saying is that everything turns out for the best in the best of all possible worlds—as Voltaire said."

He grunted morosely. "And now all the more reason for me to challenge Victor again."

"*Quoi? Quoi?*" she demanded, shocked.

"I have considered poisoning him, or perhaps throwing him into the river Seine some dark night."

"*Merde!*" Zouzou shouted. "I will tell you that you would discover only one thing about Victor. You fool, Jacques, there are many like Victor in the world and there are many others in love with you."

"In love with me?" Kelly echoed her. "Who? You're saying Victor? Oh, no!"

"Oh, yes!" she exclaimed, gagging with laughter, "And now he has achieved his highest dream—he has seen your pecker."

Kelly was reduced to misery. "You did set it up, didn't you?"

"Never! Never! I am not a pimp for Victor! If I set it up, I set it up for . . . *moi!*"

"Oh, my God," was all Kelly could say, wearily putting his head against the back of the chair.

"Why do you worry so?" Zouzou cried. "It is nothing. Victor is weak and wanton. You should not concern yourself with such worms as Victor, for you are an eagle, flying high. You are not a worm or a snake wiggling through the grass. This should not surprise you, Jacques, for you are an exciting and sensual man. . . . Do not be annoyed that a slithering worm has fallen in love with you."

"The idea is revolting."

"All right. I will tell you something. In your writing of that piece in the *RAG*, you showed contempt for Victor, and he responded desperately, as a lover will, in the only manner he could, to show to you that you cannot simply dismiss him. Now, at least, he knows you will never forget him—since you carry his mark."

"The Mark of Victor," Kelly said. "Not too impressive."

Zouzou chuckled philosophically. "Impressive or no,

you have it. Well . . . *merde!* So much for that, Jacques.
Come, open another bottle of champagne and we will
try to pull together our wilted spirits. Such worry is
unbecoming. All anxiety is of no more worth than the
sweat from the testicles of an aging Peruvian yak. Open
the bottle, sweet *garçon*, and then do walk on the
ceiling."

CHAPTER

ELEVEN

The next few days were not good. Kelly's return to the
House of Mordaunt had served only to depress him.
And Maggi—from high euphoria, her mood suddenly
and for no good reason tumbled to irritability. She tried
to explain that it was a matter of the writing. She had
developed a terrible block. She was getting too close to
sex to write about it objectively. She was with him too
much, she complained; all he thought about was screwing; he talked when she was concentrating. He wasn't
good for her. She was getting nowhere.

Gloomily, she said, "I think maybe I should go on a
field trip."

"A field trip? What exactly does that mean?"

"Well, what does it sound like? Some personal interviewing, that's what."

It was then that she began talking about his arranging
for her to meet Aristide de Bis, minister-without-portfolio.

"Why? For what?" he demanded blankly.

"Jacko," she said wearily, "haven't I told you I'm

writing about the sex drives of famous and influential men?"

Blackly, he considered what she was saying. The rank taste of fear rose in his throat.

"I've got my thing to do, Jacko. We agreed, remember? No strings . . ."

"Maggi . . ." He was not going to do any such goddamn thing. "He's got a mistress. You'd have to move in there, take him away from her."

"A piece of cake," she said.

"Oh, Maggi. Jesus, how can you talk like that?"

She laughed, jeering, and threw herself into his arms, pulling at his corduroy pants. "Jacko, Jacko," she said with a sigh, "you do know how much I want you, don't you, Jacko, you miserable rat?"

"Yes, I know," he said distantly.

"But do you really know how much?"

"I think I do."

She bit his lip and scratched his cheek near his nose with her sharply cut diamond ring, then just as erratically as before, pulled back and, without warning or logic, repeated, "I've got to get away from you." It was like being slashed across the face with a thorny whip, soothed, then whipped again. "You do want me to do what I've got to do, don't you?"

"No," he said, "I want you here."

"Yes, at your beck and call, goddamn you, Jacko, whenever you want me, falling on my back and doing your bidding."

"No, I'm telling you—I'd be very lonely."

"Why? Why?" She burst into tears and flung her arms around him again. "All we are is a sex team. Jacko, it's not really that I *want* to go. I *have* to go. . . . Maybe, for you, another woman."

"What?" She was going too fast for him. "Maybe, but . . ."

"Maybe?" She cried out and hit him a blow to the pit of the stomach. "You rat, if I catch you . . ."

Yes, a definite tension had built up between them. He had begun to notice small, insignificant faults that he would have ignored earlier. She was messy with her clothes and she ate carelessly, making chomping noises.

"Someday, you'll come back here and I'll be gone," she warned him.

"Called away . . ."

"Yes, by a force that's bigger than the both of us."

"Bullshit."

"You'll see."

Then, more often, as if creating the psychological frame to justify a rupture, she began to treat him with a certain condescension, criticizing him for not working while she, all too clearly, was working too hard. He would remind her that he *was* working. He was rebuilding his relationship with Zouzou Mordaunt and he was preparing for his interview with President Washburn.

Then she would relent a little. "You won't forget about Aristide de Bis?"

And he would grow surly again. "Even if I agreed, how would I go about that? Wouldn't it be a little strange, me trying to get you a date with a minister of the French government?"

"I dunno, Jacko. I've heard he's a very hot number."

"Oh, hell, Maggi, come on . . ."

He didn't tell her what had happened at the Maison Mordaunt, how embarrassing it had been, how close he had come to falling prey to Zouzou. She would not, he thought, have understood.

"Where's your friend Perex?" she asked him one day.

"In Geneva."

"Oh, yes?"

Her provocative smile annoyed him. She was trying to revive his doubts about Perex and Maryjane. "Perex denied that, you know."

"Did he?" she mocked. "Did he now? He would, wouldn't he?"

And, again, despite his indifference, the mental picture flashed in his mind: Maryjane, bucking and yelling, her long legs wrapped around Perex, he still impeccably dressed in his pin-striped suit and trilby securely set on his head.

"Goddamn it, Maggi, sometimes you drive me right up the wall."

She sat bolt upright in bed. "Don't get huffy with me, mister. You're mad because I mentioned Aristide de Bis. I told you what my book is about. You know, I bumped into Jack Kennedy once on a subway in New York. Christ, I wish he was still alive." She hugged her knees, thinking about it. "What about this mistress of Aristide's? Countess Beatrice de Beaupeau? She's beautiful."

"Yes," he said, "she is. Really. Classic French."

"Not like me. More beautiful than me?" she said in a small voice.

"Different."

"Yes, different—more beautiful. I suppose you'd like to get your hands on that, wouldn't you?"

"Maggi, Jesus, I've never met the woman."

"Never mind," she said calmly. "You know, I've already met him, in case you're interested."

He sat up beside her. "You did? How?"

"I went to his party headquarters and I asked for an interview. I said I was writing something about the state of French politics."

"My God." He groaned.

"Well, I can tell you—I didn't get very far." She smiled patronizingly. "Poor baby. Remember, it's all in the interests of science. Touch, touch tongues, Jacko. God, you smell of that awful Pernod again. Think of our adventures together, our lovemaking and try to relax. Forget about all those other dudes—they've got nothing to do with you."

"Aristide de Bis is a goddamn menace," he growled.

"Most powerful men are," she said. "But they can be handled. Look what I've done for you. A month ago, you were an introverted, guilt-ridden Catholic, and now I've turned you into a raging stud. I've turned you around very nicely. There may even have been a little repressed homosexuality lurking in there."

"Like hell," he said.

"Nothing to be ashamed of, Jacko. Some of history's greatest men were queers. What do you think it was bugging the prince of Denmark?"

"C'mon, Maggi, cut it out."

She chuckled and he felt her lips curling on his skin. "Our next course may be a little basic primal therapy. That'll drive you wild. It's like a little junket across two or three galaxies. . . ."

"Not for me, Maggi."

She reached down and grabbed him powerfully by the balls. He yelled in alarm. "See," she crowed, then relaxed her hold. An erotic flush spread across him. But she was already off on a new subject. "You know, we could go off to China together. There's some interesting research to be done there—the Chinese must be doing something right. There's about a billion of them."

"Naturally," Kelly pointed out, "because China is an old civilization. They started a lot sooner than the rest of us."

Maggi jabbered at him in a strange tongue. "That's Mandarin. I speak a few words of the stuff. That means you're very good at screwing."

"Indeed?" he replied archly. "Did you get to use that when you were at the Chamber of Commerce?"

"Who told you that? Oh, Perex, the big mouth. True, though. I worked for the Chamber of Commerce for a couple of years in Washington. I was still at school. . . . Jacko, do you know that I met Khruschev once upon a time?"

"Nikita?"

"Not Sam," she said airily. She cocked her leg over him and squirmed closer. Breathing lightly in his ear, she asked, "You like this full body, don't you? This receptacle of the instantaneous moment?"

But despite the good times, Kelly realized Maggi was preparing to do something rash. She was a driven being, clearly more and more preoccupied with her own sense of purpose and mission. She was not unkind but she was growing away from him.

When he came back to her flat late one afternoon in the twilight of their relationship, Maggi scarcely looked up from her typewriter. There were shadows, rings of weariness around her eyes, and smudge marks on her cheeks—she had had to change the typewriter ribbon.

"Were you to see Zouzou Mordaunt again?" she asked softly.

"I dropped in. It was her at-home day."

This was true. What was left of the Paris greats dropped in at Zouzou's on Monday afternoons. "Aristide de Bis was not there," he told her limply. He didn't confess that earlier in the day he'd arranged for a luncheon meeting with Olga Blastorov.

Maggi pushed her chair back and stared dully at him. "I am going to have to go away for a few days."

"Why? I don't bother you when you're working."

"Jacko, it's just that I'm not producing enough. And something worse is happening. When I try to work, I'm always thinking about you and that infernal machine of yours. And I get hot. And I lose my concentration."

"That's easy," he said dismissively, "just practice self-control."

"I can't, goddamn it."

She came to him and wound her arms around his chest. She was wearing a loose sweater over a pair of baggy, dirty jeans. He felt her breasts against him, the roundness of her belly. She put her head against his button-down shirt, rubbing her cheek on his pectorals.

"You know, you can't complain," she said. "We've been screwing ourselves toward the funny farm for over a month. I love it but I've got other things to do."

"Maggi, it's been marvelous."

"Jacko, you bastard, you don't care anything about my work."

"But I do," he assured her tenderly. "I want you to be very successful at your work."

"Bullshit. Next thing you'll want to do it with me sitting on my typewriter. . . ."

"Maggi! Why do you say a thing like that?"

"Because I've been thinking about it, blast you. I've

been thinking that might be a breakthrough, or a break-out of this writer's block. It'd be kind of like completing the circle of creation, wouldn't it?''

Actually, when you came to think about it, it was an original idea.

"Come on then, come on," she exclaimed. She was out of her sweater and pants in an instant. She boosted herself up on the table, then lowered herself on the portable, spreading her legs. It didn't bother her that she might damage the fragile machine. "Whoopee!" she cried, "sexologist does it on her typewriter!"

CHAPTER

TWELVE

Kelly had always liked the brasserie Coupole and it was there, a few days later, that he'd invited Count Boris Blastorov's daughter for lunch.

"Oh, and Olga," he said on the phone from the Ritz, "do me a favor and bring a dozen or so of those *RAG* reporters' notebooks, will you? I can't find them anywhere in Paris."

"And some pencils too, Monsieur Kelly?"

He arrived at noon to give himself time to settle in with a couple of drinks. Being early, he was favored with a table near the window. How he admired the place: brightly lit by long street-side windows, blond wood of a forgotten era and banquettes that stretched as if without end, facing the busy Left Bank boulevard.

"I wait for a second party," he told the waiter and ordered a bottle of Alsatian beer.

The *RAG* had once used the Coupole for a fashion layout between night and morning, one of his inventive strokes this, the juxtaposition of modern fashion and faintly thirties-ish Art Nouveau décor. Another brilliant setup in front of the presidential palace in hopes of silhouetting a model against the president's long, black limousine had misfired when they were chased away by the gendarmerie.

Ah, Kelly mused, as he took a first swallow of the mellow, but slightly bitter, beer, those had been some days. But life had moved on and, interestingly enough, now he was preparing himself by careful reading of the diplomatic columns for his interview with President George Washburn. Whatever Zouzou thought of Washburn, he *was* the president, ultimate or otherwise.

He arranged his bulky trench coat on the banquette beside him. What was it Perex had said? That there had to be a thriving business in renovating foreign correspondents' trench coats. . . . Think of the hundreds of them getting soiled and stained and holed around the world's battlefields.

Kelly lit a Gauloise and smoothed down his hair. He thought he must look well. He had dressed carefully for Olga in a tweed hacking jacket and brown flannel pants. He did want to impress her. She would be stricken when she heard about his new job, if she hadn't somehow heard already. But, Kelly reminded himself, this was to be a strictly business meeting. He'd left Maggi that morning with this intention firmly in mind after a night of frantic lovemaking. She was in a confused state of mind: frustrated, then in despair, and suddenly flying into a frenzy of want. It seemed the grind on the portable had not broken the block.

When Olga came in, Kelly recognized her immediately, as he should have. But she looked different. It occurred to him at once that this was the first time they had ever been alone, outside the office context.

She was dressed elegantly. Olga was not a tall woman

but a pair of stack-heeled patent leather shoes gave her a couple of extra inches and showed off her slim legs and the rest of her firm figure to best advantage. The legs ran to buttocks that were muscular, somehow suggestive of her Russian background. She was short-waisted and not full-breasted like Maggi, her chest being more fragile and delicate. She was wearing a black and gray silk print dress and a small string of pearls circled her neck.

Kelly got to his feet and took her hand. She slid easily into the seat beside him. "*Bonjour*, Monsieur Jack," she said.

"Olga! It's great to see you like this. God. Gosh! You're looking beautiful, more beautiful than any of the Beautiful People."

"The BP's? Yes, and for that reason I took a measure of care today."

"What have you done to your hair?" That was it: the hair.

"I have merely pulled it back. Monsieur Jack, I wished to show you I am not always the drudge you have seen in the office."

"Yes, but I knew that." He wondered how he could work the conversation back toward their aborted embrace. For a moment, they sat looking at each other. Olga modestly lowered her eyes. He put his hand on hers for a second. She pulled away.

Her words rushed to break the silence, the meaning of the silence. "I have brought your reporters' notebooks although I should not have since they are the property of *Retailers Apparel Guide*." She put the pads on the seat between them. "It was not necessary to invite me to lunch merely to secure reporters' notebooks. You could have come to the office."

"No, Olga, that wouldn't be ethical." He dropped the explosive. "You see, I have a new job."

Olga gasped. "Monsieur Jack!" He thought she would accuse him of treachery before she heard any explanation. "What is this new post?" she asked faintly.

In reply, Kelly showed her his crisp new credential.

She studied it curiously. "The *Appalachian Times* . . . *Gulch City Times* . . . These are newspapers?"

A destructive question. "What the hell do you suppose, Olga? They're not TV stations."

"I would not know," she said primly, "having never been to Gulch City."

"You should go some time. It's a hell of a place."

"All right," she said meekly. "But now, may I have a drink? Yes? I would like a vodka with a small piece of citron." Kelly summoned the waiter irritably, already feeling put down. When she had the vodka and citron nestled in her hands, she asked, "May I know how you obtained this new post?"

Kelly knew she would relay the information straight to New York. "Just lucky, I guess." She glanced at him sceptically. "You're thinking . . . what, Olga?"

"Nothing . . . Nothing. I am thinking I would like a cigarette."

"Count Boris would be very angry if he saw you smoking."

"No doubt," she said evenly. She was very displeased with him. "Now, I will tell you, I am thinking you have joined the enemy."

This remark hit as hard as the tabletop on which he rapped his knuckles. "I hope you realize that wounds me very deeply, Olga."

"I knew it would wound you very deeply, Monsieur Jack."

"Then, goddamn it, Olga, why did you say it? Why do people go out of their way to hurt my feelings?" But his hurt was not convincing. "Look, Olga, I didn't much like leaving the Flagship. But I've got a couple of good reasons for leaving. First, the Flagship threw me overboard, and second, by taking this job I'm getting an exclusive interview with President George Washburn."

She put aside his boast with another damaging remark. "Monsieur Jack, I hope you will remember the fable of the man who thought he could ride the tiger."

"As you say, Olga," he said darkly, "a fable. Olga,

goddamn it, that's the kind of female thinking that can drive a man crazy."

"Of course, Monsieur Jack. Now, I wish to look at the menu."

She studied it quickly. Olga, in her goddamned efficiency, was intimidating. But he remembered she had not been quite so self-possessed that day in the office. Glancing surreptitiously, he was able to see the faint divergence, the notch where her breasts ducked into the silk dress. He followed that in his imagination to small and sophisticated nipples, probably rose-hued. Under the table, he felt the warmth of her knee. He edged closer to her and shifted his leg. Without lifting her eyes from the menu, she flushed and her nostrils tightened.

"I will take an omelette of mushrooms, a plain salad, and a glass of Chablis," she said, "and then an espresso."

"Perfect. You're very decisive, Olga."

"An employee of the *Retailers Apparel Guide* must be so."

Kelly chuckled fondly and pushed his leg against her knee. She looked at him now with something like consternation in her eyes. He admired her openly. "I like your dress and your necklace."

"These pearls belonged to my grandmother."

"The real thing then?"

"Naturally." Olga sat up as straight as Boris would have and shoved out her chest. "I would never wear the *ersatz*. These," she said, fingering the pearls respectfully, "a poor remnant of my country. The rest, stolen, lost or confiscated over the years. Some sold."

"And that's all that's left?"

"A few other things."

They considered the sadness of it all until the Chablis arrived. Then, sorrowfully, she returned to business. Court had promised that Kelly's replacement would be in Paris in a matter of weeks.

"And what did that bastard Court say about me?"

"No word. But Monsieur Jack, the tide will turn after your interview."

"Yes, probably, but never mind about me, Olga. Look,

after lunch, I'll walk you back to the office. Is that okay?"

He was thinking forward. They would lock the door, then . . . play boss and secretary. The proposal troubled her. But it pleased her too. She opened her purse to get out a mirror, squeezing her lips together to smooth her lipstick.

Blushing a little, she asked, "Monsieur Jack, you are quite well again?"

She couldn't bring herself to be more precise. He nodded carelessly. "It was only a crease really. I guess the main worry was tetanus. I'm okay now." He smiled wickedly. "I'd show you but I might get into trouble." She recoiled bashfully. "Sorry, Olga, nothing nasty intended."

She pursed her lips and took a small sip of wine. "Monsieur Jack, you are teasing me unmercifully. . . . You always do."

"Olga, stop calling me Monsieur Jack. Plain old Jack will do. Just old Jack-off, anything like that."

She didn't get it. She was such a child, a baby really. He must remember that.

"Oh Jack," she said, "I so wish you were back at the *RAG*."

"And Olga, it would be nice to be back there. I've missed you a lot. How is your father?"

"He is well. But for you, such a shame. Your father . . ."

"I know, I know, but it had to be, Olga, my dear. Don't worry," Kelly said, putting his fingers on the back of her hand as she awkwardly knocked the ash off a second cigarette. "Time will heal all, Olga."

She seemed unaware he was stroking her knuckles. "Do you believe that, Jack?"

"Yes, I do. I'm a perpetual optimist."

She nodded, then idly looked past him toward the other side of the room and murmured, "There is Monsieur Victor sitting over there."

He turned. "Jesus!" He felt awkward, remembering

the last time he had seen Victor. "Who's that woman with him?"

Olga didn't know either. Beside Victor was a faded, very made-up and bleached blond dressed in an outlandish pink dress and floppy garden-party hat. She was speaking animatedly to Victor.

"God." Kelly groaned. "There sits my nemesis. . . . It's a good thing Count Boris isn't here."

Olga shivered and agreed. "But it is all past now, Jack."

"But not forgotten, Olga."

"I'm sorry I pointed him out to you." Nervously, she broke a roll and smeared it with butter. "Don't look at him."

"The miserable little son of a bitch." Kelly sighed.

"Jack. You have invited me to lunch at La Coupole and you must be attentive to me."

It probably would have been all right if Victor hadn't suddenly looked up, smiled delightedly, and waved.

"Smug little bastard," Kelly muttered. "What the hell he is laughing about?"

"Jack, kindly remember, you are here with Olga Blastorov."

"I should go over there and punch him in the chops."

"If you move from this seat, I will leave."

"Olga, goddamn it, ask your father . . ."

"My father is mad."

"I know that but in this case he'd do what I'm going to do. Excuse me for just one moment, Olga. I'll be right back. I'm going over and humiliate him a little."

He did not wait for approval or give her time for argument. He slid out of his place and made for Victor. What would it be? A quick smash to the chin? A napkin whipping? Should he tip over Victor's table?

Victor outmaneuvered him. As Kelly closed in, he leaped up, smiling apprehensively.

"Jack Kelly! *Mon cher . . . mon cher. . .*"

Of all the nerve. Kelly's right hand was half-cocked for a punch when Victor grabbed it and shook it convulsively.

"Allow me, Monsieur Jack Kelly, to introduce you to

one of my oldest friends, the most renowned Magda Starbright, formerly Magda Nagy of Budapest, the famed theatrical trouper. . . . Magda, an intimate of mine . . ."

Intimate? Victor should not use such words.

Magda Starbright thrust out a white-gloved hand and her puffy cheeks beamed in a showstopping smile.

"Sit down, sit down, *mon cher*," Victor urged.

"No . . . no . . . thanks. I'm with somebody." He gestured toward his table.

Olga was gone.

"Jack," Victor warbled, "the young lady has departed, such a lovely creature. . . . I believe I have seen her at the maison."

He wavered. "My old secretary, Victor . . ."

Should he run after her? Damn her. Again, it was Victor's doing. He should flatten him then and there. A new provocation. Too late: a waiter whipped a chair up to Victor's table. Kelly sat down and looked at Magda Starbright.

He dimly recognized the name. She was one of Victor's long-time couture clients. Magda had once been the subject of much trans-Atlantic gossip. She had run away with the duke of Landsend and the two had become the object of a journalistic search unequalled since Dr. Livingstone disappeared in the Congo. They had finally surfaced at the gaming tables in Baden-Baden. . . . Once upon a time, Magda had been one of the premier lays of the Continent and half of her six or seven husbands had also thrown themselves at Victor's tiny feet. Thus, the fast friendship.

Magda eyed Kelly with vapid curiosity. Her smile, the voluptuous remnant of former allure, collected in the wrinkles at the corners of her eyes.

"A young man, handsome yes," she wheezed, "but with a look of worry and anxiety in the eyes." Kelly did his best to smile back. Victor giggled excitedly and nodded. "A man of youth, yes, with a strong and dimpled face."

"It is wonderful to see you, Jack," Victor said.

Softly, Kelly retorted, "Don't give me that shit, Victor."

"What? What?" Magda Starbright demanded. "I did not hear so well that expression of friendly greeting and banter as in the plays of Noel, dear friend and writer too of so many vehicles for the likes of Magda Starbright."

"It's a pleasure to know you, Miss Starbright," Kelly said.

"You and Monsieur Victor are friends of old standing?"

"We have a little unfinished business," Kelly said.

Victor worriedly said, "Unfinished? I had hoped our business was now resolved."

Magda Starbright said, "Proceed, do, with your business then. For I go to the ladies' room for just a moment."

Victor helped her up and she flounced away. He sat down again and said, "Please put aside your hate for me, Jack. It is over and I am sorry for everything." He lifted a carafe to pour Kelly a glass of wine. As Fate would have it yet again, a bustling waiter jostled his arm. Wine surged out of the carafe, down the tablecloth, and all over Kelly's pants.

"Victor! Goddamn it!"

"*Dieu! Mon cher!* An accident. You saw that clumsy fool hit me!"

Victor jumped to his feet and shook his fists. Then he grabbed his napkin and began mopping at Kelly's crotch.

"Goddamn it, Victor, get away from there." Was there no end of it?

When Magda Starbright returned, Victor said, "We have spilled wine, dear lady."

"Heavens," she screamed lightly. "What to do? *Garçon, garçon!* Hither quickly. Monsieur Kelly is wet with vin rouge."

"No, no," Kelly said. "It's okay now. Don't worry."

"It is not to worry," she sang, "it is not to worry about spilled wine. Spilled milk, yes."

She pressed Kelly's hand, then felt his sopping trousers.

"Ugh, so clumsy to be so wet with a vile *vin rouge ordinaire.* I hope, *cher* Monsieur Kelly, that it will not stain your little birdie."

Victor turned bashfully away. Kelly stood up.

"I think I'd best be going now."

"Ah, Monsieur Kelly," said Magda Starbright, "when next in Jolly Old England you find yourself, please to deepest Lancashire do journey for a visit with Magda Starbright, *née* Nagy, always prepared, as ever, for bright conversation of the theater, past and present and future sense, as Noel would have put it, all too likely, and for amour, love in the afternoon between three and five, otherwise to feel ill and rotten, like some wasted being."

It dawned on him then that she was crazy. They were all crazy.

"Well, good-bye then," he said.

"Good-bye, *à bientôt, cher Jack*," Victor said sadly, shaking his hand gingerly. "So sorry. I am so clumsy."

"That I know, Victor."

Magda had the last word. "Remember what I have said about love, Monsieur Kelly. We must love one another for no one else will. And it is so encouraging for Magda Starbright to observe such friendship and cama-raderie as between yourself and Victor. Yes, you must kiss farewell. It is all right. . . . Yes, yes, kiss, do."

CHAPTER

THIRTEEN

After Kelly left the Coupole, sickened to his soul by Magda Starbright's suggestion that he and Victor exchange a kiss and smarting still from Olga's intimation that he had sold out and her abrupt departure, he blundered vaguely toward the river and finally caught a cab back to the rue Anjou. At least he'd had the wit to remember his trench coat and the notebooks. And he had not been physically damaged, as was often the case in the vicinity of Victor.

Life was crazy. He had recognized the lunacy in Magda Starbright and it had to be said that Victor was not really a sane man. As he was reassuring himself that he, Jack Kelly, was something of an island of reason unto himself, he began to receive signals of dread. Had something happened to Maggi? Were they so closely tuned?

He paid off the cab and hurried upstairs. He was right; something had happened. The apartment exuded a palpable (one of Maggi's favorite words) sense of absence, of departure, of *au revoir*.

"Maggi?"

Normally, if she were not asleep or occupied in the toilet, she was up and at him at the sound of his key in the lock.

He realized she had left.

Actually, the room was not very different. She had not so many possessions that their absence changed things much. Maggi was one of those creatures especially created to inhabit stark hotel rooms in distant cities. The real clue was the removal of her typewriter. In its usual spot, there was a piece of paper, anchored to the table by a dirty wineglass.

"Dear Jacko, I've gone, like I said I would, when you least expect it. That saves good-byes. I'll be working hard and trying not to think about you too much. We'll be in touch later. Love and kisses. Maggi."

He groaned and sat down in her writing chair, fancying he could feel the residual warmth of her haunches there. He lit a cigarette and drew on it unhappily. He waited; for what, he did not know. He should not have been surprised; he'd known this was coming. He told himself that her departure didn't mean that everything was over. She would be back; she'd said so in the note.

As he finished the cigarette, the phone rang. He smiled.

It was Rafe Perex, not Maggi. Perex was breathing hard and there was a barely controlled hysteria in his voice.

"Jack, we are in the bloody soup. I have just been visited by the Ministry of the Interior. That man, the man you saw with Claud Trout. He has been murdered."

"Who? Who are you talking about?"

"I told you, I told you," Perex exclaimed. "The man in the raincoat. Maxwell Maxim. He was pushed under a train in a métro station."

Slowly, Kelly said, "The guy who replaced Igl? That's incredible, Rafe."

"Not incredible, Jack, since it happened. Shit, the police, they asked me about the trust, my connection with AmFreight, my past, even about my marriage to Westerley. . . ."

"So? Be sensible. You don't have any direct connection, do you?"

"No, no," Perex moaned, "but indirect connections are even more suspicious. To be accused of being an agent of a foreign power, is that just nothing?"

"CIA?"

"No, worse, bloody shit—of Cuba! I must speak to Maggi. She will know what to do."

"Why should she know what to do?"

"She is intelligent and wise. . . ."

"She's gone, Rafe."

"Gone?" Perex sobbed. "No—arrested, my dear friend. She must have been arrested."

"Why should Maggi be arrested? For God's sake, Rafe, talk sense."

Perex stuttered, "There might be reasons. Everything is possible."

"Well, I don't believe that. She told me she was going out of town a few days," he lied. "Maybe . . . Should I call Madame Mordaunt? She could find out from Aristide de Bis. . . ."

"No, no," Perex screeched. "You must not do that. Aristide is behind all this, I know it. They are trying to fuck up the Washburn visit. It is about Mangrovia. It is about Grovival. I know it!"

"Rafe, Rafe. Crazy! I don't believe any of it."

"Oh no? First Igl, then Maxim? You don't see any

connection? Bloody shit, my friend, I am going into hiding immediately."

"Don't be stupid. Nobody's going to do anything to you."

"Stupid, am I? You are the stupid one—don't you understand they are killing AmFreight people right and left? It is very dangerous, Jack. I advise you to take cover."

Kelly chuckled harshly. "I don't have anything to do with AmFreight."

"Oh no? Kindly remember who it is owns the *Appalachian Times*."

"A very distant connection, Rafe. Besides, remember what I told you. They don't bump off reporters. Maybe secret agents and owners of mutual-fund trusts, but not reporters."

Perex whined angrily, "You dog, Kelly, you unspeakable dog. So you won't help me?"

"What can I do, Rafe?"

Perex hung up on him without answering. Quietly, Kelly lit another cigarette. If anything Perex said was true, the phone was probably tapped already. He sighed heavily, wishing Maggi were here. There was some consolation in the prospect of base intrigue at work again, but not much. He shuffled into the bathroom and took a long leak, then went into the kitchen. He found a comparatively clean glass and the remnants of his bottle of Pernod. He made himself a drink and returned to sit at Maggi's desk.

He was not disturbed by the murder of Maxwell Maxim. Naturally, being pushed under a métro train was not the greatest way to make a departure, but he had never known the man. His own relationship with AmFreight was so loose he could not conceive of any danger lurking outside the door for him. At the moment he was more concerned about Maggi's disappearance.

Could anyone have credited the fate of Jack Kelly, a man saddled with women so susceptible to making quick exits? He wondered if it had something to do with his mother, who so long ago had pulled the ultimate disappearing act: falling off the old Queen Mary on a voyage to Southampton. It was worth thinking about. First Maryjane, now Maggi Mont. But it was silly to think she had been arrested. Since when were the French police arresting American women sexologists?

There was no way of sorting it out now. He reached for the phone and dialed the *RAG*.

"'*Allo*," Olga answered promptly on the second ring. "*Ici, Retailers Apparel Guide.*"

The name of the paper always sounded a lot better in a French accent than in the coarse tones of Seventh Avenue.

"*Ici* Jack Kelly," he announced breezily. He could feel the frigid flush of her anger. "Olga, I apologize. Why did you leave? I was a perfect gentleman and you would have gotten a charge out of Magda Starbright."

"I do not think so."

"Olga, Jesus, don't you have any patience at all?"

"Monsieur Jack," she said with extreme formality, "it is not often I have so looked forward to a luncheon. But you behaved to me as if I were a peasant, a serf."

"Olga, c'mon, forgive me, will you?"

"I have already forgiven you too much."

"Olga," he said, laying it on desperately, "have dinner with me tonight, and I promise I won't take my eyes off your face."

"Tonight?" The rashness of the suggestion was enough to make her pause.

"Yes, yes. Come to my apartment. We'll have a drink, then go out."

"Your apartment?"

"Is that shocking?"

"Your wife . . ."

"You must know she hasn't been here for weeks. She's left me."

"Oh?" She thought about it and finally said, "Perhaps I will come. Perhaps I will not come."

"That's not very kind. I'm supposed to just sit there and wait?"

"Yes," she said unyieldingly, "and if you are so sorry as you say you are, then that should not be a burden on you, Monsieur Jack."

Kelly was preparing to tell her she was all woman but she had broken the connection. He was disgusted with himself for acting like such a sap. But for some reason he was petrified of being alone. He moved with his drink to the couch, that sagging place of passion. Tomorrow, he would miss Maggi and hate himself, but now, at the present moment in Maggi's Real Time, he did not. He waited. She did not call. The place was so silent. Without the presence of her powerful personality, the flat lost its vitality. Already, the lingering smell of her perfume had dissipated and even the aroma of their sex had grown old.

By 5:00 P.M. he could stand it no longer. He crumpled her note and threw it in the garbage, left his glass in the sink. He walked to the door, took a look around the room, and left.

Hands stuffed in his trench-coat pockets, he made for the Boulevard Raspail. It was colder tonight and he thanked himself for having the heavy coat with him. The tailor had mended the lining, rewoven the bullet tear, replaced the button, and removed all but the faintest traces of blood. The coat was like new. In fact, it was too new and unsoiled. A trench coat looked better, Kelly considered, and more authentic, with a greasy collar, cigarette smudges and soup stains on the sleeves, and wine and uric acid down the front flaps. In time, the coat would resume its former glory.

Dusk was lowering and the city of Paris came alive in a different way, as if a second shift of Parisians had taken over. God, he realized, he had survived everything so far, even prevailed. He was suddenly happy.

He chose a dingy café, one he ordinarily would have passed without a second glance. There were only four men inside, all huddled at a small table in the corner, berets merging over their drinks. A truly huge espresso machine dominated one end of the bar like a baroque altar. He might have genuflected as he ordered a Pernod and a fresh pack of Gauloises. He extracted one of the black beauties and lit it into a perfumed cloud as pungent as incense. The bar girl put the Pernod in front of him with such care she might have been delivering the blood of Christ. The delicacy of the licorice in the drink twisted like a fakir's magic rope past his nose toward the low ceiling.

Savoring his drink and cigarette and offering pagan prayers, Kelly noted the girl's bursting blouse, stained at beard-tufted armpits by the sweat of an honest day's labor. Her apron stretched tautly across broad hips. She was eighteen? Twenty-eight? Impossible to say, for her face was of the flat peasant variety, the Earth Mother. Screwing something like that, he thought, would be a religious experience blessed by Tolstoy himself. A virgin? Impossible: she had been had time and again over empty Chablis cases.

Kelly followed her gracefully clumsy movements as she bent to rinse glasses and stow empty bottles under the high counter. He wondered what she'd have done if he reached across the bar to stuff a hot hand down that cleavage.

He put the thought out of his mind and raised the glass to his lips. For a second, as he contemplated her, his cigarette hand shook violently and his most important scar came tinglingly alive. Muscles jerked in his leg. He gripped the glass tightly until the sensation subsided. She had not noticed his sudden crisis. If she'd had any inkling of what he was thinking, she would have run screaming into the street or fallen in a dead faint amid the débris behind the bar.

Curtly, he ordered another Pernod and drank deeply. The fever remained in his loins and he quickly paid for drinks and cigarettes and left. The unexpected clutch of lust was succeeded by a certain dizziness, but fortunately he was able to get a cab.

The apartment was as dusty as ever. He had a half hour before he could begin expecting Olga, so ran a dishcloth over the furniture, pummeled the cushions, and sprayed cologne under the smelly armpit of the décor. He turned on the radio, lowered the lights, filled an ice bucket and topped it with a bottle of Maryjane's Dom Perignon.

Feeling faint again, Kelly stretched out on the long couch by the window and closed his eyes, achingly aware of a void in his pelvic region, an uneasy concern that something was coming loose. Was he so panicked by Maggi's departure? A frightening thought occurred to him. Was it possible that Zouzou Mordaunt had slipped him a Grovival pill when he wasn't looking? Side effects: a slippage of sanity. God . . .

Then it was seven and the doorbell rang shrilly. Olga smiled at him, a question in her eyes. "Shall I come in? Are you disappointed? Surprised?"

"Not disappointed, good God! I'm thrilled." He clutched at the doorjamb. "I've just been feeling a little whoozy. . . . Come in and I'll open the champagne."

She was instantly anxious. "I will open it. You are not well, Jack?" He helped her out of her coat. She had not gone home to change. "You see, I have debated a long time and finally concluded it would be churlish of me not to forgive you. I see now your experience with Victor could not so easily be forgotten."

Kelly kissed her hand. He put the ice bucket and glasses on the coffee table and sat beside her. He commenced to remove the foil from the squat bottle. "You see, I'm something of an expert at this."

Olga smiled appreciatively, and he stopped what he was doing to put his hand on her arm. The flesh was so warm under the sleek cloth he wanted to cry. Impulsively, he kissed her cheek. She smiled with pleasure. There was no doubt Olga liked being treated as a Russian princess. He fiddled with the cork and got champagne into the glasses.

She tried it, puckering her lips. "Ah . . ."

"Not too warm? I didn't have much ice." He drank and felt unsteady again. "God, I don't know what's wrong with me. I think I'm going to faint. Jesus, Olga, I've never fainted in my life."

It must, he thought, be tension. Victor. Then finding

Maggi gone. The cry of alarm from Perex. Kelly put his glass on the table, leaned back, and then did, in fact, lose consciousness for a moment. When he came to, his feet were up on the couch and Olga was fumbling with his tie.

"Are you all right, Jack? I will get some water, a cold cloth."

"Hell, I'm sorry Olga."

She improvised an ice bag out of dirty ice and the dishcloth and put it to his forehead. It cleared his eyes of fog but he still felt dismal.

"Olga, suddenly I'm cold all over," he murmured. "I . . . Could you lie down beside me for just a minute?"

She hesitated and looked sharply at him. Then she did as he asked. She edged her body carefully against him and he shivered. Their faces were close and he watched her through slitted eyes, murmuring to himself. Little fingers of her breathing caressed his cheek. He let his arm fall across her side. Now, he began to understand what was happening to him, what had brought on the dizziness. The secondary event began to unfold. He groaned again.

"Jack, Jack? Is it all right with you? I should call a doctor. No . . . Jack, no kisses!"

"Sweet kisses, Olga."

God, the seduction was under way. Was she a virgin after all? He knew she was aware of his hardening, the stiffening ache. Her body tensed and the long kiss paused, as if in midflight.

"Olga?"

"Jack . . . Yes?"

He ran his hand lightly down her smooth, silk-covered hip, down her leg to the ankle, taut in mesh. She quivered slightly and he kissed her more adamantly, receiving the reward of heavier breathing. Carefully, he stroked her knee, found the hem of the dress, slipped fingers, then his hand, underneath.

"Jack . . ."

"Olga, you're so beautiful."

He moved his hand up another notch. It was like climbing Mount Everest: from base camp, the knee, up toward the thigh, then back to base camp. . . . He increased his pressure against her body. Then, abruptly, he moved the intrepid hand to caress her face, her lips.

"No, Olga, please, it's too much. I'm afraid. I would not want . . ."

She reacted thankfully, kissed him violently. He thrust the tip of his tongue just fleetingly between her lips, a sample of the real thing. Perfect: she nudged his tongue with the sweet, soft end of her own. Her lips were silky, like the dress she was wearing. As if unaware now of what she was doing, her body slid even closer to his. He played gently with her right ear, with one finger traced the line of her jaw to her chin, neck, as far as the cleavage of her breasts. She made no effort to escape the hand, now so precariously positioned.

"Oh, Jack," she muttered, "I think we should be going."

"Yes, yes, Olga, we should be going."

Of course, it would not have been fair to take advantage of her, and he had already considered what dangers might be involved. Olga was in no way as experienced as Maggi Mont; she was a baby by comparison. And he did not forget Count Boris. Boris was quite capable of showing up one fine day with his sharply honed Cossack sword, that weapon which had not drawn blood since the last great cavalry battle across the steppes of the mother country.

But it was difficult to remember his cautious resolution. . . . Olga's mouth was gaping open, and they were kissing in complete union of lips and tongues. He passed his dallying hand across her breast, across her subtly rounded belly, back to the hip, to the hem of the dress. He insinuated his hand underneath again, so cleverly that she was scarcely aware of it. She was engrossed in the passionate kiss. He bypassed the thigh and cupped his palm around the rise of her buttock, stroking, then edged the hand across her leg toward her belly and the lush joining of legs and torso. He let the hand lay there, unmoving, and returned to the kiss: her lips, the lobe of her ear. She had closed her eyes and was sighing softly so he kissed her eyelids. She had slipped into a drowsy softness. He was aware of the easy rise and fall of her belly. Now came the first surprise. She shifted her body so her plump saddle lifted toward his hand. He took it in his fingers, pressing, and at this, she moaned, wilted toward him. She murmured something he did not understand. But she was not telling him to go away.

So much accomplished, the front lines established, so to speak, he dangled his other hand at the collar of her dress and tried to find the zip. She surprised him again: not opening her eyes she stood up for a second to remove her dress, then lay down beside him again.

"Jack . . . *tu es vilain.*"

She was in bra and pantyhose. He was elated, yet still cautious. But Olga had no further doubt. She plastered herself against the length of him, her right hand powerfully pulling the small of his back. Kelly kissed a darkly flushed nipple through sheer bra. It was hard, a blood-engorged knob. He slipped the bra strap over her shoulder and bared the breast. He took as much of it as he could in his mouth and she trembled ecstatically. But she would not allow him to slip his hand beneath the elastic top of the pantyhose. She grunted and squirmed.

"No, no, Jack!"

"Olga, I promise you I'm going to go crazy."

"No, no."

He unzipped his pants and tried to press her hand inside his fly. But she wasn't having that either. She would not touch him with her hand.

"Put it against me, just against my leg, Jack," she pleaded urgently, "so I can feel it there against me."

Christ, he *would* go nuts now. He pulled his pants down and got half on top of her, laid the swollen thing against the abrasive nylon, next to her mound, close, yet how far away from the target. He could feel the twin segments of her opening through the nylon and scraped himself, rubbing back and forth.

"Put him there," she commanded feverishly. Her eyes were closed, teeth clenched, throat throbbing. "Put him there. I want to feel him there."

"Then feel . . . It's there!"

They looked grotesque, he supposed, but then people in this position usually did. Both her breasts were strained out of her brassiere, which was wound tightly across her stomach. His trousers were down to his ankles, all creased and messed up, his shorts ripped and stained. It was a hell of a clumsy way of protecting what he supposed was her virginity.

"Olga," he blustered, "the thought is as sinful as the act, remember that."

"I cannot, Jack, I cannot," she whimpered.

But she pressed and pulled and pushed more vigorously than before. He shoved his hand between them to relieve the pressure on himself and agitated her through her pantyhose until, quite unexpectedly, with a tightening of buttocks, a nervous shuddering of legs, and a wild yelp, she suffered—there could be no other word for it—an orgasm. It was enough to release him and he climaxed with surging abandon. He spent his fluid all over her pantyhose. But he had the presence of mind to be grateful he had not come inside her. She would not be able to charge that Kelly had robbed her of her most precious jewel.

Nonetheless, she said, "Jack, that was not nice of you. What have you done to me?"

"Olga, it was kind of mutual."

"You will despise me now."

"No, no, not at all. Don't be silly."

She started to cry. "I am ashamed. . . . I have never, never. Never before."

"What?" He was puzzled. "You never came before?"

"Never made love before."

"Well, listen, Olga, we didn't exactly make love."

"What then? What then?" He was amazed: was she so unschooled? "I had meant to retain my dignity, despite my feelings for you."

"Feelings?"

"Love," Olga said decisively. "A word you are familiar with? You may tell me what you feel for me."

"Olga . . . I . . ."

He was forced to go no further with a stuttering attempt to put things in proportion.

Their small debate was interrupted by a third presence.

" *'Soir.*" It was a tinny voice coming from nowhere. *"Ici Hercule."*

"Jack?" She had heard the voice too and started in alarm. "Jack?"

Kelly looked up, over the end of the couch, to see a man, an astonishingly small man, not a dwarf exactly, but a very short figure of a man wearing a black bowler and chewing on the end of a black cigar.

Olga pushed Kelly away, screaming, and rolled off the couch on her hands and knees, pulling embarrassedly at her clothes—trying to get her bra back over her breasts, recovering her dress, and holding it in front of herself. Kelly yanked up his pants, zipping them and turned his attention to the little man.

"Where in the fuck did you come from?"

"Ici Hercule," the intruder repeated dispassionately.

"How in the hell did you get in here, for Christ's sake? Who the hell are you?"

He edged toward the man called Hercule, his arms extended. He would throw the little runt down the stairs. Hercule quickly reached inside his tight suit coat and snatched out an envelope, which he hurled at Kelly's feet. Ignoring this, Kelly advanced. Hercule again went for his jacket, this time hauling out a long-barreled pistol, which he leveled at Kelly. His eyes were flat and unflustered.

Kelly stopped in his tracks. Holy shit, this was it. They were about to be mugged, robbed, raped, maybe shot. It was frightening. He remembered Perex's phone call, the warning: somebody was taking out AmFreight people. But then, at once, remembering Perex, he recalled the man Perex had pointed out sitting in the black car near the Ritz, a man in a bowler hat: the tiny hit man.

"Jesus . . ."

"*Silence!*" Olga screeched. "*Silence!*" She was still clutching her clothes against her. "Where may I go? I must . . . freshen up." What other expression would have been more appropriate? "And who, monsieur, is this gentleman?" she demanded. "I am mortified. I shall never forgive myself. I am dishonored." She turned to Hercule. "Monsieur, are you a representative of my father?"

An awful thought. But no, somehow Hercule was a representative of Rafe Perex.

She turned back to Kelly. "It is the worst fate. You, monsieur, had best run for your life."

"Olga," he cried angrily, "can't you see this guy has got a gun in his hand?"

But she ignored the gun and whirled away, buttocks bouncing.

The little man still had the drop on him. "Monsieur," Hercule said commandingly, "read the letter."

Kelly stooped to pick up the envelope. Yes, there was a note from Perex inside.

"Jack, my dear friend, on second thought this is to introduce Hercule. He's an expert driver and comes equipped with wheels. Speaks little English but is very effective, things being what they are now. Protectively, Rafe."

"Hercule?"

"*Oui*, monsieur."

Over by the front door sat a small suitcase, obviously Hercule's overnight things. Naturally, he thought weakly, Hercule would be moving into the guest bedroom. Kelly smiled and nodded wearily. Hercule opened his jacket and slipped the revolver back into an oiled shoulder holster.

"Jesus, Hercule, how did you get in here?" Kelly made a key turning gesture and pointed at the door. Hercule shrugged scornfully and pulled a long metal instrument out of another pocket. It was, of course, a skeleton key. "Hercule, you scared the daylights out of me, us."

He sat down and rubbed his face. It was not over. Olga would never forgive him for allowing her to be caught like this, *in flagrante*. God, he thought, if it was not one Latin expression, then it was another, if not *coitus interruptus*, then *in flagrante delicto*. Olga would go through life convinced that at her moment of matrimonial truth, Hercule would jump up in a pew in the back of the church and denounce her.

"Hercule," he said softly, "this is not something to spread around *tout Paris*." He put a finger to his lips in a shushing pantomime and pointed in the direction of the bathroom and Olga.

Trying now to be agreeable, Hercule grinned and nodded. "Monsieur desires a drink, *quelque chose à boire?*"

"A drink?" He was startled. "All right. There's Pernod in the kitchen."

"*Un Pernod?*"

As Hercule stamped out of the room, bowler firmly on his head, Olga reappeared. She sidled out of the hallway, her eyes downcast.

"How about a drink, Olga? Hercule is making me a Pernod. Then we can go on to Pipi's." For something to do, he lifted the Dom bottle out of the ice bucket. "A little more of this?"

Olga's eyes bugged in astonishment. "*Imbécile!*" She twisted the ultimate insult with the full force of its French pronunciation. "I am seduced and dishonored by you, most devious of men, and you ask me if I wish to go to dinner? I cannot decide, monsieur, whether you are the most insensitive of men or merely most stupid."

"There's no need to be so nasty," he said.

He tried to put his arm around her but she pulled away. "Cheapened and ruined am I. My life is over now. I have no wish to be seen again in your company, Monsieur Kelly."

"Olga, don't be a bore. Hercule is a friend."

She put her hands over her ears. "Bah! He is a spy and you have ruined me."

"Not at all, Olga," he said loftily. "I didn't ruin you because—thank God, in retrospect—I didn't really, you know, screw you. I never got inside, so you've got no worries there. You're intact. And think of it this way: you did get off and that wasn't the first time, was it? Tell the truth now. Are you saying you've never masturbated?"

"Oh, oh," she exclaimed, swaying in horror. "A vile person to say such things. I think it will be far better for me, monsieur, if I never set eyes on you again."

"Olga, I repeat, I'm just as sorry as you are that Hercule showed up."

"I can only thank the merciful Creator that I understood your evil intent in time to save myself."

Kelly was stunned. How could she twist things around like that? "Olga, don't give me that. You were ready for anything. I didn't seduce you. You seduced me."

Her face turned white and she hissed, "Yes, yes, it is always thus, the fate of Russian womanhood to be trodden by dishonorable men." She was close enough to slap his face. She did so with vehemence but not much strength.

"Jesus, Olga . . ."

"And the blasphemous mouth. *Au revoir,* Monsieur Kelly."

She marched toward the door, like a heroine headed for the scaffold.

But Hercule got there first. He opened the door and bowed.

"*Bonsoir, mam'selle,*" he said in a toneless voice.

CHAPTER

FOURTEEN

Hercule went downstairs for a couple of orders of take-out fried chicken and *pommes frites* and they made a feast of it, not a particularly merry one but it sufficed. Then the little man finally laid aside his bowler and unbuckled his arsenal: the holster and long-barreled pistol. They sat down to watch *Telefusion Française*. Hercule was by no means a talkative man—he had had little to say since his polite good-bye to Olga. He was truly very small but he was perfectly formed and his face, near full-sized and almost unlined, was handsome in its own craggy, heavily eyebrowed manner. It would have been difficult to guess how old he was, for he had obviously taken very good care of himself and seemed very agile and athletic. Kelly would have said about fifty. Black-haired, a small curl hung over his left forehead, as often in fanciful portraits of Napoleon.

Hercule's real power was in his eyes. Like the mouth, they were emotionless and almost opaque. He also possessed an outward utter calm. At rest, he was totally still, like a cat husbanding its strength, or perhaps a snake prepared to strike.

Kelly had often heard this would, in fact, be the physical configuration of the killer, a man with no evident feeling about anything, amoral and indifferent to life itself, whether his own or somebody else's.

He was stuck with Hercule, whether he liked it or not.

He slumped in the couch, feet up on the coffee table, and smoked a succession of Gauloises. Hercule naturally lit another of his long cigars. It was depressing. Christ knows, Kelly had had different plans than this for the evening. Olga had been stupid to take such affront. Of course, it was understandable that she had been upset and so should he be. But Hercule had merely been following orders. Perhaps he *had* rung the doorbell and they had simply not heard, having been so absorbed in the business of protecting Olga's virginity.

The telephone interrupted his thoughts. Hercule was there before Kelly had turned his head. "*Moment,*" he muttered. He carried the instrument across the room to Kelly. The voice he heard gave him something of a lift.

"Jacques, it is Zouzou here. . . ." Pause. "And who was the previous voice, may I ask?"

"A friend."

"Ach!" she cried in a terrible tone, "No mind. I hope I did not interrupt anything important." Bitch, he thought. "Jacques, I call at this hour because it is crucial that you come to the Maison Mordaunt with all convenient haste." Kelly hesitated. He could tell her he was very busy. Irritated by his silence, she cried, "Drop it! Whatever you have planned is of no consequence."

Kelly hated to give in so easily. "I can get there in a half hour."

"Good."

"What's so crucial?" he asked casually.

"Is a matter of life or death not crucial?" she demanded and hung up.

Kelly turned to Hercule. "You do have a car downstairs?"

"At your service, monsieur."

"We must drive, *comme le vent, n'est-ce pas,* to Maison Mordaunt. . . ."

"*Oui . . . rue Rimbaud,*" Hercule said, slapping his bowler back on his head.

Kelly showered quickly. He was still conscious of Olga in the pores of his skin as he toweled himself down. The memory of her body was locked in him now. . . . He dressed in a brown tweed suit he thought Madame Mordaunt would find pleasing.

Hercule's black Citroen promised amazing pickup. The driver's side was equipped with controls within reach of his short arms and legs. As they whipped across the river, it occurred to Kelly to say, "Monsieur Hercule, I'll bet you used to be a jockey, *n'est ce pas?*"

Hercule knew the word very well. The question elicited his first show of real feeling. "*Oui*, Monsieur Kelly, *un jockey* . . . Longchamps . . . Belmont . . . Le Hollywood Park. *Mais oui!*"

This was all Kelly needed to know. He had an ex-jockey hit man as a bodyguard.

Hercule braked to a stop in front of Maison Mordaunt. Kelly pointed up toward the lighted penthouse. "Wait for me, Hercule. I go up . . . there."

Hercule grunted ferociously. He would stay with the car. Beautiful, Kelly thought, he had always thought it would be the height of luxury to have someone wait with the car.

He rang the buzzer beside the front entrance and the big brass-and-glass doors unlocked. He pushed inside, closing the doors behind him. His heels echoed across the black-and-white marble-tiled floor of the downstairs boutique. A small elevator was waiting to carry him upstairs. Kelly emerged directly into Madame Mordaunt's brightly lit drawing room and an unlikely tableau of figures.

Zouzou was sitting, as usual, on the overstuffed suede couch, legs curled under her, the disgusting Charles at her side.

Standing, one arm propped stylishly on the veined stone mantelpiece, was Monsieur le Ministre, Aristide de Bis.

The surprise was the figure in an Empire chair at one side of the fireplace, legs elegantly crossed. It was the slender and remarkably beautiful woman all Paris knew to be Countess Beatrice de Beaupeau, mistress to Aristide de Bis. Kelly had never been so close to her.

"Jacques, you are here," Zouzou cried. "*Bon*—finally.

You are acquainted, of course, with Monsieur Aristide de Bis.''

"Of course." All too well he remembered the last time he had seen de Bis, that day at the Mordaunt Collection. Aristide's greeting was no more than vague and grudging. He obviously had other things on his mind.

"And this lady is Countess Beatrice de Beaupeau, Jacques."

"Yes, yes. How do you do, Countess."

Kelly took her hand. He had seen her before from a distance—across the room at the Tour d'Argent or L'Orangerie—and seen her picture often enough in the newspapers and magazines—on water skis, hopping a plane, sitting in a box at Longchamps, in the snow at Gstaad.

"Monsieur Kelly," she murmured faintly. She smiled fleetingly.

The very ordinary words were like the music of the senses: the timbre of her voice was the aural equivalent of the color scarlet. Her hand was light, lighter than a fleeting thought, a breath of summer breeze. It seemed to him warm, yet cool; strong but delicate. It spoke for the rest of her body. She held his hand for an instant, like a glove, snug and comforting. A shock ran through him.

Impatiently, Zouzou interrupted the contact. "Well, Jacques, take some champagne."

How composed, how detached from the vulgar world was Beatrice de Beaupeau. She was untouchable but no one would have said she was a haughty person. She was simply removed, as if visiting earth from a far-off constellation. Her eyes were large, gray-pupiled, moist, her hair long, silken, Titian.

"Well . . . sit down, Jacques," Zouzou said, recalling him again.

He took the chair opposite the countess, which was just as well for he found it difficult to take his eyes off her. It did not occur to him that Aristide de Bis might react to his enchantment with suspicion. As if to remind Kelly of the state of his affair, Aristide sat down on the couch beside Zouzou, reached to take Beatrice's hand, and stroked the back of it with his thumb. Beatrice jogged her eyes away from Kelly and smiled wiltingly at Aristide. Jesus, he thought, what a smile, like a flower vulnerably opening. Innocence. Beatrice was much better than the things they said about her. She was much more than a spoiled and sullen wanton stained with scandal and soiled by all manner of rumor.

"*Eh bien*, Monsieur Kelly," Aristide spoke up harshly, "it is said that you are to interview your president, George Washburn."

Kelly nodded, immediately feeling uncomfortable. He had a solid pull of the champagne while Aristide stared at him intently; Beatrice absently; and Zouzou indictingly, as if he had already been convicted of something foul.

"An interview is being arranged, yes."

"A-ha!"

"It's no secret," Kelly added. "I'll be doing it for a couple of American newspapers. It's no secret, not at all," he repeated. "But I'm surprised that such a *bagatelle* would engage even a small portion of your interest, Monsieur le Ministre."

In reply, Aristide tapped his temple, indicating nothing was so insignificant as to escape his knowledge, or attention. Words slid contemptuously from his mouth.

"Monsieur Kelly, you will find that nothing is as you say, 'small baggage.' I will explain to you some simple truths. If you troubled to read the various political journals of this country, you would know we are very concerned about American policy toward France and in particular about current American strategy as it applies to a former French colony—Mangrovia."

Kelly was under no illusion that Aristide had ever more than acknowledged his existence. The minister did not like Kelly, or any American, and it was understandable that since that day downstairs Aristide might find him even harder to accept. But, Kelly told himself, holding his champagne glass firmly, there was a certain mutuality about it.

Flatly, he replied, "It happens I do read French political journals, Monsieur le Ministre. And I'm very aware of your attitude toward the American government—and American policy in Mangrovia." He held his hand up daringly as Aristide tried to interrupt. "However, I don't know what that's got to do with me. I am a simple journalist, *c'est tout.* . . ."

Zouzou rasped, "Take care, Jacques."

But Aristide shook his head and smiled tolerantly. "Madame, no matter. It is best to be frank." But he couldn't resist a follow-up shot at Kelly, one he had probably been rehearsing all day. "You will tell me next that President Washburn, like his namesake George Washington, will always tell the truth, eh, Kelly?" He laughed derisively.

Kelly let himself chuckle in response. "No more than any other politician, Monsieur le Ministre."

Aristide's eyes lit appreciatively. "*Touché,* Kelly."

A shy smile materialized on the angular, shaded face of Beatrice de Beaupeau, a smile of encouragement, Kelly hoped.

"You understand, Monsieur Kelly," Aristide explained, "that we hold George Washburn in the greatest disrepute."

"I know that. You Europeans think he's nothing but a hillbilly truck driver. Even creating Amalgamated Freight didn't change that. A lot of Americans wouldn't disagree with you."

Aristide nodded, dropped Beatrice's hand, and leaned forward coldly.

"What is of consequence, Monsieur Kelly, is that American policy is disturbing the tranquillity of Mangrovia. Equally disturbing is that this is an unwelcome intrusion into our affairs. It should be a matter of concern to everyone when the stability of a poor nation is shattered by foreign intrigue."

"I agree," Kelly replied quickly. He was very sharp tonight. "But Mangrovia is an independent country now. Surely, it can make its own choice of friends."

This observation caused Aristide to frown with annoyance, then to proclaim, "As a government, Kelly, a moral force, France has a responsibility toward a former colony." His voice trailed away. "Kelly, we are not buccaneers operating in the dead of night. It is said Washburn will bribe this poor place to remove it from the loving embrace of France."

"I don't know about any of that," Kelly said.

He could understand France didn't want anybody else horning in on her business in Africa. But French concern had little to do with diplomacy or the niceties of maternalism. At issue was Grovival—unless there was some other vital material of which he wasn't aware. Oil . . . copper . . . cocaine?

"*Alors*," Aristide said indignantly. "You mention Amalgamated Freight—another employee of Amalgamated Freight has been murdered, thus disturbing the tranquillity of *our* beautiful city."

"Maxwell Maxim," Kelly said.

"You know?"

"I know about it. I don't know who killed him or why he was killed."

"Nor do we!" Aristide exclaimed irritably. "But it was Amalgamated Freight—this creature, Maxwell Maxim, he was entrusted with the international cosmetics affairs of Amalagamated Freight. And you, Kelly, know what *that* entails."

"Grovival," Kelly stated, thinking it was useless to play dumb.

"*Exactement!* Monsieur Kelly, you are a good friend to France, *n'est-ce pas?* You are a close and dear friend of one of our famous French women, Suzanne Mordaunt. . . ."

"Suzanne?"

"My proper name, you fool," Zouzou hissed.

"Monsieur Kelly?" Aristide pressed.

"Yes," he said slowly, "I consider myself a friend of France."

"Is it so much to ask then that you impress on your President Washburn the weight of French thought?"

"Well . . ." He laughed embarrassedly. Was that all? Washburn would pay no heed to anything Kelly might say about high policy in a such a low-rated place as Mangrovia. Chances were Washburn had never even heard of Mangrovia. Most likely, Mangrovian policy was being made in some obscure subsection of the State Department.

". . . Impress on Washburn that we will not stand for this intrusion, this murderous activity of Amalgamated Freight. We will not sit still for this imperialism. . . . And, we know your father. His voice, his newspaper, is very strong in American politics."

"I don't work there anymore."

But Aristide was not to be deterred. "We have a newspaper too, Monsieur Kelly. . . . We will accept a brief report on this interview, Washburn's responses to our serious charges. You put the salient questions, Kelly, and the *Temps de Calais* will print it."

"The *Times of Calais?*" he repeated. "I haven't heard of it. . . ."

Sarcastically, Aristide said, "Monsieur Kelly, you do not know all there is to know, *n'est ce pas? Le Temps de Calais* is a small but growing organ of French conservatives, powerfully anti-Communist. Surely that would suit you? You are not a Communist, after all, *hein?*"

"No, no . . . But I'm not terrifically right-wing either."

"Conservative, Monsieur Kelly." Aristide waved his hands. "But no matter. What would Washburn say if what you call an 'insider' informs him the French government will leave the Western alliance altogether if he persists in his Mangrovian adventure?"

"Completely?" It was hard to believe France would disown the entire Western defense umbrella. France had allowed its membership in NATO to lapse but to resign entirely? "You'd do that? You'd be defenseless, Monsieur le Ministre."

De Bis chuckled cynically. "No, *mon cher*. Between us and the Bolsheviki, we have Germany, and they are faithful to the alliance. . . . Besides . . ." He pointed his hawk nose at Kelly. "We will protect ourselves. We need no one, we French, the descendants of Napoleon."

Kelly dallied with the thought. "One of the big fears in

Washington is always that France will make a separate deal with the Russians."

Aristide de Bis leaped to his feet. He was mightily insulted now. "*Êtes-vous fou,* Monsieur Kelly? We, the French, would ally ourselves with the Bolsheviks? You are perhaps crazy?"

"Just thinking out loud, Monsieur le Ministre. . . . The prospect would scare the hell out of Washington."

Aristide nodded soberly. "You are not so politically stupid as you might seem, monsieur. . . . You might, if you wished, hint that to President Washburn. . . ."

Kelly shook his head. He had had just about enough of this. "I couldn't. Anyway, he wouldn't listen to me. It would have to come directly from you."

"No, no." Aristide waggled his large head violently. "It could not come officially. It would be something you heard from very reliable sources. Very reliable French sources indeed!" He thumped himself on the chest. "Reliable: *c'est moi.*"

"I don't think he'd pay any attention."

Aristide clapped his hands over his eyes. "*Bien!* You could tell him more: reliable sources, *moi,* say if American policy, the killing and subversion, goes forward, there is a chance of . . . war!"

Jesus, Kelly thought, the story was developing, he couldn't deny that. What a blockbuster!

"France would go to war over Mangrovia?"

Arrogantly, Aristide said, "Mangrovia is . . . symbolic. That is it." A mad stare glazed his eyes. "*Pourquoi pas?* There have been wars over lesser matters."

"That's just crazy," Kelly muttered.

"So they said in 1939 when Adolf Hitler marched on Czechoslovakia, then Poland, countries for which no one cared, Monsieur Kelly." Aristide commenced to laugh roughly, then abruptly changed the subject, leaving the vile speculation to fester in Kelly's mind. "Monsieur Kelly, we are told the health of George Washburn is very bad, that he drinks too much and that he is a weary man. What would happen if George Washburn were suddenly to die?"

Was this another, not very veiled threat? God knows who had arranged to bump off Maxwell Maxim: was this a threat of assassination?

"The vice-president would take over, Bruce Jeavens."

"Ha!" Aristide scoffed shrilly. "A weak and manipulated creature, eh, Beatrice?"

How would she know? But Beatrice nodded timidly. She had not been following the conversation very closely. She recrossed her fine legs and refolded her hands in her lap.

"A weak fool!" Zouzou said sharply.

Aristide then gave him a piece of information Kelly had not read or seen hinted at in any newspaper or magazine, the kind of information journalists would kill for: "Monsieur Washburn on his impending trip to Europe will, we understand, undergo a treatment of Grovival."

Kelly could not believe it. But if it were true, did any of the pieces begin to fall together? The equation read: Mangrovia equals Grovival. Perex thought so and obviously Aristide de Bis did too. And if Washburn himself were interested in the drug? Well! The Arabian Peninsula had become an area of the most vital importance because it was the biggest producer of another wonder substance: oil.

"Why?" he asked.

"Obviously, monsieur, because he thinks it will rejuvenate him. And he cannot, at this time, acquire Grovival in the United States of America. Ergo: he will go to Switzerland."

Kelly remembered what C.T. Trout had said. "There's a clinic . . ."

Zouzou nodded wickedly, confirming this, perhaps everything. "Yes, Jacques, the clinic Montmorency, near Geneva."

Where Maryjane had had her bosom renovated. How very odd. What a concidence. The weight of this information bore down heavily on them all. Beatrice looked sad and Zouzou perplexed. It was always the same problem: how to respond, what to say to the conceits of mankind? But there was a more shocking consideration.

If Aristide knew this for a fact, it would be no trouble for him to alert the world that George Washburn was prepared to fall for medical quackery. What would that knowledge do to the alliance?

"Monsieur Kelly," Aristide said slyly, "do you recall when Premier Khrushchev visited the United States some years ago? Are you aware the CIA managed, somehow, to retrieve a sample of his urine? Do you know that from that simple sample, you Americans were able to forecast almost the precise moment of Nikita Khrushchev's death?"

"No," Kelly said, feeling ready for a primal scream, "I wasn't aware of that."

"It is the truth." Aristide put a hand on Beatrice's knee. "What we want, Monsieur Kelly, is a sample of the urine of your president."

Kelly looked away. "I respect your sense of humor."

But Aristide was serious. "For such a sample we would be willing to pay thousands in Swiss francs. We know the Soviets would pay even more. But, after all, we are still your ally and should have priority."

"You're joking, of course." He smiled nervously.

"*Non!* It is not a jocular thought. Such a sample would be of the utmost importance to us."

"Well, you can't be suggesting I have any way of getting it for you." Aristide flipped his hands nonchalantly, saying in this way that as farfetched as it might sound he didn't consider the possibility out of the question. "My God, Minister," Kelly muttered, "pay a Swiss doctor. Couldn't your men put a tap on his toilet?"

Aristide shook his head. "American security is too vicious."

"Then . . ." He thought desperately. For his own safety, for the sake of his passport, he had to distance himself from any such project. "Good God. You French are good with your women—put a woman in his room. A woman could do it, you know, when he's gone to sleep." Thinking even faster, he continued, "A woman could even—I hate to mention this in front of the ladies—a woman could carry the sample out with her. You see what I mean? But your people must have thought of that already."

"In his semen, yes," Aristide replied crudely. "Well, we are considering all our fallback positions: the harsh threat of French retaliation; the opportunities that would present themselves to us during his Grovival cure; the urine sample. We appreciate your help, Monsieur Kelly."

It was time for the basic corrective. Kelly stood up and faced the three of them.

"No, no help. You must remember one thing: as much as I love and admire France, I *am* an American. I couldn't do anything like that."

Aristide interrupted him solemnly, "Remember, too, that you are a citizen of the world."

"I know that, I do know that." How shocking, he thought, this habit the provocateur had of appealing to your patriotism: toward your country, toward the world.

"Remember," Aristide continued, "a time may come when a man must choose between humanity and inhumanity. People have made that choice before: Brutus, Judas, Rudolf Hess. . . ." Aristide rose and brusquely clapped Kelly on the shoulder. "We have a right to expect people to make that choice, Monsieur Kelly, and we would be very disillusioned if you did not." He eyed Kelly balefully. "And I need not add, I would be *exceedingly* disillusioned if such a conversation as this one were reported. What you do with the information about Washburn and his cure, of course, is entirely up to you." His eyes glinted. It was very obvious what Aristide meant by that: use the information. Kill Washburn's credibility.

"Naturally." Kelly smiled with what he hoped was suitable inscrutability. "The greatest confidentiality."

"Confidentiality," Aristide said warmly, "the very word." He shook his shoulders, buttoned the jacket of his suit and pressed the knot of his tie. He glanced at his Cartier watch and spoke with finality. "Now, I must leave you charming people. In a few moments, I must fly to the south for an important meeting. *Ma chère . . .*"

He directed this endearment to Beatrice de Beaupeau. "The car will return for you."

Beatrice nodded and limply said, *"Très bien. Au 'voir, mon cher."*

Ma chère, mon cher, oh bullshit, Kelly muttered to himself.

"Monsieur Kelly." He shook Kelly's hand powerfully. "Monsieur Kelly, dare I hope? Sensational revelations in *Le Temps de Calais?*"

All Kelly said was, "Good-bye for now, Mr. Minister."

De Bis kissed the women's hands, lifted his arm in benediction and disappeared into the elevator like Mandrake the Magician.

For a moment, they were silent. Zouzou sat thoughtfully, nodding to herself, her dry lips pursed. Charles had gone to sleep beside her. Kelly reached for his champagne glass, thus collecting a near view of Beatrice de Beaupeau's knees. A small blue vein throbbed gently in her calf, there on the side where the flesh was at its softest. She sat as if suspended in some perfumed solution.

"Madame, mesdames, may I give you some more champagne?"

"Yes, please, Jacques," Zouzou murmured.

He poured bubbly Mordaunt 10 into the glasses. "Well, madame, I don't know what to say."

"Jacques, you are supposed to say that you will be of service to France. I speak bluntly. I am no diplomat like Aristide de Bis."

"But I can't agree to . . . all those things."

"Ach," Zouzou exclaimed impatiently, "your agreement is to me no more than whale offal washed ashore on the Adriatic shores of our Italian friends—something one cannot sit in."

"Madame—that sounds so awful."

"And so is whale offal which, as everyone knows, stinks like rotting squid after many days in the sand." Having made her point, she cracked her brown knuckles and cackled with laughter. "I cannot remain angry with you, Jacques." She winked. "Tell me, Jacques, how goes it now with your treasured genitalia?"

Kelly glanced uncomfortably toward the countess. She would be shocked. Zouzou said, "Beatrice speaks little English."

Beatrice de Beaupeau smiled and murmured, "I speak little English, Monsieur Kelly."

Her voice, enunciating his name, thrilled him.

Zouzou bade him open a fresh bottle of the champagne. He was not careful enough doing it. A spurt of foam wet the brown wool carpet.

"*Pas de tout*," Zouzou cried nonchalantly. "Now, Jacques, I would like you to walk about the room on your hands. I have told Beatrice of your marvelous trick and she is most anxious to see it. . . . We would not wish her to be bored now that Aristide de Bis has gone."

Kelly was dismayed. He could not perform his childish acrobatics in front of this supersophisticated woman.

"Ah, yes, yes," the countess exclaimed, her eyes fixed admiringly on him.

It was such a stupid thing but, other things considered, probably better than going on about George Washburn and Mangrovia. Kelly took off his jacket, emptied his pockets, and removed his shoes.

"Madame, you know there really isn't enough space in here."

"Get on with it, Jacques!" She thumped Charles's head. "Wake up, *monstre!*"

Charles snarled and spit.

Kelly assumed his usual position, head between his forearms. He jacked his knees up to his elbows, finally thrusting his legs upward until he was at the perpendicular.

"Bravo, bravo!" Beatrice clapped her hands.

Kelly took a couple of careful hand-steps forward and turned, so positioning himself, without being conscious of what he was doing, that he had an unimpeded view of Beatrice's legs, inner thighs, and—he almost collapsed— her most precious secret: for Beatrice was not wearing what the *RAG*, in its fashion reports, referred to as intimate apparel. He stood there, poised, then wavering, for what seemed an eternity, staring dead ahead at that lush place, shrouded in a silky bush of bronze-colored hair.

"Up, up, Jacques!"

Zouzou buzzed with delight, slapping her palms together like two pieces of smoked bacon.

"I'm not sure . . ."

He was breathless. His elbows began to weaken and he tottered in fresh anguish as Beatrice shifted her legs to give him a wider angle of vision. The searing, frightening thing was that she must have known exactly what she was doing. Hell! Everything was breaking loose inside him. His only hope now was to push himself higher, wheel away, before they noticed what was happening to him.

But Zouzou screamed with glee and pointed at his upside-down erection, jabbering at Beatrice in French. He heard the countess's quick intake of breath.

"Jacques, you are incorrigible!"

"Madame," he gasped.

But it was Charles who did him in. The monkey, gibbering and envious of the attention Kelly was receiving, slid off the couch and swiped at Kelly's inverted face. Charles's paw missed but Kelly was thrown completely off balance. He crashed down, one leg whacking the coffee table. A glass broke and he felt a twinge of pain. He had cut himself.

"Charles!" Zouzou screeched. "*Mon Dieu!*"

Charles scampered out of the room.

"Hell, I'm sorry, madame." Kelly groaned.

The accident removed all thought of lust from his mind. A sliver of glass had pierced his tweed pants. He felt a trickle of blood on his leg.

"I've stabbed myself," he said.

Zouzou jumped up hurriedly. "Charles, *petit monstre!* I will kill him. Quick, Jacques, to the *bain*. I will fetch a bandage."

Beatrice de Beaupeau was stricken. Her face whitened, her lips quivered. But did she know why he had fallen?

The sight of her was enough to sink a fleet of ships, let alone topple an amateur acrobat.

"Ah, monsieur," she murmured sympathetically. Her body surged forward and her hands fluttered at her breast.

"I'll be all right."

"*J'espère que oui*," she cried softly. Lightly, she touched his arm as he got to his feet. "*J'espère que oui*, Monsieur Kelly."

"Jacques, Jacques!" Zouzou had given off raving at Charles.

He tore himself away from Beatrice. Zouzou had Charles cornered in the bathroom and was whipping him with a towel.

"Miserable *con*! I will send him back to the jungle where he came from."

Kelly's bleeding soon stopped. He bandaged the wound and returned to the drawing room. Beatrice was gone.

"She told me *au revoir* for you, Jacques."

"Madame . . . she is very beautiful."

Curtly, she said, "Yes, beautiful but *très stupide*. And, as well, Jacques, the mistress of a very powerful man, a man one does not trifle with, a man who would kill. Yes, Aristide de Bis would kill."

"Madame, I merely remarked that she is very beautiful. . . . I would like to see her again though, I admit."

Zouzou hooted with laughter. "You are crazy, Jacques Kelly." Then she scowled and reminded him of something else. "Aristide de Bis is a trusted friend and confidante of many years. . . . Ah, Jacques, you fuck so much and now you wish to fuck the mistress of my friend. What am I to say to that?"

"That you are my friend too and that you understand. She is beautiful and I think she desires me."

"Oh, *merde*!" Zouzou said disgustedly. "*Merde*—I wish I were young again. You would not be able to keep up with me then, Jacques. But I am a realist and I realize my powers are limited. No, I understand, being the premier realist of France, the home of Descartes, that I could not hold you to me. But, Monsieur Jacques Kelly, do not worry. For, as you help us, I will help you. I will push you into the white arms of French womanhood and you will be happy there."

"You will? Beatrice de Beaupeau?"

"*Merde!*" she cried again. "No! Drink your champagne, monsieur." Obediently, he finished his glass and she poured him another. "Is Beatrice de Beaupeau your price? Is that so? *Eh bien alors.*" She groaned.

"Yes."

"Ah," she said softly, subsiding, "that could not be arranged. I, who could arrange almost anything, could not arrange that. Kelly, Kelly. You know most people bore Madame Mordaunt but you, Jacques, I tell you this freely, you have always been respected and loved, yes loved, by Zouzou Mordaunt. You, skillful and talented, of the upper classes of nature's own nobility, who remind me so much of Angus. And now you must ask me to do the impossible? For me, Zouzou, to complicate and ruin your life?"

Beatrice de Beaupeau, he thought dreamily, Beatrice de Beaupeau.

Zouzou approached him intently. She leaned to kiss his cheek, then perched herself on his knee.

"There is something better than momentary infatuation, Jacques, or putrid friendship. There is the exchanged anger of the bodies."

Apprehensively, he murmured, "I've never heard it put like that."

"Why are you so fearful of me, Jacques?" What could he say but deny that he was frightened of her? She smiled and like the age-old predator that she was, stuck her hand inside his shirt, put puckish fingers to his nipples. Unbuttoning his collar and loosening his tie, she roamed his chest with her bony hands. Kelly began to feel drowsy. He closed his eyes and thought of other places. He was recalled to attention by her sharp voice.

"I am not young, Jacques, and there is no need for you to look at me. I will stand now and I will go into the room where it is forever night. When I summon, you will follow."

"Madame," he said haltingly, "I don't know what to say."

She chuckled more huskily, throatily, than was usual for her.

"Jacques, all you have to say is *merci*—merely thank the good God above that he is giving you the opportunity to make love to a historic monument of France."

"But my chauffeur—he's waiting for me downstairs."

"That is of no consequence to me, monsieur."

She scrambled up and moved in the fateful direction of her bedroom.

Jesus, he shivered, what the hell! He was caught, efficiently snared. He wanted Beatrice; he got Zouzou. It was possible to get away; he had only to run to the elevator. But if he were to turn her down, he would be cast into oblivion. All would be lost. She could ruin him—and he needed her now. She was what Rafe called his pipeline.

"My Jacques . . ." Her voice beckoned him; she was ready. "Monsieur Kelly." The voice crept out for him like an old crone in slippers.

God! He drained the champagne, refilled the glass, finished that too, and burped gently.

"Yes, madame," he replied.

CHAPTER

FIFTEEN

Kelly had always supposed there must be that about Zouzou Mordaunt which in some small way corresponded to all the gossip that had been put around over the years—that she was, in brief, a very kinky individual with unlimited sexual proclivities. As was true with gossip there might be elements of truth to it, but on this night, in this single direction, she was inspired, and that was all Kelly would ever be able to say about her.

When he crept into her bed, she was waiting for him like a flowering maiden, trembling with breathless female wonder. Her heart, of course, was a bit unsteady, her respiration not one hundred percent perfect, and she coughed now and then quite racklingly. All Kelly could see of her were bright eyes flickering in the darkness. Her skin, he realized first, was smooth and she had doused herself liberally with that familiar Mordaunt perfume, Number Two.

The truly amazing thing was how untiring she was. In between, they smoked her black Gitanes.

She said: "Now, Monsieur Kelly, I will take care of you. I will see to your needs and desires, poor boy. You must forget Countess Beatrice de Beaupeau—for this love of ours will make all others seem like the noisome droppings of the giant squid."

As disarming as the metaphor was, he quietly responded, "I'm always grateful to you for your solace and comfort, madame."

How peculiar it was, for, as he spouted the formal words, he was buried between her thin but by no means scrawny thighs, and when he shifted his body for better purchase, she replied with a combination of internal actions the like of which he had never experienced, even with Maggi Mont.

"Tell me, monsieur, you are pleased?"

"God, yes."

"Ha! It is a surprise for you, is it not? You, Jacques, who pooh-poohed Grovival." He told her facilely that he retracted all doubts about Grovival. She nodded against his shoulder. "Perhaps, you will want to sleep a little now, monsieur? *Mais non!*" she cried.

She pitched her hips against him, pulling him within her as she might have some inanimate mechanical contraption. Her every movement was a ballet gesture. It was clear now why they gossiped about her, why she had been described as one of the leading courtesans of the century. She had turned many men to jelly. How many had she driven to suicide or around the bend into simple insanity?

Zouzou flattered him extravagantly with a long, guttural gasp of pleasure. But she was far from checking out. "Jacques, tell me what you think of Zouzou's body."

What could he tell her? Under his chest, he felt her breasts, the size of crab apples, the tight belly, taut as a drum, the musuclar legs pulling him forward. Her whole body was wet with Mordaunt Number Two but her private well of juices had not dried up. Inside, she was silky and firm and alive with sensuality.

Groaning, she complimented him on the bump of scar tissue which crowned his pecker, and as she was doing so, she reached sudden climax, a tiny being teetering on a cliff, then falling over, her reedy screech of satisfaction disappearing into the distance. In a moment, politely, he shot a miserly load into her.

"Ah," Zouzou whined exultantly, "I could go on forever, dear Jacques. I will not sleep. I am the Zouzou

Mordaunt of old. As my Angus would say, 'Aye, a wee fucking machine, me bairn. . . .' "

Her attempt at a Scots accent cloyed. He was not tired but to please her, he let loose a snort of exhaustion and collapsed at her side. Zouzou rummaged about in the darkness. He heard the hiss of a spray and was wildly startled by the cold impact of cologne on his balls.

"Mordaunt Number Three," Zouzou muttered, "better than the stench of tired tiger piss, *non*?" She flopped her head down on his shoulder and he caught a whiff of her Gitane-impregnated breath. "Monsieur, I will tell you that was very very good, very professionally done. But tell me why, why?" She paused for a second. "Why did you not appear in 'thirty-five, Jacques?"

"Better late than never, madame."

"Exactly . . . The anger of the body, now quenched, like a fire in a downpour of rain. Forget Beatrice," she advised him again.

"I think you are a poetess."

"I am a poetess, but of the body. And that is why I am *the* couturière of France."

Now he understood something else—her hold over such men as Aristide de Bis. Had Aristide once been her lover; had he too driven his spike of authority into this body politic?

"I guess I'm your slave now," Kelly said, "like all the others."

"All the men I have known and there have been many," she agreed, with rasping chuckle and bronchial cough, "are in bondage to me, forever."

He might, he thought, be getting near the end of her list but even now and at her age, she would have been described in the streets as a fabulous lay. He recalled Benjamin Franklin had advised a favorite nephew that when taking your pleasure with ladies of an uncertain age, merely put a bag over their head and you'll never know the difference.

Christ, and how recently had he been struggling with the virtue of Olga Blastorov and mooning over Beatrice de Beaupeau? Was there any difference between them all? Not really, for even within this sublimely experienced lady there lurked the essence of youthful passion.

"If I were really young again, tireless Lothario, you could not keep up with me—'aye, a wee bit of succulent haggis,' Angus said." Not particularly poetic that Angus had compared her to a Scottish meatball, he thought. He told her he could not keep up with her now. "Aye," she chirped. "You Kellys were ever gentlemen. . . ." This phrase bit into his brain. You Kellys? "But tell me one thing, Jacques. After all these months, can you say you love Zouzou Mordaunt in some tiny way?"

He lied easily. "I've loved you from the very beginning, madame."

"Ah, *merde*. Come, Jacques. I am the premier realist of France."

"*Vraiment*, madame," he insisted.

"Then I will tell you my secret plan. Grovival will become Mordaunt Number Eight, the precious new ingredient in perfume, cologne, balm, and deodorant. You see what it has done for me, Jacques."

"But madame, you don't have any need for it. *Vraiment*," he repeated.

"No, everybody needs it," she said. "At the moment, Grovival is caught up in the squabbles of politics. But we will acquire control. We will take it from those goddamn savages who would keep it from the world. That Mangrovian Ministry of Commerce, which exports Grovival in a trickle and then only to those who pay the highest price, whether above or below the counter. Bah! They will try to make more money than from oil, this beautiful elixir, better than any yet discovered. Will you help me?"

"I would always do my best to help you." But he knew there was a long distance between promise and delivery.

"We will be richer than you ever dreamed," she mused.

"Money isn't everything."

"You swine!" she shrilled. "You are thinking of her? I cannot obtain Beatrice for you. It is impossible." She rolled away from him irritably, again reaching toward the bedside table. She was unscrewing the top of a jar. "I will not tell you what this is, Jacques." She began massaging grease into his crotch. "People will believe this is a remoisturizer but the cognoscenti will know it is a regenerator with elastic properties for the poor man who wishes to heighten and lengthen his pleasure. Tell me, what do you feel? Does it burn?"

He was frightened. It was obvious she was applying Grovival to his privates.

"It's warm," he said. "This is Mordaunt Number Eight, isn't it?"

She didn't answer the question. "Whatever it is, the flavor is pleasant and healthful, and it will encourage *soixante-neuf*, so long out of fashion among the young."

"Out of fashion? I don't think so, madame."

"Bah!" she scoffed. "There has been no *soixante-neufing* in recent years to match that of the middle twenties.

The effect of the Number Eight was worrying. He was conscious of a smarting and swelling and his balls began to quiver.

"Is this stuff safe? I'm beginning to get a reaction, madame."

"Bien! So you are! I can feel you growing, burgeoning, like some jungle weed. *Dieu!*"

She hopped on him, perching like a bird on a branch and belabored him for some minutes until she climaxed again. His own ejaculation cooled the burning sensation and he was relieved. Zouzou continued to squeak in an incomprehensible argot which he believed had its origin in the gutters of Marseilles where she had begun her long career. It had been put about that Zouzou, third daughter of a poor French-Algerian family, had her roots in the red-light district of the port city, and Kelly could believe it.

"You do not *wilt!*" she cried triumphantly as, flailingly, he continued to thrust into her. Expertly, she turned on him like a top, presenting her behind to his face. Kelly placed his hands carefully on her tiny breasts and pinched the nipples. She yelled and swore. Then, without warning and unmindful of his continuing discomfort, she lifted herself and climbed off the bed. She disappeared into the bathroom and he could hear her making more unpleasant remarks to Charles.

Kelly seized the opportunity to get dressed. He dragged himself, still overheated by the prototype Number Eight, back to the drawing room.

Christ! Seated by the fireplace, in the chair Beatrice de Beaupeau had occupied: Hercule! Again, he had been unaware of his entry.

"Boom-boom?" Hercule asked, straight-faced, making an obscene gesture with his hands.

"Hercule, goddamn it, she's going to be mad as hell."

But Hercule merely pulled at the corner of his mouth and shrugged.

"Jacques? Jacques?"

Zouzou appeared, face drawn but lividly decorated with a fresh slash of lipstick. She was wrapped, fortunately, in a robe. Cigarette hanging from her lips, she looked like a dissolute geisha.

She was violently surprised when she saw Hercule. "Jacques! Why have you let this creature into my home?"

"Madame." Kelly sighed. "This is my friend, Hercule. He became concerned."

She glared at Hercule, pulling her robe more tightly around her body.

Returning her look serenely, Hercule said, " '*Soir* . . .'"

Astonished, Zouzou rattled at him in French. Hercule soon became more attentive. He stood up, removed his bowler, and took the cigar out of his mouth.

"You," Zouzou exclaimed, "you are a very small man. A dwarf. A deformed creature."

"*Pardon,* madame," Hercule said with great dignity. "*Je suis* Hercule."

"Hercule? Hercule? You are Hercule? You are a small man, not a Hercule. A Lilliputian. But you speak a good French."

"Sorbonne," Hercule informed her succinctly.

"*Merde,*" she replied, "the Sorbonne does not admit

such small creatures, even if they are named Hercule.
Well, well." She was still glowering, but more pleasantly.
"Everyone should sit. Jacques, give me a brandy. And,
Monsieur Hercule, you wish perhaps a small brandy? In
a . . . small glass?"

"*Merci*, madame."

When Kelly had supplied them brandy snifters, Zouzou
asked, "How long has Monsieur Hercule been here?"

"I don't know, madame. He was worried about me.
He broke in."

"Broke in? I see," she said sarcastically. "How marvelous . . . Then he must realize, monsieur, that you
were not in my bedroom for the purpose of painting
murals."

She was not being as surly about it as she might
have been, nothing like the hysterical Olga Blastorov.
Perhaps . . . Was it possible that making love had cooled
her tempestuous spirit?

"Hercule," Kelly said, "is the soul of discretion."

"Wonderful." Zouzou sneered, staring at Hercule.
"Then no doubt he belongs on my staff, so notorious
about talking too much about everything, including me,
the mistress of Maison Mordaunt."

"I'm sure he would be excellent—if he ever were in
need of a position."

Zouzou clicked with her fingers, made the sounds
again of snapping twigs. "I trust he will keep his small
mouth shut, Jacques. It would not do for all Paris to
know that you, Jacques, have been fucking the premier couturière of France. . . . It is said I am to be
elected to the *Academie*. . . ."

The French Academy? The most prestigious body of
French notables: writers, poets, philosophers, politicians?
He had not known they held seats for dress designers.

"If such became known," Zouzou continued, "it might
well ruin my chances. *Les Academiciens* do not take
lightly to French greats fucking unknowns, particularly
American unknowns. . . ."

Sourly, Kelly thought he was not anxious for word to
get around either.

"No one would believe it, madame," he said.

She drew a bead on him with her right eye, squinting. "No? Because it is so outrageous an idea?"

"No, no. Just that no one would believe someone so renowned would have anything of an . . . intimate nature to do with an American correspondent."

She had to have her little play on words. "When it comes to the matter of *corespondents*, Jacques, people will believe anything." She tossed down her brandy, snapped her fingers again with a vigor that signaled she was preparing another point of logic. "But what do I care anyway? I am old enough, Jacques, to do all the foolish things. . . . And who is so holy and superior that he can caution me?"

She laughed defiantly, enjoying the moment. He wondered when last she had had a man, or a woman, in the room that was forever dark.

"You are marvelous, madame."

She was. He meant it. He couldn't believe now he had been in there.

"Yes, I *am* marvelous," she agreed freely. "But now, Jacques . . . *et aussi* Hercule, is it '*bonsoir*'? Or do you and your small assistant wish to remain with me tonight in a *situation a trois*?" Her eyes sparkled wickedly at Hercule. "Or should I say two and a half?"

Hercule understood. His body stiffened. He stared at her in disgust.

"Madame!" he protested in a low, rumbling voice.

He was so disapproving, Zouzou seemed for an instant, and unbelievably, shamed. A rare occurrence indeed.

"I beg your pardon, Monsieur Hercule," she said.

CHAPTER

SIXTEEN

Over lunch at Chez Habanero, one of Rafe Perex's hideaways, the usually effervescent Cuban was in a funk. He appeared to have lost weight. His hair was longer, almost unkempt, and he was wearing a sloppy tweed jacket and baggy, stained flannels. Dark glasses covered Perex's face and he constantly glanced over his shoulders, toward entrance and rear exit.

But he was reluctant to elaborate on his problems beyond what Kelly already knew: that the murder of Maxwell Maxim had attracted the attention of the French Sûreté to him and that the Swiss authorities were making unpleasant noises about his trust. The situation was fraught with peril, Perex said, physically and financially. He did not know where to go. Lately, he had been traveling on a Panamanian passport, and even now was registered in a small hotel under an assumed name.

Perex insisted that everything happening was involved to a greater or lesser extent with the forthcoming Washburn visit to Europe. Trout had also gone to ground. At the moment, he was staying incognito—if that were possible for such a loudmouthed Texan—at the Weisses Rossl am Wolfgangsee.

"In Austria?" Kelly asked.

"*Jawohl*. You, my dear, are to fly to London to meet one of Washburn's advance men to arrange the time and place of your interview for the *Appalachian Times*."

171

Kelly smiled, remembering what Aristide de Bis had said about the *Times of Calais*. "Rafe," he said, trying to draw him out, "my sources are giving off what we call a heady smell of crisis."

Perex began to sweat. He wiped his face with his napkin, then held it there, concealing himself as two men came into the restaurant.

"You haven't, my friend, heard anything from Maggi?"

"Not a word. Have you?"

"No, no. *Jesu Christus*, Jack, how could they do this to me? You know the Mount Vernon Trust is on the up-and-up. I've even got a former member of the International Monetary Fund on the board of directors. But, bloody hell, that doesn't impress the Swiss. They get hysterical when there's any suggestion of irregularity."

"Grovival is supposed to be very good for irregularity, Rafe."

"Bloody shit! How can you joke about my troubles?" Perex glared at him. "Son of a bitch, somebody is putting it around that we're manipulating the stock. Aristide's minions, no doubt."

"How so, Rafe?"

Perex put the napkin over his eyes again and his shoulders shook. "That we drive the price up, dump it at a big profit, then buy it back when the price drops. It is an old trick, Jack, but, *sweet Maria*, it is very dishonest, my dear."

They were eating Cuban dishes: greasy, barbequed goat and large portions of refried black beans, not the sort of fare Kelly liked.

"Rafe," he murmured, trying to shift Perex's mind to happier things, "this stuff must make a man fart like crazy."

Perex's eyes were wet. "Insult my national food: insult me."

"Stop being a crybaby. Just tell me—who am I supposed to see in London?"

The businesslike question distracted Perex momentarily. Unpleasantly, he said, "Tom Topovsky. He's on the

White House staff. Call the embassy when you get there."

"Topovsky . . . Seems to me I know the name."

"Of course—you've seen his picture," Perex growled. "He's a fucking functionary. He's also Westerley's boyfriend. Those two assholes live together in a town house in Georgetown. But," he added urgently, "you must not let on you know me. Promise! That would only cause trouble."

Perex swallowed half a glass of dark Latin beer and reached into an inside pocket of his jacket. He passed Kelly an envelope. Inside was a stack of Swiss franc notes.

"Rafe . . . Christ . . ."

"Shut up," Perex said disagreeably. "Put it away at once! That's your advance for the trip. Trout told me to bankroll you. You're on the team now—which doesn't, for the moment, look much like the winning team, does it? Jehoshaphat, my friend, be careful."

"Rafe," Kelly said guiltily, for he took the money, "there's talk Washburn will be stopping over in Switzerland. . . ."

"So?"

"That he's going for a Grovival cure."

"Bloody balls! Where'd you hear that?" Perex demanded fiercely.

"I told you I've got some pretty good sources."

"Zouzou Mordaunt . . . that bastard de Bis . . ."

"Ain't saying."

"Well . . ." Perex appeared even more worried. "Caramba! Keep it under your hat, my friend. Anyway, what's so odd about that? Old Adenauer used to go there and I've heard a couple of popes had treatments."

"Not Grovival."

"No—monkey-ball serum. This stuff is a whole new ball game."

Kelly remembered Aristide de Bis's most insistent question. "Rafe, is there something wrong with Washburn's health?"

"No, no," Perex cried. "Shit-fire, what it amounts to

is this: Washburn really values his ability in the sack. If he doesn't wake up every morning with a hard-on, it ruins his day and makes his advisers miserable."

"Christ, Rafe, you know everything."

"Jack," Perex mocked, "there's never been any great secret about Washburn. The Ultimate President is also the Ultimate Cocksman. It's bloody spooky. You'd think the Frenchies would be sympathetic to a man like that. Plus the fact, he almost single-handedly saved this country during the war. He was with the OSS."

"A hero, yes. Zouzou told me that. So why do they hate him so much?"

Perex didn't reply at once. As a man and woman entered Chez Habanero, he trembled and held the side of his face with his hand.

"Because the French do not like being helped," he muttered. "Bloody hell, I am expecting at any moment to be spotted by that bastard de Bis's henchmen. Are you aware, my dear, that de Bis has put Madame Marceline de Winter on this case? They call her Marceline the Merciless."

Kelly shook his head. "Zouzou's never mentioned any Madame de Winter."

"Everybody in France is scared shitless of her, dear boy, that's why they don't talk about her. She's killed a dozen men with her bare hands." Perex whimpered. "Another reason, clearly, why they hate Washburn is that he wants to take their fucking colony away from them. This burns Aristide de Bis's *derrière* because he's so big on the glory of France and Greater France and all that." Perex finished his beer, wiped his mouth, and began to sidle away. Kelly stopped him.

"One other thing, Rafe—who do I see at the Klinik Montmorency?"

Perex's wet eyes bulged. "You don't intend to go *there*? My dear, promise me you won't. If this is danger, that's jumping out of a plane without a parachute. Caramba! Jack! You will be the death of me. Must you know *everything*?" He looked around furtively, then bent to whisper in Kelly's ear. "You didn't hear it from me. A doctor named Wolfgang Ehrlitz. He is associated with Amalgamated Freight."

"My lips are sealed." Kelly grunted.

"Good-bye, Jack. Take care of yourself."

Perex clung to his hand for several seconds, then sloped out of the restaurant. He had left the bill for Kelly to pay.

CHAPTER

SEVENTEEN

She was sitting beside him on the shuttle to London but she did not seem to recognize him. How could she have forgotten him so soon? His handstand, his accident? She was leafing absently through a new issue of French *Vogue* and, true to her place on the best-dressed lists, was wearing a lavender Mordaunt suit, braided at the hem of the skirt and sleeves, and under the tweed jacket a loose-fitting organdy blouse. Upon her feet were a pair of brown, patent-leather shoes with the distinctive Mordaunt buckles.

Beatrice de Beaupeau's face was placid. A cool smile played with her mouth as she read. Her lips were lightly rouged to set off the ivory tone of her skin.

"Countess," Kelly murmured as the airbus fumed down Orly airstrip, "it is me, I, Jack Kelly. We met at Madame Mordaunt's."

Her head turned quickly and light broke in her gray eyes. She opened her mouth to a small gasp, revealing the perfect white teeth.

"*Mais, oui, c'est vrai. Bonjour*, Monsieur Kelly."

She asked after his health politely, then dismissed him to turn back to her magazine. A snub. Kelly could not believe it. He thought they had established a close bond at Mordaunt's. Before he could collect his wits, the plane had landed at Heathrow, outside London.

"*À bientôt*, Monsieur Kelly," she said, smiling distantly. "Perhaps we will meet again at Maison Mordaunt."

"I sincerely hope so," he murmured, pained by her aloofness.

He lost sight of her in the immigration line and outside, depressingly, she was nowhere in sight. Kelly caught a cab into town, directing the driver to the Dorchester Hotel. Riding through the dingy London suburbs, he was saddened to consider the strange coincidences which are the woof and warp of the fabric of existence. It seemed Zouzou was right—Beatrice de Beaupeau was *not* for Jack Kelly. She had behaved with such cool *politesse* that she might never have been the woman sitting in the Mordaunt salon directing her generous beaver at his nose. Life, of course, was littered with chance meetings, many rewarding, others frustrating. Now he had to wonder if Beatrice would ever reappear on the stage of his dreamworld, this woman he so strongly admired, this sensuous beauty who had occupied his thoughts for a week now, or longer.

As it happened, she reappeared sooner, much sooner, than he had expected. For she was checking in at the hotel when Kelly came through the door.

"Countess," he called.

She turned and seemed to shrink at the sight of him. "Monsieur Kelly. *Quelle surprise!*"

He wanted to seize the moment to invite her for a drink but before he could formulate the words, she turned and, followed by a bellboy and her Vuitton luggage, walked to the elevator.

But he was elated. What an outstanding piece of luck that she had come to the same hotel. At the time, it did not occur to him that it might not be an accident. Zouzou had known of his trip, and it would not have needed a great detective to find out where he was staying. Americans usually tried for the Connaught or Dorchester if they had the money.

It was 4:00 P.M. when he got up to his room. His first job was to call the American embassy. It took Tom Topovsky five minutes to get to the telephone.

"Hiya, Kelly," Topovsky said hurriedly, "glad to have you aboard. You and I have got to get together. But I'm not here very long. Leaving tomorrow noontime. Seeing the prime minister in the morning. Hey! I got it. Come to Number Ten Downing Street about eleven. I'll meet you there and we'll chat a few minutes. . . . I'll leave your name at the door."

Kelly was very impressed, for he was to have his meeting with Topovsky at the official residence of the British prime minister. One did not easily top that, not in the journalistic racket.

Mulling it over and thinking again about Beatrice, he pulled clothes out of his bag and located his reporters' notebooks. . . . Olga. He chuckled to himself, remembering.

There was a tap on his door. What now? Flowers from the embassy, a bottle of booze?

No. Luck struck again. It was Beatrice. Timidly, she explained in halting English that she was in the next room and had overheard him on the phone.

"Why, Countess . . ." He didn't know what to say.

"Beatrice," she corrected him.

"Could I . . . could we . . . perhaps . . . have a drink together?"

God, he was so flustered. Her smile was one of the wilting variety he had watched her use on Aristide de Bis. She stood awkwardly in the doorway, accepting his suggestion with a graceful inclination of her head, her right hand fluttering, as it was wont to do, at the neckline of her blouse. She had to get her jacket, she said. Checking to make sure his key was in his pocket, Kelly closed his door and followed. Beatrice bade him come inside her room, then fiddled with lipstick and inspected herself critically in a mirror. Apparently not very satisfied with what she saw, she made a face at herself and turned, smiling shyly.

"Ah, Monsieur Kelly . . ."

"Jack . . ."

"Ah, Jack . . . Jacques," she murmured. She pouted at the mirror.

Kelly asked her what she was doing in London, alone in this strange city. He hoped he would not learn that Aristide de Bis was expected later. She had traveled to London, she said nervously, to see an English banker who looked after certain investments of her late husband's. Kelly had not known she was a widow; he'd assumed she'd been with Aristide enough years to preclude a dead husband. Her marriage must have been very early in life for she could not now be much more than thirty, if that.

Perhaps, she suggested uncertainly, it would be more convenient to call room service and have the drinks sent up. She was feeling a little *fatiguée* from the trip, and she was not a very strong woman, and there would be so many people. . . .

"A sudden trip?" he interrupted.

"Sudden? Yes . . . and no."

Kelly ordered a bottle of the dry white Burgundy she said she preferred and, for himself, three Pernods, along with ice and water.

Beatrice invited him to sit down opposite her at a table by the window which looked across Hyde Park.

"May I?" he asked, reaching for his cigarettes.

"Of course." She smiled again and watched him closely.

God, he was thinking, she was really lovely. There was this soul-searing fragility about her, an ethereal, dreamy quality. He was amazed by his good fortune: no more than an hour ago, it had been no better than a toss-up whether he would ever see her again; now they were alone in her room, among her intimate belongings. A filmy mauve nightgown had been thrown across the bed. The bed: the sight of it aroused him, and she must have sensed this for she glanced at him, eyes perceptibly widening.

The drinks were borne into the room by a stiff-necked gentleman in a white jacket. Kelly dipped generously into his AmFreight advance for a tip and signed the check with his own room number—naturally.

"Ice?"

"A *soupçon*, please."

He put one ice cube into her glass and filled it to the three-quarter mark with wine. He made himself a first Pernod and water.

"Beatrice," he said, lifting his glass to her.

"Jack . . ."

"*Eh bien* . . ." He sipped thirstily. "It is so marvelous to see you again. The last time . . ."

She knew he was referring to their meeting at Maison Mordaunt. She laughed and reminded him of how he had been standing on his hands, had fallen over, had hurt himself. He didn't think it proper, at this point, to remind her that the reason this had happened was his stunned realization that the sweet nothings she had been wearing were exactly that, nothing. Timidly, she asked him if he would care to walk on his hands again, this time in private audience.

Kelly chuckled shyly, shook his head, and explained it was a very foolish sort of thing to do.

Perhaps, Beatrice said, then asked, "*Mais*, Jack, what brings you to London?"

He told her, very sketchily, that he was here to meet an assistant of President Washburn. She nodded absently, giving no indication she even remotely remembered the substance of the conversation that night with Aristide de Bis.

"Ah, yes," she said, "President Washburn of the United States of America."

"The same."

"Ah, Jack, that will be very interesting for you, *n'est-ce pas?*"

"Yes, I think it should be."

Beatrice thrust her legs out in front of her, kicked off the Mordaunt shoes and flexed her toes luxuriously. The toenails were dusted with the same rosy color she used on her lips.

"Ah," she said, "much more comfortable."

She lifted stockinged feet and waggled the toes at him, flexed the calf muscles and laughed warmly.

"More wine?"

"A *soupçon*," she said. As he took the glass from her, she nodded appreciation and watched studiously as he chose another piece of ice and poured the wine. "*Merci.*"

He handed her the glass. Her fingers lingered on the back of his hand, and Kelly felt desire surge within him and reach out toward her.

"Thank you," she repeated in English.

"A pleasure to serve you, Countess," he said grandly.

She drank a little, then set the glass on the table and raised her arms above her head, stretching, her legs taut again, tightening all the long muscles. Under the sheer blouse, Kelly realized, her breasts were not covered. They pulled upward too, following her arms, the swell of them appearing at the top of the blouse.

"Beatrice, you're a very beautiful woman," he said admiringly, resisting no longer the impulse to say it.

Her gray eyes filled with pleasure. "You find me so, Jack."

"Yes, I sure do."

"How so?" Her smile was curious, mysterious.

"Your expression," he replied quickly, "the way your lips gather. Your eyes. Your body."

"Ah, the body," she said carelessly.

She stood up and stealthily crossed the room to the mirror. She inspected herself anew, her eyes wide, grimaced, then shrugged. Placing her hands behind her head, she gathered her lustrous red-brown hair in her fingers, flexing pectoral muscles, twisting this way and that for a different view of herself. She twirled to stare at him as, transfixed, he watched her. Was she admiring herself or finding some basic fault in her appearance? At one and the same time, she seemed indifferent and even disrespectful of her body; but also much taken with herself. It made him uneasy, worried, to think she might be so narcissistic. Beatrice ran her hands down her hips, smoothing the tweed of the Mordaunt skirt and again leaned forward to put her face up close to the mirror, as if examining the pores of her skin.

He realized she was completely ignoring him; he might have been back in his room. He wondered what, exactly, was happening. And *then* it occurred to him that it might not be a coincidence, really, that she was here in the hotel. He suddenly remembered that he had, half-jokingly, told Zouzou Mordaunt Beatrice was his price for cooperation. No, nonsense! Aristide de Bis would never have allowed his beautiful mistress to be used as live bait.

He interrupted her perusal of herself. "Beatrice, do you come here often on business?"

She shook her head. "No, not often." It had to do, she explained, with her estate, the Château de Beaupeau and the wine crop. Her property was in the Burgundy region of France and one of the many varieties of Beaujolais was made from her grapes. "You like the red Burgundy, Jack?"

"Oh, yes, very much."

Beatrice opened her suitcase which lay at the end of the bed and drew out a bottle. "You see," she said, carrying it to him.

The label read *Beaujolais de Beaupeau, Grand Vin, Appelation Controlée*, all that vinicole gibberish which meant nothing to anybody but the most dedicated of connoisseurs.

"It's beautiful," he said.

"It is a good one, Jack." He held the bottle to the fading light. The red was rich and clear. "Burgundy," she went on, "is not a long-lasting wine. It is tart, not full-bodied like Bordeaux, and it must be sold and drunk in but a few years." Her face became thoughtful. Then, verbalizing a philosophy of hedonism which, he thought ruefully, must be close to her heart, she said, "Many things in life are not long-lasting. They must be experienced early, not stored for the future." Glancing at him meaningfully, she added, "Such as love, monsieur."

"Very true," Kelly said. He evaded a direct response. "You are a native of the Burgundy region, Beatrice?"

She nodded, standing now in the center of the room, as if undecided what to do next. There was something so defenseless about her. Her arms hung at her sides, hands open, and in their way, supplicating. He wondered miserably what instructions she had been given. Finally, since he made no move, she sat down again and crossed her legs.

"*Je pense* . . ." She began haltingly and went on to say that she thought he would be very busy with this agent of President Washburn.

"No, not until tomorrow morning."

"What is the function of such a man?"

Kelly finished his second Pernod. Expansively, he said, "His name is Topovsky. His job is to arrange schedules, book hotels for the president and his party, talk to the authorities about police protection, that kind of thing."

Beatrice nodded wisely. "Yes, I understand. I have often heard such matters discussed. It would be very interesting for me to meet such a man as Monsieur . . . Topovsky, a man so close to the president of *les États-Unis.*"

God, Kelly thought dispiritedly, if she were casting about for information, she would learn little from him, nothing Aristide de Bis wouldn't have known.

"I'm seeing him for about thirty seconds tomorrow," he said. "He's very busy."

"Oui," she murmured, "one does not see these people. . . . Even Aristide . . . I scarcely ever see him. One can become very lonely living on the edge of public life, Jack." She laughed breathlessly. "I think he is more in love with the president of the republic than he is with me."

A fairly intimate bit of information for her to reveal, Kelly thought.

"And, *bien sûr,*" she went on bitterly, "he has other friends. . . ."

"Other friends?" He wanted to hear much more about Aristide de Bis.

"Women."

God, she was not the only one? What more did the man want? How could Aristide possibly handle any more than Beatrice de Beaupeau? Beatrice stared wanly at her hands. He caught a whiff of her scent: a Mordaunt perfume of which he had not heard? It hinted of body oils, the clean, milky smell of a pampered body.

"May I ask?" Kelly said. "Are you wearing Mordaunt Number Two?"

"No, no." She shook her head disdainfully. "I have no perfume on this afternoon. . . . It is so boring, all these numbers. Mordaunt Two and Three . . ."

"Eight?"

"I am not familiar with Mordaunt Eight," she said.

She was correct, Kelly thought: it did become a little boring, the unending list of Mordaunt-label products; from perfume and cologne to the body balms, deodorant and douches, the Mordaunt No. 10 champagne; then the shoes, handbags, scarves, pantyhose, stockings, brassieres. Zouzou had even designed the interior of a French car, the color scheme for an Air France jetliner, the package for a new French cigarette. And now Mordaunt Number Eight, the sex elixir, nothing more than Spanish Fly in modern disguise.

Beatrice returned without Kelly's bidding to the subject of Aristide de Bis's women. "Aristide's wife," she said. "Of course, Aristide has his wife Mathilde. . . ." Yes, she had been with Aristide at Maison Mordaunt that terrible morning. "And he is very attentive to the wife of the president of the republic," she added, twisting her hands in her lap. "Then, naturally, in the south of France. *Alors* . . ."

"You're kidding," Kelly said, feeling his heart jump at the juicy information.

It was hard stuff to believe, however. Aristide's image was that of upstanding pillar of all that was grand and sacred in church and state. Aristide, what with his political ambitions, should have trod a more careful path. He was billed as the epitome of Gallic virtue.

"And Madame de Winter, of course," Beatrice said bitterly. "His political associate."

The murderess Perex had mentioned: "I've heard of her," he said.

"Marceline de Winter." Beatrice pronounced the name poisonously. "A prostitute. Vile woman. A lover of Nazis. I say no more." Her fine mouth was drawn into a tight, angry line.

"She was a Nazi?" Again, Kelly's pulse quickened.

"Possibly, yes. But I mean a *lover* of Nazis. I say no more. But is it any wonder then that I am often so lonely?" Kelly shook his head slowly. Such a revelation: Aristide was as big a philanderer as George Washburn. Then she concluded, "Aristide is a brute!"

"A brute?"

"Yes, a cruel and vengeful man, Jack. If he knew we were here like this he would have me assassinated."

"No!"

"*Mais* yes. And quite possibly you too." She grimaced. "But, he does not know. In addition, I am here on business."

"And in addition to that," Kelly pointed out, "we are merely sitting here talking, as friends often do."

"Friends . . . Yes, we are friends, *n'est-ce pas?*"

The thought of friendship soothed her. God, Aristide was indeed a pig. Beatrice was too marvelous a woman to be treated so shabbily. Tears came to her eyes, droplets of dewy liquid gathered at her eyelids and trickled down her cheeks.

Abruptly, he asked, "Beatrice, did you know I'd be coming to London? That I'd be staying at the Dorchester?"

She nodded and confessed, "Yes, I knew, Jack."

"You knew we'd see each other? You planned it this way?"

"Yes." She stared soulfully at him.

"You planned it so we could see each other again . . . alone?"

"*Oui*, I am guilty."

Kelly grinned at her. "Yes, you're guilty of making me very happy."

Jesus! There it was, all the cards on the table. He lit a Gauloise and puffed smoke toward the window. Outside it was getting dark. Evening, a quiet London evening, was coming down. Below, in the lobby, the Arab princes and their business managers would be gathered for tea, for the Arabs didn't drink cocktails in the early evening hours, at least in public. Their long black limousines would be drawn up outside, waiting to take them off to the gaming clubs. . . . The British, and a few Americans, would be sitting in the bar, reading the *Evening Standard*, discussing the price of gold and silver, of the Pound Sterling, and cursing modern times.

Beatrice reached across the table to take his cigarette from his hand. She drew on it once and then, with such a natural gesture that he paid no heed, she drew back the sleeve of her Mordaunt blouse and planted the glowing end of the cigarette on the inner skin of her forearm.

Kelly jerked forward in alarm. But Beatrice regarded him calmly, showing no sign of pain. She puffed on the cigarette again and passed it back to him. . . . The sickening odor of singed flesh rose with the smoke. A red blister popped up on her arm, charred with ash.

"Jesus Christ! Beatrice!"

She shook her head negligently. "It is merely pain, another sort of pain, Jack. I am very accustomed to pain."

"God, what an ugly trick, Beatrice," he protested. "I'm not impressed, you know."

She looked at him almost nonchalantly. "*Eh bien?*" she challenged him.

"Excuse me a moment," he said, feeling ill.

He went into the bathroom, whether to be sick or take a leak he was not sure. She was crazy, he thought despairingly, like all the others. He flushed the toilet before he began because there was nothing more off-putting than the sound of a man urinating and no hotel was soundproofed against the walloping noise of piss hitting water.

When he returned, still shaken by what she had done, Beatrice was at the mirror again, brushing her thick hair, now golden in the twilight. "Should we go to a respectable restaurant?" she asked.

"All right. If you like."

"You are angry with me?" She realized she had shocked him beyond belief with her gesture of minor— or *petit*—immolation.

"Yes," he snapped. "Goddamn it, that's just a horrible thing to do to yourself, Beatrice."

Rising to the reprimand, she retorted, "Merely to show you that I am strong, that pain to me is nothing, that I can bear any torture."

"Torture? Who's going to torture you?"

"One never knows," she said. "I train myself to withstand all agony."

"My God . . ." Kelly put his hands on her silk-covered shoulders. She frowned and tried to pull away as he moved his hands to her back. She shuddered.

"No, no, monsieur."

"What's wrong with you?" He had an awful thought. "What have you done to yourself?" She shook her head in shame. "Have you hurt your back?"

Fearfully, she said, "*Mon amour,* it is nothing, nothing."

Holding his hands in her own surprisingly powerful grip, Beatrice came close to him and kissed him lingeringly on the lips, pressing her belly against him, lifting her pelvis to rub his leg. She released his hands and he lifted them to cup her breasts, feeling their cloudlike lilt.

"*Have you been tortured?*" he demanded. He understood now why she sat so erectly, her back so straight. "Let me see," he said gently. "I won't hurt you."

Beatrice did not move when he unbuttoned her blouse at the back and pulled it off her arms. Revealed, her breasts were slightly drooping, but rose to nipples erect and small. He turned her around and was sickened again: her backbone was laced with white, ridged scars, and they were not all old scars. Some were raw and new, livid and disgusting.

"Jesus Christ," Kelly said, "who did this?"

"It is nothing," she said, shrugging.

Kelly did not need to be told this was the work of Aristide de Bis. It was obvious—it went with what Beatrice had described of Aristide's hidden character, a man to degrade, humiliate, physically abuse. But was Beatrice such a poor fool that she put up with this? Had she no choice?

"Why did you let him?"

She shrugged again, not replying. She was completely vulnerable. Kelly understood she would have done anything he commanded. He had only to say the word and she would drop her skirt and show herself to him: more lash marks and bruises, no doubt. She was, yes, beautiful; but so damaged.

"God," he said sorrowfully. "Look, let's walk over to Les A for a bite of dinner."

"All right . . . You do not hate me?"

"Of course not."

"A moment then, *mon amour.*"

Beatrice took a black, knee-length dress from her suitcase, explaining it was a simple Balenciaga, and as Kelly watched, she changed. She was wearing no more under the Mordaunt tweed skirt than she had worn on top, no more than she had that memorable night at Mordaunt's: a black garter belt holding up sheer black stockings. He didn't ask her why she dressed so scantily; it was undoubtedly some form of French country custom. Meticulously, he studied her nude body; she seemed to welcome his attention. Her belly was full, buttocks rounded: yes, there were red welts on her backside too. Her hips were strong, slightly larger, perhaps, than they should have been in proportion to the rest of her, particularly the bosom which was virginally modest. The body, despite the stripings of old and new beatings, was luminously ivory-toned and altogether lush.

Beatrice was without shyness or sham modesty. Unabashedly, she stood with her back to him and fixed her face. She applied Mordaunt lipstick, a bit of Mordaunt underarm deodorant, a touch of Mordaunt Number Two perfume. As she toyed with her rouge, she reverted to eyeing herself ironically in the mirror, making faces, as if nothing of her secrets, including that of her nude body, had been revealed. She was without artifice. Now that Kelly knew of her innermost confidences, she seemed to be saying, there was nothing more to be hidden.

When she turned, she smiled as she had before, stuck out her tongue playfully, and coyly winked. "Almost ready, *mon amour.*"

Merde, Kelly told himself, and he had desired her so. If she had been Maggi Mont he would by now have been in a delirium. He looked at Beatrice with no emotion, no lust. So sad.

Finally, she put on the dress. It buttoned down to the navel in front, parting at the top to exhibit the beginning of bosom—*poitrine,* as the French so engagingly called it. Going to the suitcase again, she found a pair of black shoes and a black fur stole which she flipped over her shoulder. Now she looked very Parisian and very *chic,* and he was more aroused by her than when she had been naked. Beautiful. Lovely. And what? Tortured, twisted, and ruined by Aristide de Bis and God alone knows how many other perverted Frenchmen. He sighed to himself. Europe was a funny place. He kept on discovering that.

They walked through a balmy autumn evening from the Dorchester in the direction of Hyde Park Corner. Les A—its proper name, Les Ambassadeurs—was one of London's Establishment places—or at least the building that housed it was such a place, having once belonged to the Rothchilds. What had been the first of several drawing rooms had become the Les A lounge, and further inside there was a long bar and a couple of dozen tables for dining. Alcoves lined one wall. Using the magic name Perex had slipped him, Kelly secured one of the more private alcoves and they ordered drinks: champagne for Beatrice and another Pernod and water for him. They had an English-style meal, caviar and small slices of toast, then a chop with fresh asparagus. Naturally, Kelly ordered a Château Beaupeau Burgundy; it was right there, at the top of the wine list. Since C.T. Trout was paying, he thought, why not?

Beatrice sat silently, her gray eyes moist and expectant. She kept her left hand on his forearm, now and then moved it more intimately to his thigh. She appeared to take it for granted they were, later, going to make love.

Beatrice was not readily visible to the room, but from those men who could see her, Kelly could almost hear husky sighs of admiration. They didn't know, did they, these chaps, the real story of the Countess Beatrice de Beaupeau?

As they were finishing their chops, cordial voices floated in from the lounge. "Good evening, sir . . . Good evening, Mr. Ambassador . . . Madame . . ."

A man named Black, Kelly knew, was American ambassador to the Court of St. James. He, another man, and a woman entered the dining room. The second man, Kelly recognized: Tom Topovsky, thin-faced with sparse gray hair and a sharp nose. Over the years, Topovsky had had his picture taken innumerable times with George Washburn: around the country on political expeditions, in the Virgin Islands where Washburn liked to fish, or up in Washburn's native Maine, a state which the president often visited, probably hunting specimen moose turds, Harry Kelly had once joked. Tom Topovsky was always at the president's side, if he were not off on such a mission as this one, holding Washburn's hat, or fountain pen, and probably his cock too when Washburn took a piss. Yes, Tom Topovsky, formerly of the advertising business, a Washburn crony from way back when.

The woman was Westerley Washburn, a blond with a sunny, open face.

"It is President Washburn's daughter," Kelly murmured to Beatrice. "The man is Tom Topovsky, the guy I'm seeing tomorrow."

"Dieu," she whispered, "a very pretty woman."

And formerly Mrs. Rafe Perex, he thought. How

astounding to know she had been married to Rafe; but why had she left him for such a political thug as Tom Topovsky? It was easy to imagine what had drawn Topovsky to her. How many men, after all, get a chance to screw the daughter of the president?

"Which is Monsieur Topovsky?" Beatrice asked.

"The ugly one—the one with the nose shaped like a banana—or a penis."

Beatrice chuckled. He could not have been talking about Ambassador Black, who was tall, portly, and ruddy-faced.

"Ah, no," Beatrice said, "Monsieur Topovsky is not handsome."

Topovsky and Westerly Washburn did not greatly impress Beatrice. She patted his thigh and as they were drinking a demitasse, she caressed him from knee to watch pocket. *"You* are handsome, *mon amour."*

"Just passable," Kelly smiled.

"Zouzou Mordaunt thinks the world of you," she said in French. Kelly thought he had never understood the language as well as he did when Beatrice spoke it.

He studied her profile. The champagne had brought roses to her cheeks and her eyes sparkled at his look. After the fresh air, drinks, and good food, Kelly was feeling better about things. She *was* beautiful and he was lucky to be with her. He squeezed her hand as it lay on his leg. They might yet achieve the heights, he thought solemnly.

The Black table was too far from them for Kelly to eavesdrop. Topovsky leaned forward, talking earnestly and in a low voice. Then Westerley Washburn stood up. She was tall, her blond hair short-cropped. The breasts were high and prominent on her chest. She was lightly sunburned. Naturally, for she would be a golfer and probably a damned good one. Westerley Washburn looked their way as she passed and reacted with a small expression of surprise, as if, somehow, she recognized them. She nodded pleasantly.

Beatrice and Kelly strolled back to the hotel about eleven, Beatrice's fur wrapped snugly around her shoulders, her arm in his. The street was silent and slightly wet; it had rained while they were inside Les A. The air was fresh and just slightly misty, as London should be.

"Mon amour," Beatrice murmured.

They did not pause for a last drink but made straight for the elevators. Upstairs, Beatrice took his hand and led him into her room.

The bedside lamp had been turned on, the covers thrown back on one side of the bed. Beatrice removed her fur and flung it over a chair. Silently motioning him to sit down, she went off to the bath. He heard the sound of the shower. He lit a cigarette and waited.

When Beatrice emerged, she was wrapped in a large bath towel. She had removed her makeup, but she did not look very different without it. Her heavy hair, slightly wet, hung loosely on her shoulders and over the towel, which was emblazoned with the emblem of the hotel. Lightly, she came on bare feet to stand beside him. She smelled damp like the city and had rinsed herself of all but the most insidious vestiges of Mordaunt lilac soap.

"You will sleep with me tonight, *mon amour?"* her voice was soft and pleading.

CHAPTER

EIGHTEEN

Bemused, assuaged by love but troubled, Kelly left Beatrice at ten the next morning to walk in the direction of the government quarter of Whitehall.

Beatrice, Beatrice. Her name pounded in his head. Was he qualified to play her Dante?

But she was an unusual Beatrice. He had made love to her during the night and early in the morning until, drowsy with sleep and finally sated, she huddled in his arms and related things about the goings-on in the French château country of which he had never been more than dimly aware, things that would make one's blood run cold, tales of wild parties, fornication and bestiality Zouzou Mordaunt had never dared mention, she who had told Kelly so many stories.

With time to spare, Kelly strolled through Berkeley Square, window-shopped along Bond Street. He crossed Piccadilly and sauntered into the Ritz Hotel. There was no André at the London Ritz but, with winter garden or palm court, it endeavored to be a miniature of its Paris cousin.

Beatrice had told him of boots, belts, and whips, instruments for the violation of the human body forgotten since the Middle Ages or, as it was said, the days of England's own Hell Fire Club, that company of noble rowdies who had mounted orgies to shock the prudes of the nineteenth century.

As a result of her own experiences, Beatrice feared she had become emotionally blunted, her body responsive only to violent stimulation. Aristide, she charged, was by no means the worst of her tormentors, for the ugly swine had shared her with his friends. Her most terrible memory of the latter was the Man in the Black Mask, a person whose identity was a secret to all save Aristide de Bis. However, his clipped English accent gave him away as a member of the higher orders of Old-Etonian London society. There was no question he was English—not Scottish or Welsh or Irish, but pure English. Beatrice held that it was not the Celtic races which were most brutal and cruel but the English, those descendants of the Saxons and Huns, their blood unwatered by frivolous Norman strains, and of the Tudors and Plantagenets who were most decadent and beastly, the types who had made English buccaneering the sport of the sixteenth and seventeenth centuries.

"A man in a black mask," Kelly had mused, "it sounds so medieval."

"But true, *mon amour.*"

Kelly was still preoccupied by these woeful speculations as he continued on toward the river Thames and Whitehall. He walked through the verdant moistness of Green Park; birds were twittering in the trees and here and there young men kicked lackadaisically at soccer balls. Officialdom hurried past him, its umbrella hanging on its arm. A huge crowd was already in place outside Buckingham Palace waiting for the Changing of the Guard. Kelly crossed behind that tangled statuary that was the empire's monument to itself and turned left to walk down Birdcage Walk. Before him now, through the trees, he could see Big Ben, the clock tower of the Houses of Parliament.

Beatrice wanted her freedom, her release from bondage. And that she could have. But emotional release was something else. She had been so mishandled. His patience and intense concentration had been required to bring her to climax. Once, during the night, in frustration, she had shown him her private whip, hidden at the bottom of her suitcase. It was, he supposed wearily, what one would call a cat-o'-nine-tails, a sordid bouquet of rawhide strips joined in a sweat-stained handle. Had she really believed he would beat her? Her eyes had dilated with fear, and desire, and when he tapped the weighted grip in his hand, she had bleated in anticipation, then cried out when he teased the leather on her buttocks. No, for Christ's sakes, he was not into the flagellation trip. He had thrown the whip on the floor and taken her into his arms . . .

Kelly reached Number Ten Downing Street at a quarter of eleven and announced himself to the policeman at the front door. Flattered, then deflated, he overheard the mutterings of the rubberneckers: "Whoozat? Somebody?" And the murmured replies, "No, nobody."

They were expecting him. Topovsky had left Kelly's name with a secretary inside the front door. She escorted him down a narrow hallway and ushered him into a small sitting room. He was to wait there for Mr. Topovsky.

Kelly inspected the furniture, nothing that would have impressed Maryjane, and the pictures with dusty frames set on the wood-paneled walls: a large etching of a royal jubilee filled the space over the fireplace. There were other, faded prints of old-time Piccadilly Circus, Marble Arch, Nelson's Column, the Tower of London, the Parliament buildings, navy dreadnoughts, and the viceroy's palace in New Delhi—all reminders of former years of wealth and of that royal-red spotted map of the world.

Kelly sat down in a chintz-covered armchair, the mate of another facing the fireplace. In such humdrum, even dreary, middle-class décor as this were decisions of international import made. From outside, faintly, he could hear the bustle of Whitehall traffic. Inside, there was only the muffled sound of business being done. He was lighting a Gauloise and telling himself how much he'd like to know the name of the Man in the Black Mask when his musings were cut short by a new arrival in the anteroom.

It was blond Westerley Washburn Perex. "Hi," she said.

"Good morning," Kelly said, getting to his feet.

"Sit still. Some morning, isn't it?" She made the statement, expecting no answer. "You look like an Americano."

"I am. My name is Jack Kelly."

"I'm Westerley Washburn."

"I know." She made no effort to ask him how he knew. "I saw you last night at Les Ambassadeurs."

She remembered. "Right, you were sitting in the corner, hiding. I'm not surprised. That woman you were with is absolutely gorgeous."

"And you were with Ambassador Black . . ."

"And Tom Topovsky," she said, with an ironic twist of the tongue.

"I'm supposed to see Mr. Topovsky this morning. I'm going to interview your father—when he comes to Europe."

"Oh yeah?" The news did not interest her very much. She sat down opposite him and pulled out a pack of cigarettes and a gold-plated Zippo lighter. "Christ," she said, "what the hell's that you're smoking?" She didn't wait for his answer. She stuck a Camel in her mouth, flamed the Zippo, and expelled a cloud of smoke. "I'm meeting Tom here myself. We're supposed to leave for Switzerland and he'd better get a move on."

"I just need a few minutes with him."

"That's all you'll get." She eyed him shrewdly and said, "So you're a reporter." He nodded and she said crossly, "Just remember, there's no news in the fact that Tom and I travel together."

"It's no news to me," he said boldly.

"Good." She leaned back, crossing bare sunburned legs. "That beautiful lady your girl friend?"

"No," he said, shaking his head modestly, "a friend— from Paris."

"Ah, you live in Paris?" He acknowledged that he did and she continued, "Terrific city. Great food. Good wine."

Westerley was a woman with a very brisk attitude toward life, he decided. There were none of your convoluted feminine affectations here. It *was* difficult, on second thought, to imagine her married to Rafe Perex, a very emotional and volatile man. But Kelly was not going to get into that.

"Who do you work for?" she demanded.

"The *Retailers Apparel Guide*—until recently," he muttered.

Her face darkened in a frown. "Oh, you're *that* Jack Kelly. You're married to Claud Trout's daughter, aren't you?"

"Sort of," he murmured.

"What does that mean?" she asked, almost fiercely.

"We're sort of separated," he said frankly, then dodged. "I'm going to Switzerland myself on my way back to Paris."

"So if you're not with the *RAG* anymore, who you doing the interview for?"

"The *Appalachian Times.*"

Westerley hooted with laughter. She pulled on her cigarette, her face contorted with a smirk of mocking cynicism. "Oh, great," she said. "It just happens, of course, that the paper belongs to my father. Sounds kind of incestuous, don't you think?"

Now, the doubts surfaced again in his mind. It was a joke really. She was right. Miserably, he asked himself how he had been caught like this.

"I guess," he said slowly, "it all depends what I make of it."

"Sure."

She smiled more tolerantly and it was clear the subject was dropped. Perex had not told him Westerley's age, and with people of her complexion and obviously constant weight, it was hard to guess. She might have been anywhere from twenty-eight to forty-five. The fine lines at the corners of her eyes hinted at just over thirty. Her uncluttered features were bland; she was the sort who would have consumed great amounts of pasteurized milk as a child. There was a wholesomeness about her, a well-washed purity. She resembled most closely, in her blatant Americanness, his errant wife; but Westerley was a lot more sensible and down-to-earth than Maryjane. She was nothing if not straightforward.

She glanced at her watch, a Rolex for ladies, gold, like Perex's.

"Shit," she said, "that asshole Topovsky had better get a move on or we'll miss the plane."

"What's doing in Geneva?" Kelly asked.

She shrugged. "Topovsky is looking into a ball transplant," she quipped. The hint was close enough. Topovsky was probably going to be setting up the protocol for Washburn's visit to the Klinik Montmorency. Westerley grinned wickedly and asked, "Where do you stay in Geneva?"

He thought fast and replied, "The Richemont."

"Good. Us too," she said. "That's known as the French hotel. The Britishers always stay at the Beau

Rivage and the Americans, dumb as usual, at that Hotel du Rhone.''

"You seem to know the city well."

"We've been over there for a couple of summit conferences."

A person with Westerley's background was so accustomed to the world of arrivals and departures, high politics and luxury, that she dropped the phrase, of which news items are composed, as she would have reported a trip to the corner market. Now, with desultory interest, keeping clear of the subject of his new job, she asked how long he'd lived in Paris.

"About five years."

"I suppose you're one of those American guys smitten with French womanhood," she said. " 'Course you're married to an American. Some guys don't know how good they've got it at home. They seem to think the only women in the world who know more than one position are French ones. My husband was that way. Not you, though, I suppose," she said, accusingly.

Mildly, Kelly said, "I never met a nationality I didn't like."

"Really? Very cosmopolitan. A one-worlder . . . Around the world in eighty days. Huh! Now, people can make a trip around the world in an hour or two."

She watched his face for a reaction but he did not allow her to see that he understood she was trying out an old hooker routine on him.

"Speed, these days, is astounding," Kelly murmured.

She laughed loudly and was still teasing him with her blue eyes when Topovsky rushed into the room.

"Hi, Westy," he mumbled nervously. "Sorry I'm running late."

"Tom, the car is outside. Get a move on."

"Give me two minutes. You're Kelly?" Topovsky stuck out his hand. "Westy, go tell the driver I'm on my way. . . . Go on, Westy."

"All right, all right. Jack, might catch you in Geneva," she said.

She left the room, her jersey dress stuck to her behind by static electricity from the chair.

Topovsky muttered, "Jesus, rushed off my goddamn feet. You're working for Claud Trout. How is the old fart?" He pushed Kelly back down in his chair and took the seat Westerley had vacated. He rubbed his forehead. "Pooped. You know when I get in a state like this, the only thing I can think of is how much I'd like to fuck an opera singer. Kelly, I'll tell you I have this overwhelming desire to fuck a soprano. They say that hitting all those high notes vibrates their membranes—they come off the stage in a high heat."

Kelly grinned, and carrying on in the same vein, he mentioned a story he'd heard: that after Washburn's first inauguration Topovsky had been heard to mention in the bar at the National Press Club that the new administration was going to do for fucking what the last had done for golf.

Topovsky beamed. "Yeah, I did say that." Then, more seriously, he tapped Kelly's knee. "What's the outlook in France? They hate us as much as people say they do?"

Kelly shook his head. "Not quite as much. But I can tell you one thing: the French government is so mad about our policy in Africa they're ready to resign from the Western alliance."

"Yeah, those bastards," Topovsky snarled. "They can kiss our ass." Obviously, he was not impressed by Kelly's transmission of Aristide de Bis's threat. "I hate to tell you what's involved down there in the Dark Continent, Kelly."

"I hear it's got a lot to do with that crazy new drug . . . Grovival."

Topovsky's eyes narrowed. "Crazy?" He yanked at his elongated earlobes. "We hear it's not so crazy. It could be revolutionary. Frankly, we're worried as hell about it. Not so much about the French, or even the Russians. But suppose the chinks get *their* hands on it? Christ, they'd go from one billion to two billion people overnight. Insane! I'll tell you what—somebody'd do the world a big favor if they'd blast those swamps where they grow the goddamn stuff. Defoliate! Just like we get the Turks and wogs to do with the poppy fields."

"Yeah, or keep it under strict control," Kelly suggested. "You might want to allow limited supplies."

Topovsky stared. "For hospitals, and like that, you mean?"

"Sure." What Kelly was thinking was that if Grovival fell into Zouzou Mordaunt's greedy little hands, there would be no further worry. Grovival would become the aphrodisiac of the upper classes. He formed the thought. "You might want to use it to jack up the birth rate of the middle class, the aristocracy. They're slipping fast, you know."

Topovsky's eyes lit appreciatively. "Good point." He pulled a notepad from his briefcase. "I'm putting that down. *Don't wipe out,*" he dictated to himself out loud. *"Rather, cultivate Grovival as Rolls-Royce of sex drugs.* Got it! Nice thinking, Kelly. C.T. Trout said you were a thinker, Kelly. He's a big booster of yours, kiddo, and a big supporter of ours too. Not," he added rakishly, "like that old man of yours. Harry Kelly never misses a chance to drag us over the coals. But . . . no sweat. We take the good, bad, or beautiful as they come. So, you expect the French are going to jump on our ass about Mangrovia when we're over here for NATO?"

"For certain. But what do you hear from the State Department?"

Topovsky sneered. "We don't trust those fuckers. Never get straight info from them. We're running foreign affairs right out of the White House now, Jack. State issues passports—that's it!" Kelly felt his spirits pale. Was this what had happened to good government? No wonder the world was in such a state.

"Listen," Topovsky continued, "you get a chance to drop it on your sources, tell 'em if they start raising hell about Mangrovia, we'll start making noises about their tricks in Japan and—Jesus!—importing Cuban cigars and swapping French brandy for Russian caviar. Those are not such friendly acts either, kid." Kelly balanced dizzily in his chair; this was preposterous. Sharply, Topovsky reminded him, "None of this is for quotes, by the way. You can say, you know—high government officials, that kind of bullshit formula."

"Sure, sure," Kelly said. "Let me ask you another question. I know you're in a hurry. But, is Washburn going to run for another term?"

"Are you nuts?" Topovsky cried. "This *is* his second term. He can't run again, constitutionally."

"There's been talk of trying to get the third-term amendment repealed."

Topovsky laughed wildly. "Kid, you may as well ask me are we going to pull a *coup d'état* and make him president for life, like they do in those lousy Latin American countries."

"They're saying in Paris . . ."

"What are they saying in Paris?" Topovsky demanded sarcastically.

"That the president's health is not good."

"Bullshit!"

"That he's going to Switzerland for health treatments."

"What gives you that idea?" Topovsky whispered, pointing at the walls. Was he saying the British would bug his conversation? Of course, anything was possible. "Those French mother-fuckers." He grunted. "Is no rumor too low for them to peddle? I ask you, Kelly, if our president needed health treatments would he come to the continent of the Black Death, the home of syphilis?"

"I'm only reporting the tenor of feeling," Kelly said defensively.

"Right, right. I don't like to hear it but I appreciate it." Again, Topovsky patted Kelly's knee. "These things are good to know about, all beans in the information pot. Can't trust the goddamn embassies. They tell you what they think you want to hear. That's why Stalin was always so badly informed. One depressing situation report and the guy who wrote it finds his ass in Siberia or in front of a firing squad. I *want* you to level with me."

"I'm glad to hear that."

Topovsky looked at his watch. But he had something

more to say. "I got to impress on you that it would be goddamn damaging if these French rumors are given any currency—about our president even considering some goddamn kind of health cure in Switzerland."

"I doubt if anybody would believe it anyway," Kelly said.

"A lot of people would want to believe it, that's the trouble." Topovsky stood up and was preparing to leave when he thought of another point. "That kind of shit keeps surfacing—as much as we work to plug the leaks. You realize, Kelly, the glare of publicity that goes with this act? The planeloads of journalist-assholes that chase us around the globe? Jesus! I'd like to see the president operate out of a Polaris sub: Washburn sails out of the Potomac and he's gone, safe in a cloak of secrecy as deep as the goddamn ocean. Any time there's trouble in the world, he surfaces, like a missile, in front of the mike . . ."—

Kelly nodded. This was an original thought, although impractical. "Eloquent," he murmured. "Now that would be something to quote, from a highly placed aide, of course."

Topovsky's reaction was violent. "Are you nuts? Quote that and I'll have your balls chopped off. Jesus! Do you think we could really run the country like that? Christ, no, we got to operate like a Sousa band, full blast. Of course"—he grinned slyly—"we play the sections of the band one at a time. Defense: we cut their budget and they get sore. But at the same time we're sweet-talking commerce and our industrial giants and the unions. Next year, we give commerce and big business the shaft, kiss defense's ass. After that, we take on the joint chiefs of staff. . . . The lesson, and what I've always said, is don't go after them all at the same time. That's what happened to Nixon and when it came to show-down time, *nobody* would lift their hand to help him. You know what I think finally got him? I think it was the Marine Corps—they were really pissed when he took all that land away from them at Camp Pendleton."

Topovsky looked suspiciously at Kelly. "I hope you're

not going to tell me this is some kind of a cynical or immoral approach to government. Our method *works*. If you're thinking, ah, very Machiavellian, just remember that Prince Machiavelli knew where the bodies *were* buried."

Kelly eagerly agreed. These insights into Topovsky's, and Washburn's, views were so rich he didn't care whether Topovsky and Westerley missed their plane.

"What sort of questions shall I ask the president about NATO?"

"NATO? You want to know the truth? NATO bores us shitless."

"But it's vital, isn't it?" Kelly argued.

"Vital? They drain us of our hard-earned dollars, a bunch of tail-coated old farts sitting around talking about the Russian menace? The Chinese menace? Christ, boring, very boring."

At that moment, there was a knocking at the door and a voice outside said, "Mr. Topovsky, your wife asks you to hurry."

"Yeah, yeah," Topovsky exclaimed. To Kelly, he chuckled. "Wife—that's Westy being funny. Look, kid, call me at the Crillon in a week. We'll set the date then. I'll know the schedule better."

Hastily, he grabbed Kelly's hand and shook it.

"I'll call you a week from today," Kelly said.

"Good, good . . . Hey, good talking to you. I was especially interested in your thoughts about that drug. . . . They say it works, huh?"

Kelly nodded uncertainly. "Maybe—the only adverse thing I've heard is that it's grown warts on some woman's ass."

"Holy Christ." Topovsky sighed.

CHAPTER

NINETEEN

Klinik Montmorency: Kelly would never forget his first sight of that range of architectural novelties planted like random boulders in the rugged Swiss mountainside. Montmorency angled forward, receded, soared majestically, dashed horizontally, its moduled wings linked by flyways, skyways, breezeways, balconies, terraces, and gardens. Many windows were wide and shining in the hard morning light; others were small, dark, and barred as disturbingly as teeth in braces. The totality of the structure was admirable; its parts enough to make the most modern of men shiver and huddle in his trench coat.

Why had Kelly come here? He might have returned to Paris with Beatrice, followed her to Château Beaupeau as she had asked. Now, when would he see her again? God knows. They would have to be careful—Aristide de Bis was much away from the capital but he often returned unexpectedly too.

Obtaining Dr. Wolfgang Ehrlitz's approval to visit Montmorency had not been easy. The basic problem was that Kelly did not have a plan, or a good reason to travel to the clinical fortress—except for Maryjane, who had probably completed her bodywork by now and gone. What if he *could* confirm Washburn's intention to come here? Where would it lead him? The *RAG* was out of his reach and Trout would never accept a story like that for the AmFreight papers, a story charging that his political protégé was stopping in Switzerland for sex rejuvenation.

Ehrlitz had been very stubborn over the phone but mention of Maryjane's name and a hint of his connection with C.T. Trout and AmFreight had caused the doctor to cave in quickly.

Montmorency should have been an hour's drive from Geneva. Hercule, who had brought the black Citroen up from Paris, got lost in the maze of back roads through which the clinic maintained its élitist privacy. When they had climbed into final hairpin turns and cleared through a heavy iron gate to reach a high-altitude plateau, they were a half hour behind schedule. From time to time, Hercule faltered at the controls and the powerful Citroen coughed in the thin air. Kelly felt they were being watched, perhaps through binoculars from one of those modernistic turrets.

He rolled down the window as Hercule pulled up to the main entrance, a glass-fronted concrete hole in the mountain. Jesus! Was it his imagination or did he hear a scream? High-pitched laughter trickled from one of the open balconies facing what would be the sun when the latter burned through the morning mist.

Hercule shivered and looked uncomfortable. "*Je reste ici.*"

Yes, better that Hercule should protect the car. Hercule lit a black cigar and slid down in the driver's seat.

Inside, a large man in a white coat was waiting for Kelly.

"Ach," he said, "you would be Herr Kelly. I am Doctor Wolfgang Ehrlitz. Please to follow me."

Kelly fell into step beside this modified giant of a man, Ehrlitz of Mannheim and Heidelberg and points east and west. Ehrlitz was a fine specimen of a father figure, dignified, solemn, and ponderous. He bore a scar on his left cheek which ran from eye to the curl of thick red lips. A saber scar, Kelly had no doubt, acquired during his student days. Distracting attention from the disfiguration to a small extent was a pair of wire-frame spectacles which magnified his frosty blue eyes.

One knew, without asking, that Ehrlitz did not smoke, except for an occasional after-dinner cigar, that he drank wisely, and always got a good night's sleep.

"Well, Herr Kelly, so here we are, are we not?" Ehrlitz said. "And what of the man in the car?"

"He'll wait there."

Ehrlitz led him down long, white corridors which led to more long, white corridors. It seemed they were penetrating into the mountainside.

"*Herr Kelly, aus Paris,*" Ehrlitz muttered to anyone passing their way.

God, Kelly thought, the place was highly pristine, its ambiance coldly scientific. One might die here, he mused, and the act would be viewed merely as the final stage of a strict diet. He had not been with Ehrlitz more than five minutes when he asked himself again why he had come, then doubted that he would ever leave, and finally understood that there was no need to leave.

Doctors, nurses, lab technicians, all were dressed in ghastly white hospital garb. They looked so disinfected and sexless that they might have slept the night in a tray with their instruments.

A thought occurred to him. "I suppose you're familiar with Thomas Mann, doctor?" He was remembering the mammoth novel about life and death in a Swiss sanatorium, Mann's microcosm of human existence.

Ehrlitz grunted jovially. "Ach, Herr Kelly, our friend, is already talking of *The Magic Mountain.*"

When they reached Ehrlitz's office, Kelly removed his trench coat and the doctor put it on a hanger and hung it on the back of the door.

"This is the coat you normally wear, Herr Kelly?"

"Yes. It's my only coat, all-weather gear, against rain and shine. It's called a trench coat."

"So it is," Ehrlitz boomed. "For use in the trenches, during times of war."

"And in the trenches in times of peace, too."

Ehrlitz's office was decorated in Swiss modern. The

doctor proudly pointed out the views from his picture window, cut through the side of the mountain: Mont Blanc in this direction and Mount this-and-that over there.

"Coffee, Herr Kelly?" Ehrlitz produced steaming cups from a neat little machine on his desk. He sat there, facing Kelly, chewing on the strong chicory flavor. "Now, Herr Kelly, tell me instantly what is on your mind."

The silly fart—hadn't he already explained on the telephone?

"Doctor, it's simple. I'd like to see my wife. Her father, that is my father-in-law, Claud Trout, suggested I drop by."

"You could not come sooner?" Ehrlitz demanded severely.

Kelly shook his head.

"And you believe Frau Kelly to be here?"

"Yes."

"But," Ehrlitz said, flashing a patronizing smile, "if Frau Kelly is not here now—and I will tell you there is no Frau Kelly here now—then it is sensible to presume there was never a Frau Kelly at Montmorency, *nicht wahr?*"

Kelly sighed aloud and stared closely at Wolfgang Ehrlitz. What was the man getting at? Carefully, he said, "I don't see why that necessarily follows, no."

"*Donnerwetter. Gott in Himmel!*" Ehrlitz pushed forward, nearly spilling his coffee. "You do not understand the logic which says that if this woman is not at Montmorency now, the laws of probability are heavily weighted in favor of the supposition that Frau Kelly has never been here?"

Kelly smiled cautiously. Was he dealing with yet another maniac? "Excuse me, doctor," he said, "but I think you're fudging. Because, isn't it equally clear that I'm here now although I've never been here before?"

Ehrlitz groaned elaborately, shaking his head. "Of course, but in your case this does not parse, as we say in Latin, for you are here, at least in a dimension visible to me—or I *think* that I am seeing you. You are sitting in *my* chair, drinking *my* coffee. You are *my* guest. There-fore, you are obviously here, at least in simplistic terms. But Herr Kelly," Ehrlitz said fiercely, "if you were not here now, then the evidence would be almost over-whelming that you have never been here before, or since. Now, pay close attention, Herr Kelly. Frau Kelly is not here now. Ergo, it is logical to assume she has never been here. I grant you one point: I could argue more intelligently that you *have* been here before than I could that Frau Kelly has been here at all because of the fact you *are* here now, whereas Frau Kelly is not here now. . . . Do you understand?"

Kelly nodded weakly. "I understand what you're trying to say, but—"

"But? But what?" Ehrlitz demanded arrogantly. "Look around you. Do you see Frau Kelly anywhere? Is she here? Perhaps she is hiding under my desk?" Clumsily, he dropped off his chair to his hands and knees. "Frau Kelly, Frau Kelly," he called comically, *"kommst, kommst, kleine* Frau Kelly." Ehrlitz raised his head to desktop level and peered at Kelly. "No, Herr Kelly, she is not here," he announced gravely. He pulled himself up and sat down, glaring.

Stiffly, Kelly said, "I see that you're mocking me, doctor. I have two questions to ask you. The first is: when the tree falls in the forest and nobody sees it fall, does it make any noise?"

Without hesitation, Ehrlitz replied, *"Nein."*

"The second is: is my wife here or not?"

"Nein," Ehrlitz said curtly. He rubbed his hands togeth-er, satisfied evidently, that he had thrown his visitor into confusion. "Now, Herr Kelly, we will talk about you. From this small contretemps I diagnose you are suffering from a moderate anxiety syndrome."

"I don't think so," Kelly said.

Ehrlitz bashed his fist on the desk. "Herr Kelly, if you will not accept my diagnosis, then there is no purpose to our talking any more. I simply say *'Auf Weidersehen'* and *bon voyage* with your problem. If, on the other hand, it is treatment you desire, then I can recommend a course which will undoubtedly produce, as we call it, the New Man."

Now, Kelly thought, this was his chance to turn Ehrlitz toward Grovival. After all, he'd really come here to find out about Washburn. He would play along.

"What's involved?" he asked.

Ehrlitz leaned back to gaze at the ceiling. He spoke quietly. "Our methods are simple in their scientific realism. We believe in all things natural, as natural as this Swiss mountain air."

Thin air, Kelly told himself, of which Ehrlitz had obviously been inhaling too much. "Or Swiss milk chocolate," he murmured.

Ehrlitz didn't catch the sarcasm. "We use no chemicals, except in the case of the more obvious new drugs, antidepressants, for example."

"I'd heard," Kelly mentioned, "that Montmorency concentrates on ailments of a more . . . what? Sexual nature?"

Ehrlitz contradicted him sternly. "Absurd. Sexual disorders are no more than an expression of disorders more basic, glandular, the blood. Are you suffering impotency? Is that why you are here? Or are you here, Herr Kelly, in search of some fanciful or disgusting sexual adventure?" Ehrlitz was contemptuous. "I do not know what stories you have heard about Montmorency, Herr Kelly, but I can tell you they are all exaggerated. . . . Herr Kelly, are you aware that you are suffering from fatigued blood? Your eyes speak eloquently of an overloaded liver. Too much of the good life, Herr Kelly?"

"Not particularly, I wouldn't say," he replied irritably.

"Ah, yes, you see! Impatience. A sure symptom. Herr Kelly, I suggest that your employer, Amalgamated Freight—"

"My employer?"

"Is it not so? Ah, well, *es ist bestimmt,* a certainty, that we must send your tired blood out to the laundry."

"I'm afraid I don't understand," he led Ehrlitz on.

"Don't you know, Herr Kelly, that the blood can be

cleansed, sent to the laundry, so to speak?" Ehrlitz chortled.

"Like hell."

Ehrlitz stood up. "Come with me. I will show you something very interesting."

Still talking rapidly and enthusiastically, Ehrlitz led him back down several corridors and up a flight of steps into a small room, curtained across one wall. He closed and locked the door, then pulled back the curtain. Behind it was a window and Kelly found himself looking down into what seemed to be an operating amphitheater lit harshly by overhead lights and furnished with white metal tanks, huge glass retorts, a myriad of monitoring instruments, all connected by wires, cables, and tubes. In the center of the room there was a single table and upon the table lay a figure covered in towels and white sheeting. A half-dozen people, neuter-looking in sterile smocks and surgical face masks, stood watching the patient and the instruments.

Ehrlitz announced, "One-way glass, Herr Kelly. This is our observation platform. The person you see down there, Herr Kelly, is a very important countryman of yours in the process of having his tired blood laundered. His blood is very weary indeed; it is bored and lethargic blood." Ehrlitz pointed. "While his blood is being washed and shampooed in that white receptacle on the right, it is also being refurnished with useful ingredients: hormones, vitamins, minerals, and yes, some animal proteins. And, yes again, in answer to your inevitable question, some sexual fertilizers . . ."

"Grovival."

The single word caused Ehrlitz to leap back. He looked at Kelly sharply, then shrugged. "Since you know of it—yes."

"Obtained from Mangrovia?"

"With the greatest of difficulty," Ehrlitz said grimly. "We hope that will change."

"Tell me—is it the wonder drug everybody seems to think?"

Ehrlitz was obviously displeased to talk about it. "We will say it is past the experimental stage, Herr Kelly. But tell me, why are you interested in Grovival? I must tell you—it is not some secret weapon." He barked with laughter.

"A friend of mine in Paris is very interested in it. She sees a big future for Grovival in cosmetics—used carefully, of course."

"*Scheisse!*" Ehrlitz spluttered. "So are the wonders of nature adulterated."

"True enough," Kelly agreed. "Tell me, who's the man down there?"

Ehrlitz whipped the curtain back over the window. "All at Montmorency is of the highest degree of confidentiality."

That word again. Kelly was sure the man was Tom Topovsky. Any doubt of that was dispelled by the sight of the attaché case at the side of the table: a chain ran from its handle up under the sheet. It was obviously attached to Topovsky's ankle.

Drawling in a way that would be sure to infuriate Ehrlitz, Kelly said, "We hear that world statesmen of great stature come here for treatment. Can you confirm that?"

"Confirm what, Herr Kelly? I did not hear the question—and I will not hear questions of that variety. Come with me now, Herr Kelly."

As they were walking down the hall again, Kelly asked, "The treatment. How long would it take?"

"Three full days."

"That man down there, whoever he is, he'll be out like a light for three days?"

"Precisely."

"I have to tell you, Herr Doktor, I think that man down there is a close adviser of President George Washburn."

He thought for a second that Ehrlitz was going to smack him in the face. Ehrlitz flushed. He halted angrily, muttering in German.

"*Donnerwetter,*" he mumbled, taking control of himself. "Herr Kelly, you could become tiresome. Come here." He ducked into another hallway and opened another door. "Inside please."

This was a different sort of room. It was, first of all, very cold, and Kelly assumed, shuddering, that Ehrlitz had introduced him to the Montmorency mortuary. It contained two knee-high cots, or beds, one of which appeared to be occupied by a corpse. The body, concealed under a white wool blanket and swathed about the face with towels, was totally obscured except for a nose, short and stubby.

"So, Herr Kelly," Ehrlitz demanded gleefully, "where do you think you are now?"

He shook his head dumbly. "No idea. Is . . . it . . . dead?"

The body was bulky and thick and it was impossible to say whether it was male or female. As he stared, there was no movement that suggested even slight breathing.

"She is not dead," Ehrlitz whispered. "She is in a state of cryogenic suspension which is useful as preparation for the blood cleansing operation. Blood, at low temperatures, is easier to handle, you see."

"But she looks dead as a doornail."

Ehrlitz shook his head. "No, no. She has been like this for twelve hours only. We combine, for some personages, sleep cure with the cryogenic prelude. . . . You ask who she is?"

"Who is she?"

"A famous singer," Ehrlitz said respectfully, "a Wagnerian soprano from one of Germany's leading companies."

Kelly was duly impressed. And why shouldn't he have been? "Holy Christ," he muttered.

"She is resting well, is she not?"

"Very well. Does she breathe at all?" he asked.

"Once every three minutes," Ehrlitz told him. He looked at his watch. *"Um Gott ist willen.* I must see to our laundry room. Will you wait here for a moment? Commune with the peaceful, Herr Kelly. It will do you good."

Ehrlitz left Kelly with much to think about. Topovsky? Tom Topovsky was the test case. If Grovival did not destroy him, then Washburn would come to the Klinik Montmorency. But even then—what a problem of national security! Was it possible—or safe—to take the president of the United States out of circulation for three days? What of communications with Washington, the panic buttons for massive retaliation in case of enemy attack? Hell! Suppose this state of affairs were to come to the attention of the alliance? It would be a matter of one phone call from Aristide de Bis.

Curiously, he edged closer to the inert figure on the couch. He heard a macabre, lengthy sigh: the soprano was taking her three-minute breather. No, she wasn't dead; but she was the next thing to dead. This woman, whoever she was, if she never came out of her cryo-genic suspension, as Ehrlitz called it, she'd never be the wiser. Christ, had Maryjane submitted herself to this? Revolting.

Kelly lifted one end of the white blanket, uncovering a tiny foot, and above that, a narrow ankle. As he pulled the cover further, the body began to grow, first to a chunky calf, then a heavy knee. The thigh was thick and round, like a ham, and, there, above that the somnolent crotch and big belly. The hair at her mound, which in mountaineering terms would truly be a Central Massif, was matted and wet. As he silently watched, the thighs trembled and pubic hair twitched. It must have been from his breathing. He was fascinated. Then, insanely, for Ehrlitz might return at any moment, he laid his hand there. She was icy cold. He felt the frosty juices; they ran, but slowly, with all the consistency of congealed lard. His mind raced. What if he were to jump on her? But no, too risky. Ehrlitz. Yes, and the coldness; it would turn his dick into a brittle icicle, perhaps break it off. He began to laugh and told himself to stop.

Christ, this was disgusting, next door to necrophilia. But at the same time it was a learning experience. He understood how certain, weird people got their only true kicks in the worship and violation of dead bodies. Yes, but there was something incredibly, sordidly, sensuous about this body, thick and heavy though it was. Ultimate perversity. Shit, what would he have done if left alone in here for a guaranteed hour or so? No, he wouldn't. Yes, he might. All well and good to be censorious about it but how many people had such an opportunity? Put the crown aside, yes, but first the crown had to be offered. And she wasn't dead, merely suspended.

The decision was not his. For, as he stood there, hypnotized, he was startled out of his skin by her voice. Through the towels issued another three-minute gasp for air and then a burst of perfectly pitched High C notes. He thought he recognized an aria from the *Walküre,* the animal mating noises Brunhilde mouths as she leaps from rock to rock screaming for Siegfried.

Holy shit! He dropped the blanket back in place and retreated toward the door. None too soon, for Ehrlitz burst inside.

"I hear something," Ehrlitz exclaimed. "Did I hear the sound of music?"

"Not in here, doctor," Kelly said quickly. "In here, we're sleeping the sleep of the very peaceful and pure of heart."

Another thought struck him. Had the warmth of his hand set off the song? It was something to ponder. He remembered what Topovsky had said about the sex drive of sopranos. Did this indicate they did sing from a place even lower than the diaphragm? Voice box? No, no, he told himself, get off the theme. Hysteria was poking its head in the door. He grinned uncertainly at Ehrlitz. Should a message be left for Topovsky that the soprano of his dreams was waiting? Or was this why Topovsky was here at Montmorency? Was there, he wondered, such a thing as a cryogenic screw?

By the time they were back in Ehrlitz's office, Kelly was calm again.

"This is certainly a fascinating place, Herr Doktor," he said, thinking that was the least of it.

Smugly, Ehrlitz nodded. Obviously, he believed he had let Kelly in on the miracle of the age.

"Montmorency would make one hell of a story, Herr Doktor."

Ehrlitz was horrified. "I had forgotten you were a journalist, Herr Kelly. *Mein Gott,*" he exclaimed, "not a word. That is our agreement."

"Agreement? We didn't have any agreement."

Ehrlitz frowned petulantly. "When we talked on the telephone, my agreement to see you constituted *de facto* confidentiality. Herr Kelly, Montmorency wants no publicity. The good health and satisfaction of our guests is enough."

Satisfaction, the very word. "No one would believe it anyway."

"Correct," Ehrlitz said.

"On the other hand," Kelly said coolly, "there are plenty of people who'd sooner believe it than not believe it."

Ehrlitz shook his head disparagingly. "What you have seen here is very private. It would be shamelessly unethical to treat it otherwise."

Balls. There was no good reason for him to handle Montmorency or Ehrlitz with kid gloves. Ehrlitz had lied to him, about Maryjane, about Topovsky, about everything. What sort of ethics were these?

Roughly, he said, "Cut it out, doc. I can draw any conclusions I like. And I've already drawn some pretty heavy ones."

"Such as?" Ehrlitz demanded angrily.

"Such as, I think you're running a very shady place here."

"*Quatsch!*" Ehrlitz sneered. "Nonsense. I see that your delusions are so well advanced you may be beyond hope. One could easily make a case for hospitalizing you in the interests of your own survival."

There was considerable menace in Ehrlitz's voice. Kelly wondered how long Hercule would wait before coming to his rescue.

"Horsefeathers, doc. Where do you think you are? In Russia, for God's sake? Or Nazi Germany?"

It was a chance remark but it hit home. Ehrlitz's face

turned white, his saber scar blazed red. His voice, when he tried to reply, was a stutter of rage. Boldly, Kelly forged ahead.

"I think you're running some kind of a necrophiliac cathouse here, doc. I think that soprano in there was screwed by some weirdo within the last couple of hours, while she was out cold, so to speak. Was it Topovsky?"

Ehrlitz screamed with fury. He was speechless. Violently, he banged his forehead on his desk. Kelly would not have been surprised at any further reaction. Ehrlitz gripped the desk so tightly the clinic might have rolled in earthquake without budging him.

"*Du, du scheisskopf. Du Idiot.* You peeked."

"Don't call me a shithead and idiot, doc," Kelly snapped. "Sure, I peeked. Wasn't I supposed to? I'll bet you were watching, weren't you? You wanted to see if I'd bite, fall for it. Well, I didn't, did I?"

It was strong medicine, a hell of an accusation. But Kelly did not think he was out of line. He had reduced Ehrlitz, at least. The doctor slowly subsided, his face quivering. His voice was low and wounded when he spoke again. "Only a naive young boy could make such a remark as that, Herr Kelly. So tasteless. You insult all our ethics, Herr Kelly." Sadly, he continued, "What if I were to tell you, hypothetically, that certain people do fantasize about being taken when they are asleep; or others dream of the unraping rape? Human beings are a strange lot, Herr Kelly. It has been said that the human race is a freak, an accident of nature."

Ehrlitz's somber voice, his mournful face served to restore a balance between them. "What you mean is that there never should have been a human race?" Kelly asked curiously.

"Exactly. We were never meant to stand up on two feet. It was an accident that we did, nature had not intended that. We were meant to remain primitive animals, ruled by simple laws of survival. . . ."

"Of the fittest? You believe that, Herr Doktor?"

"Completely, Herr Kelly. That is why I am never surprised by the demands made of me by our freakish fellow human beings. I make no judgment on them. They are behaving as what they are: a freak of nature."

Kelly could not buy this reasoning lock, stock, and barrel. But Ehrlitz, he had to admit, had a point. "Too bad, if we are some kind of a nutty mutation, that we didn't get wings," he joked. "It would save a lot on air fares."

"Donnerwetter." Ehrlitz groaned. "I see you are not prepared to deal seriously with your own problem."

Appropriately, he began to massage his forehead with the tips of his large, square fingertips. "You see, Herr Kelly, that I too can become uptight."

"Uptight? A strange word for you to use."

"Mein Gott, you are not familiar with your own American slang?"

Ehrlitz snatched his spectacles off his nose and began to clean them so energetically with a large white handkerchief that one of the lenses cracked. He muttered disgustedly and yanked open a desk drawer. He shoved a fresh pair of glasses on his nose and clasped his hands tightly together. Kelly gave him a moment.

"Do you come originally from Berlin, Herr Doktor?"

"Close, close. I come from Pomerania, from what were formerly the eastern provinces of Greater Deutschland. Now taken by the Bolshevik swine." He stood up and paraded to the window, hands twisted behind his back, much as Kaiser Wilhelm must have done to have a look down the Kurfurstendamm in old Berlin. Speaking over his shoulder he said haughtily, "I may tell you confidentially that I have performed many operations for many of the world's leading statesmen who fear the waning powers of old age—the administration of the knife and the needle in such a way, Herr Kelly, that vigor and decision-making power are restored."

"Give me a couple of names. . . ."

"No," said Ehrlitz, turning and shaking a cautionary finger. "There are things better left to the tender care of confidentiality. But I am a bad host, Herr Kelly. Would you care to smoke? I see you are quaking from nicotine seizure."

"Thank you." Kelly lit a Gauloise and Ehrlitz stood beside him, holding an ashtray under his nose. Having had a deeper look at Ehrlitz's mind, Kelly was better disposed toward him now. "My friend of cosmetic expertise is Suzanne Mordaunt."

"Ach!" Ehrlitz bellowed with laughter. "The French couturière with the monkey. But of course, she is a favorite of mine. I am fascinated by the business of clothes, you see, particularly women's clothes."

"Really?" Kelly felt another dimension of Ehrlitz was emerging.

"Of course. The monkey has been with Madame Mordaunt for many years. Once she proposed the monkey be usefully employed to enliven her glands. Another time she proposed to me that we feast together on warm monkey brains as the sophisticated Chinese do."

"They don't. I don't believe it," Kelly cried.

Ehrlitz chuckled heavily. *"Das ist wahr,* Herr Kelly. Truthfully, it is an old Chinese belief that warm monkey brains are heaven's own aphrodisiac. It is not done much now with the Chinese Bolsheviki in power. But in the old days, a special table was prepared with a hole in the center. Said monkey was placed beneath the table so that the dome of his head protruded through the hole. Like so . . ." Ehrlitz circled his cranium with thumbs and fingers. "As *pièce de résistance* of a Chinese feast, the host with one blow, slices away the top of the skull, like the cap from a soft-boiled egg, and the guests fall to with happy abandon, devouring warm monkey brains."

"Christ, that's terrible. And the monkey is alive?"

Ehrlitz shrugged. "It hurts no one, except the monkey."

"Sickening."

"Perhaps. But it is one of nature's own foods. . . . We are digressing. Are you now more inclined to accept what I have told you about the freakish human race?"

Kelly nodded uncertainly. "I see your point, yes. But being that's what we are, we've got to live with it. And you leave out the element of love. That sets us apart."

Ehrlitz agreed reluctantly, forming a Gothic window out of his fingers and peering at Kelly through the arch.

"Who is to deny that simian creatures do not have love of a sort? I do not think this sets us much apart, Herr Kelly. Love is not an important element: if it were, there would perhaps not be so many wars, destruction, killing."

He stared coldly at Kelly. Naturally, this was the strongest argument against the power of love, and often used. "Well, we do try," Kelly said lamely.

"Man's greatest sport is killing each other, sad to say," Ehrlitz proclaimed.

"Okay. Let's skip it. We were talking about Madame Mordaunt. You don't think Grovival belongs in the cosmetics trade?"

Ehrlitz shook his head absently. "No, no, we have other plans. No, Grovival is too powerful a concoction to be used in cosmetics."

"Is it true about the growths? The warts?"

Ehrlitz looked perplexed, again undecided whether or not to confide in Kelly. Finally, he nodded. "There has been some wart phenomena, yes, but we are in the early stages of development. You see, Herr Kelly—*Gott*, how much should I reveal to you? Like most fertilizers, starting with garden fertilizers, the dosages must be minutely regulated."

"Like one drop of Grovival in a ten-gallon can?"

"*Jawohl.* That is it, in simplified terms. Also the molecular structure. Grovival in its raw form acts only in the pelvic basin. But—and this is important—not only the genitalia. Ha! Simple folk would take Grovival for the sake of sexual enhancement. It is true: Grovival has an explosive impact on male and female alike. It is true: a man's penis will grow to unwieldy proportions and women hunger for the most wanton sexual adventure. . . ."

"You make it sound almost ugly."

"Yes, some would agree but there is no limit as to what we barbaric freaks will risk," Ehrlitz continued solemnly. "What is not realized is there is another marginal effect on the pelvic environs, such as the lower bowel. Thus, the warts on the posteriors of these Swiss women—but perhaps the most unwanted and damaging subsidiary effect is the flatulence."

"Farting."

"Yes, in your terms, and most embarrassing, as you can imagine, for a statesman of world class to interrupt a high-level negotiation with an astonishing occurrence of, as you say, farting."

Kelly grinned. He thought he was finally breaking through Ehrlitz's reserve. Sure enough, Ehrlitz giggled, then chuckled, and in a second was laughing uproariously, clutching his sides. His wild guffawing was interrupted by an echoing fart. The doctor's face turned red. Abruptly, he stopped laughing and Kelly stifled his broad grin.

"We are searching even now for an antidote to the flatulence, Herr Kelly," he muttered. "Please control yourself. That noise I have just manufactured has nothing to do, whatever, with Grovival. It is the coffee, too strong this Colombian blend."

Kelly nodded, not trusting himself to speak. He wiped his eyes.

Glumly, Ehrlitz said, "I think it is time for you to be going. I think you have done enough snooping for one day."

"You're not going to tell me about Topovsky then, or what my wife was doing here?"

"Nein, kein wort," Ehrlitz said sharply. He jumped up and took Kelly's trench coat off the hanger. "Goodbye," he said, turning to leave the room. The door slammed and Kelly was alone. In a second, Ehrlitz returned. "What I mean to say is that it is time for *you* to be going. It cannot be that I should leave my own office. I will escort you to your auto."

The two marched back down the long corridors, retracing the unmapped route to the front entrance of Klinik Montmorency.

"Herr Doktor, this has been a very informative trip," Kelly said.

Ehrlitz grunted. He walked disconsolately, his head drooped on his chest, his eyes fixed on the floor. "If you break our agreement as to confidentiality," he warned, "I will have nothing but scorn and contempt for you."

At the door Ehrlitz took Kelly's hand limply, then dropped it.

"I don't see why I'd want to write anything about this," Kelly lied.

"Good. Then I will tell you that Frau Kelly did engage in cryogenic suspension. It was her wish. I will tell you only that much. Good-bye, my inquisitive American friend."

Friend? It was too late to say anything more. Ehrlitz pushed open the heavy glass door and Kelly was outside.

CHAPTER

TWENTY

Kelly was so immersed in afterthoughts about Montmorency, particularly the meaning of Ehrlitz's parting shot about Maryjane, that he did not notice Westerley Washburn Perex as he walked into the Hotel Richemont.

"A Swiss franc for your thoughts, Mr. Jack Kelly," she bantered. "Alone? Me too."

"Hey," he said, "I'm happy to see you again. I was thinking about a good stiff drink."

"That's a superior idea." She grinned. "I'm thirsty. Been out tramping the streets all day. I wanted to play golf but they've already closed the course for the winter. Hell, and I can play golf in a hailstorm."

Westerley was dressed in a heavy wool flannel skirt, a plaid jacket, and brogues. She was wearing a beret over her short blond hair and carrying gloves.

"You're by yourself?" Kelly asked politely. Of course she was.

"Topovsky had to go off last night."

"He's a busy man."

"Yeah," she agreed, "very. He's gone to Zurich, or somewhere."

Yes, indeed, he thought, somewhere. At this moment, Topovsky was knocked out under a white sheet while the Montmorency sex doctors scrubbed his blood.

They went into the bar, took stools, and Kelly ordered a Pernod for himself, for Westerley a whiskey sour.

He drank reflectively, still somewhat preoccupied by the Montmorency adventure. Westerley did not speak at once but, finally and rather impatiently, she asked, "What's your old man got against my old man?"

Kelly lit a Gauloise and held the lighter to Westerley's Camel.

"Nothing personal, I guess," he said briefly. "It's a political game he plays. He never has anything good to say about the incumbent. Anyway, like I told you, I don't work for him anymore. We had a big fight over a story."

"Yeah," she said idly, smacking her lips over her drink. "And now you work for us—I should say for C.T. Trout, because as everyone knows George Washburn has nothing, absolutely nothing—Ha!—to do with his business interests while he's serving time at the White House."

He smiled, engaged by her not so subtle sarcasm. "Right."

"Trout is some kind of a wild man," she said. "You know, kids *should* tell their parents to shove it. My father really bitches at me. He thinks I should marry Topovsky. I say balls to that!" she cried spiritedly. "I was married before to a Latin character who drove me up the wall. Jesus! Rafael Trujillo Perex! Christ, why should I change my name to Topovsky after unloading a name like Perex?"

Her voice rose in exasperation. Now might have been the time to tell her Perex was one of his closest friends.

No, he decided, it was too early. "You could hyphenate it: Topovsky-Washburn."

Westerley laughed a staccato, her eyes wide and amused. "F-word you," she said. "Tom told me your wife is nuts."

"Oh?" What would Topovsky know about it? Was he aware of Trout's story, that Maryjane had Lolita-ed Washburn? "Nuts, I don't know," he said. "Neurotic, yes. But it doesn't matter now. Trout informed me we're separated."

"Don't be bitter," she said warmly. "Jesus, the things men and women do to each other. That's one reason I'm not marrying Topovsky. I know he chases—he's probably off somewhere right now with Heidi Redcheeks. Well, screw him. Do you play cards?"

"I used to play a little poker."

"What about gin rummy?"

"I've always resisted that."

"You must be nuts too. It's a hell of a game. I suppose you're too intellectual. We play it all the time after golf."

He didn't tell her he had a mental block against golf, the result of his caddying experiences with that prick Battlen. "I just don't seem to have gotten around to it."

"Listen," she said wisely, "there are all kinds of games you've got to learn to play if you're going anywhere in life. Starting with the game of life. That's toughest of all: the rules keep changing."

It turned out that Westerley's deep resentment toward her father was rooted in Washburn's shabby treatment of Janet Washburn. Westerley's mother had been relegated to the refuse heap that littered the trail of any successful politician. Judging from what she said, she knew Washburn was a reprobate, a crony among cronies, and that he'd participated in all sorts of deals on his way to the top, indeed that he engaged in them still to maintain his place at the top.

Two whiskey sours were enough for Westerley. She

suggested they switch to martinis and then eat dinner. "You do like martinis, don't you, Jack?"

"Those I like," he said, proving he was at least to some extent attuned to the country-club set. "In Paris, though, I drink a lot of Pernod."

"French horsepiss," She scowled. "Here's to you with an American formula extradry martini." She had instructed the bartender exactly how to make it. "Here's to you, my fellow American." She sipped. "Wow! Good and strong and long, that's the way I like it."

It had been on Kelly's mind to ask her why, as far as he could make out, she had no Secret Service men on her tail. Now, he did so, adding, "I don't want to interfere in the business of protecting the president's only daughter."

Her reply was in keeping with what he was learning of her character. "I haven't had one of those creeps following me in years. If I want to have a good time, I don't want to be shadowed by some sanctimonious G-man."

"Aren't they afraid what might happen to you?"

"Of what?" She grinned. "That somebody'd kill me? Or kidnap me? That'd be a big mistake. President George Washburn wouldn't trade me for the lowest-grade Russian spy. In fact, he'd probably say good riddance."

From the bar, they progressed to the low-ceilinged dining room of the hotel. Westerley ordered them two more doubles while he was out for a leak, then excused herself for a run to the ladies' room. Kelly leaned back and thought things over. He was tired after his day in the country with Hercule. What, most vitally, had Wolfgang Ehrlitz been implying when he admitted Maryjane had taken the cryogenic cure? It had been Hercule who had recalled him to good sense. Hercules was convinced that Klinik Montmorency was a most sinister kind of place. For his entertainment while Kelly had been with Ehrlitz, there had been more crazy laughter from the balconies and at one point a white-smocked patient had come running out and jumped in the car, only to be hustled back into the sanatorium. Hercule tapped his temple, twisted his forefinger next to his ear, meaning they were all *fou,* insane. It was then that Kelly discovered that Hercule's intuition, his insight, his cynical view of human frailty, came from the fact that he was a Corsican. Not only that, he confided, but Bonapartist blood ran in his veins. *Vraiment?* Was it possible Hercule could be one of many descendants of the Emperor Napoleon? *Oui,* and that was a way of accounting for his brevity of stature.

Kelly followed Westerley with his eyes as she returned to him through the crowded dining room. She strode purposefully and with athletic gait, but she was wobbling a little. She sat down heavily, planted her elbows on the table, and lifted her martini.

"I meant to say before that C.T. Trout is a tick. Do you trust him?"

"Do *you* trust anybody?"

"Jesus, Jack, you'd trust me, wouldn't you? Would I give you a bum steer? Jack, I'll tell you something. It's maybe premature to tell you this but you've got a certain quality that I like. It's certainly not the stench of power—not like Topovsky. It comes off him like B.O." She paused, searching for words. "The smell of power really does stink you know. I'd like to see some clean politics for a change. . . . Hell, *you* could be a candidate. You look good, a little like those Kennedy characters, but you don't have that awful Boston accent. How are you at public speaking?"

"Speaking ain't my thing."

"You *ever* coming back to the good old, you know, U.S.A.?"

"Probably in the next couple of years. It depends on the old man."

She shifted her elbows to the arms of her chair and stared at him. Her speech was becoming a little fuddled but she was determined, it seemed, to tell him everything that came into her mind.

"I wouldn't marry Topovsky on a bet," she said vehemently, returning to that topic. "He's got hair on his back and he is not gentle. He thinks because I play golf and goof around at the bar with the boys that I just want it hot and fast. Bim-bam, thank you ma'am. Most women like a little tenderness, you know," she said, aggrievedly. "He's just like Washburn, the great man. I don't know what the hell it is about politicians."

"Power, like you said. The ego and conceit that goes with power."

"It takes two to do the campaign tango," she said bitterly.

They ordered Mongolian egret eggs as a starter. Kelly thought Trout would not object to his treating the daughter of his friend the president to the very best. He wed the Far Eastern delicacy to a bottle of champagne, thinking he might as well get Westerley well and truly loaded. Who knows what else he might find out? For their main course, both ordered thinly sliced roast beef from the Swiss highlands, and Kelly matched that with—what else?—a bottle of Château Beaupeau Burgundy.

"You know," Westerley said informatively, vigorously chewing her meat, "those Secret Service bastards got pictures of me and every trick I ever dated. Mr. President keeps them all stashed away in his most private filing cabinet, along with all his other blackmail. Keeping *me* in line, his own daughter. I'm telling you, Jack, I've had the SS paparazzi jump out of the woodwork in motels and hotels all across our great land. It's scared the hell out of more guys. And it gets around too. But," she said philosophically, "there are still plenty more of them willing to take the risk just so they'll be able to tell their children they slept with the president's daughter." She imparted this scandalous news with the aplomb that went with living at the social apex. Was she asking if he too thought it worth the risk? "I guess that's why I finally moved in with Tom, just to get those bastards off my back. Nobody's going to bust into the White House aide's house to get compromising pictures of me." She laughed sullenly. "There was one of Perex, though. I wish I had it. He was chasing me around the garden with a big . . . you know."

He wanted to ask her if Perex had been wearing his trilby.

They returned to the bar for coffee and brandy. By this time, Westerley was showing a distinct reaction to the alcohol, much more so than he was. Kelly had always suspected that the athletic, out-of-doors type always went down first when it came to booze. They couldn't take it. Their systems, so purified by exercise, had no resistance. Westerley's voice became more furry around the edges. Red spots glowed brightly in her cheeks. Her eyes took on a distant look, a fixity of purpose, or warmth of design. He remembered that Rafe had hinted she was a nymphomaniac.

She placed her hand on his, their first intimate contact, to make her next point. "I got a bottle of Calvados upstairs. Let's go drink it, and I'll teach you how to play gin."

"Sounds like a good idea," he agreed.

He helped her up and through the lobby. They staggered off the elevator. At once, she seemed to sober up. She didn't fumble with the key at her door. Pulling him inside, she put her finger to her lips. She went directly to the bedside radio and turned on symphony music. Whispering in his ear, she said, "I'm always afraid they've bugged me. You know who."

Kelly sat down and Westerley fetched her Calvados and two brandy glasses from one of the suitcases. She and Topovsky evidently traveled with all the sophisticated accouterments. Opening the bottle, while singing loudly to herself, she poured two sizable slugs.

But, he was thinking, if the place were bugged, there could just as well be a camera hidden in one of the pictures. That possibility did not seem to occur to her. For himself, he didn't care. He had nothing to lose.

Westerley sat down opposite him and gaily lifted her glass. She kicked off her shoes and opened a pack of cards. Kelly didn't know what he was doing, but it didn't matter. After they'd played two hands of the half-assed game, she threw down her cards and leaned across the table to kiss him. Her lips were sunburned like the rest of her, salty from the drinks, and under her lipstick, crusty.

"What say we hit the sack, Jack?" she murmured.

She took it for granted he would not refuse. She stood up, unzipped and stepped out of her skirt, pulled her turtleneck sweater over her head. She leaned over him, her hands on his shoulders, and kissed him again, more strenuously. By then, he was ready. Blindly, he reached behind her to unhook her bra. Hands resting on her hips, he lipped one rosy red nipple of the full white breast, then the other. Westerley sighed, loosed an openmouthed groan of low lust, and wriggled out of her skimpy bottoms. His face was at navel level and he thrust his tongue into her belly button, convoluted like the inside of a small seashell, a winkle. She was lightly patched at the pube, the hair wiry like steel wool. It looked as though she had recently clipped it, entirely possible, for blonds were notorious for being revolted by body hair.

Only then did he note that there was a tattoo on her belly, just above the hairline. He glanced up at her inquiringly and she nodded, eyes alight with amusement. She distended her belly so he could read the inked inscription.

PROPERTY OF U.S. GOVERNMENT.

It was a shocking insignia, yet very ironic.

"Sssh," she cautioned him. "I had it done to make Topovsky mad."

Westerley motioned for him to stay where he was. She bounded across the room to the bath and slammed the door. Kelly undressed down to his jockey shorts. She returned with a big bath towel which she spread carefully on the floor by the bed, under the symphonic sounds. This, she whispered, was so there wouldn't be any creaking. She put pillows down on the towel, and the stage was set to her satisfaction. They would be comfortable and any extraneous grunts and groans would blend with the Tchaikovsky—was it the Fifth?

Kelly gently put his arms around Westerley and they knelt. Westerley slipped his shorts down and took him in her hands, weighing him, nodding. What fascinated her most was his penile scar. She put one hand firmly around the shaft, then drew her forefinger along the scar, causing Kelly to tremble. It was a sensitive place, swollen to the same proportion as the rest of him, a ridged welt with several shreds still remaining, amazingly, of torn skin.

"What's this?" she said very softly.

He whispered his synopsis of the duel.

"Golly, that must have hurt." Probably not as much as her tattoo job, he told her. "You know, Jack," she said analytically, "this is very respectable in size. I'd say it's above average by about a half inch and it's thick as well. Topovsky—" she chuckled maliciously in his ear— "has got a short, fat cocky. I think that's why he compensates with all this power business."

Hatefully, Kelly wondered whether Topovsky was even now undergoing elongation surgery. That sort of work would be right up Ehrlitz's alley. For, as much as the good doctor railed against the Bolsheviks and the Marxists, in his own way he was a Marxist too, a believer in the dialectic which said Nature could and should be manipulated to suit Man. It was this brand of thinking, he remembered, that had led another madman, the Stalinist biologist Lysenko, to promote the theory that wheat could be made to grow in the snowfields of Siberia, oranges under water, and the human body to adapt to any environment, however unfriendly. In this way, was Western thinking coming under the influence of the Marxist dialectic. As Western religion died, it was being replaced by the quackery of such men as Lysenko, and possibly Wolfgang Ehrlitz. Rasputins like these had swept away the monarchs and now they were in hot pursuit of the presidents, the prime ministers, and the *junta* colonels. Maryjane? What had Ehrlitz done to her? Probably added a third breast to her chest. Maryjane was one who went all the way.

Westerley poked him in the stomach and demanded softly, "Why are you smiling?"

"I was thinking of something."

He wormed his hand between her legs and under her crotch to nudge her tenderest spot with his thumb. She squirmed and panted. "I've seen U.S. Army stuff," she informed him, *sotto voce*, "top secret reports that claim fighting ability is directly related to the length of men's cockies. The guys with the biggest cockies are found to be least aggressive in battle. They don't have to prove anything. When they're recruiting for the special forces, paratroopers and that, they look for guys with short ones, for they're found to be great killers and they're also not likely to get tangled up in their parachute straps and all."

"Very interesting," Kelly murmured, not believing any of it. He put a hand under her buns and linked his fingers underneath her. "What about the Chinese army?"

Evidently, this was a very serious matter at the Pentagon. "The chinks," Westerley breathlessly informed him, "are well known to have little tiny ones—and therein, my friend, lies the threat."

He remembered about Grovival. He mentioned that things might change radically when the Chinese got their hands on it. Westerley knew about the drug. "Hell, that's the whole idea," she said, "to keep it out of their mitts."

"That must be why the Japanese were such fanatical fighters."

She nodded delightedly. "Little birdie cockies. You, on the other hand, my fellow American, do not need Grovival or anything else."

Kelly was determined to establish the difference between himself and the short-peckered and callous likes of Tom Topovsky. He kissed Westerley lengthily on the mouth, relishing her lips and eager tongue, while at the same time dallying with her primary pleasure threshold. As he touched it, first with his fingers, caressingly, and then his lips as he nuzzled the length of her body, past rounded breasts, armpits, rib cage, navel, upper belly, tattoo and all, she responded with opulent grunts, much in keeping, as he had expected, with the Tchaikovsky. He mouthed the tattoo, the lower stretch of her body, where sparsely covered pube came outrageously near anal orifice and she, keyed to some sparingly used, secondary nervous system, heaved spasmodically. When he endeavored to reach into her with his tongue, she clamped his head with her thighs in a wrestler's viselike grip. Steaming with desire, she invited his deep exploration of the various and sundry membranous delicacies which both protected and concealed her most vital location, that precise spot at which reproduction is initiated.

Kelly had never in earlier years been much attracted by this part of the female body. But his tastes had changed, predictably, with Maggi Mont, his guide, his Cicero, in sexual tourism. Now, in such a personal exchange as this, he began to think there was not anything else in the world quite like it. He delighted in the notion that he was serving up breathtaking sensations to the president's daughter. For the moment, he held his own need in abeyance. This was a good thing, he told himself as he labored over her, tongue straining to an ache at the back of his jaws.

The nub of her clitoris stiffened and she made even more excited noises at each pass of his tongue. Every tiny attack elicited an answering shudder, and finally, a whimper of surrender. As he fondled her rear-sited bud with his little finger, whose nail, he knew, was carefully pared, she gasped afresh but in a different, shocked but thrilled manner. Clutching his head roughly, she thumped her thighs resoundingly against his ears. He wondered vaguely if such a pummeling was good for him; had his appetites become so voracious that he was willing to risk deafness too? He maneuvered his tongue to bring her under control. Throatily, she achieved a vaginal orgasm.

"Wow! Forty-love. Your match," she yelled, perspiring heavily, breathing as though she'd just run one hundred yards. "God, Jack, don't stop now. I'm not so sure, by the way, that it was a proper thing to do what you did around there, behind."

"You think that's un-American?"

"Yep." She grinned. "Positively un-American. That's the kind of thing people do to each other that they don't talk about afterwards." She smiled in an oddly timid way. Despite all her bravado and brave talk, she was the novice and he the skilled practitioner. It burned her a little to allow him to lead the way. "Jack, do you want me to . . . you know . . . with my mouth?"

Quid pro quo. Why not? She was willing, perhaps not eager. "That's up to you. Whatever makes you comfortable."

Blond face bashful, Westerley took the bulb of his "cockie" in her lips and tentatively touched it with the tip of her tongue. She looked up at him, as if to ask him whether she was doing okay.

"You'll get the hang of it," he said.

"I suppose this is that French thing—*soixante-neuf*. I don't like French words when it comes to love things. What's the American expression?"

"I wouldn't tell you."

She ran her tongue down the side of the shaft, underneath and up the other side. Her mouth pulled at the scar and he thrust upward. She pulled away.

"I like it," she announced. "But that's enough of that. I think it's time, Jack, to get cocky inside me."

Now, suddenly, that was what she wanted. She flopped on her back and Kelly crawled between her legs. Anxiously, she bit on her lower lip.

"It's a matter of getting the front end in first," she said.

Christ, was Topovsky as bad as that? Had she behaved so awkwardly with Rafe Perex? A nymphomaniac? He did not see how that could be possible. Kelly was put off guard by his recollection of his friend, Perex. Was this a betrayal of Perex? Was he cuckolding his pal? No, that could be only the most extreme reading of the event.

Westerley spread her legs widely and took in the throbbing bulb, which bore his scar of honor. "Gosh," she whined, "just that much would be plenty."

"There's a lot more where that came from." He allowed himself a small bit of arrogance.

"Slowly, Jack, dear," she cried aloud, "go slowly. Remember, I'm not used to this from Tom Topovsky, right hand of the president."

"What about Perex?" he asked quietly. It was an odious comparison to ask her to make.

She whimpered, "Premature ejaculation, Jack. He'd have come and gone by now."

So that was it. True to his Latin character, Perex was too excitable. Was the condition general? Were Latins, as the question had been posed, really lousy lovers?

Very carefully, Kelly lowered himself and thrust in an upward trajectory so as to intrude into, then fully occupy, her innermost compartment. He wondered if Westerley would have the will to achieve the orgasm of the unscrewing screw. Maybe later, but not this first time. By definition, she was too much the woman of action to submit to the required discipline. When he felt himself to be fully extended within her, he paused and inhaled, his nose twitching at the heady scent of their coupling.

"Is that it?" she whispered, knowing of course that it was. "Boy, I couldn't take anymore."

"Bosh," he muttered in her ear, "the female receptacle is totally elastic." His memory suddenly was of Maggi. "Can you feel the nerve ends tingling?"

"Maybe. I think so," she said doubtfully.

No, he concluded again, she was simply not experienced enough. Sadly, he understood that all her hurried moments in hotels and bargain motels along the campaign trails had netted her no more than Tom Topovsky, he of the foreshortened pecker.

"What's this rest period all about?"

"It's the highest form," Kelly told her. "You concentrate and, by and by, the nerve ends take over."

"Like automatic pilot."

"Sort of, if you can release yourself."

"I don't know if I like the idea of giving up control . . . I suppose this is something you learned from one of those French women of yours."

"No, no." He didn't want to tell her just yet that he was also acquainted with her old college chum, Maggi Mont. "It's my own invention," he lied. "I learned it from the Hindu philosophers. I had trouble at first. It's a lot harder for a Catholic to manage."

"What about a New England Protestant?"

"I don't know. Somebody should do a study of that."

She tried to be still but she could not. "You know, another reason I'll never marry Topovsky is that he's a Jew. We wouldn't mix well."

"Topovsky? I would have thought he was Polish. A Polish-American."

"No, Jack, I think he's a Polish-American Jew."

She stared up at him, waiting for him to get going again. It was up to him to satisfy the daughter of the president, she seemed to think.

"You're not ready for this just yet," he said.

"No, I'm too hot."

Kelly began to move his hips again, slowly, aware that in their moment of inertness the combined juices had begun to jell. In a second, all was warm and fluid again. He eased himself this way and that, touching, stroking all the rims and overhangs of her slick passageway.

"Ah." She sighed. "That's more like it."

Eyes closed, teeth bared, her face registered every alteration of his thrusting pattern as he started the countdown. She did not move much under him. That would not do. He hiked his hips up so that the only contact was at the precise point of entry and thus, shortening his penetration, slowly but surely drew her buttocks from the floor and toward him. In a second, she was straining upward, seeking the full length of him. She tried to pull him down with her legs, but he propped his knees and resisted, willing her to levitate. She cried out angrily once but then gave in and began to buck, as she properly should. The red flush in her cheeks heightened and her ears turned crimson with exertion. Ah, Kelly thought, she was getting there. He had dragged her down, or up, the hill, made her as anonymous as any other creature striving for release from the arm lock of physical need. So went the world: sex was the great leveler.

Westerley was not as well coordinated as one might have supposed. Her leg muscles began to jerk and the undulations of her hips and thighs became uneven. He judged that now was the time to take command in a different way. Where he had been in an aloof posture, he now pressed down. Thankfully, she rubbed her breasts against his chest. He filled her and pushed toward her nether regions. In the end, he had her beaten.

Westerley shouted aloud as she climaxed. "Fore . . ."

Kelly came in a rush, with heady, steady pumping. Westerley's legs untwined from his back and fell, heels hitting the floor with a thump. In one final passionate demand, as if to draw the last gram of pleasure from him, she pressed down with her pelvic structure, grappling for more.

"Gosh, hail to you, chief."

He kissed her parched lips. It had been good, perhaps not ultra-first-class but nonetheless top-of-the-bore; not as mind bending as an exhaustive session with Maggi Mont, but very acceptable. And wasn't that the beauty of it, after all? They were all individuals.

"Now that was what I'd call summit humpery," Westerley said. She held him there, on top of her, her hands squeezing his buttocks.

"I've always wondered," he mused wearily, "how much humpery is done at the summit?"

"Not a great deal." What came next fell into the category of relevant information. "When the wogs come to Washington, we always try to supply tail. It's helpful to foreign policy, and naturally, things being what they are, Topovsky . . ." She stopped, then apparently decided she could safely drop a few state secrets. "Topovsky and his technocrats—Nixon used to call them plumbers—believe anything goes. The pictures . . ." Her mouth twisted comically. "They can get color pictures now in dark rooms, you know."

"Technocrats?"

"Those are bureaucrats with technical training—photographers, hookers, dopers, linguists, political analysts. There's nothing more effective than hookers with linguistic training."

"Morbid," Kelly said. "Whatever happened to the Constitution?"

Westerley jiggled her pube at him. "They don't talk much about that anymore. But never mind about ethics right now." She raised her voice, as if hoping it would be recorded. "That was one of the best pieces of ass I've ever had." Abruptly, she pushed him away and rolled over on her hands and knees, her forehead down on the soggy towel. "I know this is really un-American and it's something I've only read about in a State Department memo on life in prewar Budapest. But I really want to know if it's possible from behind."

"You're kidding," Kelly said slowly. "It's not only possible but a lot of people prefer it."

It was from this angle that he could appreciate her body more fully. Her athletic haunches were smooth, unlined, and muscular. He smiled to himself, going along with her gag, and placed himself between her extended calves, slowly inserting a somewhat deflated package into her, feeling the personality of her passage from this vantage place.

"Gosh, it really is possible, isn't it?" She giggled. Was she serious? "You must think I'm a dumb bunny, Jack, a man of your cosmopolitan knowledge. No, I'm only fooling. I have seen pictures of people doing it. We got some on the Potomac one time, a girl and one of the wogs. I found it in Topovsky's attaché case. He was mad as hell, and naturally, didn't want to hear about it. He was afraid Washburn would find out somehow. But I think there's another reason—a guy with a cock as short as his probably couldn't keep it inside." Kelly murmured, crazily, that was probably the reason it was so rarely done in Japan and China. "Wow!" she yelped, grinding her teeth and growling in canine fashiom. He thought, for a second, that she might, incredibly, start barking. "Jack, do you think we could get Congress to pass a law to get this accepted as one of the national positions?"

"Like admitting a new state? I thought it was already accepted."

"Jack, this is sodomy, for God's sake!"

He wiped his mental brow. "No, no, Westerley. Sodomy is what we *don't* do. That's in the other ... place."

She was dead silent for a moment, the only indication she had heard a waggle of her hips and a deep intake of air. Finally, she collected her composure enough to speak. "If that's sodomy, what the hell is this?"

"Merely another position." Kelly chuckled. "A variation."

"Of the missionary position hallowed by our forefathers?" she cried. "God, who's been keeping me in the dark?"

"Topovsky, I guess. Did you say forefeathers?"

"No, our forefeathers were the Indians."

She should really stop talking so much and concentrate. Carrying on even the most minor sort of discussion was not conducive to passion.

But she went on. "I can see how women can get pregnant doing it this way. Everything seems much more open and vulnerable."

Kelly was aware of a tear in the corner of his eye. Westerley was charming in her innocence, her touching insouciance. She was astonishing. It did really seem to be so that she had been behind the door when the sex manuals were handed out.

"Gee whiz!" Her mouth was muffled in her hands. "It seems like it's interfering with my breathing process." But she was building surely toward another rip-roaring climax. Nervous spasms racked her, chaotic at first, then merging for the big one. She wheezed mightily and her orgasm puffed against him. "Fore!" She loosed a long, imploring cry before collapsing under him. He finished determinedly, a few strokes behind her.

"God," she breathed after a moment, "I think I came from inside my womb, my fellow American."

Kelly confessed to her about Perex the next morning.

"Son of a bitch," she said. She looked at him angrily, then shrugged, saying she was not surprised, or dismayed. "He gets around, doesn't he? Anyway, so what?

A lot of guys know the ex-husbands of women they've slept with." She frowned petulantly. "I don't know if I'd have done it with you if I'd known. Maybe it's just as well you didn't tell me. It figures, doesn't it?" she asked, rather bitterly. "All this—you working for that Texas crud, Trout, and the interview for those phony newspapers. Rafe is one of theirs, Jack, and if they were going to get at you in Paris, they'd do it through him."

"I'm sorry. You know I like Rafe. I can understand why you—"

"Never mind," she said energetically. "I hope you're not going to tell him we've been banging."

"Hell, Westerley, I'd never tell him that."

They were having croissants and café au lait on the terrace. Kelly had sent Hercule off on a wild-goose chase. He told him he wanted a map of the exact route to Klinik Montmorency. It was not a mission the descendant of Napoleon enjoyed undertaking but he was happier about it when Kelly suggested their next trip to the clinic might be with a helicopter assault force. Hercule took off in a cloud of dust; his departure gave Kelly another half day with Westerley.

"What I'd really like to do," he told her, "is go have a look at Perex's house."

"All right," she said indifferently, "if he's there, we could drop in and say hello. That'd be a surprise for the Cuban heel."

"I don't think he's here. He's taken deep cover."

The Château Perex was an impressive place, three stories of gray stone, manorial in style, with numerous chimneys leaking smoke into a slate-colored sky. Fake turrets cut the horizon above Lake Geneva. All the windows in the upper stories were tightly shuttered.

Westerley whistled. "The little heel is doing all right, isn't he? I wonder what goes on in there. Plenty, I'll bet, and not much of it having to do with the Mount Vernon Trust. You can be sure Perex is not paying for it himself."

"Shall I try him?" Kelly punched an intercom button by the front gate.

"Monsieur Perex est là?"

No, a male voice replied in English, Perex was not home. He did not ask for Maryjane because he didn't want Westerley to hear.

A few minutes later, they were sitting in a small café overlooking the lake. The weather was now fully into fall, headed surely for a gray mid-European winter. Chill sun made marks on the water and on the opposite shore the trees had turned red and gold.

"Cold." She shivered. "And I'm so sore in the crotch, I can hardly walk. That was some workout, my fellow American." Kelly muttered something inane about American citizens going astray in foreign lands. Sadly nodding, speaking in a small voice, she said, "You're wondering about Rafe and me. What can I tell you? I was in love with him once, but he got on my nerves. He's such a blabbermouth and con artist. He talks a big sex game but he's too ambitious to be much interested in it."

Kelly chuckled. "He's a funny man, Westerley."

"Yeah, funny is right. I mean, I don't mind him. I just didn't want to be married to him, Jack." She paused brightly, her eyes wet. "By the way, thanks for not calling me Westy all the time."

"I wouldn't. I hate that name. Makes you sound like a baseball pitcher."

She nodded sorrowfully. "Jack, tell me what I'm going to do now, without you?" She looked at him bleakly. "I'm so fed up. Look, we are going to see each other in Paris, aren't we? You are going to think about coming back to the States, right?"

"Right."

"Okay then," she said, her mood brightening. "In the meantime, let's go back to the hotel."

CHAPTER

TWENTY-ONE

It was a matter of extremely good fortune that Westerley Washburn Perex was not with Kelly and Hercule on the drive back to Paris. And she might have been. Topovsky, she argued, was coming to Paris anyway. She'd simply leave him a note, and meet him at the Crillon. The fact was she was loath to let Kelly leave her.

Imagine the stink there would have been if Westerley had been involved in the car crash, and possibly hurt, the daughter of the president.

Hercule had been driving too fast, and somewhere near Annecy, just on the other side of the French border, as he rounded a tight curve and made precipitous entry into the suddenly narrowing street of a small town, a truck appeared in front of them. It was only due to his skill at the wheel that the two vehicles did not meet head-on. As it was, metal screeched against metal: they were sideswiped and forced into a stone wall. The truck did not stop. They continued the journey to Paris on the train.

Now Kelly was dragging one foot after the other, suffering the aftereffects of whiplash. He had gone out during the day, painfully inserting himself into a taxicab for a ride to the rue Anjou. Groaning, he walked upstairs to Maggi's flat. He knocked but there was no reply. He let himself in. Emptiness. Nothing. There was no sign that she had been back. The rooms were exactly as he'd left them the day of her departure. Dust lay thickly on her writing table, dead flies sprinkled the windowsill, hard scum had gathered on the dishes in the sink. Heart aching as much as his body, he closed the door and left. There was nothing to do but return to the apartment and brood. Maggi was too elusive for him. He was convinced now that she was doing something for the government; exactly what he did not know. But she had known Perex long before Kelly came on the scene; and Westerley had told him Perex was in Washburn's pocket. Ergo, as Doctor Wolfgang Ehrlitz would have said.

"Monsieur . . ."

Hercule shuffled stiffly into the living room. He was wearing a red velvet robe which dragged along the floor at his heels. He sat down stiffly.

"Relax, Hercule."

"Difficile, monsieur." Hercule resumed his outraged harangue: the accident had not been an accident. The driver of the truck had been a paid assassin. The worst of it was that the French cops had booked Hercule for reckless driving.

"I believe it," Kelly said. He was willing to agree to anything just to shut Hercule up. "You saved our lives, Monsieur Hercule."

Hercule nodded, for it was true.

Kelly had begun to yearn for the honest French body of Beatrice de Beaupeau, but she would not be in Paris now. He thought of Maggi: secret agent Maggi Mont. I fucked a polar bear for the FBI and found God. Yes, that was her story all right. On orders from above, she would have fucked a polar bear.

As Kelly and Hercule were trying to settle down to watch TV, Rafe Perex called. He was so anxious he failed to note Kelly's depression.

"Jack, my dear, bloody hell," Perex wailed, "you opened a fucking hornet's nest in Geneva. It's bad. C.T. wants to see you tomorrow at lunchtime."

Perex was already there, sitting alone in the corner of a small and unfamiliar bistro near Paris-Nord, the northern railroad station. As before, he was wearing dark glasses. He had grown a ragged beard and had on a hairy tweed jacket. There was no sign of the trilby. Perex jumped up and took Kelly's hand. Hastily, he pulled him into the next chair. He was drinking white wine from a carafe.

"How was your trip, dear friend?"

Kelly smiled, thinking of Westerley. No, certainly he was not going to tell Perex. "Fine. What's all this about a hornet's nest?"

Perex shook himself. "Bloody balls, Jack, why did you have go to that goddamned clinic?"

So that was it. Ehrlitz had screamed. It had nothing to do with Westerley.

He shrugged. "It seemed like a reasonable thing to do. Maryjane might have been there. I'd heard Washburn was going there. I thought I'd check it out."

"Holy Mother of God." Perex sighed tearfully. "You asked about Topovsky, not only Maryjane."

"Bullshit," Kelly said roughly. "Doesn't it occur to you that I've got enough to write the blockbuster of the year? I've got enough on you guys to hang you all!"

"Jesu Christus," Perex moaned, "that was not the deal, Jack. Why ruin everything now? They like your work."

"Work? I haven't done any work yet."

Perex nodded miserably, his hands trembling around his wineglass.

The small restaurant abutted on a narrow alley stuffed with shops, parked cars and trucks. It was thick with pedestrian traffic. Outside, Kelly caught sight of the distinctive cowboy hat.

"Here comes the little fart," he muttered.

"Oh, mother-humper, we are in for it now."

Trout halted on the sidewalk outside and looked around. Then he opened the door and stepped inside. Kelly wondered how they could call Washburn the Ultimate President when he had so many peculiar people working for him. He understood the designation dated back to the first presidential campaign: Washburn was the ultimate, the *sine qua non*. Without him, nothing.

Trout dodged nimbly through the tables to reach them. Perex leaped to his feet, exclaiming, "Hi, C.T., hi!"

"Si'down," Trout yelped. "Hello, J.K. Understand you were using my name in vain up in Swizzerland. Little prick!" Trout slumped in his chair.

"What will you have, C.T?" Perex asked. "How was Austria?"

"Austria stinks," Trout said. "Don't suppose they got any bourbon in this shit-heel place. Give me a little of that wine there." Trout tasted the wine, made a face, and then turned on Kelly. "You little mothah-fucker," he snarled, "you ain't writin' nothin' about Monmaurice. Where the hell you get off, Kelly, invading that place?"

Kelly wondered despairingly why Trout always called him "little" this-and-that. "I was on the journalistic trail, C.T. I had a report George Washburn is going there, and I thought I'd better look into it."

"Look into it, my ass! Of all the goddamn . . . effrontery." Effrontery? That was a new one from Trout's word bank. Trout, silent for a moment, then spoke angrily again. "J.K., what you're doin' for me got nothin' to do with Monmaurice and I don't want you foolin' around with this Grovival thing. Hands off, understand?"

Kelly considered the order, weighing the alternatives. He could tell Trout to go to hell. On the other hand, there was no way Trout could erase from his mind what he already knew. When he used it, and how—that was his affair.

"Right, C.T. Okay. For the time being."

"For the long shot too, J.K. Otherwise, you gonna get your ass in lots of hot water."

Kelly nodded grimly. Hot water? "Here's one for you, C.T. Somebody tried to kill us on our way back from Geneva."

Perex's eyes crumpled and a faint shriek issued from his lips.

Trout blinked. "Who tried to kill you?"

"How the fuck do I know? We got rammed by a big truck. Hercule saved our bacon."

"Sumumumbitch," Trout said. "Who would do a thing like that?"

"I don't know," Kelly said. "Maybe Dr. Wolfgang Ehrlitz."

"Nah," Trout scoffed. He took his hat off, fanned his face, then put it down on the table; there wouldn't be any room for soup now. "Errlizz is on our side, for fuck's sake, J.K. Shee-et! First Igl, then Max Maxim, now you. Who's next? Perex, mebby you're next. I know it sure as hell ain't me."

Perex cried out, "Bloody shit . . ."

"Shaddup," Trout told him.

But Trout was not as cool about it as he might have wanted to appear. He gripped his wineglass so tightly in his hands that it shattered. Calmly, as he would have potato chips, C.T. picked up shards and fed them into his mouth, chewing contemplatively.

"Holy mother of caramba!" Perex exclaimed.

"See, boys, I'm one tough old buffalo flop."

"You're going to cut up your insides, C.T.," Kelly protested. "Where the hell did you learn that trick?"

"Up in Ostria, some of the locals in a bar." Trout irritably sized up the situation. "So you think somebody really tried to do you in, J.K.? We got to get them first, I can see it now. But that's beside the point. You got your interview set up now?"

"I had a good meeting with Tom Topovsky. I'm seeing him here in Paris again."

"Okay," Trout said. "But I'm tellin' you—just leave all that other horseshit out, J.K. Where Washburn goes got nothin' to do with you."

Kelly agreed without any hesitation. At this point, all he wanted was to get away from them. It was clear enough why Trout wanted him to steer clear of the Klinik Montmorency. AmFreight and its European cosmetics subsidiary would be using the place as a channel for Grovival, once control over the untamed substance had been established in Mangrovia. It was really an astoundingly simple scheme: Switzerland would be the cover. AmFreight had bought Ehrlitz, Montmorency, maybe the whole country *and* its neutrality. Washburn, through his conservator, C.T. Trout, was in on the deal, very obviously. Eventually, Kelly thought cynically, Montmorency would be used as Washburn's private health spa.

"Just one question, C.T.," he said carelessly, "then I'm off the subject: how in the hell are you going to take over Mangrovia?"

Trout dropped a crooked smile, his thin mouth pursed like rattler chops. "If our elegant diplomatic persuasions don't work," he said smoothly, "if our offer of guns and butter is scorned, then we'll figure out a pretext to invade the black-assed fuckers."

Jesus, Kelly thought helplessly, just like that. He wondered if Congress was aware of any of this. What about all the oversight committees? "We might get a war with France out of it."

"So? We ain't had a war with France in a long time," Trout sneered. "We'll invade these fuckers too. We done it before. We can do it again."

Kelly, despite his low feelings about Aristide de Bis, felt an immediate twinge of sympathy for his position. Aristide was up against some big guns, the poor sadist. Then Kelly was inspired by a recollection which took the whole matter from the sublime to the ridiculous.

"Ehrlitz tipped me off that Grovival makes you fart like crazy."

Trout's mouth popped open. A small sliver of glass glittered between two of his front teeth. "Errlizz is crazy! How does he know that?"

"Tests, C.T. Observations."

"Well, I never heard about a man farting from it," Trout sputtered. There was worry in his eyes, however. He could be thinking of Maryjane.

Kelly, there on the spot, invented a story to shock Trout more. "They say that in African lore, Mangrovia is called the Thunderland of the Gods."

He smiled at Trout's reaction. The Texan slammed his

Stetson on his head and jumped up. "Thunderland of the Gods? What kind of horseshit are you peddling, Kelly? Holy Alamo! Perex, did you know that?"

"No, sir."

"Well, listen, greaseball, you better find out. C'mon, let's go . . ."

On the way to the door, Kelly pressed home the outrageous point: "During the war, whenever the fleet sailed close in to Mangrovia, the place sounded like it was being bombed."

"Fuck you, J.K.," Trout growled. "You asked Errlizz about Maryjane, didn't you? I told you to forget her." In the street, he stopped to tell Kelly confidentially that Maryjane wished him well but she was out of reach. "She's off on an important mission," he whispered.

Then it happened. First a shattering explosion, the sound of a motorcycle revving up, then a heavy crackle of hail falling around them and against the shop windows. Kelly found himself flat on the sidewalk. The next remarkable sound was that of a pistol being fired. After that, it was bedlam. People were screaming and yelling. He struggled to his feet.

Trout, with a happy expression on his face, was standing in the middle of the alley, holding the shredded remnants of his hat in one hand, a smoking gun in the other. Traces of blood streaked his forehead. Someone had fired a shotgun at them, then taken to a motorcycle to escape. But Trout, Texan to the core, had been too quick for the would-be assassin. He had whipped his six-shooter out of his belt and shot back.

The assailant was dead. His body lay spread-eagled over the hood of a Renault ten yards down the street. Pieces of scalp and bone had settled on the overturned motorcycle.

Trout appeared to have been hit. His face was now covered in blood. But he apparently was not mortally damaged.

"Sumumumbitch," he yelled. He took a handkerchief out of his pocket and wiped his face. "Seems like some of that lead creased my head. Take a look, J.K. It's superficial, ain't it?"

Kelly pulled away the matted hair. True, the shotgun pellets had etched furrows through Trout's scalp, just breaking the skin and taking hair with them.

"C.T.," he said, "thumbs up! Superficial . . ."

Perex was kneeling at the gutter, throwing up.

"Sumumumbitch," Trout complained bitterly, "ruined my hat. Looky that, J.K."

The crowd gathered with the suddenness that gathering crowds or rain clouds are noted for. Men and women poured out of the little shops; restaurants and pawnshops emptied of customers. People stared in shock, several muttering about *bon chance,* a lucky occurrence. For it was rare these days for an urban guerrilla to be cut down in the act of terrorism.

Trout stopped complaining about his hat and began to curse in a senseless fashion. People pointed at him, marveling that he was still on his feet, for, from a distance, it looked like blood-splattered Trout had to be a goner.

Perex finally stopped heaving. He crawled across the sidewalk and propped himself against the wall.

"Put your coat over him, Jack, bloody shit!"

"Like hell—use your own coat."

It was then that Kelly spotted Hercule. The little man was lurking, hardly visible in the dense crowd, in the vicinity of the corpse. Calmly, he was lighting one of his cigars. When he saw Kelly watching him, he patted the place near his left shoulder where he carried his rod. Kelly understood at once: Hercule had fired the deadly retaliatory shot. Or had Trout and Hercule fired simultaneously? Of one thing he was sure. Hercule had knocked him to the sidewalk, out of harm's way. But they could let Trout take credit for the kill.

The police arrived within minutes, one of those very specialized antiterrorist squads now so popular in world capitals, and then a meat wagon to whose personnel fell the gruesome task of collecting the pieces of the gunman. Arms extended and already stiffening, the body looked like that of a body surfer brought to sudden rest.

"So they *are* after us," Trout muttered.

"Who's they?" Kelly asked.

"They . . . They, for Christ's sake."

The police climbed out of their cars with machine guns cocked and ready. Brusquely, they ordered people back, clearing the area, as police are so good at doing. A plainclothesman approached them warily.

"Messieurs . . . Police."

Trout immediately exclaimed, "That fucker tried to kill me. But I got him."

The plainclothesman murmured something in French. "He's saying, C.T., that it was a close shave," Kelly translated.

"Oh yeah? Yeah?" Trout yelled. "It was more than a shave. It was damn near a scalping." Then the policeman wanted to know who had finished off the would-be assassin. "I done it," Trout yelped. He held up his revolver.

"Donnez-le moi," said the cop. Trout handed it over.

So it began, at about 1:00 P.M. By six in the evening, Kelly had been grilled, and regrilled at Sûreté headquarters. Calls were made to the embassy, to the *RAG* office, finally to Zouzou Mordaunt. Having been separated for their interrogations, Kelly learned later that Trout had flown into such a rage at the questions and the charge of carrying a concealed weapon that they had had to restrain him. But when his connection with George Washburn was confirmed, he was quickly released. The gun was merely confiscated. What had happened to Perex, Kelly didn't find out until later.

The police gave up on Kelly in the early evening. He was merely a journalist, *alors,* who happened to work for the Claud Trout newspapers. At five-thirty, Kelly's interrogator poured him a stiff Pernod, for by this time shock was beginning to set in, that on top of the remnants of his whiplash. Altogether he was not in great shape. By now, a report had come down from Interpol, the international police headquarters. They had not succeeded in establishing the gunman's identity.

"Bien, merde, alors," grunted Inspector Marcel Gaston, or was it Gaston Marcel? *"Merde, alors,* Monsieur Kelly, this is a great mystery."

"He was a terrorist?"

"Oui, guerrilla urbain," the inspector said, shrugging violently, and lighting a cigarette even more filthy than those to which Kelly was addicted. "In all probability, monsieur."

"But of which terrorist group?" Kelly asked.

"It is possible it is the American terrorists, *les Weathermen,* or equally possible, the Communists, *Marxistes ou Maoistes.* Perhaps the Italians, *le Red Brigade,* or possibly the PLO or *les Basques* or *les Israéliens.* Or, Monsieur Kelly, one could speak of *les thrill killers.* But of one thing we are certain, monsieur: it was not an accident. *Et* Monsieur Trout *qui est cet homme?"*

Ah, there was the question. "An intimate of President Washburn," he answered simply.

"Ah, oui." The inspector sighed hopelessly. *"Bien sûr."* He flipped his hands in an expressive gesture: what could he do? Nothing. *"Mais,* Monsieur Kelly, we think it is also likely it was *un groupe Africain* called the Cou-Cou Macoo . . ."

This was a new one on Kelly. "Cou-Cou Macoo? I don't think I've heard of that group, Monsieur l'Inspector."

Gaston, or was it Marcel, waved his hand. *"Les terroristes nationalistes Mangroviens."*

Olga Blastorov was waiting for him downstairs in a reception room where Kelly was to sign a statement to the effect he had not been beaten up or otherwise molested during his hours at the Sûreté.

Olga's eyes were red. Naturally, she had been weeping. "Oh, Monsieur Jack," she wailed when she saw him.

He tried to be nonchalant. In fact, the terrible sight of the dead body had already begun to recede in his memory, as ugly things have a habit of doing. "Olga, thanks for getting me out of here." Of course, she had done no more than pass along telephone messages. She had probably already informed New York of his close call. He signed the required piece of paper and was handed back his trench coat. It was not too desperately soiled except for driblets of C.T.'s blood and a few splatters of Perex's vomit. But that was enough for Olga. She put her hand over her mouth as if to cut off sickness. The cop impatiently motioned them toward the door.

"Come on, Olga, you didn't even know the guy."

"I am crying for you, stupid man."

He took her arm. She leaned on him, her eyes shining with relief. But she stopped smiling when they got down to the courtyard, for parked there in the midst of a dozen police cars was Madame Mordaunt's vintage black Rolls-Royce. A rear window purred down.

"Jacques!"

"Madame Mordaunt! What are you doing here?"

"Get in."

"This is Olga. I'd like you to meet Olga Blastorov."

"I know Olga Blastorov," Zouzou said furiously. "We have spoken on the telephone enough times today. Get in, blast you!"

They climbed into the backseat of the Rolls. He saw Victor was in the driver's seat.

"Hello, Vic," Kelly cried jovially. He was feeling so wildly relieved, he forgave Victor everything. He had never called him "Vic" to his face before.

Victor nervously put the car into gear. It jerked and stalled. Kelly laughed uproariously.

"Well, bloated one, well?" Zouzou screamed. "Drive on. Do we sit here all night, or what?"

Kelly's elation heightened as they drove out of the fortress. He was free. More than that: he was alive.

He kissed Zouzou on the cheek. "I feel wonderful now. Thank you."

She sneered at him spitefully. "You are in euphoria, Monsieur Kelly? I am not impressed. Do you think that I have never seen the brains of men spewed across the bricks?" Kelly felt Olga shake. "And you, girl? You are the daughter of the despicable Count Boris Blastorov, is it not so?"

"Despicable? Madame!" Olga protested faintly.

Christ, Kelly thought, did Zouzou Mordaunt know Boris Blastorov too? Was there no one who was a stranger to her? He felt obliged to come to Olga's aid. "Surely Count Blastorov is not a despicable man."

"All men are despicable," Zouzou retorted icily, "and if not despicable, then very *stupide*. As are you, Monsieur Kelly, for consorting with a known scoundrel."

"Which known scoundrel?" he asked wonderingly.

"All of them. *Phui!*" she shouted. "Monsieur Victor, where are we now?" They were approaching the center of the city. "When we reach the Madeleine, stop the car quickly and we will let this poor thing alight, so she can take the métro to return to her dear father."

"Madame," Kelly said coldly, "I cannot leave Miss Blastorov on a deserted corner in the middle of the night."

"*Merde*, Jacques, it is barely seven o'clock."

"No matter."

Furiously, Madame Mordaunt changed her orders. Victor would drive them all to the Maison Mordaunt. "And make haste, Monsieur Humpty-Dumpty."

When they arrived at the rue Rimbaud, Victor hurried to open the rear door. Zouzou shook his hand away when he tried to help her out. She took Olga's arm instead. Up to the penthouse, where with a sigh of relief Zouzou lowered herself into the couch.

"*Eh bien, finalement*, Jacques, do open some champagne. You know where it is." Her eyes flicked at Olga. "You there, girl. What do *you* think of Madame Mordaunt's hideaway?"

It occurred to Kelly that Zouzou looked very old. She showed the strain of the day. But she also, unquestionably, was taken by Olga Blastorov.

"It is beautiful, madame," Olga said shyly.

Zouzou nodded smugly, then said something that might ordinarily have seemed surprising. "You are a beautiful young woman. I was once enamored of a woman who looked very much like you. You must give the count, your father, my best wishes." It was very like her to be contradictory. But a near confession of a past lesbian attachment? That was laying it on the line.

Kelly filled four glasses with Mordaunt No. 10, one for Victor too who sat slumped in a chair well removed from Madame Zouzou.

"Champagne, thank God," Zouzou cried. "Sometimes I fear you will be the death of me, Jacques. Was it very terrible?" Terrible, he asked himself? He had been through the dark valley again and had come out unscathed. "Who was that man, now fortunately dead?" she demanded.

"The Sûreté thinks he was an African terrorist, a member of some weird group called the Cou-Cou Macoo."

"Dieu," she breathed in alarm. "Was he a black man?"

"No, that's what's funny. He was white."

She nodded angrily. *"Naturellement. Merde.* Now that too. *Mais oui,* the Cou-Cou Macoo are secret police recruited from an albino tribe in the densest swamps of Mangrovia, whence Grovival is harvested. He was not white, Jacques. He was an albino black man, descendant of a German pirate, called Rotbart, meaning Red Beard, who raped many Mangrovian women in the eighteenth century. . . . *Merde,* our police are so stupid."

Kelly leaned back, nodding soberly. Not a very reassuring piece of news. The opponent in this mixed-up affair was not only Aristide de Bis but a band of left-leaning African albino killers.

"Charles!" Zouzou called. She had noted the absence of her pet. There was no answer. Charles was asleep most probably, Zouzou explained. He was so old and bad-tempered, she explained to Olga. "He eats little, watches some television, sleeps again. But, *c'est la vie.* I may say Charles has been with me longer than any of my so-called lovers."

Victor startled them by gasping, almost in grief. He put a hand over his eyes and crouched miserably.

"Ach, merde," Zouzou cried irritably, *"alors and weider-mal,* again we have a weeper in our midst. Victor, I tell you: snap out of it, or fuck off!" Turning to Olga she grinned maliciously. "The world is collapsing around his head. *Dommage, hein?* Too bad. It is no more than such a swollen pederast deserves." She dredged up a spiteful chuckle, then grinned lasciviously at Olga. *"Eh bien,* cutie pie, you have perhaps much to learn, *n'est-ce pas?"*

Kelly shifted uncomfortably but Olga handled Zouzou with equanimity. "Madame, I am not a baby in the forest." She stared quite boldly at the old lady. Kelly felt more uneasy. It was possible, even necessary, to change the subject.

"Madame," he said, "you will find it fascinating that my life was saved this afternoon by none other than Monsieur Hercule."

Zouzou nodded complacently. "We will give him a very small medal then, Jacques." She lifted her hand and her bracelets sounded off like firecrackers. "I know of the whole incident. Even before I heard from Mam'selle Blastorov, *petit* Hercule was here to advise me of your predicament. I sprang into action. I contacted Aristide and I can tell you, Monsieur Kelly," she said pompously, "that Monsieur le Ministre was astounded at your foolhardiness. But appreciative too, Jacques, for Aristide is a man who honors bravery."

"So he's back in town?"

"Yes." She looked at him inquisitively. But she was not going to ask about London. Pensively, she turned to stare at Olga, to take Olga's hand in her own and stroke it. Her next words were a true revelation. "Monsieur Hercule, now, *zut alors,"* she exclaimed delightedly, "there is a man. A lovely little creature. He has the body of a doll, a perfectly formed doll." Zouzou's bosom heaved and she raised her glass on high. "A toast to the greatest of the smallest. A veritable hero of a man. Victor! Raise your glass, I say." Victor, so absorbed in his own misery, did not hear. Zouzou tossed champagne at him; it dashed against his balding pate. Victor straightened in alarm. "Top me," Zouzou shrieked, "top me to the brim with fresh champagne. Now, to Hercule, abbreviated angel. My Punch and Judy man. Yes it is true: Madame Mordaunt is in love again."

Kelly felt his mouth gape. He watched, stunned, as she quaffed almost the whole of her replenished glass. "Madame, you say that you are in love with Hercule?"

"Yes, yes, Jacques, is it not too much? Hercule will come to the Maison Mordaunt. He is to manage my entire corporation. Victor, you see, is talking of retiring again to the south of France."

"Ah, madame," Victor wept. This accounted for his suffering.

"Silence! Your protestations are to me no more than the croakings of a senescent cock."

Kelly tried to protest. "But, Madame, Hercule is my—"

She interrupted. She did not care that Hercule guarded Kelly's life. *"Merde,"* she exploded. "Whether you know it or not, Monsieur Kelly, from today you are under the protection of the House of Mordaunt, and I will yet have you as my *directeur des relations publiques,* serving *les dry martinis* to our friends of the press and otherwise. . . ."

CHAPTER

TWENTY-TWO

At his knock, this time the door swung open and there she was, Maggi, tanned and stunning, perhaps a little thinner than she had been. She stood silently for a moment, one hand on the doorknob, the other planted on her swelling hip.

"Well, Jacko," she said amusedly, "I was beginning to wonder what had happened to you. How come you didn't call until today?"

"Maggi . . ." How she twisted the truth. "I did call. I was even over here a couple of days ago. You haven't been here."

"True," she admitted, "I just got back."

Hesitantly, he asked, "How's the book coming?"

"Good, good . . . Come in, for Pete's sake." When she had closed the door, she put her arms around his waist and hugged him tight. "What's up?" she asked brightly.

Kelly snorted. "Exciting events, my dear. Car accident, then somebody tried to shotgun me and Perex and Claud Trout."

"Oh, shit," she said, "I heard about the shotgun. Come on, take off your coat. Christ, it's all filthy again. Well, at least not another duel."

"We goddamn near got killed." It had been a close call both times. "We . . ."

"We?" she asked suspiciously.

254

"Hercule and me. You don't know him. He's my driver. We got hit by a truck outside Geneva and then . . ."

"Geneva?" Her voice was perplexed. "Did you go see Perex?"

"No, no, that was a stopover on my way back from London. I was arranging my interview with Washburn. You remember."

She looked concerned and held him to her gently, put her hands under his jacket, and massaged his chest. "You sure it was an accident? Poor baby, you've gotten yourself caught in a very tangled web of intrigue, as they say."

"The shotgun thing was sure no accident," he said, "and that goddamn truck never stopped. Hercule is convinced they were trying to kill us."

"Jesuschirist," she said disgustedly, "this whole thing is getting out of hand. Somebody's going to have to put a stop to it." He asked her who was in a position to do that and she replied curtly, "Forget it." She lifted her face and smiled. "I've missed you, Jacko. Traveling, coming up here on the jet, I was so horny I couldn't sit still. This full and voluptuous bag of bones has been possessed by memories, much as I've tried to relegate them to the Past Tense."

Her typewriter was back in its place on the dusty table, where the farewell note had been.

"Did you see the note?" she asked, reading his mind.

"Of course. I was devastated. Maggi, I don't understand you."

She chuckled and pouted her lips. "Do you smell what's cooking? That's beef stroganoff. Are you hungry? Would you like to eat or slip into something more comfortable? Namely—me."

"I think I'd like to slip into you," he said.

"Good, you said the right thing. Get undressed."

She waited until he was unzipping his trousers to toss her wildly patterned at-home smock over her head. She had not changed, what a comfort, she had not changed at all. If anything, slightly trimmed down, she was more succulent than before. Her body was completely tanned, the large nipples of her breasts shadowed velvety scarlet under the brown. Her belly tilted toward him, the muscles taut at the navel and the black mount of bush and berry luscious enough to make him drool.

"The receptacle, Jacko, here it is. The receptacle of everlasting joy." She flounced into his arms, ran her fingers across his loins, palmed his belly, and shifted her legs so that his personage was between her thighs. Kelly noticed for the first time that there were marks on her shoulders, abrasions and scratches.

"Somebody's been biting on you."

She laughed disarmingly. "No, I was sunbathing and I slipped on a rock and scraped myself, Jacko."

"I see," he said stiffly for he did not necessarily believe her. "Tell me where you've been."

"On my mission, doing my research," she said warily. "You'll never guess who I ran into down south. But I won't tell you if you're going to be so prickly about it."

"Maybe I don't even want to know."

"Okay, so you won't know then. It doesn't matter anyway. You may not believe this, but I've been true to you, in my own fashion."

"Great," he said flatly. "What the hell does that mean?"

"It means what it's always meant. I do my best with you. Maybe that's unfortunate, being that you're so misunderstanding. What in the hell is wrong with you? You know that when it comes to my work, I'm not a sentimentalist. Come on, Jacko," she pleaded, "give an inch, will you?"

"And no more," he said unwillingly. No, he could not resist her.

She pulled him to the bed-couch and down beside her. But the suspicion that someone else had been with her, even in the interests of science, unmanned him. He was jealous, yes. He felt loose and weak in the stomach.

Maggi was determined to drag him out of it. Black hair swinging, she set about him with her mouth, taking him up with her full lips, all she had to do, really, to turn him back into a creature of the ever-present Present Tense. He dropped his hand on her bottom and felt the heat rising off her, something like steam exuding from her lower regions. He slipped his hand under her. Her femaleness pulsed against his fingers, her moisture slid down the fingers into the palm of his hand.

"Oh God," she whispered, "it's been much too long." Then, in such a pathetic voice that he would have forgiven her any transgression, she said, "It's not even been good doing what you have to do when you've got to do it. It's at times like that when you remember doing it when you don't have to do it, when you just want to do it for the sake of doing it."

He smiled to himself. "Give me a minute to sort that out, please."

Her mouth was so full of him he wondered that she could speak at all, let alone put together a complex aphorism. In seconds, his personage was throbbing, and seeing he was ready, Maggi crumbled beside him and yanked him on top of her. She tucked him efficiently inside and at once began a shattering sequence of maneuvers, beating her heels on the small of his back. Kelly aligned his forearms at her sides and extended his fingers to fondle her breasts, to squeeze and stroke the nipples into rigid peaks. Again he had the sensation, the Maggie-wrought sensation, of approaching the edge of a cliff, or the universe, or truth itself. He strained against her gyrating mons, trying to adapt to its contortions, to gain control, if he could, and, by the raw force of his body, to direct her wantonness. But Maggi was unpredictable in the sweep of her physical ability. Again, he was minutely conscious of her zone of the interior, the grip of the giant membranes pulling, releasing, grasping again and laboring to throttle his erection. In the end, he could not control himself as he might have wished to do, or as he could have done with Westerley, or Beatrice, or Olga, if he'd actually had her, or, horrid to think of it, Zouzou. Orgasm was wrested out of him, as with one last staccato drumming of her heels he was projected into the gallop. Maggi, an expert on timing, let herself go at the same time, venting a wild war whoop.

Their bodies subsided as darkness came down on the

litter of massacred desire. Maggi's eyes were closed but her eyelashes batted against her cheekbones. She sought his mouth and kissed him, tongue overlaying his. Then, dropping her head to the side, she muttered, "Don't retract, Jacko. Stay inside, in that place of mystery where lovers finally are well met, where the tall forests whisper, swamps wash with sticky scum, misty meadows suck life from trickly streams . . ."

"Maggi, I think you've been writing poetry."

"Yes." Her lips curled with satisfaction. "Couplets to our coupling. Sonnets to our screwing. Epic poems . . . what? Never mind. I wish I could carry that disfigured thing of yours around inside me all day long."

"Get a couple of those little stainless steel balls they sell in Japan . . ."

"Miserable, unpoetic clod," she said happily. "Now, let's relax and see if we can climb Mount Sublime again. Do you remember?"

"Could I forget? It changed my life."

They arranged themselves in a less numbing position and Kelly eased himself toward passivity. But he had a last question.

"I've really been wondering. Do you do some kind of part-time work for the government?"

Her body tensed. "Why do you ask?"

"Well, you're always talking about a mission. People who go on missions ordinarily do them for somebody or other."

She stretched her body against him. Her reply was straightforward. "Whatever I do, and I won't tell you what it is, I'd rather be with you. Say you want me, Jacko."

"I do." He thought that he did. Yes, he did. Maggi was best of all.

"A good reply," she said comfortably, "for two characters like us who love to make love. Now, do you take this receptacle to be your receptacle forever and ever?"

"I do."

"All right then. Shut up and kindly allow the force to take over."

"Amen." It seemed that his pledge was enough to seal the success of their ascent of Mount Sublime. They were to make themselves ready, she murmured, for the force of universality to envelop them, in fact to requisition their bodies for its own purposes. Gladly. It was, he thought, as if he were burrowing into rich, rich earth, floating in a pool of fecundity or sprouting wings in some supercharged solution of inchoate fertility from which heaven and earth had sprung. Was this the stuff of creation then, this bubbling, gaseous reservoir of juice and static electricity? There had to be a jolt of power in there somewhere to bring the monster to life. And, indeed, Kelly felt his personage, like a lightning rod, absorb low voltage, to ache thunderingly as the heavens must have, if you believed in the Big Bang theory of the birth of the universe. His impulse was to let fly without delay into Maggi's quivering body, to obliterate everything that stood in the way of simple fulfillment. But he managed to rest quietly within her magnetic field, this holding him, indeed, like the universal fist. Her grip seemed to find its strength from every corner of the room, from every *arrondissement* of the city of Paris, and to draw power from the earth below and the sky above. This did not begin or end, he understood devoutly, where they were joined. It reached far beyond them to the unknown. Infinity was in between.

Maggi's mouth had fallen open and for a second he marveled at the mystery of the gods who had created this lovely thing. Her face was vacant of recognizable expression and a strange voice began to speak through her lips. Was this possible? He knew, with that part of him still capable of knowing, that she had passed into a trance, that the universal force had taken over.

"You, you." He did not know this voice. It sputtered words he had never heard, perhaps from some prehistoric language. "Inside . . . outside . . . within . . . without."

Kelly knew nothing made any sense but he didn't care. Her body began to shake convulsively. She was possessed. Inside her, yet another complex being was speaking. Kelly felt it, a presence, babbling an unknown dialect but clearly enticing him to explode and form a new unit of the universe, one uncontrolled by human reason or the conventions of passion. Was this what Doctor Faustus had understood to be the reverse of Truth?

Tiny hands invited him to join in the great adventure. He felt his body sliding away from him. He too was being drawn into nothingness and, unwillingly, he succumbed. At once he became conscious, in reward, of huge pulsations, of surf crashing on the rocks of unformed continents, a chill wind blowing through a primitive atmosphere, of rippling land masses as flatland and mountain ranges were determined, rocks flying off toward the sun as gravity faltered, of blazing sun, burgeoning stars, a quaking moon.

The detonation arrived unexpectedly, unbidden, and reverberated. A savage scream, triumphant cry, which might have been uttered by the gods or devils, broke from inside Maggi's chest. It was more than mere climax, or orgasm. It was fusion and fission at one and the same time. The heat of it, he supposed desperately, had welded them together like Shakespeare's two-backed creature. Darkness, twilight, dawn, swept across his face.

Maggi came back more slowly. "What the hell happened, Jacko? There must be something wrong with me. I was out like a light. Jesus, the power of this man's nuts."

"Remember the time," he said. He looked at his watch. "It's eight-thirty. Remember that."

"What the hell for?" she demanded, sounding like herself again.

"Because I think one or the other, or both of us, have made some kind of a pact with the devil." He was not sure this was not so.

"You're crackers," she cried disgustedly. "Eight-thirty? Jesus, you've got to get the hell out of here. Holy shit! Jacko, I'm expecting . . ."

Dryly, he said, "I wouldn't be surprised, after that."

"Idiot!" But she patted his face. "Come on. I've got

to go out. Promise you won't ask where. You've got to leave. No arguments."

"You go out," he said. "I'll stay here and wait for you."

"No, goddamn it." She got out of bed and faced him, not realizing her thighs were still shaking. "C'mon! Go wash and get dressed. I've got to take a shower."

"Where are you going? I want to know. You've got to tell me."

"I don't have to tell you anything. I've got an important meeting."

"Who with?"

She was annoyed. "Never mind. Why do you want to know? There are things it's better for you not to know. Didn't you ever hear about the right *not* to know." She wiped her hands across her bare stomach, like a butcher in the nude, yes, the butcher of his equilibrium.

"All right," he said humbly, "I'll go."

"Call me tomorrow. I want to see you tomorrow."

"I don't know," he said dully. "I've got to go out to the airport. My old man's coming in."

"He's coming to town? You didn't say. I'd like to meet him sometime."

"Maybe you will, if you're around," he said, too nastily. "He's coming to check out all the shit that's happened. I don't know what I'm going to do . . . I may bail out of this can of worms."

Maggi began to cry. She sat on the edge of her writing table and openly cried. "Leave me, huh? You son of a bitch, you don't understand, do you?"

He couldn't reply. He shambled into the bathroom and splashed water on his unraveled parts. When he was finished, she had stopped sobbing. She was still sitting there, though, staring at the wall. "Maggi . . ." He grabbed her, lifted her and buried his face between her breasts.

"Come on, you." She struggled against him. "Let me down, or I'll kick you in the balls."

There was no use arguing with her. She went limp

and he let her down. Without a word, she marched to the shower. He got dressed.

"I'm leaving," he called miserably.

She came out in a towel. "Okay, hit the road. If you don't want to call me, then don't. If you don't want me to meet your old man, that's fine too." Implacably, she stared him down. "Just be careful. No more accidents."

Kelly knew what he had to do. He could not help himself. He left the building, walking in a slouch, buried in his trench coat. He went a block until he was out of view of her window, stopped and crossed the street. He came back and slid into the shadow of a doorway opposite the entrance, carefully lit a cigarette, and settled down to spy on her.

He had not long to wait. In no more than fifteen minutes, a long gray limousine pulled up. Its horn sounded once and a chauffeur got out, circling, to stand on the curb by the rear door. A light blipped on in the hallway and in a moment, silhouetted, Maggi appeared at the top of the steps. She was elegantly dressed, he could see, in high heels and a fur coat over a clinging black dress. In the brief time it took her to get from steps into the car, he observed she had pulled her black hair back and fastened it behind her ears, gypsy style. For all the world, she looked like a call girl going off to a rendezvous. His heart tumbled into his shoes.

The car sped silently away. He could not read the license plate but there were official-looking decals on the back bumper and stanchions on each front fender from which diplomatic flags would fly.

CHAPTER

TWENTY-THREE

For Hercule, Kelly realized, the Maison Mordaunt was a great opportunity, a way for the rootless little Corsican to secure his future. He could not object to Hercule's leaving him. After all, the little man had saved his life, twice that he was aware of, and had promised to watch over him still as best he could when free of the scaly comforts of the Maison Mordaunt. But Kelly was disillusioned to a small extent: he had not conceived of Hercule as a fortune hunter.

"Well, Hercule," he said conversationally on the way to Charles de Gaulle Airport, "I guess this is our last ride together."

Hercule nodded abruptly. He would not be emotional about good-byes.

"God, Hercule," Kelly said, as they progressed through the evening traffic, "what a dark and noisome place is the world of espionage, that trading company of bodies and souls."

"*Oui*," Hercule said.

Kelly fell to thinking about Maggi. He did not know it for a fact, but he was sure she had now succeeded in meeting Aristide de Bis. How had *she* come from the harmless business of writing sex manuals to this joyless work? The compromising of Aristide de Bis would be a far more dangerous job than the surveillance of Jack Kelly.

There had been a bomb scare at Charles de Gaulle, something to do with the Basque separatist. Police were everywhere, but showing his press credentials, Kelly was able to get inside after submitting to a body search.

Harry Kelly was waiting for him in the TWA VIP lounge. He was sitting in a cushioned corner as if he'd been there an hour or two, twisting a martini glass in his fingers.

Harry was a little taller than his son, broader at the shoulder and now, in middle age, beefier around chest and waist. At Yale, Harry had gone out for football and the weightier track-and-field events while Kelly had contented himself with the less competitive gymnastic categories of jockstrapping. Harry was wearing his usual uniform—a gray, vested suit, white collar, club tie, and a broad-brimmed Borsalino hat—the latter still very much in style at the *RAG* and elsewhere at Kelly Communications, despite its decline in the outside world. Harry's face was what people described as very Irish, wry and high-colored. Harry drank just enough gin and good whiskey to keep it that way from season to season. People sometimes assumed Harry was a yachtsman. He was not.

Swinging his trench coat on one arm, Kelly walked toward him. How distant their relationship had become; yet, he thought, they remained close, despite all the sound and fury. He understood the old man and he saw at once that Harry was very displeased with him.

"Sit down, Jack."

"How are you?" Kelly was determined not to be browbeaten, not like the old Jack Kelly.

"Fine," Harry said sarcastically. "Great to have to fly over here to see your kid is still in one piece."

Kelly chuckled nonchalantly. "I ducked. You always told me to remember to duck. Remember?"

"You ducked? They were after that scum Trout. I'm referring to the fact you might have got plugged by mistake."

Harry's cold blue eyes ate at him like driblets of acid. The old man already had the drop on him. According to theory, and practice in the *RAG* newsroom, Kelly was now supposed to break into a cold sweat.

He shrugged. "Whatever . . . I wasn't scratched."

"Very cool, aren't you?" Then Harry let him have it. "You lousy little bastard. What the hell do you mean by traveling with that no-good Trout? Are you deliberately trying to blacken my name?"

Kelly felt his face burn red. Fortunately, a waiter strolled over and Harry took time off to order *two* double martinis. Did that mean Harry had finally certified him as grown-up?

"I'm working for Trout," Kelly said defiantly.

"I know that! You call that thing a newspaper? It used to be owned by the CIA, maybe still is."

"Well, it's a newspaper, goddamn it. I needed a job someplace. I'm not working for that fucking *RAG* of yours anymore, you know."

Christ, insubordination! It was as if he'd dropped a hand grenade between them. For a second, it seemed Harry might reach across the table and backhand him. But instead, he drew a deep breath. His eyes became troubled and he quickly reached into a vest pocket for a pill which he popped in his mouth and swallowed with the dregs of his martini.

"All right," Harry said slowly, "maybe I had that coming."

"I'm sorry," Kelly said. "Are you okay?"

"I'm okay," Harry said shortly. "But tell me, little man, just what is it you're going to do for Claud Trout?"

"I'm interviewing Washburn when he comes for NATO."

Harry cocked a mocking eye at him. "What you mean is they've bought you off. They got scared when you wrote that cosmetics story, the thing you started and never finished."

"It died on the vine. . . ."

"You should have pushed for more. We needed better confirmation. We could have gone after that bastard Washburn with a vengeance. Although it doesn't matter much. He's going to be out in a couple of years. He'll never get his amendment through. People are fed up with him. He's messed up everything, from the economy to foreign policy."

"Tom Topovsky told me in Geneva there's nothing to the amendment story anyway."

"Topovsky is a goddamn liar," Harry growled.

"Maybe . . . Anyway, if you're interested I've got Mangrovia nailed down tight now. You know what's involved, don't you? The French and the Washburn bunch both want that drug, Grovival—"

Harry cut him off with a snort of laughter. "I read your story. What bullshit! There's some cockeyed yarn every year about a new sex rejuvenation drug."

Kelly smiled cleverly. For he had the information in his pocket. "Maybe so, boss, but right now—that is, a week ago, Topovsky himself was trying it out in a Swiss clinic AmFreight controls outside Geneva. If it doesn't pop his buttons, the plan is for Washburn to stop there when he's in Europe. It's a three-day treatment."

Harry's eyes flared cynically. "Bullshit. How do you know that?"

"I was there. I saw Topovsky on the table having it done."

"Holy Christ." Harry grunted. "Can I believe that?" He whistled. "What will these presidents of ours get up to next? Are you kidding me?"

"No, no," Kelly said urgently. He'd already forgotten his ethical allegiance to the *Appalachian Times,* so eager was he to impress the old man. "The point is the patient is out of circulation; he's practically unconscious for three whole days. That means Washburn would give up command of the ship while he gets his glands jazzed up. Think of the implications."

Harry sipped luxuriously at his fresh martini. His eyes sparkled. Kelly knew then he was on to a big one. Harry nodded, too ponderously, and he realized that the old man was slowing down, like a car coming off the high-speed straightaway. A distant look came into Harry's eyes as he thought of the fallout from such a story, the media explosion it would set off: the denials, the threats, the subpoenas. But again Harry shook his head.

"Listen, I don't want to be responsible for bringing down another of our great presidents. I felt bad enough about the last one."

"What about the amendment?"

"No, there's no way they can get that through in time. But if it looks like it, then we'd go after Washburn with hammer and tongs. Look at it this way—if we ran your story now, Washburn would only change his plans and call us a bunch of troublemaking sensationalists. And even if he does go to that place, how could we confirm it? You'd have to see him going into the clinic and you'd have to be in the room with him. You'd need affidavits from a dozen people saying he actually got injected with the stuff."

"We could try for that. . . ."

"You wouldn't get near the place," Harry growled. "Besides . . . the whole thing is nuts. I doubt anybody would believe it even if you did have affidavits. All this commotion over a goddamn drug? You sure there isn't something else involved—uranium, gold . . . oil?"

"No," Kelly said hastily. "It's become . . . like a *cause célèbre*. It's a matter of French honor. And you should hear Trout talk. We're ready to buy Mangrovia, or invade it. Trout says the Washburn boys are deathly afraid the Chinese will get their hands on Grovival and set off a population explosion. Same with the Russians."

Harry shook his head, ticking off his scepticism. "I still can't buy it, not entirely."

"Then why should somebody try to kill us on the road from Geneva?"

Harry's eyes widened. "There too? Son of a bitch! Who?"

"I don't know. A truck tried to run us down. Then the shotgun . . ."

"I told you they were after Trout."

"Trout wasn't in the car coming from Geneva."

Harry looked more worried. "Maybe you should get the hell out of here."

"No. I can't now."

"And you're going to work for Trout?" Harry asked sorrowfully.

"That's my entrée into the mess. See what I mean?"

Harry signaled for the waiter again. "How much is he paying you?"

"Better than you ever did," Kelly muttered. This was not quite so. All he'd had so far was the advance. He hadn't any idea what size his paycheck would be.

Harry leaned back and nudged the brim of his Borsalino with his thumb.

"You're really something," he said sardonically. "My own son talking to me like that. Your career has had its ups and downs lately, hasn't it? Makes my blood run cold, sonny boy. That business at Zouzou's, the duel, a truck trying to run you down, shotgun pellets whistling around your head. Who?"

"A member of the Mangrovian Secret Police. An albino from the Cou-Cou Macoo," Kelly said flatly.

Harry's face strained. "An *albino* from the *Cou-Cou Macoo*," he repeated. "I think somebody is coo-coo macoo. I'm trying very hard, believe me, to suspend my disbelief."

"I know the whole thing sounds nutty. But they tell me Grovival is the greatest thing as a perfume ingredient since whale puke."

Harry grimaced. "Truth is stranger than fiction. I could see the cosmetic monsters fighting over it—but they don't have armies. Or do they? I hope you're not just being used by all these bastards, Jack."

Kelly nodded smugly. "That's the thing—*both* sides think they're using me. That's the beauty of it. The info comes pouring in. Aristide de Bis . . ."

"I know that son of a bitch," Harry interrupted.

"He's using me to pass along threats. . . . Topovsky is using me to scare off Aristide de Bis."

Harry looked wearily at him. "Jack, you're in the middle of the goddamndest barrel of red herrings I ever heard of. So, okay—stay with it." He smiled frostily. "Your replacement for the *RAG* office will be over here in a couple of weeks. We picked him carefully, a man with good experience. Knows his fashion, he's okay on people pieces, and he loves gossip and scandal. In short, he sounds just like you."

"I suppose he's going to make a lot more money than I ever did."

"He's got a lot more experience than you did when you came over to Paris," Harry said gently. "And remember, I pay what I want. I don't go by precedents. His name is Maurice Moody."

"I'll fix it so he doesn't get in the front door at Mordaunt."

"Don't kid me. Zouzou will love him." Harry chuckled. "By the way, how is the old tramp?"

"Tramp?" Mention of Zouzou's name made him faintly uneasy.

Harry chuckled fondly. "Didn't you ever hear her story? She was working the dance halls before the war—I mean the First World War. They say that's where she got her start . . . well, you know, goddamn it."

"You're such a gentleman," Jack observed.

"Well, yes I am, Jack. They used to say Zouzou Mordaunt was so patriotic she took on Marshal Foch's whole army. There was even a World War I song about her. I got to know her in the thirties when my old man, your grandfather, sent me over here to learn the ropes." Jack felt himself blush. What was his father suggesting? "Listen, Jack, I was single then, remember."

"And I suppose *your* father made a couple of trips to Paris?"

Harry's face stiffened. "Jack, are you suggesting my father had something to do with Zouzou Mordaunt?"

"Well," Kelly said bravely, "mine did."

Harry burst into laughter, appreciating the irony. "I was young. Anyway, I can assure you that *my* old man never made the trip to Paris, Jack. Not that I'm aware of anyway, although I suppose it's possible. Too bad for him too, come to think of it. Zouzou must have been marvelous way back then. She was still damn good in the thirties. I don't remember seeing her during World War II. I should have looked her up."

"She's still an outstanding woman," Kelly said daringly.

It was too outlandish a thing for Harry to conceive that three generations of Kellys had quite possibly. . . . Anyway, Jack, of course, would have denied it. Harry looked at his watch.

"My plane back is at nine P.M. We've got time for a couple of more. I am happy to see you alive and kicking."

"You mean you're not staying?" The truth dawned on him. "You flew all the way over here just to see me for a couple of hours? Dad . . ." Christ, that hit hard. He choked up.

"Goddamn it, Jack, you do happen to be my only son. If you ever have one of your own, you'll know it cuts a little ice to be an only son. If I had two or three of you, it might be a different story."

Harry waved for a waiter and ordered the same again.

"I saw your wife in New York, by the way," he said abruptly. "About a month ago, I guess. On the run. She told me you're finished, you two." Harry frowned. He did not want to hurt his son's feelings, Kelly realized. "You're well out of that, in my opinion. I've always thought she was a crazy, just like her old man."

"I don't give a damn."

"Okay then," Harry said. "She told me she was going to divorce you, for mental cruelty. At least not for adultery. She was on her way to Haiti, or somewhere. You weren't married in the church anyway," Harry observed with satisfaction. "Just remember, when you do it in the church, you better make damn sure it's going to stick. . . . Let me give you a little advice. Don't worry too much about what women say or do. And, for Christ's sake, don't ever feel sorry for them. Any one woman is tougher than five men. Tell me, does that Maryjane take some kind of dope? I hardly recognized her."

Kelly grinned. "What? A different nose? Little bigger in the . . ." He modeled a bosom with his hands. "She's supposed to have gotten herself retouched at that same damn clinic. I know she smokes grass. I wouldn't be too surprised to hear she'd graduated to coke or something, the opium of the privileged classes."

"Martinis are a hell of a lot cheaper," Harry commented sagely.

Kelly debated whether to tell Harry about Maryjane's teenaged boff with George Washburn. No, the old man was still very shockable. Should he mention Westerley Washburn? No. He thought instead of something that might amuse his father.

"They tell me Grovival . . . a doctor at the clinic admitted it has some strange side effects. For one thing, it causes an awful lot of uncontrolled farting."

Harry guffawed. "I have to tell you I can't really believe half of this stuff you're telling me. But . . ." A follow-up idea occurred to him. "If so, why are they worried about the Russians or Chinese getting it? It'd be a hell of an early-warning system. Can't you just see the great armies advancing through the night letting divisional-sized farts? No, no, I can't believe any of this." His eyes grew cautious. "Tell me, with that nutty wife gone, are you seeing any interesting . . . action?"

"You mean action in the sense of—"

"Sexual sense, for Christ's sake. Do I have to spell out everything?"

Pleased to be able to tell him this, Kelly muttered, "Well, there is a certain lady of the French nobility."

"Good. Good." Harry grinned conspiratorially. "I wouldn't want my kid to be involved with a mere commoner. A good looker?"

"A knockout." He thought that was how Harry's generation would have described Beatrice de Beaupeau. "Dad, come on, what about hanging around a couple of days?"

Harry lifted his hand like a traffic cop. "Nah, Jack, I've gotta get home. It'd be fun though. I'll be back, maybe sooner than you think. They tell me I should take it a little easier now."

There was something in his expression that moved Kelly. "We don't always have to argue about news stories, Dad."

"No, of course not," Harry said. "But there is one thing I want to ask you—why did that bastard de Bis use you to leak the Mangrovia story? Why not the *New York Times?* I've heard their correspondent here will fall for anything."

"Because I'm close to Zouzou. And I didn't just fall for it, you know."

"Okay, okay. I'm not knocking you. Who do you think actually killed that man Igl, then Maxim? Don't say the Coo-Coo Macoo, please."

"I figure it's the French and they'll try to pin it on the Mangrovians. The French are simply not going to stand still for Washburn."

Harry picked at his teeth with his thumbnail. "Jack, it's really *weird.* I mean we all expect to have trouble with our enemies. But when we start having trouble with our friends, well, need I say more?" He pulled his Borsalino back down on his forehead. "If we could pin it down better, that'd be good."

"Yes, okay—but, remember, I don't work for you anymore."

"Don't give me that malarkey! I'd like to have the whole story in the house—just in case. Suppose there is an invasion of Mangrovia. God! Don't tell me we're going to set out to get our asses burned in the tropics again." Harry grunted sadly. "No reason why you should discuss any of this with Moody when he gets here. Just put it all together. I'll keep banking your money in New York."

"I'm back on the payroll?" Kelly brightened. He had not, after all, been forsaken. "Since I'm forgiven—"

"Who says you're forgiven?" Harry demanded. "Some of those stunts of yours . . ."

He was embarrassed. The old man was right. "I don't know—it just seems like I got mousetrapped. . . . What I wasn't going to tell you was that I got to know Washburn's daughter when I was up in Geneva."

"Holy Christ—more yet." Harry groaned. "Frying pan into the fire."

"She's not a bad woman."

"Shit! She's Topovsky's girl friend, isn't she?"

Kelly shook his head. "Not exactly. She doesn't like him much."

Harry was confused. "What are you trying to say?"

"Straight to the source, Dad. I got a lot of dope out of her."

A smile spread across Harry's face. "Well, well . . . don't tell Moody any of this. Nothing."

"So you won't be compromised if anything goes wrong. Right?"

Harry didn't reply. He polished off his martini and drummed his fingers on the tabletop. The hands were heavily veined and speckled with telltale liver spots. But Harry's eyes were still all right, Kelly judged. They were lively and direct, not rheumy and red-lidded like those of the usual heavy, middle-aged drinker.

"Are you taking care of yourself?"

Harry scowled. "Yes, I am, to the best of my ability, to the best of my needs."

One of their problems, Kelly thought, was that they'd always lacked a woman to mediate, to interpret, to translate for them.

"I know one thing," he said, "you're going to have double jet lag by the time you get back to New York. Why don't you stay over for a couple of days? No kidding, why don't you? I'll get you a date."

Harry chuckled moistly. "That's what I don't need. No, I told you, I've got a bunch of newspapers to run. . . . What have you got available?"

"All sizes and shapes," he said lightly.

Harry smiled, almost affectionately. It was phenomenal, Kelly thought, outstanding. They had never been as close as they were right now. He felt a wet knot in his throat. Covering it up, he asked, "How's that bastard, Court?"

"I'll tell him you asked after him," Harry said sarcastically. "One of my oldest hands, Jack."

"Yeah, I know."

"Jack, just remember this." Harry pointed at him for emphasis. "A friend of my friend is my friend. An enemy

of my enemy is my friend, and so on—you know how
that goes. Court is a loyal friend. Always remember
that."

"That hasn't always been your rule. What about the
guy I'm named after? Jack . . ."

Harry compressed his lips and stared down at the
table. "Okay, I've made mistakes too. I kicked Jack's ass
out because he was getting drunk all the time. I thought
it was for his own good. It was a mistake, because he
turned around and died, one of my oldest pals. I hope
he forgives me, wherever he is. . . ." Harry's voice
trailed away, then returned strongly. "Don't think you're
not going to make any mistakes, because you'll be
making them every day."

Harry's startling blue eyes bit like pieces of metal.
Seeing him vulnerable, Kelly was apologetic. "I'm sorry
I mentioned it. I'm sorry I've been such a pain in the
ass."

"Hell." Harry dismissed his contrition. "I don't expect
you to crawl. I don't care if you're a pain in the ass.
Everybody's entitled to that. Just try to be a loyal pain in
the ass."

"All right, you can count on me. I'll do my best."

"Good." Harry lowered his eyes again. "That's good
for you to say."

The substance of the conversation was beginning to
bother both of them. The old man was being uncharacteristically soft.

"Let's not get maudlin, kid," Harry said gruffly. "You
can take off now, if you want to. You've probably got to
meet that girl. Yeah? Good luck. I'm sorry I can't stay
over a couple of days. But there'll be another shot at
that. Maybe Christmastime. Or maybe you'll be back in
New York. Don't forget to get that story together. If you
do, we might have to pull you out of here for your own
safety." Harry grinned. "So long now. I'll be seeing
you."

"Come on," Kelly protested. "I've got nothing to do.
I'll stick around 'till the plane leaves."

"No, go on," Harry insisted. "I'm going to have another

drink and I don't feel like talking anymore. I don't mind being alone. I kind of look forward to being alone sometimes these days."

Kelly was shocked. What had happened to Harry's old gregariousness? It occurred to him, painfully, that Harry was a lonely man. The impulsive plane trip in and out of Paris? In the old days, any worry he might have had for Jack's well-being would have been settled quickly by a terse phone call.

"No," Kelly said determinedly, "I better put you on the plane. You'll fall on your ass from all those martinis."

"Are you kidding? You know it's an insult to doubt a man's capacity. I want you to leave. We've covered our agenda. . . . Except for money. Do you need any money? Like right now?"

"No, Christ, no."

"Then twenty-three skidoo. I hate good-byes."

Kelly knew when to quit. He stood up regretfully, unwound his trench coat from the back of his chair, and slung it over his shoulder. The sight of the soiled garment was enough to make Harry get tough again; it was a diversion from farewell.

"Holy Christ! What is that thing? Jack, you better retire that coat."

"No, I love it. Look . . ." He pointed at the bloodstains. "There's the true blood of your great good friend, Claud "C.T." Trout."

Harry scowled. "Burn it. Here . . ."

He tossed a bundle of French franc notes on the table. "Take the money and buy yourself a new coat at least. I don't care if you starve to death, but do it in a new coat."

Kelly knew he could not disagree. He picked up the money and shoved it in his pants pocket.

"And listen," Harry growled, "try to be more careful." He waved him away, shoving out his hand brusquely for Kelly to shake. Harry held his hand and his son realized Harry would not object if he kissed him. Wavering a moment, he did so.

CHAPTER

TWENTY-FOUR

As October turns toward November in Europe, there is an inevitable period of seasonal hiatus, an indefinable few weeks when it is as if nothing has been decided about the weather one way or the other. Autumn is running down and winter lags cautiously behind. Bastille Day is long since past, but it is too early to be thinking about Christmas. The waiting game seemed much more trying this year.

Kelly was waiting: waiting for Washburn, waiting for Topovsky, and for Westerley Washburn to show up in Paris. He was trying to piece together in his mind the tangled AmFreight and Grovival story. There was nothing but bits and pieces of information, his own conjectures, and a few rumors. He endeavored to speak again with Inspector Marcel Gaston (or was it Gaston Marcel?) at the Sûreté, but the police had put the lid on the Coo-Coo Macoo story. Zouzou Mordaunt was not her usual, chatty self, being far more occupied now with Hercule, who had moved in with her at the Maison Mordaunt. At any mention he made of Beatrice de Beaupeau, Zouzou became fiercely annoyed. All she would talk about was when he was coming to work for her at the Maison Mordaunt. Once, they quarreled and she ordered him out of the penthouse.

Kelly lay on his couch, thinking it over, taking a *soupçon* of Pernod and water. Maggi? He'd called and called again; there was no answer at her flat. Harry Kelly? Kelly felt sad and mournful when he thought of his old man.

Blackly, he contemplated the past and the future. It was a gloomy time. Storm clouds had gathered. Was the world into that perilous hour of dusk before darkness? Was war really in the offing? If not over the highly suspect drug, Grovival, then something else? Perex called Grovival more strategically vital than oil: oil simply ran machines while Grovival would twist men's souls. In the wrong hands, Perex said, Grovival would be a more threatening weapon than anthrax bacteria. Imagine the teeming, farting masses breeding like rats. Population soars and global food war breaks out. Genocide grips the earth and still they breed, forced on by this beaten and boiled vegetable root from Mangrovia. And why? Because President George Washburn wants an aphrodisiac, Zouzou Mordaunt a powerful new ingredient for her cosmetics, and Aristide de Bis to rebuild the glory of the French nation. Meanwhile, the world quakes with flatulence. . . .

Perhaps that was stretching the point. But world crises had often been set off by unlikely events. What if there were to be a war between America and its ancient ally, *la belle France,* for control of a drug? Was that any more unlikely than a war over Jenkin's ear or rebellion in Ireland over the colors orange and green, or civil war in America because of a Mason-Dixon line on a map? It was unthinkable, ridiculous . . . yet possible.

And, he thought sourly, he was not ready. His trench coat was back in the shop.

Whatever the silly potential, it was obvious that relations between Washington and Paris were on "hold." The French press was still talking angrily about *L'Affaire Igl, L'Affaire Maxwell Maxim,* making much of an intriguing linkage between the Washburn-family conglomerate, AmFreight, and American political ambitions in West Africa and sneering over such evidence of corruption among the mighty. That morning in the Paris *Trib,* Don Cook had written a doom-haunted think piece: the assassinations of Igl, Maxim, and the attempted murder of presidential adviser Claud Trout had caused everyone in both capitals to pause and draw a worried breath. Yes, Cook said, there was talk now of calling off the Washburn mission of reconciliation.

If this happened, Kelly realized, he might well wind up working for Zouzou Mordaunt, crueler than all the Medicis, more wanton than a Pompadour, more feudal than the Romanoffs. At the Maison Mordaunt he would remain close to the story; but he was depressed by the prospect.

The phone rang, interrupting his brooding.

"Hello, you bugger!"

"Westerley! I was just thinking about you," he lied.

"Tom and I got in last night," she reported. "We're behind schedule. His work in Switzerland took longer than he expected. Then he had an attack of intestinal flu. What are you doing for lunch?"

"Meeting you, I hope."

"You've got a date," she said. "I've got nothing to do until five. We're going to a cocktail party at Ambassador Capone's. Come over."

"I'll be there in a half hour," he sang out. Seeing her again would at least break the monotony of waiting.

Westerley was still in a blue jogging suit. "Been out this morning running," she said. "Ran around the Tuileries garden, across the bridge to the Left Bank—even though Topovsky doesn't like to see me anywhere to the left."

"You look marvelous," he said.

Topovsky, she explained, had come down with a bad case of the Swiss diarrhea and now, of course, the whole matter of arrangements for the presidential tour had been hopelessly complicated by the attempt on Trout's life. "Poor baby," she said, "you were there too."

"And Rafe. It was a close call."

"And C.T. shot the gunman. Wow!"

Westerley put her arms around his waist and kissed him lightly on the cheek, then the mouth. He tasted the lingering salty sweat of her morning workout. "Let's have lunch right here," she said. "It'll be okay. Topovsky is with the foreign minister and half the French cabinet, I gather. Who cares a goddamn anyway? It's good to touch you again, Jack."

"You feel good too."

"Ummm," she murmured. "Topovsky's been such a pain in the ass these last few days, really off his feed."

Kelly hesitated, not knowing what or how much to say. Was the Grovival having such a bad effect on him? Should he warn Westerley? Best not. He kissed her briny lips, then the flesh under her chin.

"Gosh, Jack, oh, gosh." As was her habit, Westerley's eyes remained watchfully open as desire built. He moved his hands across the fabric of her jogging gear, feeling her buttocks tighten. Under the top of her suit, her back was warm and still moist with perspiration. Her brassiere was already open. "My jogging bra," she muttered. "It busted in the Tuileries. My tits were bouncing like a set of tennis balls."

He advanced his hands to her ribs, gathering her breasts up and squeezing them gently. The nipples rose. "Seem all right to me," he murmured. "The complete woman."

"Except for one thing and that's what I want." Her eyes became very serious. He pulled the drawstring of her sweat pants, and they dropped to the floor. She gasped with approval. All her blondness was revealed south of the navel. She was bare-assed, of course. Women had no need to wear anything under their sweat pants. Her cheeks drew in, as he ran his thumb caressingly along the fleshy indentation. "Jack," she said, "would you mind very much taking off your splendid duds?"

By the time he had undressed, carefully folding his pants at the crease and hanging his freshly laundered shirt and underwear over the back of a chair, Westerley was breathless.

"Should I take a shower?"

"No," he said, "I like 'em sweaty."

He was hard now. He thrust his personage between her legs, against the rosy lips of her pube, bending his knees a little to accommodate the movement. Slowly, she wove a pattern with her hips, clasping him between her thighs. "Cocky feels good," she said. She wasn't worried about Topovsky but, nonetheless, the situation was not unprecarious. Her finishing-school lust won out.

"Westerly, I've been needing this."

She responded with a look of gluey passion. "You missed me! Shall we do it? I have an idea about doing it with Topovsky's attaché case under my ass."

"Doesn't he have it with him?" And if he didn't, then he might be back any minute to pick it up.

"Topovsky's got attaché cases within attaché cases," she said. "I'd like to leave a big come mark on it, tell him it was mayonnaise."

"First, please, on the bed for a change. Is *this* place bugged?"

She shook her head, telling him, no, the Frenchies were in control here. She sat down on the edge of the bed, sparse patch of blond hair scarcely covering the split of her center. The tattoo puckered in her seated posture.

"You're not really the property of the U.S. government." She shook her head, smiling. "You could have that taken off."

"Why? It's my souvenir of the White House years. But Jack, F-word it, are you going to stand there, forever staring, or what?"

He dropped on his knees before her and did what he had done so well in Geneva. He tongued the property sign, and as before, it worked like a release mechanism: her hatches flew open, gears engaged, and desire's wings began to flap wildly.

"Wow!"

Kelly worked his lips to her pube, tasting the pungence of her morning's exercise.

"Wow! Jack! Do you want me to . . .? Shall we? You know . . ."

"*Soixante-neuf?*"

"Around the world," she corrected him. "What about the attaché case?"

"Later."

"Jack, would it be too much to ask . . ."

He lifted himself so she could reach him. She fondled his personage for a moment, shyly running her fingers along the scar, then pushed him down and eased him inside her. Very slowly he entered to her long exhalation of breath and made snug contact. Her hips ground down. She clasped him behind with her legs and rocked. It was only seconds before she climaxed.

"Birdie," she cried hoarsely.

"Fore," Kelly replied, not holding back.

"Wow! Gosh, I guess we both needed that, Jack. We really got it off fast there."

He rested beside her, handling her left breast, fingers playing with the nipple.

"Gosh, Jack, why *don't* you come back to Washington? Or New York? If you were in New York, we could see a lot of each other. Hell, and we're leaving tomorrow."

Her face was sorrowful. She stared glumly at the ceiling, then at him.

"You wouldn't be satisfied with a mere affair," he said.

"It could be more permanent if you wanted. I mean, if we wanted to, we could easily enough. I can do whatever I want." She put her hands to his face and absently stroked.

"Well," he said vaguely, "we'll see what happens."

"Shall we go to the showers?"

"No, I want to wallow." He slid down her belly, mouthed her solar plexus, then covered his face in the spent juices of their mating. In a thrice, Westerley was straining again.

"I want . . . I want to do it that illegal way again, Jack."

"Westerley, it's not illegal. I explained that."

"Whatever it is," she moaned, "get off a minute." He released her and she knelt beside the bed, presenting herself to him as primates do in submission, haunches high and her hands clasped on the floor. He entered her from behind, pulling her back with his hands at her stomach so that the penetration was total. "You know," she whispered excitedly, "if you came down to Washington once in a while. . . . What would you say to having a screw at the Supreme Court or maybe the Pentagon?"

"What about your father's desk in the Oval Office?"

Now that would be a true expression of defiance, a real kick in the ass of authority.

She giggled. "We could do it when he goes to Japan."

"He's going to Japan? What about Europe?"

"No," she said, biting off the word with a choke of ecstasy. "He's giving up on these yokels over here. The new focus of the alliance is going to be the Far East. Besides . . ." She groaned softly. "Besides, he's heard about the wondrous power of the geisha."

Kelly chuckled and kissed her between the shoulder blades. Another piece of ill-gotten information. "Your old man is quite a boy-o."

"God, oh God!" She whimpered. "All he thinks about is screwing. Not the affairs of state. All the papers just lie around on his desk. It's a good thing he's getting out of there. Too bad . . . it's not sooner."

Kelly bore into the smooth convolutions of her interior, swaying from side to side, touching all the degrees of her compass. She was close to swooning now.

"Oh, Jack, Jack! Oh, gosh. Here I go again."

She commenced deep orgasm as stuttering, spluttering pockets of trapped air exploded like tiny fireworks against his personage.

"Oh, oh, oh . . ." She gasped as the last convulsive shudder shook her and collapsed under him, beating her fists on the carpeted floor and puffing in a purely human sort of way. "Jack, if you don't come home, I'll go crazy. I am spent, ruined, I'll never be the same again. I won't ever be able to walk around the golf course again."

"You'll be all right in a minute, you'll see."

"No, I won't be all right," she exclaimed petulantly. "You think it's easy, but it's not. Men just want me for who I am, not for what I am. You're different, Jack, because you don't give an F-word who I am."

She was right in saying that. Kelly was not impressed that she was the Washburn daughter. His interest in her was purely sexual. But now was a time for great caution. He would soon be a free man, if he was not already, and he did not know that he was ready to pledge a new allegiance. It was good fun, certainly, and informative, but was he ready for Westerley Washburn Perex and all that went with her? Her father, for example, his father's enemy? Her mother, distraught and half-potty. The party politicos of Washington where people waited for your first slip, then leaped like famished Bengal tigers? Kelly remembered what Perex had said: it was not necessarily a bed of roses at Blair House or wherever. It could be a bag of nails being married or closely allied to the daughter of the president. And who could say how Westerley would weather the storm? Remember, he warned himself, what she had done to Perex; she had damn near ruined the Cuban's machismo. Kelly had a feeling Westerley might be a demanding and not easily satisfied woman once she had you in her power.

She had already forgotten her proposal. "Now, Jack," she said, her voice muffled, "now I want to go on an around-the-world mission." So saying, she rolled away from him and onto her back and began to do things which surprised him. Eyes glazed, she jolted him with a final demand. "We've done everything now, haven't we? Everything that's legal. I've heard stories about wanton women who've been screwed in every orifice. And, remember, I won't be seeing you for a while. Please, let's do it illegally now."

"Westerley," he reminded her uneasily. "I don't know. Remember, we don't have an amendment on that yet."

"Never you mind. I won't tell if you won't. And I know you want to hear all my secrets. There's a lot more."

Kelly was startled. She was bribing him. Was it worth it? What else could there be?

For one thing, he soon discovered, Westerley's mother, Janet Washburn, was going to marry the Secretary of State as soon as George Washburn was out of the White House. Another thing was that George Washburn had a big Swiss bank account. Thirdly, the seaside mansion in Maine had been bought for Washburn by a consortium of crooks and furnished at great expense to the nation. Hell, he and others had always suspected that.

"It hurts," Westerley muttered, "but I don't see why this should be illegal."

He grunted, "I think it's illegal for the same reason that it's illegal to stuff the ballot box. It's just not done."

Despite all his knowledgeable chatter, Kelly had never done this before and now, doing it, he was not sure he cared for it. If one orifice was much the same as another, then why not stick to the purist method? Naturally, there were always variations on any theme but that applied mainly to music.

"If I said I liked it, then you'd think I was terrible, wouldn't you?"

"No," he said.

"I hope I don't get pregnant. I don't think the pill works back there."

He could not help laughing. "I doubt it."

"But one never knows, does one?" she demanded. She did not like being laughed at. "Strange things can happen."

"Let me know . . ."

"I *don't* like it," she decided. "And I'm surprised they make so much of it."

They were sitting on their haunches, recovering, she stiff, he sore.

"Another secret I have to tell you," Westerley said, "is that I think your wife plays around."

"How would you know that?"

"I had Topovsky check her out."

"Who with then? I'd like to know." If she said Rafe Perex . . .

"With my father," she said, blinking rapidly.

Steadily, Kelly said, "I've already heard that. It was a

long time ago. She was a dumb kid. You know who told me? Trout himself."

"Uh-uh," she insisted. "It's still going on, I promise you."

"Jesus," he swore, "that cunt . . . All those trips . . ."

"Jack—that's a no-no word." Westerley took his hands in her own and squeezed them sympathetically. "It's not a nice thing to hear, I know. Of course, I have my own motives for telling you." She stared into his eyes. "Topovsky says she's a political groupie. She'll screw anything in striped pants. I think you should get a divorce."

"So do I."

"And then . . ."

"We'll see," he said.

They had forgotten all about lunch and it was about 3:00 P.M. when, sufficiently recovered from their last experiment, Westerley slipped Topovsky's number two attaché case under her butt and invited him to join her there.

The rat-tat-tat of knuckles on the door threw them into total confusion. Westerley jumped up and dashed into the entryway.

"Who's there?"

As Kelly had feared, the reply was, "It is I, Tom Topovsky."

Kelly was on his feet and into his shirt before Topovsky had finished giving his name. He buttoned his shirt and had his pants back on before she spoke again. Shoes . . . shit, where were his shoes? He slipped them on, ignoring the socks which he stuffed in his pants pocket. He kicked his underwear under the bed and grabbed his tie.

"Just coming in a second, Tom," Westerley bawled. She pulled on her jogging suit and ran her hands through her hair. She cast a despairing look at the bed, then returned to open the door. "Oh," she said nervously, "it's you. Hi, Tom."

Topovsky hustled into the room and drew up with

what would have been a scream of heels on anything else but a carpet. He began to breathe very heavily. "Kelly—what the hell are you doing here?"

Westerley smiled sweetly and said, "We were going to play a little gin, waiting for you, Tom. Jack dropped by to talk to you about his interview."

Topovsky ground his crooked teeth like a cornered animal. There was no doubt he knew. He was not that stupid. "What's my White House attaché case doing out there?" he demanded.

"I don't know," Westerley said.

Kelly lit a cigarette with an unsteady hand as Topovsky picked up the attaché case, twirled the combination, and opened it.

"Kelly, I'm glad you've come over," he said in a hollow voice. "I got some things to say to you. Come in the other room."

Glancing questioningly at Westerley, Kelly followed him into the sitting room of the suite. Topovsky did not look any different than he had in London, perhaps a little more tired and drawn, Kelly supposed, and of course much flustered at finding him here, alone, with Westerley.

"Well, Kelly," Topovsky said, "so you've come to collect on the promise of an interview with President Washburn?"

"Yes," he said carefully, "we were going to arrange. . . . You told me to check with you here at the Crillon." He realized boldness was the only course. "He *is* coming over, isn't he?"

Furiously, Topovsky exclaimed, "Who says he's not? *Her?*"

"There was a mention in the paper. Don Cook . . ."

"What's he know?" Topovsky snarled. "Never mind—whatever happens, you're not getting any interview, no way, you loathsome bastard! And for a couple of very good reasons. One is that you were snooping around up at the clinic where you had no business being. And, to think of it, you're working for *our* newspapers. We took you on with great hesitation, Kelly, in the first place, I can tell you, and against *my* better judgment. It was that goddamn crackpot Trout with all the smarts of a gnat who insisted . . ."

Kelly began to perspire. No interview, no job. It was his visit to Montmorency that really disturbed them. Not Westerley. Nevertheless, he determined his only strategy now was to play it through. "I didn't realize you White House people feel that way about Trout. . . ."

"Shut up!" Topovsky yelled. "You ain't working for the *Appalachian Times* now, Kelly, you decadent louse! The second reason for that, Mr. Smart-ass, is that you busted security. Yeah, *you* busted security." Topovsky's face was red and his eyes rolled in his head.

"I don't get that," Kelly said slowly. "Busted security?"

"So you think you didn't bust security?" Topovsky laughed crazily, showing wolflike incisors. "I'm going to get your ass fried for this, Kelly."

"I do not understand," Kelly said angrily.

"Well, then, let me put it this way," Topovsky yelled. "Do you think you can philander around with the president's daughter and not bust security?"

"Just a minute, sir . . . Miss Washburn and I had a couple of drinks together. That's it. . . ."

"Bullshit," Topovsky exclaimed. "Bullshit! I've got the tapes right in this attaché case, right in here, to prove conclusively that you fucked Mrs. Westerley Washburn Perex. You fucked her in Geneva and I know for a fact that you been fucking her right in that next room while I been out attending to the affairs of state. What do you say to that, Mr. Kelly?" Topovsky sneered.

Westerley's voice intruded unpleasantly into the conversation, if it could be called a conversation. "And F-word you too, Tom!"

Topovsky strained for control. The muscles were tight in his neck. He grunted and wiped his forehead. "Neither of you are going to be feeling so brave when I get back to Washington and play these tapes for the president."

Kelly had to say something. "I don't think that'd be so wise," he mumbled.

"Oh, yeah?" Topovsky exclaimed. "Let me tell you something, Kelly—that nympho in there. Yeah, I mean her. . . ."

"I beg your pardon?" Kelly said in a low voice. Surely this was the point at which he had to take umbrage.

"You don't think she is, I suppose?"

"No, I don't."

A fierce, dogged, expression came over Topovsky's face. "Well, maybe you should know, you bastard."

"All right," Kelly agreed, "maybe I should. But let me tell you something, something you guys should have learned by now. Making tapes, eavesdropping electronically, is immoral and unconstitutional."

"Bullshit!" Topovsky jeered hysterically. "We'll release them to the public. Then we'll see what that sanctimonious old man of yours has to say. . . ."

"The Supreme Court—"

"Supreme Court nothing—they released Nixon's, didn't they? Why should yours be kept secret?"

"I came over here to find out about that interview," Kelly yelled, "not to be abused by a blood-sucking bureaucrat."

There could be no worse insult thrown at one who earned his living from the tax rolls. Topovsky blanched.

"Kelly, I'm going to get your passport yanked. I'm gonna get the IRS to audit your returns from the year zilch. I'm gonna get defense to go over your service records. I'm gonna get a charge of treason laid on you. I'm gonna get the Federal District Court in New York to indict you for . . . sodomy." He turned even whiter and gaped as he pronounced the dread word.

"Sodomy? You're crazy, Topovsky," Kelly said scornfully.

"I've got it on tape—the two of you bastards discussing it."

Kelly got another Gauloise out of his jacket pocket and took his time about lighting it. "You got pictures of it too, Mr. Topovsky?" From Topovsky's face, he knew there were no pictures. "Well, Mr. Bureaucrat, kind of hard to prove it without pictures. Talking about it is one thing—but you don't have the smoking gun on film, do you?"

Topovsky shook his head uncertainly. Kelly pursued him. The best tactic now was to throw Topovsky off guard.

"Doesn't seem your little session up at Montmorency helped your disposition very much, Mr. Topovsky."

The casual comment had the desired effect. Topovsky's face tightened and his eyebrows drew together anxiously. "What the hell are you talking about, Kelly?"

Kelly knew then it was true, whatever doubts he had had. "You were at Montmorency getting your tired blood washed and your pecker straightened, weren't you? Now, there's a hell of a story. I don't need your goddamn *Appalachian Times* to sell that one. Didn't work, did it? That Grovival has set you right on your ass. So Washburn won't be going there after all, will he? Right, so might as well cancel the trip to Europe . . ."

Topovsky exploded fearfully. "You're crazy, Kelly. You could never prove it."

"I can prove you were at Montmorency, sir."

"So what? That don't cut any ice, Kelly. Lots of people go to clinics, fat farms, tennis ranches. I been feeling low. . . ."

Westerley burst into the room, unable to contain herself. She pointed accusingly at Topovsky. "You bastard! You lied! You told me you were going to Zurich to vist the bank account."

"Shut up, Westy! For Christ's sake!"

"Bank account?" Kelly repeated, thanking her silently.

"Never mind about any bank account," Topovsky muttered.

Westerley's nose twitched. "What's the smell in here?"

"Smell?" Topovsky shouted. "What smell?"

"Don't you smell it, Jack?" Westerley asked.

He sniffed the air. It was not his cigarette. The acrid aroma of powerful gas cut through the room. It was an insidious smell, not unlike skunk perfume. He shrugged. "Maybe there's a gas leak somewhere." Then he remembered something Dr. Wolfgang Ehrlitz had mentioned at

Montmorency. "How'd your meeting go this morning, Mr. Topovsky?"

Topovsky looked embarrassed. He shrugged. "Okay."

"Good." But he was still in hot pursuit. "There's something else I wanted to ask you, Mr. Topovsky—about AmFreight's investment—I guess that's the proper term—in Klinik Montmorency. . . ."

He got no further with the query. Topovsky began to curse and went for his throat with two thin hands, much wizened by his career as a paper pusher. Kelly dodged but Topovsky seized him by the lapels of his jacket and, in a frenzy, started shaking him. Curiously, at these close quarters, the odor Westerley had noticed became much more pronounced.

"Goddamn you, Kelly!"

Kelly had no choice and he had no wish to participate in an exhibition of violence in front of the president's daughter. He planted a firm right fist in Topovsky's gut. The president's right-hand man reacted with a loud fart. But, like a bulldog, he held on. Reluctantly, Kelly followed through with a classic right to the jaw. Topovsky toppled to the left and went down on one knee.

"Jesus," Kelly gasped, "I'm sorry."

Topovsky picked himself up, retreated to a chair, and sat down breathlessly, glowering. Westerley finished the job.

"When we get back to D.C., you bastard, I'm moving out. You and I have reached the end of the trail, you deceitful—"

Topovsky interrupted her nastily. "Fuck you, Westy. You've had it."

Westerley turned to Kelly. "Did you hear that? Did you hear what he said? That fucker used the F-word."

Kelly almost laughed. "Mr. Topovsky, it's not nice to say things like that to a lady. And, damn it, sir, you can't attack a member of the press just because he asks you a direct question. I could make a complaint to the press office at the White House."

"Goddamn you, Kelly, I *will* get you for this," Topovsky muttered.

"Butt out, Topovsky," Westerley stormed. "I've got a good notion to stay right here in Paris, not even go back to D.C. with you. What the hell do I care about appearances?"

"With your lover, yeah," Topovsky wailed. He was close to the end of his tether. His hands were shaking, sweat rolled down his face, and a wretched exclamation of grief choked him. "The shame of it, the horror. The president's own daughter, behaving like a slut."

Westerley almost gagged with ferocious laughter. Kelly coughed and got out a handkerchief. The presidential assistant's body odor was becoming unbearable. Was this the smell of humiliation and defeat? He felt sorry for the man. There was little more to be said.

One thing: "Mr. Topovsky, I'd like those tapes."

Topovsky gasped. "You expect *me* to give *you* those tapes?"

"Yes."

"I won't." His look, even in defeat, was determined. "Pair of goddamn perverts."

"If you don't," Kelly said evenly, regretful he had to be so cruel, "I'll blow the whistle: on you being at Montmorency for a Grovival treatment, on AmFreight, on a potential invasion of Mangrovia, on the bank account, on my wife being seduced by Washburn when she was nothing but a sprite of a teenager. . . ."

As Kelly recited the litany of corruption, Topovsky shuddered, then brokenly began to nod. Finally, he reached down for his attaché case, opened it and drew out spools of recording tape. Without speaking, he handed them to Kelly, who in turn, passed them to Westerley Washburn.

"Thanks," she said bitterly. "I'll play them whenever I get lonely back in D.C. You won't be around to hear them, Tom."

Topovsky did not reply and truly there was nothing for him to say. He dropped the attaché case on the floor and sat limply, his hands dangling over the arms of his chair, chin sagging on his chest. They left him there, returning to the adjoining bedroom, and Westerley slammed the connecting door.

She shook her head. "Jeeze, some scene. What the hell's wrong with him? He even smells funny; like laundry detergent."

Westerley put her arms around Kelly, wanting to be comforted. She pressed her face against his chest. But Kelly felt sick and dirty. They had sullied themselves, almost beyond repair. All that he could think was that there was no danger, now, of any sordid revelation of their affair.

"I'm sorry," he muttered. "That wasn't a pretty sight."

"It never is," she said soberly, "watching a man destroying himself."

"I'm sorry you had to hear it."

He felt her tears through his shirt. "Jack, please, please, come back." He moved his chin against the top of her head. She continued, "Not to work for the administration. I wouldn't want you to. You shouldn't have anything to do with those morons. Where Topovsky comes from, there are five or six more just like him. No, just come back to D.C."

"If I come back, I'll be working for my father," he said wearily.

"So—I'll move to New York. I'll buy a place in River House so we can look at the Pepsi-Cola sign." Gosh, Kelly thought, the most prestigious address in the city. But would the residents' committee let her in? Could they turn down an application from the president's daughter? Yes, if they wanted to, they could. "Or," Westerley continued persuasively, "I was thinking. For you: the State Department. I've got that good connection there. State is a lot cleaner than the rest of them. In a couple of years, an ambassadorship. That would be a kick. Traveling, an embassy residence with butlers and all. And you and me, Jack, making great love and good diplomacy. It would be my salvation. Of course, we'd have to get married. . . ." Her voice trailed away sorrowfully. "And I don't think you even love me."

He smoothed her short blond hair, stroked her back. "Westerley, I've got to make it on my own."

Westerley rubbed against his leg, her eyes glowing with hope. "And you will. And you'll be back, Jack, and we'll get together. I know we will. When I set my mind on something, it always turns out. Just promise me one thing: you'll not close the books on Westerley."

"I promise."

They got no further with this unbinding exchange of vows for, from the next room, there was a crash, the sound of shattering glass, a scramble of feet . . . a wild yell.

"Topovsky!"

Kelly jumped to the door and pulled it open. There was no sign of Topovsky. The window was broken and a chair was upside down, against the wall. He understood.

Topovsky had smashed the window, and jumped. Careful of protruding pieces of glass, Kelly looked down into the street in front of the Crillon. A body, arms and legs in a sprawl, lay on top of a black limousine. Westerley pressed against his back.

"Oh, gosh, oh goddamn," she said.

"Don't look," he said.

She squirmed, her hands clutching his shoulders. Her face was wet on his neck. She didn't know what she was doing. Her hands dropped and she grabbed him through his trousers and squeezed until he wrested away, turning. Her eyes were violent, burning.

"You're alive," she whispered. "Yes?" Something about the manner of Topovsky's end sent her mind reeling. She dropped to her knees, tore at his pants and gobbled him.

"Westerley!" he cried. "Not now. We've got to call the embassy."

She sobbed imploringly and continued at him, as if to reassure herself there was such a thing as continuity in the world. "Why are men so weak?" She paused, wet eyes staring at him. "Even if we'd been in there screwing, so what? That's not the end of the world, is it? Is it?"

"He couldn't handle it."

"And a guy who manipulates world policy, sends men to their deaths without blinking an eye. Horrors!"

"What are we going to say?"

"The truth of course," Westerley said callously. "Topovsky has been under a hell of a strain. I've noticed myself how nervous and depressed he's been, Morose, that's it! And then the diarrhea. That's Swiss diarrhea, well known, from too much chocolate. Sure, sure," she kept on rapidly, still on her knees in front of him. "But mainly the pressure. He broke. Gosh, goddamn, so suddenly, just when we were sitting in the other room, chatting. A hell of a thing, Jack, a hell of a thing. You come around to say hello to a couple of pals and then *this*. . . ." She paused again. "Come on, come on, just two more minutes, that's all I need. Let me do it," she pleaded. "You can call the embassy while I'm doing it."

CHAPTER

TWENTY-FIVE

Kelly had not been aware that Air Force One had gone to war. The normally sparkling white skin of the presidential aircraft had been camouflaged in desert hues: sand colors and streaky black.

George Washburn, in a classical Roman gesture, had flown to Paris to pick up the body of his dead lieutenant.

At Westerley's urging, Kelly went out to the airport with her and a security man in a nondescript embassy station wagon, loaded with hers and the late Topovsky's extensive luggage. Alone with him in the backseat, the watchdog's eyes busy with evening traffic on the fast speedway, she rested her hand on his thigh. She had warned him in the elevator that she would never let "cocky" be far from her grasp.

A sparse crowd had gathered outside the gates of the aerodrome but inside the security cordon there were less than a hundred people. Across the way, Kelly spotted a black line of Élysée Palace cars and a knot of men standing in front of them. He could make out the president of France and several of his more prominent ministers. The lard-ass silhouette of Aristide de Bis was not in evidence. A select contingent of reporters, TV people, and photographers had been admitted to the area: they were penned in an enclosure to the left of the nose of the plane. Flashbulbs popped, and now and then TV lights blinked on as cameras whirred. A long hearse which obviously contained Topovsky's body was drawn up at the right of Air Force One. The circumference was ringed by shoulder-to-shoulder security police in black helmets.

"What happens?" Kelly asked.

"What do we do, Frank?" Westerley asked the security person.

"We wait. The president is coming down in a minute to say hello. He'll say a few words, then he gets back on the plane and away you go."

Lights blazed from within the giant plane and its generators hummed eerily above the level of ground noise. The jet was being refueled from a truck parked at its bosom. A short red carpet had been unrolled from the bottom of the gangway to a small platform. On this, someone placed a stanchion with microphone.

The security person listened intently to his walkie-talkie, nodding, finally saying the word, "Roger." He turned around to Westerley. "You'll go up after they finish speaking, Miss Washburn. Ambassador Capone is over there talking to the French president."

Capone and President Fernand Cachet stood together, hands clasped behind their backs, their hair blowing in the slight wind.

Westerley had fallen silent, her eyes fixed on the cabin entrance of Air Force One. Her shoulder touched Kelly's gently and then, daringly, she shoved her hand into the pocket of his trench coat. God, he thought, must she?

At this moment, Washburn appeared in the cabin light. He paused to wave and slowly descended. Capone and Cachet moved to meet him on the red carpet at the bottom of the steps. Washburn was not a particularly tall man but he was authoritatively built. He was wearing a dark suit, dark tie, and white shirt. His hair was very black under the TV lights, and two triangles of white skin cut back from the forehead. His face looked pasty, heavily jowled, in the unflattering light. People said Washburn had great charisma. Certainly he gave off power, as if he were walking in the center of an electrical field. Washburn shook hands first with President Cachet, then with Capone. They exchanged a few words. Then, his hand on Washburn's arm, Cachet guided him to the platform. The French president took the mike first very briefly. He greeted Washburn and, rather curtly, made reference to the sad reason for this lightning trip to Paris. He paid small tribute to Topovsky who, Cachet reminded them all, had been in conference with French ministers only the day before. Finally, Cachet expressed disappointment that President Washburn was not staying longer in France, especially since his reconciliation mission was being indefinitely postponed: The tone of Cachet's voice, Kelly judged, would make it very clear to French TV viewers that Cachet could not care less if the mission ever came off and that, indeed, the sooner Washburn was airborne and on his way back to Washington, the better.

Washburn's knowledge of French was still sharp enough for him to catch the nuances and his back was stiff as he replaced Cachet at the microphone. Flashbulbs popped again and the TV cameras homed in for close-ups.

Washburn's address was to the point. "My dear French friends," he began, his words, in English, flatly New England in accent. "I am in your country tonight only briefly, to perform a painful duty—that is to recover the remains of one of my most faithful associates. . . ."

Westerley's fingers bit into Kelly's hand.

"Tom was a valiant warrior and yet another victim of the unending struggle for world peace. He was here in Paris discussing with your government matters of great importance to our alliance, which, regardless of administration and policy, will go forward. . . ."

Jesus, a crack at Cachet.

"My fellow citizens of the free world, pressure and high tension has taken my friend Tom." Washburn carefully wiped away a tear. "But his work will continue, I promise you. No sacrifice is too great, no journey too far, no schedule too agonizing in the service of our alliance and of peace. I myself had intended to visit Europe in the near future. Unfortunately, that is now impossible. Recent discussions have shown that a longer period of preparation will be necessary before our road to reconciliation can be paved."

This was blunt stuff. What Washburn was saying in other words was that no purpose would be served by talks now because differences were too strong. He watched Cachet's reaction; the French president's head turned and he stared at his ministers.

Washburn continued, "But let me say this. American policy will never be directed against the vital interests of France. I hold our friendship sacred and this must be so because we are surrounded by enemies. And let me say this too—whatever the shocking reports and rumors being given currency by our enemies, the United States of America will always be a friend of France. We will not be provoked into ill-considered action. We respect the honor of France. But we will guard our honor. We will proceed in mutual respect. . . ."

Washburn shifted his stance to glance at Cachet. Unmoved, the Frenchman returned the look. Suddenly, it was much easier to understand the significance of Aristide de Bis's anti-American influence in the cabinet. All these guys hated Washburn's guts.

Warmly, Washburn continued, "Our hearts are welded

together unbreakably. We have stood together against tyranny for two centuries. And it was my own great honor to serve here among you during the darkest days of the war against Nazi tyranny, to serve with the valiant fighters for French liberation—from the Nazis and your own Vichy collaborators. . . ."

It was either a tremendous boner or a calculated slap in the chops to mention Vichy, to remind the French nation that only very recently the country had been severely divided along ideological lines. He could almost feel the hackles rise on the other side of the tarmac.

Then Washburn concluded. "Although my mission to Europe is being postponed, let me say that I have invited your president to visit with me in Washington. I hope he will come soon. . . . *Merci* . . . *Au revoir* . . . And God bless you all."

Washburn stepped back. Cachet clapped exactly three times and from the group in front of the black cars there came only a hint of applause, like gull wings briefly whipping. Kelly shivered. If he'd been Don Cook, he'd have written in the next day's *Trib* that on this night an avalanche of ice had smothered Franco-American relations. Washburn and Cachet shook hands perfunctorily; it was not certain that even polite good-byes were exchanged. They stepped down from the platform and, with Capone trailing, took up a position at the foot of the gangway. Men opened the rear door of the hearse. Topovsky's coffin was covered with an American flag. Washburn placed his right hand over his heart. The men carried the coffin to a freight elevator and it slowly disappeared into the bowels of the plane. When this was done, Washburn shook hands once more with Cachet, turned, and walked ponderously up the steps.

"Okay," Westerley's security man said, "we can go on board now."

Nervously, Kelly took Westerley's arm to escort her to the plane.

"Come on up for a second," she said.

They mounted the steps. Washburn was already sitting in an easy chair in the forward section.

"Hello, Westy," he said. He stared at her pleasantly, then at Kelly.

Kelly was surprised, although he perhaps should not have been, to find C.T. Trout in the chair opposite the president. Trout leered at him.

"Mr. President," Westerley said formally, "I'd like you to meet Jack Kelly."

"Hi, there," Washburn said. He stuck out his hand. "You're the Kelly . . ."

"Yes," Westerley said, "Jack was with us when Tom . . ."

Washburn rubbed his cheeks with the tips of his fingers. At short distance, his skin was even pastier than the TV lights had made it seem. The line of his jaw was pouched with sagging flesh and his upper lip was beaded with perspiration.

"C.T.," he said, "see about some drinks, will you? Well, I guess this has been a trying point in time for you, Mr. Kelly."

"Yes sir," Kelly said, "but nothing like it's been for you, sir."

Washburn cleared his throat raspingly. "Tom was a good man. He was tried and true. Tom never deserted my side. He was a faithful friend, politically and personally."

Kelly nodded humbly, glancing at Westerley. "I can't tell you how sorry I am." He warmed to the subject. "We were just arranging for my interview with you."

"Interview?" Washburn's heavy eyebrows elevated and his forehead creased.

"The plan was for me to interview you, hopefully, while you were in Europe. I guess that's all off now."

Trout handed Washburn a large tumbler of what looked like bourbon and water. "Sure looks like it's off, don't it, J.K.?" he sneered.

"You are Harry Kelly's son, right?" Washburn demanded. "Um . . . not one of my greatest supporters." Kelly said nothing, merely moving his head in moderate agreement. "Yes, you're *that* Jack Kelly. Yes, C.T. is your father-in-law, isn't that so?" Badly concealed smugness glinted in Washburn's eyes.

The son of a bitch. Kelly nodded coolly.

Trout cackled spitefully. "No more, Mr. President. Maryjane messaged me that the knot is untied. She done it in Haiti."

"Oh?" Washburn said indifferently.

Kelly made his voice flat and unemotional. "Perfect. That's perfect." He was not going to give these men any satisfaction. He smiled faintly at Trout. So he was loose of her; now it was his ex-wife who'd been playing around for years with the most powerful man in the world, the man who controlled the ships and the planes and the subs that carried the missiles that could destroy the world. So what! And all the poor fool was interested in was a piece of tail, tall-in-the-saddle Texas tail. "We're still friends though, aren't we, C.T.?" he added sardonically.

"Sure," Trout spit, "but what you done for me lately, J.K.? Where were you when they tried to shoot my ass?"

"I was at your side, C.T.," Kelly drawled. The shotgun-pellet furrows in Trout's scalp were still visible.

"Hold it!" Washburn ordered. "What'd you think, Kelly? How did it go out there tonight?"

Kelly bunched his lips. "Frankly, I think we've got trouble, Mr. President."

"What!" Washburn's face was anxious. Then he pouted, turning to Trout. "These bastards have all but wrecked our foreign policy, C.T. Did you see that creep Capone? Put his name down now, C.T. He's going to get it." He made a chopping motion with his right hand and a whacking sound.

"Right, Mr. President."

Westerley did not speak. Caustically, she observed the scene. She was standing close to Kelly's shoulder.

"Well," Kelly said, "I guess I'd better say good-bye. Mr. President, it's been a pleasure to meet you. . . ." Then he had a brilliant thought. While he was here, he might as well chance it. "Mr. President, may I ask you a question?"

Washburn glanced at Trout, an odd look of discomfort on his face. Trout nodded and Washburn cautiously said, "Yes."

"You mentioned vital French interests. They'll interpret that to mean you're declaring a hands-off policy in West Africa. Would that be right?"

Washburn, relieved, smoothly smiled. "We've never had any other kind of policy in West Africa, my boy."

"Well . . ." Kelly hesitated. "From what one gathers around town, the whole strain in the alliance seems to be centered on Mangrovia . . . and that drug, Grovival."

"J.K. . . ." Trout's eyes hardened.

Washburn repeated the word Grovival as though he'd never heard it before. "Jack . . ." He chuckled mirthlessly. "Do you suppose at this point in time we'd run the alliance into shallow water just over a drug with an impossible name like that? C'mon, be reasonable."

"But the French are making an awful big thing about it," Kelly persisted. "People say Grovival could change the whole pattern of world population growth. . . ."

"How do you know about this, Kelly?" Washburn demanded. "C.T. . . ."

"Mr. President, Kelly is talking through his goddamn hat," Trout said angrily.

Washburn's face became dark and threatening. "Our only interest in West Africa is to see basic human rights preserved."

"I see," Kelly said. Then he thought he might as well shoot the works. "I have good reason to believe that Tom Topovsky was experimenting with Grovival. I think that's what happened—"

Washburn exploded. "What the hell do you mean? Are you suggesting a member of my staff was on drugs?"

"Not drugs in that sense," Kelly stammered. "This is a different kind of drug. It's a rejuvenator and it comes from Mangrovia. Why I'm making a point of it is—the stuff could be very dangerous. Some people say it's the ultimate secret weapon. Slip it into Canada and overnight the population would triple. They say . . ."

Washburn held up his hand, his face sullen. He wiped

perspiration off his upper lip. "I don't want to hear anymore. What you're saying about my friend Tom is blasphemous. I'll tell you this much, Mr. Kelly. If it's so bad, we'll get an international convention against it—like for poison gas or germ warfare. Make a note, C.T."

"There may not be time," Kelly said. "The French . . ."

"Mr. Kelly," Washburn warned, "you're walking dangerous ground."

"Mr. President, the French have reported that we're assembling an invasion fleet off the coast of Mangrovia."

Washburn lifted his right arm, pointing at him. Kelly saw it then: the paranoia. "Get the fuck off my airplane, Mr. Kelly. Get off right now, or I'll have the Marines throw you off."

Kelly flushed. His knees were shaking. "Yes, sir, Mr. President."

"Now!"

Washburn's arm was shaking in his fury, his facial muscles twitched, and sweat seemed to boil in the creases of his forehead. He wiped his face on his sleeve. A hunted, haunted look came over his face.

Kelly backed away. Smiling, now that her back was to her father and Trout, Westerley followed him. She winked. It was not as bad as it seemed, she was saying. Unmindful of the observers behind her, she put her hands on his shoulders and kissed him on the mouth.

"So long, cocky," she whispered. "Jeez, you really riled him."

"Yes . . . good-bye, Westerley," he muttered, saying loudly over her shoulder, "Good-bye, Mr. President, C.T. Have a good trip."

Trout's voice was blistering. "You're fired, J.K., you goddamn polecat."

And again Washburn's voice: "C.T., put his goddamn name down. Put it down. He's going to get it." Kelly heard the guttural chopping sound again.

Westerley followed him down the gangway to say a last wet good-bye, and then alone, Kelly went back across the tarmac to the embassy station wagon. They drove off before Air Force One began to taxi.

"How was he?" Frank, the security person, asked. "Very broken up?"

Kelly nodded. "Yeah, Christ, he was in a hell of a state."

CHAPTER

TWENTY-SIX

Kelly's name was mentioned in the French press in connection with Topovsky's suicide, but only insignificantly in a bottom paragraph. The story had turned out innocently enough: Westerley Washburn, the president's daughter, had been in Paris with Monsieur Topovsky to see about French participation in an annual Washington charity event called Salute to Lafayette. Jack Kelly stopped at the Crillon that afternoon to say good-bye to these two dear friends when . . . *Zut alors* and the rest was history, already rewritten. Only the most reckless of scandalmongers would draw the wrong conclusion. And, as the paper said, gloating over the drama of it, this was not the first, nor would it be the last, time a government functionary had buckled under the weight of office.

Olga Blastorov called to inform Kelly that her father, Count Blastorov, was convinced Topovsky had been killed by Communist agents. "Monsieur Jack, his is the devil theory of history: that nothing, absolutely nothing, happens as it seems. Count Boris believes it was a defenestration—meaning that Mr. Topovsky's fall was really a *push* out of the *fenêtre. Fenêtre* is the French word for window."

"Shit, Olga, I know what it means. I can tell you it was suicide."

"How can you be so sure, Monsieur Jack?"

"Because there was no way a murderer could get into the room, Olga," he said patiently. "Don't forget, I was there."

"Count Boris says they would have come down the chimney or over the roofs. . . ."

"Olga, please, I've got to get some sleep. I'll be all right in the morning. . . ."

But it was Zouzou Mordaunt who possessed the most shocking, worrying theory about the demise of Tom Topovsky. Sitting next to him on the brown couch in her penthouse, she whispered, "I will tell you something very important—Aristide believes you killed Monsieur Topovsky." She was very solemn. "If that is so, Jacques, then you have gone too far."

"Me?" He might have dropped his champagne glass. "Madame, surely you don't agree."

Impatiently, she shook her arm, rattling her bracelets, "Jacques, bother what I think. It is what Aristide thinks. He believes that following your London rendezvous, having been paid your price, you did this drastic thing."

"I didn't do anything." At least he had a witness to that: Westerley Washburn.

Zouzou shrugged imperiously. "No matter. The demolition of the American threat to Grovival is in motion. For Beatrice de Beaupeau, there may be a decoration."

Kelly cried, "It wasn't that way at all: Beatrice hates Aristide's guts. She's in love with me."

"No," Zouzou said decidedly, "she loves you not. She sits in seclusion at Château Beaupeau pining for Aristide, who is now so unfortunately entranced with your American harlot friend."

"Madame, she is *not* a harlot! You've got everything wrong."

"No mind, no mind!" Zouzou sniffed. "Now we shall begin planning for our new product, L'Élixir Mordaunt, formerly Grovival."

Kelly nodded slowly. There was no purpose in debating with her on any subject.

"Yes," she went on complacently, "all now remaining is when you will commence work here at Maison Mordaunt." She clucked and put her hand on his thigh. "You will not mind to be paid in the French way? You are not so patriotic you will demand payment in *les dollars Américains, eh, mon petit assassin*?"

"Please don't say things like that, madame. I am not an assassin. I'd like to ask you . . . but where is Hercule?"

She smiled fondly. "He is having conversation with Monsieur Victor. You see, I have relented. Monsieur Victor will remain. He will continue to design dresses for his disgusting women, notable only for their bad taste. But he will be silent, a very silent partner."

"I want to get in touch with Beatrice."

"You are crazy. Aristide would not stand for that."

"We will see what we will see," he said stubbornly.

"Jacques," Zouzou said grimly, "you do not know what an uncomfortable position you occupy here in Paris."

"I think I do."

There was no chance for her to elaborate. Hercule entered the room. "*Bonjour*," he growled, noting that Kelly was seated next to Zouzou. Hercule had changed. His little body had expanded to fill the importance of his office. His chest, stomach, arms, and legs filled a miniature suit, this one, Zouzou proudly informed Kelly, from the great Monsieur Pierre Cardin—it was a small, from his Japanese line. Kelly was amazed at the transformation. Hercule had arrived: he was what the French called an *arriviste*. The sky was the limit now for his ambitions. Kelly could foresee him entering French politics. The country might acquire its shortest president; it had already had the tallest. Hercule sat down solemnly and drew a long panatela from an inside pocket. "*Très bon*," he murmured as he lit it.

Zouzou purred. "I do love so the smell of a fine Habana. Ah, Hercule, *mon petit amour*, all my loves smoked fine cigars."

A disturbing thing happened then. At Hercule's entrance, Charles had awakened from a sound sleep. He had been stretched out like a sunbather in front of the fireplace. Now he cringed when Zouzou tried to pat his head, hissed and gnashed his rotten teeth.

"*Alors,* silence," Zouzou commanded, "mangy beast, we may have a special long good-bye for you too, my friend." Charles understood the substance of the threat, if not the words in which it was phrased. "Well, Jacques, so it is settled." To Hercule, she explained, "Monsieur Jacques will be joining us soon as *directeur des relations publiques.*"

"Ah, *bon,*" Hercule said, nodding gravely.

Kelly squirmed. "Madame, I'm working for the newspaper. . . ." Of course, this was not true. Trout had fired him and he was not yet restored to the *RAG.* "I've never done any PR work."

"You do not work for a newspaper," she glowered. "There is no Washburn interview. Washburn will not come to Europe." Her face grew livid. "*Enfin!* When will you finally understand, monsieur, that I, Zouzou Mordaunt, and only I, stand between you and disaster? Do you not understand that you could be implicated in the death of this Topovsky? It is not impossible that you could end your days in the Bastille." She sneered. "Just as your dear friend, Rafael Trujillo Perex is now incarcerated in the Bastille de Genève."

That news stopped him cold. "Perex is in jail?"

"Of course, you didn't know? He was arrested for terrible violations of Swiss banking law. It happened only hours after the death of . . . Topovsky. Mr. Perex is no longer immune to the European legal ststem, monsieur, as are you also not."

Kelly's face burned. Alongside his heart he felt a dull throbbing. "Madame," he said faintly, "Topovsky committed suicide. That's a fact."

"So you say," she shrilled. "What I say is that you now live under the protection of the House of Mordaunt."

Kelly felt a chill trip down his spine. He shivered. Christ, she might have been scrounging lines from a nineteenth-century romance: protected by the House of Orange, the House of Aragon, the House of . . . Mordaunt. D'Artagnan and his musketeers had survived intrigue and danger under the protection of one or another armed house of feudal France.

"If Aristide de Bis tries to involve me in Topovsky's death, it would be a frame-up," he protested weakly.

"That word is familiar to me," Zouzou said scornfully. "What you must appreciate, Jacques, is that Zouzou Mordaunt has only to turn her back and you are *kaput*." She sliced her finger across her throat.

Impassively, Hercule agreed. "*Vraiment.*"

"I think I'll have another glass of champagne, if I may," Kelly said. "I just might try for the protection of the House of Beaupeau."

"*Ach, merde,* Jacques," Zouzou droned disgustedly. "For now, I expect you at the House of Mordaunt Monday next."

Beatrice de Beaupeau reentered his life of her own accord, ironically on the day following the first Tuesday after the first Monday of November, American election day. At midterm, thanks to his own aloof refusal to campaign and what were perceived as blunders in both domestic and foreign policy, Washburn lost control of Congress. Any dream he might have entertained of repealing the third-term amendment was demolished. French political commentators were elated at his electoral embarrassment. The right-wing papers laid his defeat to the stout resistance of the French government to American colonial ambitions in Africa. Monsieur le Ministre-without-portfolio Aristide de Bis was quoted. "Washburn," he said, "and his running yokels, the carrion birds of international imperialist machination, have been soundly thrashed by right-thinking Americans. France is supreme in Africa! *Vive la France!*"

Reading such ugly words in a Parisian morning newspaper was enough to make the most hardened political observer shake in his shoes. Of course, Aristide's sneering anti-Americanism could not come as a surprise, but still, to have it stated so baldly in print. . . . Kelly could imagine a frantic morning meeting at the embassy.

He was dressing to go off to his new job at the Maison Mordaunt when Beatrice called.

"Jackelly? Aristide is a monster to say such things about your country," she exclaimed.

"Beatrice? You? I was beginning to think you'd forgotten me."

"*Non, non.*" Her voice trembled. "It has been . . . inconvenient . . . for me since my return from London."

"Where are you?"

She was at her château in Burgundy, she said. "I have been reading of your escapades. *Mon Dieu,* this is no joke. I am very worried for you. But I have been working on my memoirs day and night. Tomorrow, I return to Paris. Could I trouble you to visit me at the Villa Peau? I am feeling very low. My life is in a splinters."

"Don't say it, Beatrice. That cannot be so."

He was not in the sprightliest of moods when he arrived the next night at the Villa Peau, although, naturally, he was yearning to see Beatrice. Already Zouzou seemed somehow to be extracting revenge for the months of no mention in the *RAG.* She had warned him again that very day to stay away from Beatrice.

The Countess de Beaupeau was waiting for him in a St. Laurent hostess gown out of Yves' chinoiserie period. She collapsed into his arms. The last few weeks in the country had brought a rose garden of freshness to her face and her gold-red hair was brushed to lustrous perfection. Kelly felt grubby and intimidated for he was in her sophisticated territory, not a neutral hotel room. And he could not escape the suspicion that Aristide de Bis was plotting to use him again, that this might be a second round of inducement, of political seduction.

Outside, seen from the street, the Villa Peau was formidably characterless but, as Kelly would have known from past experience in this fashionable *arrondissement,* the inside was a treasure house of art and decoration. Beatrice led him through a flagstoned and dimly lit hall and into a huge room where table lamps and crystal chandeliers competed to reproduce broad daylight.

"Jackelly, *mon amour,*" Beatrice whispered, "there is no one in the house save us. Please, sit down on the couch."

He lowered himself into a broad, blue velvet-covered divan to the right of a modestly warm fireplace. Beatrice, without another word, handed him a tooled leather folder within which lay a sheaf of notepaper inscribed *Memoirs de Beatrice de Beaupeau.* He began reading. The memoirs were disturbing, although he admired them for their sincerity. In their own, unusual way, they could be taken as an addendum to the book he'd been reading, off and on, about Nazi Germany, *Warped Walhalla.* The similarity was in the continental sickness they attempted to delineate. This is a rough translation of what he read:

I, Beatrice de Beaupeau, am a beautiful and titled member of the French aristocracy and my lineage goes back to the beginning of time. My father, a war hero, dead at the age of thirty-five in Germany, was one of the premier nobles of France, tall, insanely handsome, lordly; also proud and, if need be, cruel and ruthless to a fault. A leader of the peasant masses. Father introduced me to the French *philosophes,* those writers upon whose work our ethics are based, and to the classics. Since then I have been one obsessed by the search for truth. Being alive, as I am, and a survivor of the grim harvests of history, our lineage in several of its branches having been lopped off at the guillotine, nothing significant happened to me until I wed my first husband. I was seventeen. He was an onologist from the region of the Rhone, visiting Beaupeau to study a chance occurrence of the *noble rot,* a vinicultural phenomenon of some importance. After five years of besotted union, this clumsy and ugly man joined the heroes of France. His misfortune—my good fortune—was to fall into one of the larger tuns of Nouveau Beaupeau Burgundy, a very good year for the wine but not for my deceased spouse. There had been no offspring and I was twenty-one.

My second husband was an *avocat* of France, a graduate of the *École Normale*, an elderly man too, unsure of foot and three-quarters blind. That is to say, *Maître* Gaston de Bis. My second husband died one evening in the library whilst I was at evening prayers in our chapel. Reaching for a heavy volume of the works of Pascal, the latter fell, striking the *Maître* on the cranium, surely an ironical departure for one of the law. Gaston's brother, Aristide de Bis, known to many now as a minister of the French government, albeit without portfolio, became foremost in my life following the burial of Gaston and a requisite period of mourning. Like my father, Aristide de Bis is a proud and arrogant man but the cruelty of his nature far surpasses any I have known. His life story is not an honorable one, this I have learned, to my regret. However, the truth will out. As a mere youth, Aristide de Bis was an adherent of the Vichy régime, allied with Adolf Hitler or perhaps, better said, the servant government of the Nazi occupiers. Aristide de Bis's politics are of the far Right and his inclinations are to the restoration of the French monarchy, I being one of the leading candidates to become a queen of France, one of the last of the House of Bourbon.

At the time weakened by tragedy and of a malleable character, I allowed myself to be swayed by Aristide de Bis's ambitions. He has stated that none will stand in his way. Among his supporters, there has even been mention of seizing power by *coup d'état*. Aristide de Bis has traveled the country, canvassing military and civilian support. I fear for this nation. Aristide's royalist dreams extend to the reestablishment of the French Empire by laying claim to former French lands: colonies in the Orient, the Moyen-Orient, Africa, and even North

America—as to the latter meaning Quebec, Louisiana, and Mexico. France, in the eyes of Aristide de Bis, is the land of Charlemagne, and more.

But I, I Beatrice de Beaupeau, was becoming disenchanted with this risky adventure even before the entry into my life of a very new element: Monsieur Jack Kelly. We, Jackelly and I, collided on a dreary and formless day in November, and thus, Jackelly lifted the state of seige on my emotions. Jackelly strode into my fashionable villa in an extremely *chic cul-de-sac* in elegant Paris Sixteen, rapping with demanding knuckles on the threshold of my love, entering to me with the powerful scent of Want, Desire, Passion, but also of Honesty, an aroma still, by heavens, unbottled. Jackelly, this American, took me in strong arms, first of course kissing my soft hand as custom requires, then boldly carrying me into my *Louis Quatorze* salon where, only weeks before, influential Fascists were wont to gather for medieval royalist songs and toasts to many a bygone monarch. Jackelly lowered me gently to a couch by the fire and gazed into my delirious eyes. . . .

Kelly put the manuscript down and drew a deep breath. "Gosh, Beatrice," he said, "this is dynamite stuff. Aristide plans all that?"

She nodded, stirring languorously inside her St. Laurent, hand to her hair, deep red now by the firelight. "*Mon cher,*" she murmured.

"He really wants to restore the monarchy?" She nodded and said this was true. "Beatrice . . ." He winked. "You left out London."

She blushed slightly. "Merely for decorum, *mon cher.*"

"I thought so. You know, you'd have to say Aristide de Bis is what they call an *irrédentiste.*" He explained to her that irredentism meant an ambition to put the political pieces back the way they had been centuries before. "Do you remember when de Gaulle made that big thing about Quebec française? All hell broke loose. I can't believe Aristide could pull it off."

Beatrice reminded him that the monarchy had been restored in Spain, that the Germans were crazy about anything to do with royalty, and that there was always a chance Russia would return to the rule of the Czars.

"Would you be queen, Beatrice?"

She shook her head. "No, I would not be queen. I would not want that, Jackelly. I am more Socialist than Monarchist."

"I have a feeling these activities of de Bis's might be . . . illegal." That word again. Beatrice moved beside him, caressed his hand, then swiftly drew it under her hostess gown and against her bare skin. "Have you told Aristide you don't want any part of this?"

"Yes, I have told him," she said. "I have banished him from my life. He is looking for a new queen. Some say it will be Madame Marceline de Winter. Have you heard of her?"

"I've heard she's a very unsavory piece of goods. If she's in on this, you could be in big trouble, Beatrice."

She shrugged. "Life's journey is dangerous."

Kelly agreed by kissing her cool cheek, the corner of her eye, feeling beneath his hand, under the silk gown, the murmuring of her flesh. Again, she was bathed in an undefinable scent, not Mordaunt but with a hint of Mordaunt Number Two in it. To think Beatrice had once seemed so unobtainable.

The Villa Peau at this late hour, secluded as it was in a wooded district and cul-de-saced in privacy, was a place of great tranquillity, but almost too quiet, so still as to send a shiver of apprehension through him, as knowledge of an inhabiting spirit might well keep one on a fearful anticipatory edge. Was there something he didn't know?

"What of my memoirs?" Beatrice asked. "Will you edit it for me?"

"It'll need work," Kelly said thoughtfully. A lot of work, he thought. "And we'll have to get you an agent."

He paused to change the subject. "You are aware that I have a post at the Maison Mordaunt?"

"With that fearsome woman?"

"Yes." Kelly nodded blackly. "You see, it's a matter of some small extortion. Aristide de Bis professes to think I had something to do with the death of Tom Topovsky."

"Ha!"

"The fact is it was a suicide, pure and simple."

"And when everyone knows," Beatrice said scornfully, "that Aristide himself was responsible, and also for the deaths of those men, Igl and Maxwell Maxim."

"No, no, Topovsky jumped."

"It seemed like suicide. But nothing is as it seems," she said.

"I was close by."

"No, no, I am certain. Aristide's agents did it. Come ..."

Beatrice removed his hand from her gown and stood up. Above the fireplace there was a large, oval-shaped antique mirror with beveled glass, heavily gilded frame and, atop it, a Napoleonic imperial eagle superimposed on a *fleur-de-lis*. As she had done in London, Beatrice went to stare in the mirror. Standing on the fireplace fender, forearms propped on the mantel, she studied herself, ran her tongue around her lips, pushed her cheeks up with her forefingers. She sighed, turned her head, and examined a mole on the line of her jaw.

"I will tell Zouzou that I wish you to be here with me," she murmured over her shoulder.

Kelly chuckled. "She'd have a fit. She says Aristide de Bis would kill us both."

Beatrice frowned. "Here you would be under the protection of the House of Beaupeau and in Burgundy you will be protected by my loyal servants. They are fiercely faithful."

Beatrice thrust out a pink tongue and critically looked at it. This was not a useless enterprise. Ridging or discoloration of the tongue meant many things in medical diagnosis. But she seemed altogether better physically than she had been in London. Despite a grain of anxiety, there was more of a calmness now. She was stronger and more self-possessed, perhaps because she had made her irrevocable decision not to pretend to the throne of France. Kelly remembered her frightening propensity for self-abuse; at least she had not reached for his Gauloise to burn another scar into her flesh. With a languid motion, stepping off the fireplace, she unzipped her long gown and dropped it to the floor. He saw that the welts on her back had faded and there were no new ones in evidence: ah, the recuperative power of the skin. She was coming around, he thought, and perhaps now her body would be more responsive to the normal needs of passion.

"I am more beautiful now, *n'est-ce pas,* Jackelly?"

"More than ever, Beatrice."

The sight of her slim nakedness aroused him mightily and at once, but he determined to let her make the first move. She did so, frankly.

"Shall we make love now, Jackelly?"

"Gladly."

Beatrice returned to sit beside him, seizing him around the chest and pressing her breasts against him. She kissed him, exhaling a sweet perfume into his mouth, then moved to kneel between his legs. He held her breasts in his hands, lifting them, first one, then the other, to his lips.

"Oh, my Jackelly," she said huskily, "my American barbarian will revive the tired genes of France."

She slipped off the divan to the carpet before the fireplace, the latter now washing them in warmth, properly contradicting the outside chill of November.

"Here we will make love," she said, "before the eyes of my ancestors. Do you think they will be shocked? No, they were passionate creatures too, lusty and loving."

She kissed his body, lipping the length of him to the crotch and finally taking his personage in her mouth and nicking him with sharp little teeth. Apprehensively, he remembered she was capable of sudden unexpected action. There were stories. . . . But, no, she was gentle, so much had her personality changed. She transported him close to the crest, then alertly stopped. Sinuously, she eased herself to eye level, wrapping one leg across him to position the personage between her legs, tip of it against her mons. She tittered happily, the agile lips of her secret self grasping teasingly for him. He flamed, wanting now only to complete the connection, to prove himself before the haughty eyes of her ancestors. But then she leaped up.

"*Momento, prego,*" she cried, lapsing into the Italian, "I have in mind a *beau geste.*" She bounded across the salon into the adjacent library and returned with a heavy volume. "You see," she said gleefully, "it is the *Almanack de Gotha,* wherein are registered the names of lineage of all European nobility. I have in mind, Jackelly, to make this gesture of *amour* whilst astride these noble forebearers." It was a childish, yet delightful, idea. Only Beatrice could have thought of it. She put the hefty register in front of the fireplace and sat down on it, her hands on the floor behind her, legs, gleaming in the firelight, extended. "Now, Jackelly, to the horses, *mon amour.*"

Carefully, deliberately, respectfully, Kelly positioned himself to enter her splendidly prepared private quarters, she in a presentation which arched her pelvis upward. Perhaps it was this posture, or the symbolism of the seat, but in any case he realized that she had become more willing and eager, less inhibited and haunted by the past molestations of her body. The nexus of her passion had come to life. Under her, the heavy volume wheezed and creaked in its binding.

"Oh, Jackelly," she moaned.

Her groin, seemingly gratified by the revival of simple, uncomplicated sex, twisted, her hips rose off the fat book, elevating, then falling stickily on the vellum cover. Her head lolled backward on her outstretched arms, veins in the white throat pounding, and her mouth opened. Saliva poured down her chin. Her eyes were tightly closed, but behind the lids muscles twitched. Her breasts quivered and her breathing progressed from timid gasping to long hoarse panting.

The reward came soon, her first honest-to-God orgasm in months, perhaps years, discounting the long-drawn effort in London. It was cataclysmic, yanking her inches off the *Almanack,* then dumping her back and pulling her up again. She began to scream, lightly, in a reedy voice. She fell, then reached blindly for his shoulders. Not so astonishingly, the effort, the sheer power of the event, had riven her of control and she issued a tiny fart against the leather cover of the *Almanack.*

A fart of any dimension can be disconcerting to lovemaking and Kelly was momentarily distracted. But, thank God, it was not of the Grovival variety, he was sure of that. He dismissed the sound, at the same time thinking he understood Wagner better now. For in the crescendoing buildup of Wagnerian music, there were often enormously loud crashes of cymbal and drum as hero and heroine met either love or death—both, after all, a way of orchestrating climax, orgasm, or the wrath of the gods.

Beatrice's climax seemed to go on and on, to extend to a full minute, maybe longer, as Kelly pursued it through her vaginal tunnel and finally, with a final thrust of his own, released a storm of ejaculation into her yearning body.

"Oh, Jackelly, *mon cher,* I have never. . . . It is never . . . *rien, jamais.*" She kept repeating the French exclamations for "never" and "nothing."

She initiated the movement off the *Almanack* and their juices, left behind, glistened on the leather. The beginning of another new world, it might have been, Kelly thought gravely. Mother Universe had laid an egg on the recorded history of the great families of Europe and now was standing back, hands thrust into the pockets of her jeans, to watch it germinate, grow and mature. Some day this edition of the *Almanack* would be brought to auction, in mint condition, except for this mysterious stain and fart print in the rich leather cover. How were these marks made, do you suppose, Messrs. Sotheby, Parke and Bernet? Of course: a long-dead and skeletonized monk spilled candle wax there and killed a fly in it while perusing the genealogy of the Middle Ages.

"Jackelly," Beatrice breathed, "you have given me joy everlasting. You are my knight in shining armor, the lancer of my delight. You are my champion home from the Crusades. My protector, my enjoyment, my dalliance. Come, dally with me at the castle moat, swordsman of my keep, jouster supreme."

"That was good, Beatrice," he said, "but I can't match your poetry."

"For me, marvelous, Jackelly."

Kelly was much taken by her now. Her fine body moved against him and her eyes sought his, a touch of naiveté in her woman's expression, all knowing, yes, and understanding better than any man from whence all life sprang. The old vulnerability was still there. It would be easy to hurt her. But he would not. Gazing down into her gray eyes, he thought it was surely Beatrice who pleased him most.

Feeling him growing tumescent again, she muttered, "Oh, my brave knight, come with me to the land of Beaupeau. Soon? But now, I have in mind visiting the Napoleon Salon where I will make love to you on the emperor's battle flags."

CHAPTER

TWENTY-SEVEN

Winter was closing in on the City of Light. The weather through October and most of November was clear, unseasonably warm in the daytime but restoratively cool at night. But now, like a horde out of the plains of Central Europe came a foggy dampness dressed in a gray-yellow tunic, and rain, turning now and then to soggy sleet. A continental low-pressure system had trapped Paris between the mountains and the sea.

This, the usual early-winter fare, did not distract the city from an optimism abnormally bright for this time of year in the last quarter of the century. France was again supreme. A heady sense of national accomplishment had grown out of the put-down of the American president. The economy had been buoyed for the time being by a rich oil find in the French Alps and the inflation rate, for some reason, had settled back to the ten-percent mark.

Europe, and France, so accustomed to living with crisis, to living more happily with crisis than tranquillity, reeled with the good news.

The season for hedonism was approaching. The institution of the bank account had become a dead issue. If they could afford it, people bought gold and silver, postage stamps, works of art; or, if they were poor, as so many are, they spent all their money on worthless things, knowing that even worthless things would be worth still less tomorrow. The holiday season of balls, small parties, trips to the skiing grounds of Europe or the sand of North Africa, the midwinter cruises, had begun. Shop windows in the more elegant *arrondissements* were chock full of the newest, most outrageous luxury goods. *Son et lumière* had been switched back on Notre Dame on the basis of new oil wealth. Restaurants, cafés, nightclubs, and sporting palaces were jammed. Taxis were harder than ever to find. There had not been a political assassination in several months, and it seemed the present government of Fernand Cachet was strong enough to continue in power at least until summer.

The few American tourists who still came to Paris were stunned by the high prices and the money, which seemed in unending supply. "How do they do it? How can they afford it?" The answer was: "They don't give a damn. They're living it up. . . ."

On the other hand, there were loud whispers of political intrigue, rumors of the organization of yet another right-wing royalist group whose first declared goal would be to demand from the British the return of the true bones of Napoleon the First from their present hiding place in a crypt in Westminster Abbey in London.

There were things that never changed and there was constant change.

Charles, Madame Mordaunt's long-time constant companion, died December the seventh, victim of depression, then of simian suicide. The latter, a veterinarian told Zouzou, is rare but not uncommon among the lower species. Animals are as susceptible as humans to extreme reactions to their environment. Charles, the doctor said, could bear life no longer. It did not seem, in short, to have been an accident. Charles had hung himself on a garter belt in one of the second-floor dressing rooms.

Zouzou was very nearly inconsolable. Worse, she confessed to Kelly and Hercule, Charles had spoken his first, and last, word to her the night before the desperate act.

"It is too much," Zouzou wailed. "I cannot tell you

what he said. Yes, I will tell. He called Zouzou Mordaunt a word: *Con!* Yes, Jacques, in English, cunt!"

Kelly tried to comfort her. "Madame, it was a word he heard so often. Perhaps he thought it was an endearment."

"*Quoi, quoi?*" she howled. "What? Endearment? You think? No, Charles was very unhappy with me."

Kelly glanced at Hercule. "Jealousy, perhaps."

Hercule drew himself up, his small body tense, and he protested vehemently. "*Non! Alors . . . Monsieur! Pfui!*" Outraged, he strutted across the room and slapped his hand on the stone mantelpiece.

Hercule, now addressed as Monsieur Hercule by one and all at the Maison Mordaunt, was strikingly sleek in his well-tailored business suits, striped shirts, and loud ties. He puffed continuously on long, thin panatelas and issued orders and rebukes in a powerful voice of authority. But wisely, except for cracking the whip, he did not intrude into the area of design or style and thus kept tenuous peace with Monsieur Victor. Much of Hercule's day was spent with Zouzou in her penthouse, and if one believed the eavesdroppers and house wags, a good deal of rasping, gasping, and rattling of bracelets went on there, in those rooms now *interdit,* or forbidden, to anyone without an appointment.

Despite Zouzou's distress, life at the Maison Mordaunt went on, as did her new life with Hercule. Unchanged were the preparations for her annual New Year's Eve party to which faithful Mordaunt customers from all over the world were invited. All these were friends as well, for, by and large, to be a friend of Zouzou Mordaunt one must also have been a customer.

Thus, the house on rue Rimbaud was as busy or busier than ever in these preholiday days. Red-eyed and drooping with fatigue, thinner than he had been in recent years, Monsieur Victor was worked like a slave from morning until night putting rich fabrics to the poor bodies of his affluent clientele. It had been Hercule who pushed him to the limit. Victor, trapped now, had no recourse but to respond with even harder work. For it remained a fashion maxim that owning a Mordaunt by Monsieur Victor was second only to possessing a Mordaunt by Madame Zouzou, and a badge of distinction in an equalizing world.

Ironically, too, where Western Europe had possibly grown jaded in its attitude toward *le Couture*, the *nouveaux riches* of the Communist party élite of a dozen countries across the other half of the Continent had more recently learned to love it—and their Mordaunts as well. In matters of high fashion, it was sardonically said, the privacy of the official Soviet dacha had come to rival the Parisian drawing room.

Women saved their Mordaunts over the years, never threw them away, hardly ever handed them down, and certainly never donated them to the cause of charity auction, as they might have done a Dior, Lanvin, or even a Chanel.

Business was very brisk on the ground floor of the rue Rimbaud headquarters. Here, Zouzou sold her *Mordaunt-à-porter* line, the ready-to-wear clothes modeled after the couture originals but not comparable in fabric or workmanship, and certainly much less expensive. Everyone was dressing up for the holiday, as though there might never be another. Suits and dresses sold out, along with hundreds of dozens of the popular Mordaunt signature scarves packed in their slick boxes slashed with the Zouzou script. The niceties of intimate apparel were also moving well: the Mordaunt slips, bras, stockings, panties and pantyhose, nightgowns, robes, seductive "at-home" items, and in the other departments, shoes, bags, umbrellas, rain gear, and sporty hats.

"And," reported Jack Kelly, new public relations *chef* chez Mordaunt, "gallons of perfume and cologne, literally gallons of Mordaunt Numbers Two and Three, even Mordaunt Four, the body-soothing balm." He told local business reporters that Mordaunt figures were running at least thirty percent ahead of the previous year and far better than two years ago. This despite the fact that the year had been one of inflation and creeping recession. "Does this mean France is in for a period of economic

boom? Is that the question? Well, I can say this: Madame
Mordaunt is superconfident of the future. She sees a
new spirit arising in Western Europe.''

It was tried and true, this classic PR bullshit, he admitted to himself, the kind of thing he'd heard so often
when he'd been on the other side of the fence. When
he was not dishing it out, he and Hercule worked on the
guest list for the New Year's party, the *fête de Zouzou*,
as it was traditionally called. Altogether, things were
going well, very well. Even Zouzou, habitually dissatis-
fied, admitted that. The only fly in the ointment, so to
speak, was the delay in bringing the new cosmetic ingredient to market: L'Élixir de Zouzou, formerly Grovival.
Zouzou had counted on launching it for the Christmas
season.

Charles's conclusive departure was forgotten soon
enough. At times, Kelly could not help thinking mischievously that Zouzou might have been better served with
Charles's warm brains, according to the Wolfgang Ehrlitz
recipe—or had Charles, as Kelly suspected, been con-
taminated by excessive doses of Grovival? Kelly had
tried again to warn Zouzou about the drug and its apparently destructive effect on Tom Topovsky. But she would
not listen.

In a mere few weeks at the maison, Kelly congratu-
lated himself, he had done well, even though the occupation of PR flack was not his proper work. In that short
space of time, he had made love to two writers from one
French fashion magazine, to the beauty editor of another, and he had thrilled the living daylights out of a
woman fashion buyer from one of the biggest of the
American department-store chains. The girl who covered couture for *Womens Wear Daily* hadn't been around
yet.

But he paid only scant attention to this conventional
aspect of his position. Sex was *not* the whole answer.
Although he acknowledged what a big part sexual favors
played in the fashion business, it did not delight him to
trade his body for headlines or fat orders. He thought

now, as unbelievable as it seemed, that he had fallen in love with Beatrice.

Kelly had not openly discussed Beatrice with Madame Mordaunt in the days at Maison Mordaunt, but he was sure the high priestess was aware of what was happening. Her often huffy manner, her frostiness, disturbed him. He had fulfilled what Zouzou had claimed was her fondest ambition when he had joined her staff, but he knew how her mind worked. She was besotted with Hercule but nonetheless she considered Kelly to be her private property. And, again, he would become aware of her Grovival habit. She began to show signs of physical wear. During the summer and through September, her revived sexuality had seemed to slow, perhaps even to reverse, the aging process, but now the demands of passion—and there could be no doubt Hercule could be very passionate when he slipped out of his small suits—appeared to have accelerated her decline. At times, she was a spectacle of senility in action: one day her usual, decisive self, the next day she might be weak, irritable, and tearful. Such swift changes in character were a matter of concern, or should have been, for she was the rock on which Maison Mordaunt was founded and on whom they all depended. But Hercule did not seem to worry. He was kind to her, he tolerated her moods, and he soothed her. He was an Olympian of patience.

Through all this, the Villa Peau was Kelly's refuge and Beatrice his companion in peace and quiet. He deserved this now, he thought, for the past few months had been very eventful. Beatrice did not fight him intellectually, analyze his emotions down to every sigh, or rack him with comparisons of her own efficiency and his predilection toward procrastination and simple laziness. She accepted him as he was, like the weather, and loved him as trustingly as she did the church. He did not have to amuse her, but only be there. She had no desire to go out on the town; she'd had enough of that. The extent of their ramblings when he returned from Maison Mordaunt was a stroll in the manicured garden behind the Villa Peau. Their evenings were hours of solitude, food, and drink: country *pâté,* quail eggs and Château Beaupeau wine, brought to the city daily from her country estate.

Now and then Beatrice turned, but less frequently of late, to the subject of Aristide de Bis, and Kelly began to hate him even more than he had. She warned him repeatedly that Aristide was murderous and treacherous. She told him in grueling detail how Aristide had first violated her: in the wine cellars of the Château Beaupeau; how he had twisted her vision of love; then exposed her to the English lord, the Man in the Black Mask. God, Kelly groaned and writhed in pain as he listened. What he'd like to do to these swine! She reminded him that Aristide was as pragmatic as Talleyrand, and as corrupt as the Balkans.

Kelly could not understand why Aristide de Bis had not been disgraced, tried and hung after the war. Beatrice explained by giving him a lesson in European realism, *realpolitik,* as the Germans called it.

"You must not forget, Jackelly, that many Frenchmen were *collaborateurs.* It is a cancer that eats still on the body politic. There are many bitternesses dating from those days. And Aristide was very careful. His cruelties were perpetrated at second hand. Bah! Aristide and his friends: Zouzou Mordaunt and her wartime lover, Colonel-General Ulrich von Unterstutzen. Yes. Jackelly, does that shock you?"

Aristide and his friends believed a cowed and ruined Beatrice would never reveal their secrets. And the fear of revelation, she said, was what protected Victor; Victor knew where the bodies were buried. He had been part of the ruined and debauched group that had danced on the lip of the catastrophe.

"The darling of the perverted Nazi SS *Oberleutnants,* Jackelly, that was Monsieur Victor. Monsieur Victor spent the war years in German staff cars being ferried from one orgy to another, dressed like a French chorus girl, drunk and whining the *Horst Wessel* song."

God, was Europe such a decadent place? Was there really no hope for the Continent? Bitterly, Beatrice said that behind the monuments, Europe was alive with death. But, sadly, wasn't this true of every country in this century of the decline and fall of Western civilization? No, Kelly proclaimed, there was hope for America just because American civilization was not as old and tangled in nationalism and historical feud. Having heard his argument, Beatrice would frown and ask him, what then, of men like Washburn, Topovsky, and C.T. Trout?

One night, shyly, she wanted to know whether it was true, as Aristide de Bis had told her months before, that Madame Mordaunt had forced Jackelly to make love to her. Kelly denied it. Typically Beatrice believed him instantly.

He kissed her on the lips and they made love in her big brass bed on the second floor of the Villa Peau as a small fire sparkled in the wall, surrounded by her collection of French Impressionists; or wrapped in the Bonaparte battle flags; or on top of the grand piano Beatrice said had belonged to her ancestor, Louis XVI.

It was in these long hours of sensory satisfaction that Kelly was inspired to a new marketing scheme for Maison Mordaunt's coming spring-summer collection. The slogan came to him like a shot out of the night: Erogenous Springtime. The new designs would highlight the erogenous flash points of the female torso through clever use of bias seams, cutouts, wedges of color, and fabric pointing to a particular location of erotic potential. The line would be modern and daring, Kelly predicted, and it would be highly promotable.

He presented the concept to Zouzou during a stormy council of war, as Zouzou appropriately called their meetings. She had taken to flailing him openly.

"Jacques, you have written much about me. But now I think you must do better." Brusquely, she threw a *WWD* clipping on the coffee table. MORE OLD HAT AT MORDAUNT was the headline.

"Madame," he protested, "this rotten thing was written in October, before I even got here."

She paid no attention. "Do you not understand, Monsieur Kelly, that such trash as this is damaging to my dollar earnings? *Merde* like this and my American clients become discouraged, and when they are discouraged then there are no more cakes and ale, *n'est-ce pas*? It must not be thought in New York that Zouzou Mordaunt is an old hat, Jacques, clever boy. We must do much better in the spring."

Victor, naturally, had to say, "Madame, truly, it is damaging for the *cautions*. . . ." He twisted the word dramatically.

Cautions were the advance monies that stores put down for the privilege of merely seeing the collection, against the final tally of purchases. The theory was that heavy *cautions* discouraged the cheap knockoff artists.

Zouzou spit at Victor. "It is nothing to do with you, monsieur. But, Jacques, are you so intelligent after all as I have thought?" She sneered. "Where are your *gimmicks* to attract attention to us?"

Again, Victor made the mistake of nodding in agreement. Zouzou exploded at him, "*Silence, cochon!* Stop bobbing your head. Your approbation is to me no more than the turd of the aardvark."

Victor gasped and went white. Behind a curl of cigar smoke, Hercule faintly smiled.

Kelly pointed out calmly, "Madame, gimmicks have a bad habit of backfiring in your face. When I was at the *RAG* . . ."

He got no further. She whirled, in a rage. "You are not at the *RAG* now, monsieur. You are at Maison Mordaunt."

Kelly was amazed at her fury, and mortified. She spoke the truth, however. He did not work for the *RAG* anymore. Olga had called, rather spitefully, probably because of his indifference to her, to tell him his replacement, Maurice Moody, had arrived in town.

Zouzou grinned hatefully. "Do not be sensitive, Monsieur Jacques. That is but a small taste of my medicine. There can be only one prima donna at Maison Mordaunt—*et, c'est moi!*"

Cautiously, he lifted his eyes to face her. "I do have in

mind one idea for the new line. . . . What about calling it Erogenous Springtime?"

"*Quoi, quoi?*" she screeched, as if she had not heard him right. "*Merde!* What is that you are speaking of? Erogenous Springtime? What means that, Monsieur Kelly? To me, it is meaningless. You call that a *gimmick?*" She laughed mockingly.

"It refers to the erogenous zones of a woman, madame," he said tersely. "My idea, as stupid as it might sound to you, was to have that as a fashion theme for spring-summer."

She interrupted fiercely. "I know what means it," she cried. "Why not say, then, the season for the fuck, Spring Fuckers?" She pealed out an ugly laugh, looking to Victor and Hercule for support. Victor dared a chuckle but Hercule did not blink. "Then these stupid people would know what you were talking about, Monsieur Kelly."

Hercule held up his hand, telling her to calm herself.

"*Madame, alors,*" said Victor, the sycophant.

"Silence, fool."

"Madame," Kelly said quietly, "we must always consider your image: elegance with dignity."

Zouzou made a face. "I spit on image. To Zouzou Mordaunt image is the sewer water of the holy city, unsanctified. Image is only important as it signifies money."

"*Moderation,*" Hercule again softly counseled.

"Correct," Kelly said, more confidently. "That's why I've suggested 'erogenous.' It's a word with dignity, but it's also suggestive. It's a scientific word; one finds it in the textbooks. Yet it implies sexuality. Let me explain, *please,*" he said as Zouzou splutteringly tried to stop him. "I see our erogenous woman as about thirty-five. She is slim, mature, well dieted, the type of woman who drinks a vermouth before lunch and a half glass of white wine with her meal. Often she does not touch her dinner. She eats no bread, never a potato, takes her protein in the form of red meat. She is a predator. She prowls. She is ready for adventure. She is a lurking sexual tiger.

Her teeth are well honed, sparkling white. Her tongue is pointed. . . ."

"Bah!" Zouzou exclaimed, "you are describing a woman with anorexia? Or a female Dracula?"

"No, no, she wouldn't have anorexia. She *does* eat—but only when she's hungry."

"*Scheisse.* You make her sound . . . yes, as though she eats men's peckers."

"Please, madame," Kelly insisted. "Just let me go on. . . . Her light tan is no surprise, for this woman spends a good half of her year dug into the sand, nude, at St. Tropez or spread out to cook in the mountain sun at Gstaad or St. Moritz. If she becomes bored there is always a side trip to be made to somewhere steamy and sordid in North Africa. Her eyes are tainted by scepticism but she has retained a certain innocence. There is little she has not seen or personally experienced. What she has not seen or done, she understands with her unsurpassed intuition. She is cosmopolitan but bears none of the low scars of passion. . . ."

There—he had rattled it off with a growing conviction that this was a gimmick that would work. At last, the old fool was impressed. Her reaction changed from scorn to enthusiasm.

"Jacques! *Dieu!* I apologize. You have described the Mordaunt woman."

"Exactly. The woman ready for her Erogenous Springtime."

Zouzou snapped her fingers excitedly, rattling the bracelets. "I buy it, Jacques."

"Bravo, Jacques," Victor murmured.

Hercule nodded approvingly at Kelly.

But an objection occured to Zouzou. "How, Jacques? We cannot make our clothes with holes for the tits to stick out or zippers at the cunt."

"No, no, madame, only a few items done with much cleverness of design. The rest of the collection toned down, modified. I don't think Victor's ladies are going to accept see-through and ass cleavage."

Zouzou shook her finger. "Do not be too sure of that,

Jacques." She was torn by a sudden memory and stifled a sob. "We will dedicate the Erogenous Spring to my beloved Charles." Hercule nodded sadly. "But, yes," Zouzou went on, her mind flying from grief, "I see nothing wrong with a small sensation. Yes, the Erogenous Spring of Maison Mordaunt. I think it is proper, in keeping with the times. After all, everyone now does *gimmick,* except Monsieur Balenciaga, and he is dead." She turned swiftly on Victor. "Monsieur, return to your drawing board. I will want sketches immediately. And remember: Erogenalia. Yes, Jacques, why not *Erogenalia? Erogenalia du Printemps!* Yes. Beautiful. It suggests the nerve ends, a bacchanalia of the ancients. *Dieu!* It calls up a vision, without saying so, of the genitalia. Erogenalia. Genitalia. Heavens above, a stroke of genius. Victor, remember fat one, we are banishing the dirty browns and *merde* tweeds. I realize, monsieur, this might rob you of your earnings from the fabric merchants of Lyons. . . ."

So simply, so directly, her eyes snapping vituperatively, was she charging Victor with taking kickbacks from the French fabric industry.

"Madame!" Victor gagged.

"*Merde!* Do you suppose I did not know this, monsieur? I know to the *sou* how much you have taken."

"*Non, madame,*" Victor sobbed.

"Take note of this, Monsieur Hercule, he denies it. Monsieur, it is only by the grace of God that you have not been arrested." She nodded, making noises in her throat. "Now, Monsieur Hercule . . ." Her mind jumped again. "I think it would be appropriate for us to reward Jacques with a pittance for his idea, now refined by Zouzou Mordaunt. I would say one hundred francs."

Thinking, the parsimonious old bitch, twenty dollars, Kelly mildly said, "Madame, this is my job. I want no reward."

"No, no, I insist. Hercule will arrange it." Again, she moved her eyes to Victor. "Now, you, Monsieur Embezzler, to your designs. I will have no browns. I will have pinks, reds, scarlets, tangerine, rose, the hue of the most personal genitalia, the colors of passion. For Zouzou

Mordaunt decrees Fashion Rebellion, *Fashion Anarchy!*"
She leaped off the couch, clicking her fingers and clatter-
ing the bracelets. "I am restored, *mes amis.* I am thrilled!
Let us have some champagne, *mon petit Bonaparte.* . . ."

Hercule, his face a Corsican mask, got up and went to
the cooler for her champagne. Zouzou was falling for his
story about being a descendant of the emperor.

"*Au revoir,*" Zouzou said to Victor and Kelly. They
were dismissed.

As they walked downstairs Victor moaned, "Jack, do
you believe I took money?"

Kelly considered what he should say. Should he be
kind, thus passing up his only opportunity to repay
Victor? "I suppose not," he said.

"Thank you, Jack." They halted outside Victor's stu-
dio, a stuffy room facing a back alley. Bitterly, Victor
said, "With her, it is always money, money, money. I
did not steal or take bribes." Kelly nodded, not wishing
to incite him, but Victor was in a foul and vengeful
mood. "What do you think the plan is, Jack? I will tell
you. She will sell Maison Mordaunt to one of the big
perfume companies. There have been approaches."

"You mean one of the multinationals?" AmFreight
again.

"Of course," Victor said, "this is the reason for her
fascination with *gimmicks.* She wishes to build the maison
to unprecedented profits to make the financial arrangement more attractive . . . and then to sell. And"—Victor
smiled contemptuously—"where will the money go? I
will tell you. Zouzou will pay her debt to Aristide de Bis
and his royalists."

"Victor, are you saying she owes de Bis money?"

Victor crowed, "She owes Aristide de Bis *everything.*
It dates back many years, this association. What I am
saying, Jack, is that by inventing this madness, this
Erogenalia du Printemps, you are performing a valuable
service to the royalists. Something you, no doubt, did not
plan."

"Not your favorite party, I take it," Kelly observed
calmly.

That did not quite make sense, if one believed that Victor had been a Nazi whore. But Kelly tried not to think of that aspect as he later analyzed what Victor had said. It was true Maison Mordaunt was a monument of Parisian couture and would be a jewel in the crown of any of the multinational fashion and cosmetic corporations. Maison Mordaunt was starred on the tourist maps, and there were few local historians who could remember a time when there had not been a Maison Mordaunt to shock and thrill the *beau monde*. The Mordaunt mystique was powerful and it would survive the old lady. Maison Mordaunt would be a blue-ribbon investment—just acquiring the worldwide rights to Mordaunt One, Two, and Three would be a solid piece of work, for the cosmetics sold like wildfire in every hemisphere.

Kelly knew there had been talk before of merger, or takeover, and he had received Zouzou's denial that any such thing was in the works many times. Had she changed her mind now? And why? In prior days, it had always been enough for Zouzou to rule the fashion pack, to set the pace for the Beautiful People, to dictate the direction of fashion in everything from hat pins to the flavor of douches and the smell of deodorants. But evidently things were different now. It was horribly true that the emergence of Grovival had altered the equation. If Zouzou did manage to corner the Grovival market, then Maison Mordaunt would become an even juicier takeover plum.

He wondered if AmFreight had made its approach.

Downstairs, the ground-floor boutiques were crowded with the before-lunch shopping crowd. One could recognize the first-timers by the agonized expressions on their faces. They feared they would be recognized for what they were, novices at Maison Mordaunt, and be ejected. They were frightened by the prices. Little did they know, Kelly thought sadly, that their money was as good as anybody else's. The *vendeuses*, sales ladies, experienced and merciless, took advantage of them, shamed them into purchases beyond their means.

There was a well-worn magnificence about the place. The boutiques had not been seriously renovated since

1946. Wooden fixtures had been oiled and revarnished so many times that they gleamed with memories of better, and worse, times. The shining beveled-glass cases were heavy and of a quality no longer obtainable. To the right, in the *Mordaunt-à-porter* salon, favored—that is, repeat—customers were served brimming glasses of Mordaunt No. 10 champagne, this calculated to engender light-hearted recklessness; if taken to extreme, they could stagger across to the shoe bar to collapse in deep leather and try on shoes until they had sobered up. And on the way out, for they did not escape so easily, they were lost in a maze of accessories: the scarves, lipsticks, costume jewelry, Mordaunt-brand stockings and tights, the Mordaunt "Groping Fingers" brassieres, Mordaunt "L'Invitation" nightgowns, the eye shadow and nipple tint, Egyptian oils from the secret formulas of pharaohs, and much more—including, as the joke went around town, under-the-counter Fabergé-style pillboxes lined with the Mordaunt "slip-on," her specially prepared French "letters."

So, Kelly thought realistically, *Erogenalia du Printemps* was more than a gimmick. It fit the tone of the place. So would "L'Élixir de Zouzou."

CHAPTER

TWENTY-EIGHT

Rain was beating the slate roofs of Paris One, the fashion *arrondissement*. The city dripped with humidity and held its nose against the stench of wet clothes and smelly shoes.

Kelly had two appointments that gray and miserable afternoon, the first to meet the *RAG*'s new bureau chief, Maurice Moody, and the second to brief well-known fashion writer Erika Plimsole on the matter of *Erogenalia du Printemps*.

Maurice Moody would have rubbed Kelly the wrong way even if the man had not replaced him at the *RAG*. Moody was a product of the New York rag trade, a child of Seventh Avenue with no subtlety or fine tuning.

Viewed objectively, Moody might not have been considered totally disgusting. But he made such a good try at it, Kelly judged after their first five minutes together. Moody was loud, pushy, and conceited, just the man to jolt French sensibilities and deep-freeze Franco-American relations. Kelly knew at once there was no possibility he could bring Moody up to the penthouse to meet Madame Mordaunt.

Upon sitting down opposite Kelly, Moody belched and explained he had been drinking a little more at lunch than was absolutely necessary. His raincoat hung limply over the back of the chair, his suit was wet at the cuffs and needed pressing, and his tie bore the stains of slopped soup leading to piss-dribble marks down the legs of his trousers. Moody plucked at his nose and fiddled in his ears in search of wax, sometimes successfully, as evidenced by the exhibition of a gummy ball of it on the tip of his forefinger.

Kelly thought Moody was probably so nervous from lunchtime brandy that his feet tapped a continual, annoying pitter-patter on the floor. His eyes were a cloudy blue and bloodshot. He put on and removed a pair of dirty glasses. He had little, if any, chin, and as he now and then stopped drumming his feet to cock an ankle over his knee, Kelly noticed with distaste he was wearing short yellow nylon socks which left hairless calfs uncovered. Moody's shoes were unshined and naturally were stained a blotchy white at the insteps, whether from the rain or splashed urine Kelly did not know. When Moody extracted a snarled handkerchief to blow his hairy-nostriled nose, Kelly saw it was sticky and soiled brown with ancient snot.

There was little else that could be said about Maurice Moody upon such superficial study, except that the stripes on his dirty tie ran counter to the stripes on his shirt and that, across his shoulders, there was a rich field of fallen dandruff.

"Your fly is open, Mr. Moody," Kelly was able to advise him.

Moody chuckled, showing irregular teeth and pink gums. He stood and zipped without shame or embarrassment. "So you're Jack Kelly?"

"Yes," Kelly said, "we finally meet. What can I do for you?"

"What can you do for me? You mean, what can I do for you, pal."

"Pal?" Kelly said frigidly, "I don't even know you."

"Wait a minute," Moody said jovially, "you worked for the *RAG*, for that son of a bitch Court, so I consider we're pals. More: soul mates." Kelly waited and Moody told him he brought greetings from everybody in New York. "Including Court. Hard to believe? I guess so, when you consider the cloud you left under."

Kelly looked up at the ceiling. "I don't see any clouds."

Moody laughed familiarly. "Maybe not now. What I'm trying to say is, no hard feelings, okay? I'm only here because they sent me."

"My old man?"

"I never met your old man. He doesn't associate with the riffraff. Court sent me. Anyway, I want our relationship to be a good one. Because as you know, Maison Mordaunt is, was, and always will be the apple of the *RAG*'s eye. Amen. So if I can't work well with the old bag, I'm nowhere, right? I want to meet her."

"Not today—pal."

"Okay, later then. I'm easy." Moody beat his heels on the floor. "So what's doing for spring? What's all this shit about erogenous zones?"

Kelly folded his hands, put his elbows on the desk, and stared at Moody. "What the fuck do you think you're covering here? Some shit-ass Seventh Avenue designer?"

But Moody only grinned, unimpressed. "Bullshit," he said pleasantly. "From what I hear you're fucking all the fashion press to get word around." His eyes were taunting. "Not that I blame you. But since you can't do it to me, who do I send? Olga Blastorov? Would you pass the info to her, pal?"

"Jesus," Kelly said disgustedly. "I *like* your approach.... I've got nothing to tell you, no details. We're calling it *Erogenalia du Printemps*."

"What's it going to look like, for Christ's sake?"

Why should he help this punk? Let Moody sink. "We won't know for a while. It's going to be very sexy stuff."

Moody was not convinced. "I would have thought she's so old by now she'd have forgotten what a bung-hole is."

Kelly showed himself to be irritated. "I don't want to play games with you, Moody. I'm working for Madame Mordaunt, so skip all the horseshit. We don't need the *RAG*. You can tell Court that too."

Moody received the message without blinking. "All

right," he said harshly, "I guess there's no reason to expect cooperation from you."

"You come on kind of strong, you know."

Moody worked up another defiant grin. "My New York training."

"Shit."

Laughing shakily, Moody said, "Come on, Jack, don't take it so seriously. I'm just seeing how far I can get with you. Say, where do all the models hang out? I hear the ones here are a lot better than those New York dogs. I bet you got a peephole somewhere."

"For Christ's sake . . ."

"Come on, don't hold out on your pal."

"Shit," he said again. "One look at you and they'd puke. Why don't you come back when you're sober."

The crowning insult. No one more than a drinker hates to be told he's acting like a drunk. "Sober?" Moody cried. "I am sober, goddamn it. What the hell are you saying? I suppose you're going to get on the horn to your old man. You're that kind of a prick, aren't you? You're sore because I got your job. I didn't have anything to do with getting you canned, Jack."

"I didn't get canned, you asshole," Kelly said. "I quit. . . ."

"Not from what I heard."

"You heard wrong."

"All right, all right! Forget it. Where's the snatch around here?"

Kelly for a moment considered tipping the desk over on Moody who, in the meantime, seemed to have been taken by nervous seizure. His feet beat the floor, dancing in place. Much later, Kelly was to learn that upon his arrival in Paris, Moody had tumbled down the gangway of the Pan Am plane, having spent the entire flight in the cocktail lounge trying to overcome his fear of flying.

"Mr. Moody, did you take the elevator up here?"

"You know I did, you superior prick."

"Let's walk down." Kelly stood up and before Moody could agree or disagree, he was leading him down the hallway.

"The models are down here, right, Jack?"

They met Hercule at the head of the stairs. Moody stopped and commenced muttering. Then he made a terrible mistake. "Hi, there, shorty," he cried. "Who's this guy, Jack, your token midget?"

Hercule probably did not understand precisely what Moody had said, but he did know the words were derisive. "Monsieur?"

"How's the weather down there, short stuff?" Moody's supreme faux pas was to reach out and pat Hercule on top of the head. Now and then Kelly had seen Hercule's face triggered from serenity to cold rage. It happened now. Moody made a tentative step off the landing, intending to pass Hercule, saying over his shoulder, "See you later, pipsqueak," but suddenly there did not seem to be room enough for both of them on the steep, narrow staircase.

Their legs became entangled and Moody tripped, twisted, hit the wall and grappled for a railing that was not there. He fell. He toppled and rolled all the way down to the next landing.

"Jesus Christ, now you've hurt yourself. I knew you were drunk."

"Kelly, goddamn it, I think I've busted my leg."

"Ah," Hercule said gently, "*dommage*. I will call a doctor." His lip curled in a regretful smile, also in its way an explanation. No, it did not do to make an enemy of Hercule.

"Kelly," Moody roared, "my leg is busted. It's gone all numb."

"Monsieur Hercule is going to call a doctor. Don't move."

"You're going to leave me here like this?"

"We can't move you."

"Get me a brandy or something. It's beginning to hurt."

Kelly thought he had no option as PR chief but to go with Moody to the hospital. After the ambulance attendants had given the rumpled *RAG* correspondent a painkilling shot, Moody grunted vindictively that he was going to get even. "That little fucker pushed me. Who is that little bastard anyway?"

"That was Monsieur Hercule, Madame Mordaunt's closest associate. . . ."

Moody began to whimper. "Shit, Jack, I really blew it. Shit . . ."

"Yeah, you did," he said. "You'll be out of commission for a while, I guess." Kelly looked at his watch. "I can't stay. I've got to see Erika Plimsole. You know her, don't you?"

"Sure I know her, the bitch. I suppose you're going to give her the whole scoop now, along with some hot pork."

Kelly chuckled gently. "Moody, you're a gentleman to the end."

Back in the office, Kelly called Olga and told her that Moody, her new boss, was in the hospital getting a broken leg set. Olga laughed bitterly. That was good, she said, for Monsieur Moody was a pig of the first litter. Unwillingly, she agreed to go to the hospital and help him home.

Erika Plimsole was next on his agenda. She got straight to the point. She wanted to know all about this "erogenalia business." Kelly tried deftly to explain without revealing too many details. It happened actually that as some people grew old, Madame Mordaunt grew younger, and *Erogenalia du Printemps* would be her youngest collection in years, all, of course, within the strict boundaries of good taste and in keeping with the classical verities of the carefully escalated elegance for which Maison Mordaunt was so noted.

"Balls," Erika Plimsole said crudely, "get to the point."

Erika was a big woman with a small head and a boy's haircut. He thought acidly that she was, indeed, about the size of Field Marshal Hermann Goering, and appropriately, she was wearing a close-fitted leather coat. Erika's face was broad, blue-veined at the cheekbones. Blue eyes were planted rather too close to her nose.

Erogenalia du Printemps, Kelly tried to tell her, would

be girlishly feminine and at the same time femininely girlish. Madame Mordaunt, he continued, thinking to tickle her fancy, had become an explorer of the previously forbidden hinterlands, the unexplored zones of the erogenous.

"Erika, think of earlobes, toes, the nostrils, as well as the obvious ones which I don't wish to mention for fear of embarrassing you, darling."

"Don't 'darling' me, Jack. I've known you too long for that."

Casually, he mentioned the navel. He invited Erika to think of the erogenous possibilities as a Chinese doctor might think of acupuncture, of the caress at the right place: the tip of a finger, an elbow, behind the knee to bring the human body to the edge of delight. "Our designs will simply be meant to point the direction. How, you ask? By cutouts, a slit, say a slit at the elbow, opening the way to a caress of the funny bone. . . ."

"I think," Erika said dryly, "that you're having me on. I suppose one touch in the right place and she comes in her pants just walking along the street."

"Well, it's not impossible, is it?"

"Cut it out, Jack. What are you doing here anyway, handing out this PR crappolo? Tell me—we hear stories that at her age Zouzou has taken on a new lover, a funny-looking little guy."

"Don't let Monsieur Hercule hear you say that," he warned her, remembering Moody.

"Also that you're selling your ass to all the women editors."

"Selling it? God, Erika, that's libelous. What more can I tell you?"

"You can stop beating around the bush—speaking of which there's a zone you haven't talked about yet."

He allowed himself to blush. "We haven't figured that out yet."

"What about the tits?"

He stuttered an explanation. They were thinking about windows to reveal glossed nipples, a lot sexier than slit-to-the-navel dresses.

"That could be," Erika agreed. "And if you could, decide how to do the same thing at the crotch in a tasteful way." Pencil clamped in her teeth, Erika's eyes twinkled. "All the little tootsies are saying you're really the director here of pubic, not public, relations. What if I said, a piece of ass or no story?"

"I'd say you were very ruthless."

She laughed heartily, slapping her leather-covered thigh. "Don't worry, stud, I don't swing that way. You know who I'd like? I'm honest. I'd like the blond model."

"Simone? You want Simone?"

"Yeah. Does that embarrass you? I could hardly stop from throwing her down on the runway at the last show."

Kelly said, "I'll introduce you. Now?"

"Yeah, what about right now?"

He walked Erika downstairs. Luckily, Simone was there. She was standing, as usual half-dressed, in her changing room. "Simone," Kelly said, "I'd like you to meet Erika Plimsole. Erika is with the fashion press and she'd like to talk to you about . . ."

Erika was already unstrapping her leather coat. Underneath, she bulged within a loose blouse and ruffled crepe skirt.

Simone smiled professionally. "*Ah, oui, bonjour . . .*"

Kelly began to back out but, paying no attention to him, Erika had taken Simone in her arms and was violently pulling at her smooth breasts. Simone winked broadly at him over Erika's shoulder while the fashion reporter made wild, rutting noises. As he got to the door, Erika dropped to her knees and rubbed her face against Simone's belly. He slammed the door and ran up the stairs. He wanted to see no more of that.

Breathing hard, Kelly tried to reassure himself that this was merely the way of the fashion world. It was a rough and tough industry and nothing should have surprised him. But he never ceased being surprised. Fashion was an art based on esthetics, form, style, beauty. But among the practitioners of the art and their adherents, or hangers-on, there was little of artistry or sophistication. So many, like Moody, had been schooled in New York, in those sodden sweatshops and showrooms of Seventh Avenue where human cargo rode in the hole. Bodies were meat, bought and sold by the pound. The models were the dancing girls of the industry, always available to the biggies, the lustful moguls, and the media.

He felt very soiled. He knew Erika would deliver, for she had just been bought. And Simone? Simone did not give a damn. She was indifferent to male and female alike. Simone considered the whole sex thing ridiculous, more ridiculous even than eating. Keeping her figure and money in the bank, that was the important thing.

The flattering stories were already coming in from the clipping services, and that same afternoon, while Erika Plimsole enjoyed the luscious but sexless body of *la belle* Simone, Zouzou gloated over the reception by the world press of *Erogenalia du Printemps*.

SEX RAMPANT AT MORDAUNT
ZOUZOU SPELLS SEXSEX
FOR SPRING ZOUZOU SAYS E.Z.

"Jacques, it is a triumph!" Zouzou chortled. "The press is swept off its clumsy feet. Like footless lepers, they scramble to the altar."

"It has gone very well, madame," he said. He deserved some credit.

She cocked her head at him like a brown bird and put a sly finger to her lips. "I am not sure, however, that I can approve of your *modus operandi*. It is said in the local *blague*—"

"I know, I know," he said impatiently, "that we're giving sex away. A lie. Those bastards at Maison Cuir and Chevaux . . ."

"No, no." She chuckled, "not that you give it away. You barter it. . . ."

Hercule's chubby lips were wrapped around a long panatela. He snorted with amusement. Bribery would be nothing new to him. Madame Mordaunt asked him to give Kelly some champagne. She was pleased with him, finally. He had been readmitted to her world. Kelly grinned. "All for the greater good of the maison, madame."

She laughed so hard she could not contain herself. He heard, muffled though it was in the suede of the couch, the sound of a dull fart. Hercule looked startled. But Zouzou paid no attention. Christ, Kelly thought, hadn't he tried to warn her?

"Is it true, Jacques, that the fat ones are most passionate? *Oui?*" Then, abruptly, her mood changed and she began to glower at him. "A pity you cannot take all your sex here at the Maison Mordaunt, monsieur. Yes, I say it, monsieur. And how *is* Countess Beatrice de Beaupeau, shameless traitor?"

Hercule looked pained.

Kelly frowned. "I'd better be going now."

"No! You will listen to what I have to say. *Mon cher* Hercule, he knows what I will say. Aristide de Bis is in Paris and this affair of yours has reached a serious stage. Aristide will insist that you stop this trysting with Beatrice de Beaupeau."

"As simple as that? I happen to be in love with Beatrice de Beaupeau."

She screamed in frustration. "Fool! Are you one of those willing to risk your life for love? I have warned you before about the vile temper of Aristide de Bis. There are some things that even Zouzou Mordaunt cannot change. Jacques! I would have thought by now you would have enjoyed enough of the neurotic countess, the perfidious slut."

Kelly walked angrily to the window. Rain was pouring down, drumming a tattoo against the window. "Madame, unkind. I won't listen to this. I thought you were Beatrice's friend."

"*Merde.* Idiot! I have no friends! Jacques," she pleaded, "this is not good for you, nor for the maison. *Mon Dieu . . .*" She sidled up behind him, running her hand down his stiff back. "I never thought it would lead to this. *Au fond,* a few episodes, a little sunshine into Beatrice's life. I did not contemplate heatstroke."

Miserably, he asked, "Why can't de Bis let her go? He doesn't need her. He doesn't want her. He's got . . ." He could not utter the name.

"You will say he has this Maggi creature. But you do not understand, Jacques. Aristide is a man with a mission. He *cannot* allow her to be free."

Kelly knew why. It was clear enough. Even a blind man could see it. Beatrice knew too much of his nefarious past, his corrupt present, of his terrible potential. He turned. Hercule was studiously staring at his hands. Hercule felt bad for him. Kelly knew that Hercule was his friend, whatever happened. "I won't desert her now," he said.

"Fool!" Zouzou bawled again. "They will be the death of you—Aristide and Madame de Winter."

"Madame de Winter?" He was furious. "Goddamn it, I'm sick and tired of hearing about Madame de Winter."

Worriedly, Zouzou said, "She is a powerful and strange woman."

"Another of the royalist pretenders?" he asked sarcastically.

Zouzou jumped away from him, her eyes snapping. "From where do you know this?" Hercule straightened in his chair. He became very attentive. "Did Beatrice tell you that? That is something you should not know. Never mention it to me again."

It was perhaps to have been expected, given the way the day had gone, that Kelly should run into Aristide de Bis in the first-floor boutique that very evening as he was leaving for the Villa Peau. The minister stopped dead, his cold, hard eyes surveying Kelly from head to foot. Aristide was wearing a large, black, floppy-brimmed hat on his big head and a yellow rain slicker over his lumpy body. At his side was a woman in a shoe-length black cape, the cowl drawn over tight curls. Her face was drawn, lined, and ugly, the eyes bulging as if from a terminal thyroid condition.

"Ah." Aristide sneered. "If I dare believe my eyes, it is Monsieur Jack Kelly. . . . I would like you to make the acquaintance of Madame de Winter."

She made no sign of recognition other than a still more disturbing bugging of her eyes.

"Madame," Kelly said in a low voice, bowing. He did not take her hand.

The eyes goggled at him and her lips parted over yellowish teeth. She looked ready to bite.

"Monsieur le Ministre," Kelly said nervously, "what are you doing here?"

"Doing here? Doing here?" Aristide exclaimed, almost frantically, as if he had forgotten why they had come. "We have business here, of course, with Madame Mordaunt—and especially Monsieur Hercule. À bientôt, Monsieur Kelly. Perhaps one fine day we three will also have words."

CHAPTER

TWENTY-NINE

Deep in his trench coat, umbrella over his head, Kelly dodged puddles and pedestrians along the rue Rimbaud. He was walking in the direction of the Madeleine to catch a cab.

Seeing Aristide de Bis again was disquieting, more than that, worrying and frightening. And meeting Madame de Winter would have been terrifying under any circumstances. Even though he had, in a certain way, served Aristide's purposes—for, after all, Washburn and company now seemed resigned to giving up their African adventure—the game was obviously not over. Zouzou was right. Aristide would never forgive Beatrice, or him.

Near the corner, as Kelly neared the glut of traffic in the boulevard, a hand came out of nowhere to pluck at his sleeve. He recoiled; he was that nervous. It was Maggi. She smiled sardonically at him.

"Where you going, big boy? Wanna have a little fun?"

"Maggi! Is it really you? Where have you been? I called—"

She frowned. "I'm busy. Research," she growled, looking around uneasily. "Let's grab a cab. Come on."

They hurried across the street to the Hotel des Scribes and finally got a cab discharging passengers at the front door.

"Where to? Rue Anjou?"

"No, no," she said nervously, "back to your place. They're watching rue Anjou."

"Who's watching? What are you afraid of?" But he knew.

Maggi shook her head, indicating with her eyes that they must not talk in front of the driver. The cab took a side street, avoiding the chaotic Place de la Concorde, and crossed the river at the Pont de Rien. Over her right shoulder, the Eiffel Tower glimmered through the rain and mist. "You surprised the hell out of me, Maggi."

"I had to do it that way." She said nothing more as they followed the circuitous route to his apartment. He paid off the cab. Maggi darted ahead to stand in the shadow. "Come on, come on, hurry up. Let's get inside," she urged.

Upstairs, she slammed the door and made sure it was locked and bolted. Then she relaxed a little.

"Jesuschirist, Jacko, this place smells like a cathouse." This was the first reminder of the old Maggi. "What the hell have you been doing here?"

"Nothing. I'm not here that much anymore."

"It smells like two mountain lions have been in here screwing."

Kelly put his hands on her shoulders and looked

closely at her. There were dark circles under her eyes, and sadly, deep worry lines around her mouth. Kelly helped her out of her raincoat, heavy twill lined with mink. Underneath, she was wearing a black turtleneck sweater and black slacks.

Maggi sat down, crossed her legs, and folded her hands in her lap. "I hope they didn't follow me."

He knew. But he asked anyway. "Who? Screw them, whoever they are."

"Whom," she corrected him, "whom do you think?"

"The agents of Aristide de Bis naturally."

"Correct."

"Your assignment," he commented bitterly. "Aristide de Bis."

"Correct," she repeated, no expression on her face.

Kelly paused. He tried to register sorrow. "I suppose you know about everything that's happened."

"I know Tom Topovsky jumped out of a window—and you were there. Jesuschirist, Jacko, you're getting into a bad habit of being in the wrong place at the wrong time."

"A pure coincidence," he muttered.

Maggi shook her head knowingly. "No, not if one knows you were humping the president's daughter all over Europe, my old schoolmate. . . ." He started to deny it but she stopped him. "Don't bother to sing me a song, Jacko. I know. Aristide knows. Topovsky caught you screwing her, didn't he?"

He looked away, embarrassed. "No, he didn't. . . . I suppose de Bis had the goddamn place bugged after all. It was . . . all an accident, Maggi."

She hooted. "Sure. All an accident. Bis thinks you pushed him."

"You don't believe that, do you?"

"No, I don't believe it. That wouldn't be your kind of thing."

"And what about you?" he demanded. "Miss Lily of the Valley?"

"Me? So I've been humping Aristide Bis. What of it? I didn't have any choice."

"Well, you do now. This whole thing is falling apart."

She shook her head. Anxiety, the prolonged risk factor, had drained her face of vitality. "The trouble is Aristide Bis is still alive. One does not lightly withdraw one's favors from Aristide de Bis. No, it's not over yet, not by any means."

"You can't get away?"

"Uh-uh," she said wanly. "The only reason I dared go out today is I know for a fact that he's at Mordaunt's talking to Hercule Bonaparte. Then he and de Winter are taking off to Corsica to study birth records."

Kelly slowly nodded. The deduction was not so complex. "Hercule is going to be the Pretender? Hercule wouldn't have any part of that."

She laughed briefly. "He might not have any choice. You saw that cow de Winter? If Hercule said no, she'd sit on him."

"Holy shit."

"Yeah, holy shit is right. See why it's not over yet? But . . ." She grinned a little more hopefully. "In the meantime, I've got Aristide jumping like a flea on a hot tin roof. . . . You know, Jacko, before it's over this whole goddamn thing is likely to go to the United Nations."

Kelly groaned. "Nothing would surprise me. Washburn said they might try to get a U.N. convention to ban Grovival."

"Yeah, if they can't have it, they'll turn the problem over to the United Nations. Some hot potato, this Grovival crap."

"Jesus, Maggi, de Bis is such a louse. It's dangerous for you."

"I'm not worried," she said. "Fortunately, he's also a hell of a masochist. He likes to be whipped better than he likes whipping. Too bad your friend Beatrice de Beaupeau didn't find that out."

"My friend?" he repeated weakly.

"Jacko," Maggie said patiently, "everybody knows you've been laying her nonstop. That's one reason I'm here—to give you a very serious warning. You're going to have a lot of trouble if you keep that up."

"That's what Zouzou says too. . . . Is that the only reason you're here?"

"No," she said slowly. "I wanted to see how you're doing."

He understood what she was saying. "How about a drink? I know you don't like it much, but I've got some Pernod here."

She seemed too weary to argue. He made the drinks and sat down beside her on the couch. Maggi shifted away from shoulder contact. Seeing he was aware of the movement, and disappointed, she patted his hand. "Jacko, I'm sexed out. . . . I'll tell you something. The more I think about this, the more I'm convinced Beatrice is the key. She must know everything."

"Yes," he said gloomily, "and that's why he won't let her go."

"You nuts about her?" Maggi asked bluntly. He could see a twinge of hurt in her eye.

"I guess so," he admitted, "but, Maggi, you were always first."

"Balls! It was purely physical. I'll admit I half fell for you, Jacko, but I pulled myself back. That's just not done. Never, never done!"

"How can you be so callous about it, Maggi?"

"Look," she said brightly, "this whole thing is just a little sabbatical they talked me into. It seemed like it'd be good background, particularly as it involved Aristide Bis. The truth is I *am* writing about the aphrodisiac of power. Working title *Political Balls* . . ."

"Great! Just great!"

"Just a working title, Jacko," she said impatiently. "The problem now is Bis. Playing around with a maniac like that can be risky."

"Maggi, the man is a total son of a bitch. Christ," he said angrily, "I'm practically a prisoner in Paris. I don't think I could get out of the country if I wanted to."

She nodded. "Could be. Most likely he thinks Beatrice has dumped all the information on you. But you could probably get over the Swiss border all right. That's how I'll do it. Jesuschirist, Perex is safer in a Swiss cooler than he'd be here." She laughed amusedly. "Rafe is some kind of covert agent, ain't he? He's convinced it was the Cuban Secret Police taking a shot at him the day the Cou-Cou Macoo tried to nail Trout."

"So it was the Cou-Cou Macoo then?"

" 'Course. But the hand on the trigger was Aristide Bis's."

"What about AmFreight? Have they thrown in the towel on Mangrovia?"

"Who knows? I'm not much clued in on the Mangrovia and Grovival aspects of this. I'm working my own street— which happens to be the royalist ambitions of Aristide Bis."

Kelly tried to calculate. "How many people are involved, for God's sake? And what the hell do we care if Aristide brings back a queen or a Napoleon?"

Maggi sniffed disparagingly. "Listen, personally, I couldn't give less of a shit. But they worry in Washington. You know those guys don't like to be surprised. They always want all the strings in their hands. They claim the Western alliance is already fucked up enough without Aristide Bis making more waves."

Unwillingly, he had to agree. "The whole thing is a comic opera."

"Seems that way sometimes, doesn't it?" she asked cheerfully. He knew she was feeling better already, being here with him. "But even high comedy has its moments of tragedy, Jacko. Think of Igl, Maxim, Topovsky. Maxim had a wife and kids, you know."

He leaned back, depressed. "I don't know anything about Maxwell Maxim. Christ, Maggi, things could have been so simple."

Maggi hesitated, then chuckled. "As simple as your wife getting herself knocked up by the Mangrovian foreign minister?"

Kelly almost squealed his shock and disbelief. He jerked forward. "How . . . How do you know this?"

Calmly, she said, "That's the word."

"The last I heard she was in Haiti."

"Sure. I guess it happened before that, up in Switzerland. Then she went to Haiti, from there to La Minge—that's the old French capital of Mangrovia."

Kelly smashed his fist into the cushions. "Goddamn it, that clinic. It must have been that cryogenic sleep cure. Holy shit! How did all this happen to me?"

"You? *You* didn't get knocked up. I guess Washburn just wanted her to give that guy a little bang. He's evidently mad as a hornet about it."

Kelly crouched miserably, chin cupped in his hands. Maggi put her arm around his shoulder. "What do you care, Jacko? There are worse things. At one point there, I even thought you'd knocked *me* up. Now that would have been a pretty kettle of fish, wouldn't it have been?"

"Why?" He stared at her despairingly. "Would that be so bad?"

"Guys in my profession—"

"Profession? What the hell are you saying? How can you talk like that?"

"Well," she said easily, "Aristide thinks I'm nothing but a hooker out of Las Vegas. And maybe that *is* all I am. When you come right down to it, Jacko, we serve our political masters, subvert whole parties, undermine the opposition. You remember the time Washburn, as rumored, set up the floating whorehouse in Miami Bay? I was there." She laughed modestly. "We even had a kind of a motto: we hook for history. Not exactly for history, more for the historical process. So the good guys come out on top, so to speak." She chuckled raucously, defaming herself, he thought. He put his hand over her mouth.

"Don't punish yourself," he said. "There's a big difference. You're working for your country now."

"You think so?" She frowned, her face white, slashed with vivid lipstick. "No, I'm hooking for the higher purposes of Washburn."

"Corrupt . . ."

"Sure, it's corrupt. But Rafe's not so bad. Why don't you use your influence with Westerley Washburn and get the State Department to put some pressure on the Swiss, get him the hell out of there."

"And you?" he demanded. "Why don't you run? Take a plane and get the hell out of *here*? Maggi, I do love you, you know."

He turned to kiss her cheek, put his hand softly on her breast, feeling its lushness, the answering pressure of the nipple.

"Jacko, forget it," she said forlornly. "I don't have a good screw left in me. Don't talk about love. Look, I've got to go. I've got to get back before one of his spies reports me absent too long without leave. Christ, Aristide is a jealous and suspicious man. And that de Winter! Ugh. She's nothing but a big dike. So far, I've managed to keep out of her way."

"God, this is bad."

"Yeah," she jeered, "what do you think now of this receptacle of joy everlasting, Jacko?"

"A lot."

Maggi sighed and smiled and he kissed her again. But she edged away from him. She was determined to leave. "Uh-uh."

Perhaps it was just as well. Once they had been so joyous together and now they were reduced to an anxiety which overrode all erotic thought. "Maggi," he said again, "he's a son of a bitch."

"I know. We've got a dossier on that character that just won't stop. It dates way back to 1945 and the OSS days when Washburn was trying to nail him. You know, that's true—one of Washburn's prime objectives was to get Aristide Bis. . . ."

"Aristide *de* Bis," he corrected her, adding the noble touch.

"*De,* my ass," she said. "He tacked that on. He's nothing but a two-bit adventurer from Brussels. He's not even French, if the truth be known. I think he's Dutch or a Walloon or something."

"But Beatrice was married to his brother Gaston."

"Gaston was *not* Aristide's brother. We've researched that," she informed him icily. "Gaston was gaga and a ding-a-ling even before Beatrice got him. Aristide convinced Gaston that he had a brother. Hell, none of his name was real. During the war, he had another name."

"Holy shit," Kelly said. "Doesn't that explain a lot?"

"What would it explain?" she asked blandly, "except that he's a crook and an imposter."

"He's probably Zouzou's brother."

"I wouldn't be surprised at anything," she said disgustedly. "Anyway, he's gotten away with it because the French don't like to stir the slops for fear of what kind of crud will rise to the top."

"As simple as that?"

"Yes, but we're about ready to blow the whistle on him. We'll make such a stink, they won't dare cover it up any longer."

"The government will fall," Kelly said soberly. "Cachet and his mob will be out on their asses."

Maggi looked at him as if he had suddenly proven himself daft. "My dear, that's the purpose of the whole goddamn exercise, don't you know."

Forgetfully, in the heat of the conversation, Maggi had crept closer to him on the couch and they were huddled together, whispering, her arm around his shoulder and his arms around her. Again, he cupped her breast and she drew a deep breath. Her eyes melted.

"Jacko, you bastard . . ."

"Maggi . . ."

She did not resist as he put his hand under the turtleneck sweater. Her breath fluttered on his cheek.

"Jacko, just remember to be very careful. And I'd be very careful of that countess of yours too."

"Never mind," he said. "What about you?"

"Me?" Her eyes were closed and her hand was at his belt. "Don't worry. I'm about ready to do my disappearing act. When the bomb goes off under Aristide, I'll be long gone. Don't look for me. But you wouldn't. You've got little countess. . . ."

"Maggi . . ."

"Jesuschirist," she murmured, "I thought I'd never get horny again. Damn and blast you, Jacko, get out of those clothes."

CHAPTER

THIRTY

"Voilà!"

Zouzou Mordaunt threw a copy of *France-Soir,* the Paris evening paper, down on Hercule's desk. Her face was pointed and weary. Her hands were shaking.

It was seven o'clock on a Monday night, one week before Christmas. Kelly and Hercule had been working all day on the guest lists, checking invitations against RSVP's for the *fête de Zouzou.*

"Merde!" Zouzou shrieked, *"c'est ça. Morte!"*

Somebody was dead, she was saying. She had circled an item on the bottom of the front page. The headline read: *L'Affaire Mystérieuse au Seine*; and under that a smaller-sized caption: QUI EST MAGGI MONT?

Kelly trembled as he picked up the paper. The story was brief, skeletal, because there was so little information. A pocketbook containing documents and an American passport made out to Maggi Mont, of Las Vegas, Nevada, had been discovered in the shallow water beneath the Pont de Rien. Of a body, there was no trace but even now the police and *les frogmen policiers* were dragging the river. Nothing was known, according to *France-Soir,* of the occupation of Mlle. Maggi Mont or how long she had been in Paris. Was she a simple tourist or involved in some despicable espionage affair? The American embassy had not been able to supply any clues.

"Jacques," Zouzou said dully, "this was a woman with whom you consorted."

"And so did Aristide de Bis, or whatever his name is," he said bitterly.

This last remark caused Zouzou to gasp. Hercule's head lifted. There was an enigmatic expression on his face.

Kelly slammed his hand down on the newspaper. "Goddamn it, she was scared to death of him. He was having her followed. I'm going to the police. . . ."

"No," Zouzou screamed in alarm, "you will not. I have already spoken to Aristide. It will not be necessary for you to go to the police. It is his urgent wish that you do not go to the police, for obvious reasons. Aristide is taking care of this matter himself."

"I'll bet he is, the son of a bitch," Kelly yelled. "Goddamn him!"

Zouzou by now was quaking with fright. She could hardly speak. "He is . . . he wants . . . to save us all from embarrassment."

"I've got nothing to be embarrassed about," Kelly cried. "I didn't kill her."

Tears had come to his eyes. He felt as though he were choking.

Hercule took command. He removed the panatela from his mouth, slid out of his chair, and went to stand at the window. He could barely see over the ledge. After a moment, he turned, his mouth tight, and broke the silence. "Aristide de Bis *et* Madame de Winter . . ."

Zouzou's body seemed to sag. "Hercule, I forbid . . ."

Hercule ignored her. "Monsieur," he said to Kelly, "I would advise you to depart Paris, with Countess Beatrice de Beaupeau."

"Hercule!" Zouzou screamed.

"*Silence!*"

Zouzou's head wobbled. She stared at Hercule with dread in her eyes. She backed toward the door.

CHAPTER

THIRTY-ONE

From his place by the window, Kelly had a view of approximately thirty degrees of rooftop, a horizon of ragged chimney pots where a black cat ruled supreme, and two floors of shining, dead windows. Of life itself, there was no hint, just as there was no sign of life at the flat on rue Anjou. He had almost crossed the street and let himself inside to check Maggi's typewriter. But he'd decided that, somehow, the police would be watching.

He could not believe she was dead. The search of the river had been thorough: no body. But what if she were dead? Goddamn. To think she might well be, buried in some unmarked hole in the ground, her papers thrown in the river, the thought of it made his body ache and sorrow play like barbed wire across his highly strung nerves. Maggi had discovered that he loved Beatrice and she had understood, too, that he loved her as well. Most women would not agree that it was possible for a man to so split his emotional equity. But Maggi did understand. And if she were dead. . . . Was it his fault? He might have kept her here, locked in the apartment.

How would he ever know? *Don't look for me,* she had said. Whatever happened, Aristide de Bis, despite hypocritical expressions of sorrow transmitted through Zouzou Mordaunt, would be accountable. That much, he did know.

The sadness was that their paths had not crossed at a star-blessed time. . . .

In a few hours he would be at the Château Beaupeau. Beatrice had already left the city to seek safety. Hercule was to pick him up later in the evening to drive out of Paris under cover of darkness.

Kelly had been at this observation post most of the afternoon, wary of changing position or making a noise of any kind. Even now, Aristide's men might be lurking in the hallway. When he reached from couch to coffee table to replenish his glass of Château Beaupeau, slightly chilled, the mere gesture seemed to thunder in the quiet of the apartment. Red wine—probably best over the long haul. It would have been suicide for him to start drinking Pernod or brandy at a time like this. He had to keep his wits about him. If tragedy it truly was, it would be a mistake to wallow in it. Maggi had been doing her job and that would be her salvation. He took a memorial sip of wine, for making much of mourning did not help the dead, however enjoyable the strokings of grief might be for the living.

He sighed and caressed his subconscious once more with misty speculation on the meaning of life and finality of death. Aristide was a man to strike from behind. Had Maggi been thinking of him? He knew she had loved him very much.

A sob forced itself through his chest. Shit, and he had promised himself he would not cry. He closed his eyes, holding the wineglass on his chest. No, she was not dead. He preferred to think she had merely pulled a fast one on Aristide de Bis, pseudonymed monster.

He must eventually have dozed off, for when the doorbell rang he started up, spilling wine all over his shirt. Christ, it was too early for Hercule. He stood well away from the door, out of the spread of a shotgun or machine-gun blast. "Who is it?"

"Olga," a voice whispered at the crack in the door.

Cautiously, he peered through the peephole. Olga. Like that other day, so long ago, she had gathered her hair in a knot at the back of her head. She was wearing a raincoat and under it layers of sweaters, a wool skirt and calf-length brown boots. Her expression was anxious but also expectant, in her eyes a warm glitter and in her smile the expanse of the Russian steppes.

"*Bonsoir*," she announced briskly. "I have come to say how sorry I am. It is not a pleasant thing to lose one's mistress. . . . All Paris is talking. Did you love her very much?"

"Slow down," he said.

But she would not stop. "I realized you loved her very much when you would not see me again, Jack."

"No, no, Olga, it wasn't that. I just got very busy. Come, sit down. Have a glass of wine. A Château Beaupeau."

"All right," she said, "yes, a glass of that, please."

She didn't take the bait. She did not know about Beatrice. *Bon.* Kelly guided her to the couch. She drew back for a second, remembering, and looked furtively around the room.

Kelly laughed. "Have no fear. Hercule isn't there. He is with Madame Mordaunt, his new love."

"Grotesque." Olga sniffed. "And, Monsieur Jack, I have brought you the latest airmail copy of the *RAG*." She clicked her tongue. "This evening *France-Soir* speculates further on the mysterious affair of the Seine. They allege Miss Mont was an agent of the American government, somehow mixed up in the turgid *affaire* of Grovival and Mangrovia. Is that possible, Jack?"

"That's horseshit," he said.

"Is it dangerous for you?"

"Could be."

"Oh, *mon Dieu!*" She put down her wineglass and surprised him by throwing her arms around his neck. She kissed him frantically. "It is exciting, you in danger," she cried. She slipped his hands between hers and rubbed them until his knuckles were warm, then clapped one of his palms over each of her breasts. Her voice gurgled, as if she'd been dunked under water. "Feel me, alive! I have missed you so. Maurice Moody is a pig. Do you have any feeling for me, Jack?"

"Of course," he said softly.

"I want to make love to you," she said urgently. He felt the rush-rush of her breathing against his face. "Now! I do not have much time, Jack."

"Nor I. I've got to go out in a couple of hours."

"A rendezvous?" He nodded. "Dangerous? So exciting," she repeated.

Their lips folded comfortably together, like glue on an envelope, and her wet kiss swept through him. Kelly drew her forward, his hand on her arm, the sweater, and around the breast—firm and round and goose-pimpled at the nipple. A deep growl broke in her throat. "Jack," she gasped, "uhhh." She pushed his hand away and shoved her bosom at him, squirming. Her hips strained, as if against a void which, they were saying with their movements, must be filled. Olga was not only prepared to give herself to him, she positively insisted on it. "I will be your mistress now, Jack. I will make you forget those bad times," she grunted.

Her belly heaved and Kelly put a calming hand on it. She rolled the belly under his hand, the bare hand, after all only a hand, being nothing by itself. He stroked the wool skirt, then underneath it her thighs, encased in those low-voltage pantyhose. Again, her body climbed toward the hand, as her fingers groped at his crotch.

"Uhhh," she groaned, a garbled statement of desire.

Quieting her loins as best he could, Kelly unzipped and removed her long brown boots and loosened the back of her Mordaunt-copy skirt. She arched her hips so he could pull it from beneath her, and he did the same with the pantyhose, tugging them over the roll of her ass, past her thighs and knees, and finally, in a balled-up knot, from her feet. Underneath, she was wearing black pants. Her legs thrashed, and then he had it before him, finally, free and clear, the glistening brown bush and its hidden split, the mons, vibrating with its own nervous energy.

Absently, Kelly kissed her belly, running his tongue around the fine concavity of her navel.

Although he was not interested in hearing about it, she hoarsely cried, "Maurice Moody is an awful man. In the office, he asks me to do vile things."

"Such as?"

Olga opened her eyes briefly. "While he is working at his typewriter, Maurice Moody will suddenly stand up and say, 'Hey, Olga, take a look at this . . .'"

"At what?"

Her eyes blazed. "At what? At his thing, in enormous proportion."

"How can he? How can he do that in a cast?" Briefly, Kelly was envious. Was Moody so well hung?

"No matter," she cried. "Then I have to help him down the stairs and he feels me."

"That son of a bitch," Kelly grated. "Listen, Olga, he won't be around long."

"No, I have told Count Boris."

"Boris will kill him."

"I do not care," she said bitterly. "It is not proper that I should be made to do terrible things because Maurice Moody is my superior. Oh, Jack, I miss you."

She tugged at his clothes, then in a fury of desire jumped up and pulled her sweaters over her head. She was wearing no bra and had no need for one. The fine, firm breasts pointed at him, nipples rust-colored and small. She stood before him, her muff, as they appropriately called it in Russia, land of sable and mink, looking like a fur hat with a moist crease down the middle of it.

"Hurry, hurry, Jack!"

It was as if the train, plane, the trans-Atlantic steamer were leaving gate, runway, dock, and that Olga had been running all the way with this something to do before it was too late. As Kelly stood to remove his pants, pull off his loafers and socks, Olga threw herself backward onto the couch, her body twitching. In this convulsion of pent-up desire, her hand drifted. She began caressing herself, the breasts, taut with excitement, the solar plexus and pubic arena—heavily furred, strands of hair straggling up her belly, reaching for the navel but never quite making it.

"Jesus, Olga, wait a second, will you?"

She was masturbating herself, grunting and panting, and he feared she might accomplish the deed before he got there to do it for her. But in a second, her legs spread to make room for his body, she was taking him in her hands and ramming his personage into her, whimpering, in Russian, he supposed. Her hips were so wild she almost tossed him on the floor.

"Stick it to me, baby!"

Jesus, he thought, that was distasteful. "Olga, you shouldn't use expressions like that."

"It is American—I heard it on 'The Voice of America.' "

More likely, she had learned it from Maurice Moody, he thought wickedly. "You never heard that on 'The Voice of America,' " he whispered. "Shame on you, Olga. It's better you speak Russian . . . or French, the language of love. What about the French verb: *embracer*?"

"I'm only trying to please you, as a mistress should," she exclaimed impatiently.

She drew him in deeply, then not satisfied with that, she stretched her arm to seize him by the scrotum and pulled. Holding on as best he could, Kelly willed himself to reach the ends of her, but still not assuaged, she slid a hand between their sweaty bodies and stroked herself above the mass of his personage. Her eyes were tightly shut. She bit her tongue in concentration.

"Jazz me, baby, eight to the bar!"

"Olga, no!"

She giggled hysterically, racing him to the finish line, and precipitously, her strenuous effort paid off. Her fingernails raked his back and she climaxed with a hefty bellow—and again and again, he could not count the times, with each one her convulsion decreasing until eventually, it became a weak tremor accompanied by an animal whine of some thirty seconds' duration.

God, Kelly thought, gentle Beatrice was his point of comparison and she did naught but love in a quiet place, as passionate in her reticence as Olga was in her delirium. In fact, he thought, in the silent thundering of her desire, Beatrice was more violent than these noisy, pushy ones.

"Ram it home!"

"Olga, please . . ."

As she had before, Olga kneaded his balls like baclava dough. He resisted, trying to get out of her reach, but her fingers initiated his own orgasm. When he felt it, she responded forcefully.

"I'm coming too! Like a freight train. Toot-toot!"

He didn't bother to reprimand her now. Olga humped and bucked and yelled. If it went on much longer, he would be torn to pieces. Then, at once, her body surrendered to control, her breasts relaxed, and the driving force of her mons diminished to placidity.

"Jack," she murmured, her accent breaking up the words, "*Quel* fuck!"

"Yeah, really." He had to say something. "Olga, that was worth waiting for. You're a very active woman."

She opened her eyes at last. The pupils were flooded with fulfillment and her smile was self-satisfied. It worried him a little, what he saw. Was it a victorious little smile as well? Yes, no doubt. Resting a moment on her slightly chubby body, he wondered if he should tell her that this might not only be their first, but last, sexual encounter, that he did not want or need a mistress, that it would make him feel cheap and even, yes, adulterous, to meet her in that relationship, particularly as she mouthed the guttersnipe argot of the American school system.

Slowly, he withdrew from her plush enclosure, and as he was doing so, the truth came to him: Olga was not a virgin after all. "Olga, have you known many men?"

She shook her head. "But one," she confessed softly, "many years ago, before you arrived in Paris."

Kelly was willing to accept that but he also understood that when it came to the delicate matter of virginity, one was as good as a hundred. If a woman had lost it, she had only to admit to the one. "What happened?"

"My poor boy was the victim of a dread disease. It was in the summer, on a beach in Bretagne. We were in love. I was very young."

"And he died? I'm sorry, Olga."

"Of tetanus," she said, closing her eyes with the pain of it, or something like pain. "And now, Jack—you make me crazy. Give me a little wine."

He held the glass to her lips. Red wine flowed down her chin, onto her chest, staining her breasts. Kelly bent to lick it up and her heart began to pound. Yes, there was, he admitted, something to be said for simple desire, desire not entangled with the emotion of love. This small *contretemps* with Olga had no bearing on his affair with the mistress of Château Beaupeau. This was primitive, a reflex action existing only in the body, not the heart and the mind.

"So all these years I have been waiting," Olga said. "And now you, Jack. It is wonderful."

Waiting, he thought, remembering, and masturbating, a sorrowful thing to discover. He drew his thumb along her chin, down the cleft between her breasts, following the line of her stomach, almost like a seam, where the Creator had joined the skin covering the human frame. With his fingertips, he played with the knotted patch of brown hair that grew up her stomach, placed his hand lightly over her sopping pube, and sensed the tingling of nerves as he did so. In afterglow, she was not as resoundingly wanton. Her body moved luxuriously under his caress; she clamped his hand between her thighs, tightened the muscles of her pelvis, and held him locked there.

"It is unforgettable," she whispered. Her eyes changed color and tone. They became mischievous. "So this is the fabled *équipage?*"

"Fabled? What do you mean?"

"Madame Mordaunt told me Monsieur Jacques has been passing his days in the service of love in every *arrondissement* of Paris."

Kelly laughed modestly. "Slanderous old bag."

"But I do not think you have made love like this before, Jack?"

He had to lie to her. Did any woman want to be told she was not the best? "Never so good as this, Olga."

"Put some more wine in my mouth, Jack."

He tilted the glass carefully, allowing the Château Beaupeau to trickle between her teeth. She gulped a little of it, swishing the rest on her tongue. "Now Jack," she said. She bent forward to close her mouth tightly over the burgeoning bulb of his personage and whacked it with her tongue. The tart body of the wine inflamed him; it stung like an antiseptic. But it served her purpose. In a thrice, he was revived, and Olga, for her part, was writhing on the cushions. Pausing for a second to take a deep breath, she fastened her tongue to him, spiraling, jabbing. Kelly ran his hand down her back, fingers through the dividing pass of her buns, and followed filmy patches of wet hair to the sweetly split pube, each lip swollen as if by bee sting, creased like a cheerful smile leading to her base of merriment. Was this the smile at the foot of the ladder, of which Henry Miller had written? Olga dripped with sticky fluid, not as viscous in texture as Mordaunt Number Four but nevertheless a lubricant smeary enough to ease the way for all but the heaviest of *équipages*. He slipped his hand back toward the other orifice, feeling the knot of it tighten into unopened rosebud. Her ass shook in response.

"Sorry about that," he murmured. "I was just wandering."

But she was not at all put out. "No matter. My body is your body now, to do with what you please."

"What do *you* please?"

She removed her mouth from him and cocked an eye devilishly. "I wish you to tell me that it is not true, as Count Boris suspects, that you were making love to the president's daughter on that awful day at the Crillon."

Kelly chuckled. "Olga, there's your old devil theory again."

Reassured, she resumed her intimate act, pulling at his personage with her cheek muscles, huffing and puffing against his roots. She wound strands of hair around it, twisting them into little bows and slid on him to place the personage between her breasts and smack them together. He replied with renewed pressure on her cherub-lipped pube, puckering the lips together and rolling them like ball bearings on his fingers. This got to her: she cried out in an ecstasy.

"Jack, this prick of yours is very lovely and beautiful," she wailed. God, he thought, she didn't waste words, did she? "Do you think it is possible to make love again so soon or must one wait for a day or so?"

He didn't believe such naiveté. "I think if we wait a little while, like thirty seconds or so, we could manage it again, Olga."

"Ah, that is good. Please be so kind as to insert and *embrace-moi.*"

He felt better about her now. She was wild but, after all, that wasn't a sin. Yes, he could accept her like this, with no commitments, merely for the sexual thrill of it. He bent his head to take her nipples again. Close up, he noted a fine brown fur growing within the rust-colored coronas, several individual hairs quite long and needing clipping. But whatever their hirsute quality, they were undoubtedly sensitive. As his tongue jarred them, the nipples stiffened attentively. She gasped again and implanted tiny bites on him, causing him to shudder with terrified delight. Her buttocks flounced against the cushions, another reflex action, he noted. She had him entirely in her mouth but, surprisingly, she could still speak. Speak she did.

"Count Boris is convinced that the death of Miss Mont . . ."

"If she is dead . . ."

"Yes, her death, or disappearance. It is the work of the most depraved Aristide de Bis, minister-without-portfolio."

"I agree."

"Count Boris told me that during the Nazi occupation of France many years ago, during which time Count

Boris was a hero of the Resistance, Madame Mordaunt was the mistress of a Nazi general. . . ."

"Heard that one before, Olga . . . old news," he mumbled in the lushness of her belly.

"That Aristide de Bis, a brutal teenager, was a police chief loyal to the Vichy régime . . ."

She was getting warmer. "I've heard talk of that, Olga."

Whatever the novelty of her revelations, it struck him as absolutely remarkable that some of the most astounding bits of gossip, even tendrils of truth, emerged from the mouths of aroused women. She worked over his personals with both hands and her mouth, in an intensely curious, almost impersonal manner as she plied him with information. Kelly swooped down her odalisque figure, brushing his cheeks across her thighs. She shifted smoothly to take his head between her legs, his face into a hairy growth as thick as any beard. He could say one thing about Olga for certain: she had hair that just didn't stop, a full mane of it. She was like a lioness; or better, a Russian bear. Her movement to accommodate this most confidential of gestures was so seemingly natural, it occurred to him that she and her youthful lover must have practiced considerably on the beaches of Bretagne all those bright summers ago.

"During the war," Olga growled, having taken his testicles in her lips, "Monsieur Victor was a slave in a Nazi bordello."

"I know."

Thoughtfully, she chewed on his scrotum, as she might have an overripe fig. Kelly bit her thighs, nibbled on her lush mons.

Olga continued fulsomely, "During the war, your president was a member of a secret organization. He was parachuted into France to work with the *Maquis* in the mountains and it was there Count Boris met him." Kelly gazed at her through the fleshy "V" of her legs. She was regarding him solemnly. "It is said that during those months, George Washburn was a hero."

"Yes, so I believe." He lisped slightly through a mouthful of hair. "The mystery is why the French despise him so much now."

"Yummy!" she cried before replying. "Because he learned too much of the inner workings of French politics, of the *collaborateurs,* such as Aristide de Bis. He was also responsible for the destruction of many installations—bridges which were most expensive to rebuild—and some historical monuments used as Nazi offices. And the jail, a seventeenth-century edifice, where Aristide de Bis tortured many true Frenchmen. This is why Aristide de Bis hates Washburn, and it is why Count Boris hates Aristide de Bis above all else. He also has contempt for Monsieur Victor and harbors a deep resentment even for Madame Mordaunt."

"Hatred runs deep in this country," Kelly summarized.

But then she imparted her really gigantic piece of information. She spit out his balls and tears ran down his genitals.

"Count Boris is *not* my father," she said weeping. "Do you know when I learned this, Jack? Only a few days ago. Count Boris told me the entire story. I am the daughter of George Washburn."

"No, you're kidding! I don't believe it!" He hiked his head up so he could see her more clearly.

"It is *true.* I am half-American. And that is why I decided today to become your mistress."

He was well and truly shocked. "How did this happen? I must know."

Holding his balls in one hand and wiping away tears with the other, Olga said, "During the time of the *Maquis,* my mother and Count Boris and a troop of patriots lived in the mountains of eastern France. There, my mother fell in love with the dashing Captain Washburn. One night, while Count Boris was out with his *troupe* blowing up an enemy pontoon bridge, this love was consummated. I am the fruition."

"Well . . ." Good God! "How could your mother be sure?"

"Because Count Boris was captured that night and did not escape from Aristide de Bis's jail until three months later, when said jail was blown up by Captain Washburn. You see, three months . . ."

"I know, Olga, I can count. Is this possible? Olga, I have to think this is one of the biggest coincidences I've heard in this most coincidental of worlds."

He was almost overcome by the realization of how incredibly confused was the history of Europe, how much he had yet to learn about the hates, passions, and memories that governed the fortunes of the Continent. And he was well nigh swept away by the flood of another coincidence: he had now made love to two of Washburn's daughters. That fact was most unbelievable of all.

Olga finished her tale: her mother had died in an artillery bombardment only weeks after her birth.

"And Count Boris raised you as his own daughter. God, what a fine man."

She nodded. "For years, he preferred to think that I was a very premature baby. Now—I do not know why—he decided to tell me the truth." Olga sniffled.

"So you're Russian-American. Does George Washburn know about this?"

She shrugged her bare shoulders. "He was gone. He was taken away by night plane before my birth."

"You should meet him, Olga, tell him who you are."

"No, I would not wish to embarrass the president of the United States. And it might kill Count Boris. It would shame and humiliate him if he thought everyone knew he had been cuckolded by a president."

Kelly nodded wisely. "Yes, I can understand that," he murmured, again allowing himself to be taken by the marvel of coincidence and the central part George Washburn played in all their lives. Surely, this man had the stature of a historical figure, whether good or bad.

Mournfully, Olga returned to the solace of his loins, and Kelly tenderly tried to take her mind off these doleful matters. He savored each part of her twittering mons, devoured each sector as he would have a segment of fruit. "Olga, we should really make this a joyful event, if we can."

"Yes, yes," she agreed, happy to be diverted, "what should we do?"

"Your body is too much for me, like marble or ivory, a work by Michelangelo. Let's get up a minute."

He helped her climb on the coffee table, stood her there like a piece of sculpture. It was true—her body did have the sensuous dimension of sculpture, the hardness but fluidity of stone. The harmonics of her sexuality echoed from deep within her, vitalized the skin and provided the dynamic of her uplifted breasts, her thighs and belly. As he greedily surveyed her, she wheeled to show him her rear, the dimpled seat. She was indeed a wonder, and making love to her, now that she was quiescent, would be a form of worship too, akin to delving into more of the mysteries, translating the ultimate riddles, solving the equations of existence, implanting one's self into the center of the life-force.

"Gosh, Olga," he said. The word made him think of Westerley Washburn, the president's other daughter. Kelly clasped her hips and buried his face in her belly, hearing the pounding of her life against his forehead.

"Again, Jack! Again!"

He stooped to sweep everything off the table, then spread her upon it, pausing to absorb the message of the flesh. Her eyes were smilingly closed, her mons twitched, and her ass gently slapped against the wood.

"Please, Jack, put my Cossack boots on me."

"Yes," he said. He was breathing hard. He slipped the boots on her tiny feet, zipping them up the sides. Moving around her sprawled figure, he stroked her from head to toes. When she was seething, he assumed a position between her thighs and lowered himself in a docking maneuver. It was no big trick, for her Venusian bulge reached to meet him and draw him almost magnetically.

Strangely, Olga began to count to herself: one, two, three, as though she were standing in the prow of a riverboat measuring the depth of channel, Mark One, Mark Twain, sounding off the extent of his penetration. "Very slowly, Monsieur Jack. Please, by little, little steps."

The velvety smooth muscles at the verge of her passage took note of every nudge of progress, and as he neared the end of his potential, she held back for a second, then yawned open to envelop him. She screamed thinly and kicked her boots in the air, crossed her ankles behind him to hold him there, encased. The veins in her chest jumped and very slowly she gyrated, each turn of the convoluted bore pulling him further forward. She wrenched her right hand free of his grasp and slipped her fingers down, again seizing his sack of balls. Kelly did not think this could be done. He had evaded her before but this time he could not. It was not easy, or painless, this part of her lovemaking requirement. However, the gesture added an additional dimension of pleasure with which he could not argue: she pushed one ball, then the other, inside her . . . searched for a third—was she mad? Kelly's structural muscles began to ache. Olga expelled a raw mixture of cries and jungle exclamations. Her eyes flicked open: yes, he was still there, no doubt of that, for it would have been impossible for him to escape from the trap she had closed behind him. All her attention now was directed to a grinding action to which he could do nothing but respond; to do otherwise would have been self-destructive. Finally, after what seemed an eternity of numb connection, merely a twinkling of time, her drugged familiarity with his *équipage* brought her to another dramatic climax. Next, the mashing contractions of her muscles forced from Kelly an excruciating orgasm and a cry of hurt from his throat as sure as if she had stuck her hand down his esophagus and yanked on his windpipe.

She screamed pitifully, "No more, no more! I can stand no more! You are killing me."

But release lay with her, not him, and she did then set him loose of the wringer. Personage and balls free, Kelly collapsed upon her. It took him time to recover. "Olga, that was something I'll never forget."

"Bah!" she scoffed lovingly, "it is the Russian way."

"The Russian-American way," he reminded her.

Once more, he was aware of the sex drive inherent in

the Washburn line. Surely there could be no pure Russian as horny as this. He began again to doubt her protestations of innocence—she could not have perfected such articulation in one fling with a pimply youth. Nor was he sure such an extreme of intimacy had been described in the sex manuals. Certainly, Maggi, the expert sexologist, had never hinted at the engagement of the entire genital armory during the act of love.

"Ah, Jack," Olga gushed, "that was quite marvelous. I am subtracted by joy."

"Distracted," he corrected her. "I'm the one who's subtracted."

"But it cannot hurt," she said knowingly, "our bodies would not hurt each other. They are for bringing rapture. Our bodies know no shyness or embarrassment. They are united now. If I could, I would swallow all of you in my body, so you would become another of my organs, living perhaps between my womb and heart."

"I think I've already been there," he said.

She chuckled. "I have hidden in my boudoir a fat book relating to the love affairs of our Catherine the Great."

"Mae West always said that Catherine was great," he said lightly.

Olga bit his arm. She didn't take kindly to jokes about the Russian royalty. "I am referring to the secrets of her passion and how she expressed them to her many lovers, of whom Count Boris's ancestor was one." Kelly did not interrupt; he thought it best to let her run her course. "Do you know, *par exemple*, Jack, that Catherine once made love to a dancing bear?" He shook his head, although everyone knew Catherine had been a sickie. "The bear was later beheaded. It is also written that she once made love to five of her noblemen at the same time—not the same day, or week, but in the same moment of time."

"Good God," Kelly said, feigning surprise. "Olga, you're marvelous."

"Yes," she said, "as always. I never change. What next? I do not think we have yet covered what we Americans call the waterfront."

* * *

Their cheerful postcoital chat was inevitably disturbed by the sound of the doorbell. Again, Kelly was thrown into near panic. It was still too early for Hercule.

"Oh, *merde*," Olga yelled. "It must be that doctor. I forgot to tell you. He said he would be calling."

Olga was lying in exhibit like one of those porcelain dolls used by Chinese doctors and shy women patients to establish the location of aches and pains. She grabbed her clothes and ran into the bathroom. This time, she was not going to be caught *en déshabillé*.

"Yes?" Kelly spoke toward the door, standing, as before, to the side.

"Ehrlitz!"

Of course, it would be Dr. Wolfgang Ehrlitz of Mannheim and Heidelberg. Kelly dressed quickly, checked to be sure Olga had left nothing behind, and whispered to her to be sure to stay in the bedroom.

He scarcely recognized Wolfgang Ehrlitz. It was not a matter of the esteemed specialist having changed physically. Surgeon's smock laid aside and now dressed, so to speak, in civilian clothes, Ehrlitz seemed to have altered in personality. At Montmorency, his home ground, he had been coldly scientific, an ageless automaton. Now Kelly saw a man of about sixty, a man who eagerly shook his hand and then sat down very carefully in the center of an inner tube he pulled from his briefcase and inflated.

"Herr Doktor," Kelly asked, "are you suffering from hemorrhoids?"

Ehrlitz flushed. "No." He squinted curiously around the living room but made no remark about the squalidness of the place—the ashtray overflowing with butts, the bottle, two glasses overturned on the floor. "It is a great pleasure for me to see you again, Herr Kelly." He clasped carefully manicured hands in his lap.

Kelly offered him a glass of wine but Ehrlitz declined, explaining that he never drank while traveling, which he said, as Kelly would know, was a very dangerous occupation.

"I suppose you're referring to the accident I had on the way home from Geneva."

"I was not aware of that, Herr Kelly," Ehrlitz said uneasily.

"But I suppose you have heard what happened to your patient, Topovsky?"

Ehrlitz groaned and studied his hands. "I know from the newspapers that a presidential assistant named T. Topovsky . . ."

"Suffered a breakdown and jumped out of a window at the Crillon."

"The pressures of high office are mutilating." Ehrlitz sighed.

"I trust it had nothing to do with the Grovival treatment."

"Certainly not," Ehrlitz exclaimed. He stared reprovingly at Kelly from behind his shiny spectacles. "Mr. Topovsky obviously suffered a personality challenge with which he could not cope. But that is not why I am in Paris, Herr Kelly." Ehrlitz hummed to himself, eyeing the rumpled sofa. As composed as he tried to seem, it was obvious there was something on his mind that made him nervous. He took a stubby Swiss cigar out of a leather pocket packet, cut it carefully, and put it between his teeth. Eventually, he would get to the point. When the cigar was evenly lit, Ehrlitz announced, "I have come here for an appointment with Madame Mordaunt. I thought I would tell you this, and ask your advice, since you are very close to the House of Mordaunt."

Kelly shook his head. "Not like I used to be. I suppose you've come about Grovival. . . ."

Ehrlitz shrugged irritably. "Maybe yes, maybe no. I would like to ask you—has Madame Mordaunt developed any idiosyncrasies, since last I saw her?"

"You mean during the war, when Zouzou was mistress of Colonel-General Ulrich von Unterstutzen?"

"Herr Kelly, *Donnerwetter!*" Ehrlitz cried. "That is impossible. Where could you hear such a loathsome story? The Herr General was, as everyone knows, on the Eastern Front during the war."

"Along with you, I suppose, Herr Doktor."

Ehrlitz's face darkened from blush to blood clot high in the cheekbones. He muttered that *Jawohl,* as a matter of fact he too had served on the Russian Front. He sprang off his inner tube in agitation, thus liberating a floater; the odor was so heavy as to be almost visible, like smoke from dry ice. His face flushed an even darker red.

"Well, doc," Kelly said laconically, "I can tell you Zouzou's taking the stuff too, and she doesn't seem to be any the better for it."

Ehrlitz marched up and down the room. "I can see, as before, Herr Kelly, that you are quite mad." He resumed his tricky seat. "I would say that what is past is past. I would remind you that during the war and afterwards I have served as a man of medicine, true to my Hippocratic oath. I bring also a message of Let Bygones Be Bygones, *nicht wahr,* or *n'est ce pas,* as we say in France. That is one of my purposes in Paris today."

"I don't understand you," Kelly said easily, "but I'm willing to listen. No wine? I need some more. Just a minute, please."

From the kitchen, he could see Olga's face in the partially opened bedroom door. She smiled naughtily and shook her head. She appreciated the comic aspect of Ehrlitz's delivery. When he returned to the living room, Ehrlitz was studying documents he had spread on the coffee table.

Kelly opened the bottle and retrieved a glass from the floor.

Sternly, Ehrlitz said, "Do you care so little that you are not going to ask after the state of the health of your wife?"

"Ex-wife."

Ehrlitz waved his arms. "Let no man put asunder," he exclaimed. "You, Herr Kelly, are the father of her child!"

Kelly smiled broadly. At least on this one, he was ahead of the good doctor. "Oh, no. I've already heard about that, doc. The father is the Mangrovian foreign minister."

"Nonsense!" Ehrlitz glared at him. "What if I told you that your wife wants to return to you here in Paris?"

"Frankly, if you told me that I'd be very surprised. I'd be even more surprised if I agreed. The last I heard was she picked up a quickie divorce in Haiti, then went on to Mangrovia. . . . Tell me, when is the baby due?"

"Next August."

Kelly's smile widened. This was too much. "Let's see, then, doc, a little arithmetic, shall we? Normal incubation is nine months, I believe?" Ehrlitz agreed without hesitation. "Well, then, since Maryjane Kelly, née Trout, left here last August and I haven't seen her since, wouldn't it seem slightly impossible . . ."

Ehrlitz's chin muscles stiffened. "Not if the child was artificially inseminated, Herr Kelly."

"How, pray tell, was that done?"

It was Ehrlitz's turn to smile. "If you admit the possibility of artificial insemination, then is it not just as logical to conjecture that your wife was artificially fertilized by your . . . fluid?"

"Doc—I'm not playing that game again."

Ehrlitz, however, was not discouraged. "What if I were to tell you, then, as a second possibility, that her father, Herr Trout—forelle, in German, and a very delicious fish plate, as you know—is aware of her pregnancy but does not wish her to become another in a line of Mesdames Foreign Minister of Mangrovia, Madame Cinnabar Macoo?"

"Macoo? He's one of that Cou-Cou Macoo tribe?"

"So I believe," Ehrlitz said.

Slowly, Kelly considered the proposition. "Trout wants her to come back here and for me to be the father, in quotes, of this little albino-black bambino?"

"Yes, I believe he is an albino."

Kelly paused. "To hell with that, doc. Tell C.T., no dice. I'm not available. And naturally, you know," he said sarcastically, "that little gambit would completely screw up your plans for Grovival. I mean, if Maryjane deserts Monsieur Cinnabar Macoo, the Mangrovians will be so pissed off you'll never do any business with them."

Ehrlitz coolly said, "That is up to the authorities in La Minge. Cinnabar Macoo does not have the last word. Besides which, Herr Kelly; at this point it seems Grovival will be outlawed by the United Nations' World Health Organization. It will be dropped from our schedule. . . ."

"Like a hot potato."

"The subsidiary effects of the drug have proven very hard to manage," Ehrlitz said reluctantly.

"The farting and the warts," Kelly said. "Doc, I have a feeling the reason you're sitting on that inner tube is you've got a big, fat wart on your ass."

Face glowing with embarrassment, Ehrlitz lowered his eyes. "Your powers of observation are quite extraordinary, Herr Kelly," he muttered. "Grovival, we have also found, works with normal bodily fluids to produce a quite nauseating odor. . . ."

"Topovsky—I noticed that."

"Yes, perhaps, and other things—pronounced personality disorders."

"Topovsky again! Wonder of wonders! Well, at least you're going to cut your losses. What I don't understand is how the natives handle it."

Ehrlitz shrugged disgustedly. "Over the centuries, those savages developed a tolerance. Climatic, or to do with the inferior African genes. As is known, hepatitis doesn't strike in the same place twice."

"Really? I suppose too that a bad smell wouldn't be as noticeable in the wide open spaces as in a city. The warts, I don't know. They might think warts were worth it if they grew big penises. . . . How long does it take for the stuff to wear off?"

Ehrlitz grunted and said, "Approximately a year." Petulantly, he took a damaging shot. "At any rate, it aroused your former wife to quite basic instincts. . . . You will not cooperate?"

"No," Kelly said. "You've got to understand, doc, it wouldn't be any good. Maryjane and I don't get along, and having her back with this little stunt in her *curriculum vitae* wouldn't help matters. I mean, I don't think I could handle it. Shit, she'd be all pumped up with

Grovival, most likely some kind of a sex maniac and emotionally disturbed—more than she already was. Jesus! The more I think about it, the more impossible it is. And, besides, I'm in love with somebody else now. Oh, shit, he had forgotten Olga was listening; but she would assume he meant her. "Another thing, doc, Maryjane can't just pick up and go trotting around the world laying everybody in sight—for all I know, you probably fucked her too."

"Herr Kelly!" Ehrlitz jumped up again.

"What I'm saying is I don't want her back and that's the end of it."

His hands behind his back, Ehrlitz strode to the window and stared into the street. "Ethically, it is impossible that I would have touched a patient!"

"Not even when they were in deep freeze?" Kelly taunted.

"Scheisse, nein!" Ehrlitz growled. "However, since you are being so unpleasant, I will tell you we have certain reason to believe there was dalliance in Geneva between your wife and your dearest friend, Señor Rafael Trujillo Perex."

Kelly's stomach tightened. So it *was* true. Rafe, the two-timing son of a bitch. The sight of the Perex château flashed through his mind and the imagined scene, again, of Maryjane scampering nakedly through the baronial building, Perex in pursuit, then catching her, flinging her down, and jumping between her Grovival-crazed legs and pumping away, pin-striped suit and trilby undisturbed by the exertion.

"Do you know that for a fact?"

"No, what is there that is known for a fact? But if it is true, then it would be reasonable to assume, or postulate, that Señor Perex is the father of the child, not Foreign Minister Cinnabar Macoo. I wonder if Señor Perex will do *his* duty?"

"Why don't you ask him?" Kelly suggested angrily. "And if he won't, then *you* do it."

"I do it?" Ehrlitz turned furiously. "No, I could never marry. As much as I admire your lady-wife."

"No longer my lady-wife."

"No, I could not. That is impossible."

Disgustedly, Kelly said, "I thought there was no limit to what you people will do for your leader, George Washburn." Ehrlitz trembled. "Well, you *are* on the AmFreight payroll, aren't you, doc?"

"No. I am paid by the foundation. Washburn's political days are numbered," Ehrlitz said crudely. He sat down carefully on his inner tube. He leaned forward, an ingratiating smile on his face. "Let us change the subject. . . . I have designed some dresses. Do you think Madame Mordaunt would be interested in looking at my sketches?"

Weakly, Kelly said, "You want to be a dress designer now, doctor?"

"Yes, and why not? The practice of medicine can become a bore, Herr Kelly. I thought the design of sundresses and lingerie would be an interesting hobby. Now it has become my passion." Kelly did not speak and Ehrlitz grinned foolishly. "I will make a small confession, since we are such close friends. In Berlin, in the thirties, a most decadent time, I became fond of wearing silk against my body, and since I am a large man, it was necessary for me to design my own underthings. A youthful silliness, yes, I admit it."

"Just panties?" Kelly asked.

Ehrlitz giggled. "Later, in older years, the breasts of a man enlarge, as you will discover one day, Herr Kelly. . . . So now also, I confess, what we Germans call the *Bustenhalter.*"

"That is brassieres?" Kelly asked wonderingly. "Silk must have been damn cold on the Russian Front."

"*Jawohl.* But I wore what you call woolies over them." Ehrlitz's face was agonized. He suspected now that he had told Kelly too much.

"Well, all I can suggest is that you talk it over with Zouzou."

"Yes, I will." A frightful thought occurred to Ehrlitz. "Herr Kelly, do not conclude from this that I am a homosexual, for I am not."

"No, I wouldn't ever conclude that," Kelly said. "Simply because you enjoy wearing women's underwear would not logically lead one to conjecture that you—"

"Herr Kelly, you are mocking me!" Ehrlitz was very wounded.

"No, I'm not. I wouldn't." Kelly fell into silence. "You know, I think you should let Maryjane stick with the foreign minister. To hell with her."

"And leave her in exile in that godforsaken swamp? What! How can you be so unfeeling, Herr Kelly? A youthful indiscretion and you would make her pay for it the rest of her life?"

"She might like it in Mangrovia very much. . . . Is it true you enlarged her tits?"

Ehrlitz nodded. "But not by much. We redesigned the nipples and restructured her fatty tissues."

Ehrlitz was poised, waiting for more questions. "Is AmFreight going to buy Maison Mordaunt, doc?"

"I do not know. That is up to Herr Forelle, Trout I mean."

"Well . . ." Kelly had had enough. He hoped Ehrlitz would leave soon. But he couldn't wait for him to make a move. He shouted, "Olga, come out here a minute. . . .I want you to meet somebody."

Ehrlitz was displeased when Olga came from the bedroom. Since she had dressed, he would never be able to say anything of an intimate nature had occurred this afternoon. "Good day, *fraulein*," he said.

"Doctor, this is Olga Blastorov, my secretary. Olga, this gentleman is Doctor Wolfgang Ehrlitz."

Ehrlitz's face was set, the long saber scar looked ghastly on his cheek. "I see you do not trust me, Herr Kelly. You thought it necessary to have a witness, also a witness to my indiscretions."

"No, no, don't get the wrong idea. Miss Blastorov is more of a friend than a witness."

The second mention of her name caused Ehrlitz to go white in the face. "Did I hear the name to be Blastorov?"

"*Oui,*" Olga said snippily, "and what of it?"

"Nothing, *fraulein*. Sometimes, Herr Kelly, I am drawn to the conclusion that you are not a gentleman."

"Really? Sometimes, doctor, I'm drawn to the conclusion you are not a doctor."

"Gott in Himmel! Donnerwetter! Verdammt!" Ehrlitz barked. "I see one cannot do business with you. I have here a paper for you to sign but I see you will not sign it."

"A paper?"

"A document of a paternalistic nature," Ehrlitz muttered. "You have just missed an opportunity for what you Americans call *Das Jackpot.*"

"So Trout was ready to pay? So what?"

"So, good-bye, Herr Kelly. It is extremely doubtful we shall ever see each other again."

Kelly smiled in a way that would make Ehrlitz sick. "Doc, if we see each other today, isn't it really logical to think that we might see each other again another day?"

"Dummkopf!"

When Ehrlitz had gone into the hall and his angry beating at the elevator cage had ceased, Kelly put his arm around Olga and drew her down on the long couch. He had not been prepared for Ehrlitz. Normally, one can anticipate almost any kind of accident or disaster: car collision, measles, stroke, blood poisoning. It was always the totally unexpected that threw you.

Olga twisted the gold wedding ring he wore on his left hand. "You are, I understand, a free man now, Monsieur Kelly. You are no longer married. Perhaps you will not feel so guilty now about our love affair. Is it true what this doctor said about . . ."

"Maryjane? Yeah, I think so. Although, who the hell knows? All this is very surrealistic, Olga."

She nodded vehemently. "I know that I do not feel so guilty now. Now my passion can be fully unleashed."

"Did it bother you before?"

"Making love to a married man? Yes, naturally. Each time I undress, I am made to feel sinful. When I allow you to touch me, I receive the shock of knowledge of the venal sin and when I allow you, so unbalanced by love, to enter my body, I am aware of mortal sin of the worst kind. Now I will not have to worry. I will not have to stop at the church when I leave you, for it is only a little thing in the eye of God."

Kelly watched her warily. He thought perhaps she did not fully understand. "Olga, I don't know about the Russian Orthodox Church but in the Catholic Church when two people make love outside marriage it's considered a mortal sin. More than that, Olga," he said, slipping his hand under her sweater for a feel of the Rubenesque breasts, "I was taught that the thought is just as sinful as the act. We discussed this—before."

She brushed aside the comment. "That has changed now, Jack. In the new Catholic Church where Latin is no longer said at the Mass, the pope has also decided that when two people embrace it is not so bad. It would be better, yes, if they were married. But the *papa* hopes that if they enjoy each other very much, then they will marry and have many, many Catholic children. . . . No, no, it is not bad anymore."

There was a yearning look in her eye that disturbed him. "I see you're very modern."

"*Très.* You see, previously I have been holding back. There is much, I am told, that we have not attempted. There are variations—they are called *les Positions.*"

"Really?"

Olga began to undress again. Really, Kelly thought, there had to be some limit to his endurance. Olga's eyes closed and she swayed heatedly, murmuring, stringing together unrelated thoughts.

"I will be your mistress. . . . But what will I do if Monsieur Maurice Moody makes demands on me? He speaks of the *droit du seigneur,* that by which the master demands the sexual compliance of the slave. . . ."

Carelessly, he said, "Tell him you're under the protection of the House of Kelly."

"All right. I will always be your mistress. Even if I marry and you marry again, I will continue to be your mistress."

"What do you mean, if you marry?"

"Well, being your mistress does not mean I cannot marry. That is the European way, Jack. Marriage has nothing to do with making love, Monsieur Jack."

"Olga, please."

"It is not so bad, Jack."

In her own junior statuesque manner, Olga was as deeply mysterious as any other woman. Kelly was seized by the notion that he could roll her up like a piece of pastry, then thrust into her sugary center as into a juicy éclair. He had the exciting sensation of making love to an amoeba, all center, no arms or legs. He could fold and compress her parts like a plastic-wrapped and refrigerated chicken, all creased and wrinkled around her pliable mons. She would have totally surrendered to eroticism, to her motor, his driving shaft and cylinders, to the hot blood that coursed through her. All began and ended there at this one tiny jeweled place, like a Fabergé box which opened to become a vast chamber of delight as large as the solar system. Olga was rare, disembodied sex and theirs a merger of blood, marrow, bone, tissue. They were two deliquescent jungle blossoms, male, female, or hermaphroditic, ground together, all petals crushed and then compressed in the giant hand until all passionate dribblings had been blended into one superheated mulch powerful enough to refertilize the earth in the eons after Apocalypse. Thus stunned, as if stoned to death by her orgasm, he was vaguely reminded of the stories told by the ancients about the thunder and lightning produced when Hera, well caught and well screwed by Zeus, blasted mountaintops loose from their moorings, unhinged the stars, and laid waste to what had once been the green belt of the Sahara Desert.

Olga lay panting, kicking her heels in the air, like a turtle on its back scrambling for purchase where none could be found, that is in thin air.

"Jack! Jack! You have killed me now for sure."

"Olga, it is the sweet death—death by orgasm. The way they punished the ancient queens."

"Jack! You have burst into my womb and I can feel you have started my menstrual cycle, with which you are familiar, I think. You see, every month . . ."

"Shut up, Olga. I know all about that."

"The violence of your attack has brought it on two days early. I keep a calendar, Jack," she said efficiently. "Jack, that was a bang heard round the world."

"Olga . . ."

"Like Catherine"—she laughed hoarsely—"I could feel you inside me, like a stallion off the steppes, like a band of Cossack dancers, a dozen pairs of marching boots, all stamping."

"Olga, was it that fantastic for you?"

"Yes, fantastic. For you?"

"Yes." He was flattered, of course.

"All the balalaikas were playing. I could feel the strings, the strumming of the strings. I was Murmansk and you were the icebreaker opening the channel in the dead of winter. You were the Volga boatman, Olga's Volga boatman . . . Peter the Great."

"Olga, come on, cut it out. You sound like a tour of Russia."

She snuggled up to him. "I am your mistress now. We will see each other every day, for the *cinq-à-sept.*"

She was referring to the traditional French interlude, the 5:00 P.M. to 7:00 P.M. screw, stolen by Frenchmen immemorial on their way home from the office; a quick one with the mistress to prepare for an evening with the wife and kiddies.

Kelly didn't like the concept. He never had. "Call it what you want, Olga."

"Yes, Jack. Do you think mistresses love better than wives?"

"I don't know for sure," he said tiredly, "but it's very possible."

CHAPTER

THIRTY-TWO

"You see before you," Perex murmured, "a far more cynical man than you have seen before."

They were strolling the gravel paths of the formal garden within the walls of the Château Beaupeau. It was cold winter now, a few days after Christmas. A light layer of snow, more like heavy frost than snow, crunched under their feet. Above them, the branches of the bare winter oaks seemed woven like dark veins into the gray matter of the sky and the topiaried shrubbery, clipped and pruned into evergreen species of the animal world, was shrouded in the frozen sleet. Behind, the gray eminence of the feudal edifice, Château Beaupeau itself, loomed protectively for them, menacingly to the stranger. High-fluted and flanged chimneys added more gray to the sky.

In the long room nearest them, the library, wood-paneled and lined with leather-bound books, where Gaston de Bis had met his end, Beatrice would still be sitting at her table, so long after breakfast, going through the heavy ledgers in which she kept the facts and figures relating to the autumn vintage. It would be a good year, she said, for the long days of sunshine had filled the grapes with mellow juice: the transmogrification of sunlight into energy and, in due course, alcoholic content, the transformation of energy to matter, the dream of the alchemist, never yet realized.

Perex shivered in his British "warm" and stamped his feet in their thin-soled Italian shoes. The trilby did not look quite so cocky perched on his head as it used to. He had lost weight and his face was pallid from his weeks in the cantonal jail. He had arrived last night.

"Well at least you're out of that Swiss cooler," Kelly observed.

"Yeah, out of the frying pan and into the bloody fire," Perex said cryptically.

"What do you mean?"

Perex only shook his head. Kelly wondered if this meant Doctor Ehrlitz had made his approach, or if some kind of word had come from the boss, C.T. Trout. It served the bastard right.

"You might know, my dear, that the bounders wouldn't let me out until the day after Christmas, one of my favorite holidays." Wistfully, he added, "You must have had a good time here."

Yes. It had been a very private time, however. Beatrice had directed a tall spruce be cut and shaped for the library, and they had decorated it with candles and tinsel. A priest had come from the village to celebrate Midnight Mass in the château chapel, and then Beatrice had asked for the servants to gather around. She gave them small gifts and envelopes of money. This accomplished, they had gone to the second-floor sleeping apartment to drink a final bottle of champagne, a very exclusive Beaupeau Brut made for consumption on the estate. Only a few hundred cases were bottled each year. Alas, it would not travel past the village without spoiling.

But traveling was not so important, Kelly had pointed out. Beatrice agreed that "home was best."

"Fuck it, my dear," Perex muttered, "it sure took those bloody shits in Washington a long time to get me out of there. It was purely political, you know."

"Yep." Kelly knew this was the case for he had called Westerley Washburn to ask her aid in getting the machinery rolling. Why he had done this for Perex he did not know and he did not tell Perex about it.

"Bloody balls," Perex said sadly, "life has turned into

a turgid porridge, my dear. Topovsky dead, my God, a suicide! I cannot believe it."

"And Maggi," Kelly remarked softly.

Perex stared moodily at the gravel path. He shrugged and glanced at Kelly. "Is she? Somehow, I doubt it, *cher*. Maggi, you must know, is too smart to be dead."

Kelly shuddered with faint hope. Would Perex know? "Do you think . . ." he started to say, then stopped. What was the good of talking about it? "And Maryjane?" he threw the name out gamely.

"Yes, yes," Perex muttered, kicking at the gravel with his pointed shoe.

They stopped to light cigarettes. The smell of the burning tobacco intruded pungently into the fresh odor of pine and spruce trees sweating in the cold.

"Remember the last time we were together in the woods?" Kelly reminded him.

"Yes, bloody history. It seems like a hundred years ago."

"That's where all this began, Rafe, in the Bois de Boulogne."

They talked a little about Grovival, and Perex roared with malicious appreciation when Kelly told him about Ehrlitz, the warts and floater farts.

"I was hoping you and I could get some of the action, Jack," Perex said. "But now . . ."

"It'll be banned . . . too dangerous for the human race. Although, who knows? So is the atom bomb. It looks like AmFreight will buy Maison Mordaunt and C.T. might just decide to go ahead with Grovival, the crazy bastard."

Cautiously, Perex asked, "Do you think Maryjane was on it?" Kelly nodded silently. "Bloody shit, that's awful."

"Listen," Kelly said, inciting him, "that's her problem. It's probably turned her into some kind of sex fiend. . . . I suppose she farts a lot too, like Ehrlitz. Warts . . ."

"Holy Mother of God," Perex said miserably.

"Oh, well, that *is* her problem, isn't it, Rafe?"

"Yes. Well . . . It probably wears off."

"In a year, according to Ehrlitz," Kelly informed him

cruelly. "But, the hell with that. What about Aristide de Bis? I'm afraid he's not finished with us yet. If Maggi is dead, you can be damn sure it was de Bis and Madame de Winter who did it."

"That misbegotten swine," Perex said viciously. "Christ, my friend, we're risking our asses just being in France. Why did I come? And the Cubans are still after me."

"No, not here," Kelly assured him. "It's too cold for the Cubans. And Aristide? Beatrice's peasants are very loyal. There'd be a revolution if Aristide tried anything on Beatrice in Burgundy."

Perex nodded, somewhat comforted. He took off his trilby and smoothed down his hair. "She is a bloody power, isn't she?"

"They worship her. It all dates back to the twelfth century."

Perex whistled. "Caramba! You are a lucky man, *mon vieux*. Tell me, though, are you going back to Mordaunt? You might get in on the merger."

"Nope. We're going down for the New Year's party. We'll take some of the Burgundian heavies with us. But that's it."

They walked for a while without speaking. Beaupeau was quiet, so peaceful. Winter's work had been done in the vineyards: grape stock cut back and the earth between the vines given a year-end harrowing. The tractors and carts were stored away, hibernating in grease. The only sound now came from the pastures where hardy cattle rummaged under the frost for their fodder, gently lowing. Beaupeau was nearly self-sufficient. The dairy supplied all necessary milk products, and on the other side of the wall there were barns, pig sties, and slaughterhouses which turned out varieties of meat and sausage. Chicken, ducks, and geese came from the rustic farmers who labored in the vineyards of Beaupeau in return for their land, rent free.

"This place is a bloody fortress," Perex said.

"See that tower?" Kelly pointed to a stone turret located at one side of the front gate which had once opened to a drawbridge over a moat, long gone. "There's a guy up there, day and night. We're on top of a little hill and the place being surrounded almost entirely by the vineyards, he can see for miles, right into the village of Beaupeau sur Beaurive, the local river. If Aristide showed up with his army, the sentry would see them long before they got here. He'd start clanging his bell like a son of a bitch to warn the neighborhood. They use it for a fire alarm too.''

Perex was impressed but nevertheless he chuckled nervously. "Can't you see de Bis riding across the plain with his merry men? We'd blast his ass, wouldn't we, my dear Jack?" He paused. "Are you in love with this chick?"

Chick? A strange way to describe Beatrice de Beaupeau, the countess. Kelly nodded. "I guess I am, Rafe."

"Lucky guy," Perex said, adding, "I suppose now there's no chance of you and Maryjane getting back together." There was little hope in his voice. "Well, Beatrice is a hell of a beauty, my dear. A real bloody aristocrat, ain't she? You can tell her blood dates back a long way. And to think she used to be Aristide's mistress," he said innocently. "Bloody hell, you really moved in on that asshole."

Kelly agreed. "You know, I'd just as soon not be reminded he was her boy friend, Rafe."

"Sorry, my dear. I won't mention it again."

"That was politics too, you know," Kelly explained. "His idea is to restore the monarchy. Beatrice was going to be made queen."

Perex gloated, "Surely you josh, *mon ami.*"

"No. Beatrice has no interest in being fucking queen."

Nodding strenuously, Perex said, "Good thinking. It could be one hell of a risky job, the way the world is. Somebody'd take a shot at her for sure. But what the hell, Jack. He won't have any trouble finding another pigeon. Europe is loaded with Pretenders; there's one in every capital city. So—are you going to marry her?"

"Yep, it looks that way, after all this settles down. You know the rest of Aristide's strategy? The first thing is to start raising hell about Napoleon's bones. I never knew this before but the theory is that's not really Napoleon buried there in Paris. It's actually his valet, a guy they say looked just like him. The British apparently pulled a fast one on the Frenchies. After Napoleon died on St. Helena, about twenty years after the Battle of Waterloo, the Brits substituted the remains of the valet, a man named Francis Cipriani. Paris got Cipriani and Napoleon went into a John Doe vault in Westminster Abbey in London."

Perex repeated, "Surely, you do jest, *mon ami*. Why would they want to do a thing like that? I wouldn't think the British would want any part of Napoleon after he'd been such a pain in the ass. . . ."

"Rafe, *mon ami*," Kelly said ironically, "*you* of all people don't believe in intrigue? The idea was clever. British reasoning was if the Frenchies ever got ambitious again, the British could shoot them down. Don't give us that stuff about the monarchy and empire, they'd say— you don't even have Napoleon. Your relic is a phony."

Perex admitted there was something to the idea.

Kelly laughed. "There's another theory you might like better. It goes like this—the French excavated Napoleon to bring him back here. He looked so terrible, decayed and all, after thirty-odd years, that they pulled a fast one on the British. It seems that after Napoleon died, the valet, Cipriani, killed himself with rat poison, arsenic in those days. The arsenic acted as a preservative and scared away the maggots and worms and all. So, since Cipriani looked so much like Napoleon, handsome as hell although slightly bigger, the Frenchies took him and palmed Napoleon off on the British."

"Jesus, my dear, that is disgusting. Can you believe it?"

"I can believe anything about this continent," Kelly said. "But there is a final irony. According to the British Foreign Office, Cipriani worked as a British spy in Napoleon's camp to the bitter end. So tell me, who finally got the shaft?"

"Not Cipriani," Perex said drolly. "He's got a hotel in Venice. Ha!" He stopped to light another Benson &

Hedges. He was too much a man of the present to be interested much in history or historical ironies. "So, where does Aristide de Bis stand? Is he a Bonapartist, Bourbonist, or what?"

"Just a simple royalist. Napoleon is considered part of French royalty. Hell, he did have himself declared emperor and I guess the rest of Europe accepted it, even though he was never connected with any of the Louis gang."

Perex came to a weighty conclusion. "Nothing is as cut and dried as it seems."

"Correct," Kelly said. "That's what Count Boris Blastorov calls the devil theory of history. Nothing actually happened as we were taught it." Kelly asked himself whether he should give Perex the rest of the facts.

"Ehrlitz gave me a bit of news from Geneva," he continued solemnly, watching Perex's reaction. "He told me he did a silicone job on Maryjane along with the Grovival treatment and cryogenic suspension."

Rafe shivered violently inside his coat. "Dear friend, could we go inside? It is bloody cold out here. I must rest. I could be going on an arduous mission after the new year."

They walked from the garden up a flight of stone steps, flanked by huge urns now empty of flowers, and across a broad terrace to the heavy oak door set in a twenty-foot-high portal.

"Sit down by the fire," Kelly told Perex. "I'll send Villars along with your scotch and soda. I just want to go see how Beatrice is doing."

"Yes, thank you," Perex said. He held his wet shoes toward the flames.

Kelly strolled down the hallway toward the library, passing his new friends—suits of armor standing at attention, their arms wired to the walls. Above them and stacked in the corners were their weapons: maces, broadswords, and rusty pikes.

Beatrice was sitting next to the fireplace in the library, staring at her ledgers. "Ah, *mon amour.*" She sent him a fragile smile.

Kelly crossed the long room and put his hands on her shoulders. He kissed the top of her head. "How is everything?"

"Ah, much work, Jackelly, and always so confusing. It is too bad I am not a better bookkeeper and less suspicious." She leaned back, resting her arms on the old, marred wood of the chair. She was wearing her warm corduroy trousers and a roll-necked sweater. "Jackelly, is your friend, Monsieur Perex, enjoying his stay with us?"

"He feels safe here, Beatrice—and so do I."

"And I too." She laughed musically, showing the tips of her white teeth. She was looking at him in a peculiar way. "Jackelly, I have been writing this morning. I wish to tell you that when I die you will be master of Château Beaupeau."

"Beatrice! Don't say things like that."

Her gray eyes were amused. "Do you not realize what you have done to me, the act you have perpetrated?"

"What do you mean?" This was an alarming thing for her to say.

"You have ravaged my fair body, Jackelly." She slipped out of the chair and went to look at herself in a mirror by the fireplace. "I will tell you what you have done, Jackelly," she said sharply. "You have made Beatrice de Beaupeau, descendant of the French kings, a distant granddaughter of Charlemagne. . . . You have put this same Beatrice de Beaupeau with child." Then she laughed and began to cry. She rushed across the room and fell into his arms. "It is what I want," she wailed, "and therefore Beaupeau is yours."

Christ, he was chilled, happy but chilled. Had she some sort of premonition?

"Beatrice . . ."

"This makes you happy too, Jackelly?"

"Yes." But did it? "Yes, Beatrice, very happy," he said.

So, it seemed they would be married. He hoped

Maryjane's Haitian divorce was binding. It wouldn't be pleasant to be booked for bigamy at some later date.

She stood back from him a little, her eyes shining. "It is fantastic, Jackelly. To think that only a few months ago, I accepted that I was doomed forever to be merely the mistress of Aristide de Bis, living a life of unfruitful frustration."

He frowned. "I'd just as soon never hear that bastard's name again."

"Now," Beatrice cried, "there is no question—I could never be queen of France bearing an Irish-American child. The common folk would not stand for it."

"You think so?" Hell, he thought, there could be nothing wrong with a little rugged Irish-American blood to fortify this tired old French stuff. But she was right; the French were very sticky about diluting either blood or wine. "Let's have Villars open some house champagne so we can celebrate."

"I will have a little," she said. "I must be very careful now." She rubbed her corduroy trousers against his leg. "Should we tell your friend?"

"No," Kelly said. "Perex has got enough on his mind."

His arm around her slender waist, Kelly led her back to the drawing room. Perex jumped to his feet. "Good morning, Countess."

"Monsieur Perex," she whispered.

Beatrice went to the wall by the door and pulled hard on a bell cord. Villars was there almost instantly. He was tall, a heavy man with a round Burgundian face. He was dressed in striped trousers and a white ticking jacket. "Madame rang."

"Villars, please bring us a chilled bottle of Beaupeau Brut." Villars shot off on his mission. "Sit down, Rafe," she said. "May I call you Rafe, or Rafael? And you will call me Beatrice."

Perex took his chair and Kelly and Beatrice sat down together on a red, velvet-covered sofa facing him. She put her hand on Kelly's arm and he covered it with his own.

"Well . . . Rafe? What do you think of my ancient château?"

Perex's brown face was wreathed in an ingratiating smile. God, Kelly thought sardonically, he was really such a kiss-ass. "It is simply magnificent, Beatrice." His eyes darted at Kelly, back to her. "It's so beautiful here, surrounded by wine, champagne . . ."

Beatrice admonished him, "No, we cannot call it champagne here, Rafe, for we are outside the champagne region. But, *alors,* it is champagne nonetheless."

Villars returned with bottle and glasses on a silver tray. With strong hands, he wrested the cork from the bottle and poured the foaming Beaupeau.

Beatrice held up her glass. "*Eh bien,* Jackelly, now we will drink—to what?"

Perex suggested, "Good health and happiness?" And then, moodily, "The success of all our endeavors?"

"Also to what, Jackelly?"

"Well, Rafael," Kelly said, drawling over the name, "we have a little surprise and you're the first to know."

Perex looked anxious. He was a man who always expected the bad news first. "I suppose . . ."

"Suppose no longer, *bloody hell*! Rafe, Beatrice and I have decided to get married."

Perex seemed to falter. He whipped the handkerchief out of his breast pocket and blew his nose.

Beatrice exclaimed, "See, Jackelly, he weeps for us. In happiness to be sure."

"Jack, you bloody f—" Perex began to say. He almost said it: fucker.

"Listen, my dear," Kelly said breezily, "pay no attention to Rafe's tears. He cries over television commercials."

"No, no," she protested. "We are very happy."

It was not the imperial "*we*"—she was speaking for both of them.

They had lunch in a bright dining room overlooking the silent garden, Perex and Kelly doing most of the drinking. They finished another bottle of the Brut with a light garden soup, then moved to a tarty Beaupeau red and roast pheasant shot in the woods a half mile from the château and hung for two weeks in the cellar until it was on the edge of rot. Over coffee, Beatrice offered them an old brandy, another fine Beaupeau product not for general sale.

"Mes amis," she said, "this brandy dates from 1855, during the years of Napoleon III . . ."

Perex glanced stealthily at Kelly at the mention of the emperor's descendant, then slumped comfortably in his chair. Perex was enough of a hedonist to sink without trace into this morass of luxury. The brandy was spectacular, delicate and smooth. All traces of sediment had been removed by rebottling over the years, and moreover, it had to travel no farther than from the cellars down below. It brought greetings from the past and caressed the soul. Perex, his eye ever fixed on commerce, murmured to Beatrice that she could make a pile if she put it on the market. She merely smiled.

Beatrice left them for a few minutes then. Her secretary, Madame Crochet, had arrived from the village, and there were certain business matters to be attended to.

When the door was closed behind her, Perex could contain himself no longer. "Bloody fucker, Jack, my dear, you have struck it rich." There was envy in his face, tears of jealousy in his eyes.

Kelly nodded idly and then, when Perex was least expecting it, he said, "I hear you were laying Maryjane up in Geneva."

"What!" Perex's body came to with a start. His mouth fell open. "I—are you mad, Jack?"

"No," Kelly said quietly, "I'm told it's true. That's this mission, isn't it? Trout is sending you off to Mangrovia to get her out of there. It's your kid, isn't it?"

Perex could not summon the strength to deny the charge. He fell back in his chair and put his hands over his face, moaning. "Bloody shit, my friend, yes, that is the mission. But it is insane. Do you know anything about the Cou-Cou Macoo?"

"Only that one of them fired a shotgun at us."

"Yes! Caramba! Shit!" Perex's voice quavered. He

began crying freely. "They are murderous. It is a suicide mission."

Flatly, Kelly said, "You'll have to buy them off."

"Yes, yes," Perex whispered, "if I can. But who knows how this Cinnabar Macoo will react?"

"The question really is," Kelly said sardonically, "whether he'll sell Maryjane to you."

Perex's eyes were wet, wide, and wild when he looked up. "Jesus, Mary, and Joseph," he whined, "*mon ami*, Jack, do you believe . . ."

"Yes, I do believe, Rafe. I think you did screw her. But look, I don't care. Get that straight. I don't give a good goddamn. . . . I'll tell you something now. We're *even* because I screwed *your* ex-wife. What do you say to that?"

Perex stared at him blindly, trying to absorb the news. He was astonished, there was no doubt of that. His brown cheeks went slack and his milky eyes, brown polka-dot pupiled in the center, dilated with outrage. But without warning, he began to laugh. His voice cracked and moved toward hysteria.

Gasping, he finally exclaimed, "Marvelous. Oh, my dear! Priceless! Yes, you are right. We are quits!"

"So you *did*, you son of a bitch," Kelly snarled. "Tell me—how was she?"

"Possessed." Perex tittered. "And Westerley?"

"Abandoned," Kelly told him, "completely wild and horny . . ."

Perex was surprised again. But he retaliated. "Maryjane was like a maniac. I have never known a woman so . . ."

"Westerley . . . She . . ." But then he stopped. "None of this goes beyond this room, Rafe, you no-good son of a bitch. . . ."

Beatrice's private apartment had been built to dovetail perfectly into that portion of the château directly above the library, its fireplace vented into the same chimney. The room was lit by wide, leaded windows which drew in what was left of the gray afternoon. The ceiling was vaulted and beamed, the whitewashed walls decorated with ancestral portraits, a grouping of Impressionists, and a few pieces of modern art. Persian, Chinese, and old Flemish rugs covered the oak floor. Between the windows on the west wall, there was a gigantic four-poster feather bed, covered by a down comforter and a plethora of pillows. A distinctly nonmedieval accouterment in the bathroom was an eight-foot-long tub with brass fittings.

Beatrice locked the door behind them. "Ah, Jackelly, you and your friend Rafe were having your chuckles, weren't you? I could hear you in the drawing room."

"Yes, we certainly were having our chuckles."

She paid no attention. "Life is beneficent. Let us not be too serious, Jackelly. Let us gather rosebuds while we may. I will give thanks."

Unabashedly—and why should she be embarrassed?—she knelt at the side of the bed, an altar too in its way, crossed herself and prayed. He had known she was religious, how deeply religious was a revelation. She attended the little church outside the château wall for vespers every night with the peasant women; there was a private chapel at the other end of the house which, she said, had once belonged to Marie Antoinette and had been saved from the revolutionary mobs two centuries before. Thus, he thought, was history perpetuated, belief carried forward, whatever the odds. Continuity . . .

"*Cher* Jackelly, I am praying for our passion. I am praying to the Almighty and to my sainted ancestors that our passion will always be electric. For, without passion, there is no life. I am praying that within me, we will be made immortal. . . ."

"Yes, Beatrice, I'll leave you to it." Christ, she was like a nun or some other category of pious being.

She had not asked him to join her, so while she was about her religion, he strolled the twenty yards to the bathroom, closed the door and took a leak. He did not need to pray. He readily acknowledged that some form of higher being had brought him here and made this happen. He undressed, for they would be taking advantage of the midafternoon drowse, and put on a Chinese robe. He felt, jovially, after the wine and the brandy, that he might have tucked an ascot into the top of the robe and emerged with a long cigarette holder to play a few bars on the piano.

She was waiting patiently. "A little sleep now, Jackelly?"

"Yes . . . You know, Madame Mordaunt is going to say I've been chasing your property and title all along."

"Bah! I do not care what she says, for I know she is only a creature of Aristide de Bis."

"Beatrice, I told you—fuck Aristide de Bis!"

She grinned. She had come to appreciate this American expression.

While she was preparing herself, Kelly poured himself another shot of brandy off a sideboard by the wall, thinking no boudoir should be without a bottle, and sat down on a love seat before the fire. It was warm and cozy, facing the flickering flames, and he took care to follow the route of the Beaupeau brandy down his gullet and into his gizzard. He lit a Gauloise and hazily contemplated the situation to which the higher being had carried him. Maggi . . . His final interlude with Olga, before the flight from Paris. He was nodding by the time Beatrice returned to him, in an embroidered pegnoir, dipped to reveal the rise of her breasts, so full, it seemed, already.

She stroked the side of his leg. "Are you happy, Jackelly, and do you love me as I love you?" She glanced at him shyly. "I am told that being pregnant doesn't eliminate the possibility of making love."

"Beatrice, I'm almost afraid to touch you."

"But you do not need to be afraid, for women are strong. And it is good for the child too."

Yes, he had heard women were even more sensual when they were *enceinte*, and that there were men who liked nothing better than pregnant women and the screwing of them. He thought he understood why: pregnancy added another dimension to femininity and turned loose a deeper passion in women. He felt the tension of Beatrice's heart issue through her arm. She flexed her fingers and put them on his thigh, two fingers around the bulge of his personage under the robe. Blood rushed to the point of contact.

"Oooh-la-la," she said, "he is saying hello." One could understand why this article of furniture was called the love seat; it was made for playing around. Now, however, she brought up the matter of their return to Paris for the *fête de Zouzou*. She reminded him that the House of Beaupeau was strongest in Burgundy. "*He* may have the police on his side by now."

Kelly shook his head. "Hercule is going to let us know if it's safe."

Tearfully, she pleaded, "I want to stay here always, Jackelly. I have seen enough of the world, the *beau monde*, as we call it."

He remembered how exhaustively the media had covered her. "I used to see your pictures in all the newspapers, so beautiful—in the nightclubs and restaurants, the hotels . . . St. Moritz, London, Paris . . ."

"We have been in London together, *mon amour*. . . ."

"Yes. Remember? I was surprised that day."

Her brow furrowed. "I was so ugly then and so neurotic."

"Yes, you wanted me to whip you." Her eyes teared and she looked away shamefully. "You wanted me to humiliate and hurt you. . . ."

"And you became my savior, my knight, Jackelly. . . ."

His name, as she pronounced it, had an antique quality harking back to the Norman tongue, like the diminutive for some deadly animal, a wild dog or bird of prey tamed for hunting. Jackelly? Jackal? Was that its origin?

"There were pictures of you from everywhere. Cairo. Vienna . . ."

"Yes," she said, not interested in hearing about it, "and all of no consequence. Now I want to be here, with you. We will manage our vineyard, make good wine and much love; eat, drink, and be merry. Is there anything else?"

He shook his head. But he knew there was more.

People could not cut themselves completely away from the world. "You'd get bored with me."

"No! Never!"

"But, once in a while. . . . Eventually, I'll have to go back to New York to work for my father. You'll like him."

"New York?" she cried fearfully. "So noisy and barbaric."

"No, no, you don't have to see the people," he promised her. "We'll get a place on the East Side and something in the country. Beatrice, you'll never have to go on the subway."

She continued to look doubtful but his enthusiasm made a difference. "I will go where you want, my *cher*." She leaned forward so he could kiss her lips. "Umm, the flavor of Beaupeau brandy."

Lightly, he joked, "It's the Beaupeau red that got you pregnant, Beatrice. I was drunk that night."

"Oh, no, you cannot say such naughty things. I am pregnant because you seduced me, the flower of France." But she wasn't being serious. She eased away from him and made for the bed, whirling out of her pegnoir.

"I can see it already," he said.

"No, that is impossible." But her belly was, in fact, bigger. This was evident at the hip and there was no doubt: the breasts had begun to blossom. He bent over her and watched as she smiled the smug smile of incipient motherhood. It was slightly disquieting. But he put away his worry and took her nipples in his mouth. "Oh, Jackelly, what am I to do about you?"

"Stay perfectly still. I'll do everything."

Clasped in each other's arms, they sank into the cocoon of light feathers. Kelly had already noted that while it was extremely comfortable for sleeping, a down mattress was not the most efficient place for making active love. For the latter, a firm, modern surface was best. On the other hand, when it came to the unscrewing screw of blessed Maggi Mont's invention, down was perfect. Once completely engaged, the down became formfitting, preventing cramp or other muscle seizure. It was even possible to fall asleep like that, coupled, with nary a bit of discomfort.

Beatrice gathered him in her hands and he was aware of a new scent. Something had been added to the tangy hint of the wine of the country. It was, he knew instantly, the peculiar smell of motherhood, of milk coming in, slightly sour perhaps but deeply stirring.

"This scar, Jackelly, will it disappear like the welts on my back?"

"Maybe, in time." He hoped not. He thought it would fade but not disappear, for the stitching had been somewhat clumsy.

Beatrice slid along his body to kiss the scar, then to bite gently where bulb joined shaft of the personage. He was not frightened now that she would dig deeply with her teeth. Lazily, relaxing, he ran his hand across the wide river of her belly and between her legs, feeling the wispy Titian hair, lightly coated with desire. The lips of her place were soft and wet.

"Please, Jackelly, do not agitate me too much," she bade him. She closed her finely skinned eyelids, like membranes covering two eggs. Nature, Kelly thought, was a very delicate affair. "Ah, Jackelly, it will not take me long to want you. I am very near to my emotions these days. Please to allow me to introduce you, once again, to my passions."

She eased her body toward him, like melted butter, and her anointed pube accepted his devotion. She uttered an archaic word of approval. The heat inside was intense; even now, gestation was at work and he was party to it. He would want to remember some of these sensations for a later day.

"Jackelly, *mon amour.*" She sighed, producing a thin whistle of satisfaction, then lapsing again into some incomprehensible ancient French, perhaps even the vernacular of the Druids for all he knew, emptying herself of exclamations.

She lay her hand against his face, a finger at his lips. Her softness gathered him up and he felt life surge through him. There was a fluttering from within her, an unusual movement, as if they were opening the chest where she stored her pearls, jewels, her tiara, her holy vestments. Released, these treasures spilled over him. Her fingers trembled against his face as, inside, the nerves quivered. She was alive with it: all her physical attention was directed to the spot of stimulation. She was an object and a force at the same time, inertia *and* momentum. The instincts had taken over. This was what made women different from men, despite anything Maggi Mont—Maggi, gone, lost, dead, goddamn it—might have tried to tell him.

Beatrice's raw womanhood conquered. A rippling shudder ran through her body. Groans, prayers, and mouthings of passion were coarsely produced and her bodily movements were far more elemental than those to which he'd grown accustomed. She gasped, breathed shallowly, and climaxed. It was a marvel, for he had not moved a muscle—so close now were all her thresholds. Once, twice, three times she heaved in orgasmic after-shock and Kelly expended himself within the deep catacomb. A torrent of seed, now superfluous, swept out of him to fill her. She wailed silently: her lips moved but no sound emerged. She was giving thanks again, for Beatrice was a woman who believed in giving thanks at every turning.

It done, muscles soothed and nerves battered to insensibility, it done again, yet to be done again and again, to be remembered as having been done so often and then yet once more, with the promise of doing it still again and having pledged faithfulness to the process of doing it and shown appreciation for the blessing of having done it, Kelly fell asleep. But even in his sleep, he dreamed of it. Not a bad thing, thus, to have joined the legions who unendingly march over the Chinese cliff, leaving untold other legions behind, the latter reproducing other legions so that, as it was well known, the race never lacked men and women to march over the cliff.

He remained inside her as they slept, for Beatrice had arranged her body in such a way that he was held fast. God, it was Maggi Mont who had taught him this. Had she somehow passed along her gift to Beatrice? God, to think this could happen in the midst of all the rest: the danger and intrigue, the slapstick stupidity of it all.

Hercule called after dinner that night. It was all right, he reported. Aristide de Bis would not be in Paris at New Year's time. Under great government pressure to cease and desist in his political splintering activities, Aristide was removing himself to the countryside for a period of reassessment. Moreover, Madame Mordaunt was not well. She asked particularly that Kelly come back to Paris, for it was a matter of some meaning to the future.

"Beatrice," Kelly said, after the call, "we've got to go. Rafe . . ."

"Dear boy," Perex said, "personally I think we could have a hell of a party right here."

"I owe it to Zouzou."

"So noble," Perex growled.

Beatrice reluctantly agreed. "We will take my man Villars."

"And Hercule will also have his men at the House of Mordaunt," Kelly said.

"We will stay at the Villa Peau and if we feel we can without risk attend the ball, we will go in disguise," Beatrice said. "Black masks . . ."

"Black masks?" Kelly was reminded of the vile Englishman.

CHAPTER

THIRTY-THREE

"Shall we stop for a small apéritif, Monsieur Hercule?"

"And why not, Monsieur Jacques?"

The two were walking through the Ritz, headed for the rue Rimbaud.

"*Alors,* Monsieur Hercule, you are looking very elegant tonight."

Hercule was dressed in a midnight-blue velvet tuxedo, a bountifully pleated silk shirt of ivory hue, and a floppy velvet bow tie. His hair was slicked to his head, the latter hardly clearing the top of André's oak bar.

"Champagne, Monsieur Hercule?"

"Why not, Monsieur Jacques?"

To André, Kelly said, "A bottle of the Dom, if you please."

André was all politeness in front of Hercule. Word of the little man's power had passed through the *arrondissement.*

Hercule asked softly, "And Madame la Comtesse? Monsieur Perex?"

"They'll be along later, Hercule, if the coast is clear."

That was what they'd decided. Beatrice and Perex would wait at the Villa Peau until they heard from him. He hoped he could trust the son of a bitch with her.

"All will be well, Monsieur Jacques."

"But we must be sure. Tell me, how is Madame?"

Hercule shook his head. "Very worried, very nervous . . . Grovival, *c'est merde ça!*" He made a disgusted face. "But, Monsieur Jacques, will you come back to us? I am worried too."

Kelly hedged. He did not want to disappoint Hercule. He did not say no outright. He cited the imponderables and added, "A lot depends on Aristide de Bis. We know now that he is very dangerous."

"Perhaps not so dangerous as you think," Hercule said.

It was barely 8:00 P.M. but already the rue Rimbaud was clogged with traffic. In another two hours, the police would be forced to close the street to all but guests invited to the *fête de Zouzou*. This was not something they liked to do but their Christmas bribe had been generous. From now until midnight, the guests would be alighting from long, chauffeur-driven limousines, out of freshly washed cabs, embassy Mercedes, and Rolls-Royces. As the night wore on, they would arrive by motorcycle, their evening clothes a mockery of the establishment and unwashed masses alike, many in horse-drawn carriages shanghaied from the parks. . . .Once a few years before, an intrepid Italian producer had tried to bring a hot-air balloon down into the rue Rimbaud and, less recently, the dissolute Duc de Tijuana had actually succeeded in landing a midget helicopter in the street outside Maison Mordaunt, this to the fury of the Paris *flic,* the Parisian underworld designation of the cops.

Would-be gate-crashers even now were congregating outside the brightly-burnished brass front entrance of the maison. But they had small hope, if any, of getting past a phalanx of guards. Tickets were numbered, assigned names, and there were supposed to be no transfers. There was, however, and it had to be admitted, a brisk black-market trade in tickets to the *fête de Zouzou,* and Madame Mordaunt's philosophy had always been that if one were so desperate as to shell out five hundred or a thousand dollars to a scalper, then what the hell, let them do it. There were other stories, unconfirmed of course, that Madame herself sold a certain proportion of the invitations at higher than scalper prices to defray a good bit of the expense of the party. She was no fool. It was a story Kelly had once considered writing, but wisely shelved.

Kelly saw colleagues from his former life: representatives of most of the boulevard papers across the Continent, from the international press and news magazines, a scrimmage of photographers waiting for both the notables and the notorious. Zouzou kept the press list deliberately and infuriatingly small: thus, the favored few would be so grateful they would write about her through the next year. Only the most influential magazines had been sent invitations, as well as the more powerful fashion publications: *Vogue, Harper's Bazaar, Elle, Womens Wear Daily,* and naturally, the *RAG.*

"Snotty and arrogant morons, one and all," Zouzou often remarked, "so stupidly frivolous. They believe women are interested only in clothes, spending money, going on expensive holidays, and fuck-fuck perfume. But alas, we need them, these harlots of the printed word. Try to be polite, all my staff."

Kelly and Hercule pushed through the crowd. He was hailed by a few of his acquaintances, shouted at, sworn at, and mocked.

"Animals," Hercule snarled. "*Schweinhunde . . .*"

"You speak German, Monsieur Hercule?" Kelly was surprised.

"A little," Hercule muttered. "I was in a prison camp of *les Boches.* I escaped through a drainpipe—being small has a certain advantage, Monsieur Jacques. I liberated a horse and rode all the way back to my homeland."

"Hercule, I know so little about you," Kelly observed.

"Now is not the time to exchange life histories, Monsieur Jacques."

There were last-minute things to be checked and verified: the uniforms and morale of the *commissionaires* who would be holding back the mob of crashers, drunks, hookers, pickpockets, spies, and voyeurs. Were the models ready? They would be circulating in prototypes of

Erogenalia du Printemps, their assigned jewelry either Mordaunt property or on loan from Van Cleef, Cartier, and Winston. It was essential that the plainclothes security men be on station to watch the valuables. They were to have two orchestras. Were the flowers in place? It was said Zouzou spent fifty-thousand dollars for the flowers alone. And the caterers. Were they ready? Had the passages to the penthouse been blocked off and the elevator closed down?

No one had ever been known to send regrets for the *fête de Zouzou.* Only serious illness, family tragedy, or death were acceptable excuses. Anything less persuasive in the way of RSVP meant one's name was crossed off the list for next year. They came to Paris by ship, train, and plane, by car from the depths of France and the Continent, from Near and Far East, from the Americas, Tierra del Fuego, and Nome, Alaska. This year, Hercule had told him, Zouzou had gone so far as to invite the Soviet lady-minister of culture, a woman dangerously famous for her high-flown fashion ideas, a Mordaunt customer by monitored long-distance telephone. Was her seat on the Politburo worth coming to the party? They would soon know.

The glass display cases had been removed from the ground-floor boutiques and stored away. A bar had been set up at the bottom of the shimmering, glass-tiled stairway: a first glass of champagne, naturally Mordaunt No. 10, was pressed into one's hand as furs, top hats, cloaks were consigned to a guardroom in the shoe salon.

"A glass of champagne, Monsieur Hercule? Monsieur Jacques." It was comforting to be so well known.

In this year of the Lord, Zouzou Mordaunt had determined to make a splash with her new gimmick, *Erogenalia du Printemps.* Sex was to be the theme of the *fête de Zouzou,* pure sex. The house models were close to total exposure in the new creations. Nude movie extras, artists' models, and male and female strippers, had been recruited to stand, in black and white body paint, on the steps of the glass staircase; eventually they would circulate through the crowd with cigarettes, drinks, and party favors. It was still early and for now they were covered with G-strings and modeling jocks. Later, everything would come off. The girls' nipples, Kelly noticed appreciatively, stood up pertly in the drafts of cold air coming in the opening and closing front door. They appeared lackluster but a few murmured words from Hercule, as he and Kelly went upstairs, caused the girls to smile and the men to straighten their spears.

The large second-floor salon had been turned into a nightclub where a contemporary band would entertain for dancing on a small spot within the jumble of tables. Strolling minstrels and something South American would be playing upstairs where the dressing rooms had been transformed into cafés.

One thousand invitations had been mailed. There were seats enough for six hundred people. The overflow, Zouzou said carelessly, would have to make do at the bars: potential trouble spots. "Suppose the duke and duchess want to bring a couple of extra people?" Kelly had asked her. "And who's to say what that little asshole, Duc Turbot, will do?" But, never mind, he told himself, it was not really his problem now. And, so far, at any rate, everything seemed to be in order.

"Hercule, you've done one hell of a job."

Hercule nodded his satisfaction. "Yes, Monsieur Jacques, it will be beautiful. But so much work. Any mistakes tonight—and tomorrow it is the guillotine." He smiled savagely. "Monsieur Victor is to bring the insane Hungarian, Magda Starbright. It is said Victor will go with her to England."

"Not a bad move for Victor," Kelly said. They walked through the double archway at the rear of the salon to sit for a moment with their champagne on the thronelike settee where Zouzou would hold court later in the evening. "Well, Hercule, here we are at the end of the year. Here's to you, your good health."

"And to you, Jacques." Enigmatically, he added, "Let the dead bury the dead. . . . Now, best I go upstairs to see how Madame is progressing."

* * *

The main salon was filling by 9:00 P.M. A dozen tables had been reserved for the contingents from the other houses of couture. Downstairs, the guests were beginning to arrive from the small parties preceding the *fête*. They trooped up the steps past the array of black and white slaves whose last flimsy coverings had been removed, exposing them to smiles, stares, giggles, and now and then an emboldened tweak of private parts— the girls responding with a jab of their feathered swagger sticks, the men with a rattling of spears. It was all in such good fun. At least at this stage of the evening.

Later, Kelly expected, there would be trouble. Chaos was inescapable. Hercule had told him Zouzou had ordered a live sex act for a time just before or after midnight, to leave no doubt that *Erogenalia* was for real, not just a special effect. "It will be a Danish couple," Hercule said. "They are best at it. They will not be shamed if people laugh or try to join in." Hercule was a curious man, Kelly decided again. He had no feeling about it one way or the other; he was truly amoral.

Kelly was downstairs close to the front door at nine-thirty, a fresh glass of champagne in hand. The party from the House of Cardin was the first of the couture contingents to arrive. Pierre's people were dressed entirely in black, women in long, tight black dresses slit extensively at the leg and cleaved so spectacularly at the bosom as to offer competition to Mordaunt's own *Erogenalia*. Kelly was startled; had Pierre somehow been tipped off? The Cardin men were in black silk dinner suits, black shirts, and black silk ties. Altogether, they looked a dangerous group, sullen and unsmiling.

Hard on Maison Cardin's heels was the jolly team from Maison Chevaux, led by plumpish Marco Chevaux. They were dressed as one, all clowns, white-faced and with big red knobs attached to their noses. Marco must have hired help, for one of the Chevauxistes did a clever somersault as he came through the door.

"Ah, Monsieur Kelly," Marco himself bawled, "we are here, you see, the House of Chevaux."

"So I see, Marco," Kelly replied, saying to himself: asshole.

The next of the couturiers was the House of Givenchy, all nearly as tall as the maître himself, the men in white tailcoats, white ties, and shoes, the women in white dresses, with white carnations woven in their hair.

The arrival of the other houses became almost monotonous: the Chanelistes, all small and, even in evening clothes, managing to look tweedy; the House of Cuir, menacing in leather like Hell's Angels, shoving their way through the downstairs boutique toward the stairs, prodding the slaves with their whips; the House of Lanvin, smelling like a perfume refinery, carrying atomizers and draped in costumes made of Lanvin signature scarves.

The cosmetic magnates drifted in, dressed splendidly but already yawning, trailed by mysterious lackeys and unidentified figures of international conglomeracy.

How had Pete Fink gotten an invitation, that knockoff artist?

"Hi, Kelly, how goes it, pal?"

It was too crowded now, much too noisy. The voices, screams of laughter, the loud music from upstairs would soon buckle the walls and spill everybody into the rue Rimbaud. Kelly's inclination was to run for it, to return to the Villa Peau for a quiet glass of champagne with Beatrice.

He had promised he would call her at ten and it was time. Kelly scrambled through bodies to get back upstairs. Tables set against the wall and in an alcove overlooking the street were laden with food. The squads of waiters already looked desperate. The shopping lists for the *fête* were lengthy, the bill of fare broad enough to satisfy any European or international palate, all manner of seafood, meat, and game, a dozen cheeses, the beverages of every country, pastries, cakes, after-dinner drinks and cigars from Havana. And for every party guest a party favor of some value: expensive pieces of jewelry designed by Zouzou herself, suggestive and rude and again underlining the message: *Erogenalia.* Bags of cosmetic samples, including Mordaunt Four body balm, were available for the women and for the men special packages of Mordaunt "slip-on" had been prepared, each condom printed with an expandable *Erogenalia* logo. There were choruses of oh's and ah's as the gifts were distributed. Zouzou did not care that the supply would soon be exhausted. Let them fight over it, she said. . . .

One of the security men reported a fistfight in the third-floor bar between stocky, sadomasochist Emil Cuir and merry Marco Chevaux. The forces of Cardin, Givenchy, Lanvin, Chanel, and the rest of them had taken watchful positions around the big room. Christ, Kelly told himself, Zouzou was crazy to invite them all at the same time, for it was well known that the maison fashion gangs were hateful and unrelenting enemies, vicious in attack and lethal in reprisal. Even as he watched, Cardin put a calming hand on one of his hot-blooded assistants. Givenchy glared balefully at the seedy Chanel-istes. But all fell silent when the Arabiques swarmed up the stairs, these of the House of Hammoum, swarthy and disdainful, reeking of oil money, in baggy black caftans and checkered headdresses. *Merde,* Kelly thought, they would all be carrying daggers. It was the Cuiristes who hissed them the loudest, sensitive to their gas-eating motorcyles, and loosed a barrage of bread rolls at the Arabs. The latter replied with native curses, turned and headed for the bar, squealing for fresh orange juice. When any of the rival houses danced to the deafening music, they did so to the laughter and mockery of their rivals.

"Marco—putrid rat catcher . . ."

"Cuir—balding pederast . . ."

A ragged chicken leg whistled past Kelly's ear. Champagne splattered on the dance floor.

To make matters even more tricky, the House of Molotov, named in honor of the late Stalinist foreign minister, marched up the stairs in close formation. Maison Molotov supplied cheap rubbish to bigwigs of the Italian and French Communist parties. The Molotovistes were greeted with ideological taunts and screamed insults.

They replied with their clenched-fist salute and revolutionary epithets.

If there was a left-wing couture house, then there of necessity had to be a right-wing house: Versailles. A small house, it was represented by a mere trio of men, each dressed in a demothballed black tailcoat with tarnished decorations pinned on the lapels. With some relief, Kelly realized that if Aristide de Bis had intended to attend the *fête* he would have come with the Versaillistes.

But there was more. Groaning in alarm, Kelly recognized the Texas representative stumble up the steps and totter into the salon. C.T. Trout was obviously very drunk. Kelly turned but it was too late. Trout waved his ten-gallon hat and shouted.

"J.K. J.K. C'mere, J.K."

Trout smelled of a twelve-hour plane ride, of bourbon and down-home sweat. His eyes were red and he needed a shave.

"Hello, C.T."

Trout sneered. "All dressed up like a little French pansy, ain't we? Who's all these fuckin' people, J.K.? Why am I here? Because Missus Mordaunt sent me a ticket, that's why. 'Cause AmFreight is going to buy this fallen-down business. Here, here's your Christmas present."

Trout dug a small box out of his pocket. Kelly knew what it was: another set of cheap cuff links emblazoned with the Trout brand, his usual Christmas gift.

"Gosh, thanks, C.T.," Kelly said sarcastically. "I suppose you want a drink." He could not escape; there was no use trying. Trout trailed him to the bar. Kelly got a bourbon for C.T. and his first Pernod of the evening. He would need it. "I hear M.J. is in Mangrovia, C.T."

"Yep," Trout said, unconcerned. "Knocked up in Africa, that's right. Bound to happen sooner or later, J.K., way she fucks around. . . .Trouble is I'm gettin' a little coon for a grandson. . . ."

"Albino," Kelly pointed out. "In other words, white."

Trout's eyes were perplexed. After a moment and painfully, he said, "Yeah, that's the mystery, J.K. Is an albino coon still a coon or is he a white man? I haven't been able to figure that out."

Kelly enjoyed his problem. "Way I see it, C.T., is we're all coons, some white, some black."

"I ain't a coon," Trout said.

Kelly shook his head doubtfully. "I dunno, C.T. I always thought you were something along that line, a very albino coon, yeah."

"Shit," Trout exclaimed. "You lily-livered little Catholic turd." He had trouble focusing on Kelly's face. "Unnerstand you ain't taking her back. Not that I blame you, goddamn eastern establishment effete turd that you are."

"No, Maryjane and I are out of sync, C.T."

Trout became very quiet as he tried hard to concentrate. He looked like a Texas snake about to strike. But whatever he was working himself up to say or do, he was interrupted by the entrance of another of the maison groups, this one from the House of Billy, makers of sports couture. If anything, Brooklyn-born Billy Bostwick had always been more daring in his collections than the projected *Erogenalia du Printemps* of Maison Mordaunt. The House of Billy was known around Paris as the House of Ill Repute, so obscene were some of its creations. What went on at Maison Billy was only to be guessed at. But tonight, Billy and his boys and girls were undoubtedly doped to the eyeballs and as undressed as they could be without risking arrest. Billy and the boys wore costumes of shocking simplicity—wildly colored cotton sheaths over their peckers and balls; the girls, pasties on their nipples and skimpy threads at their crotches, these apparently anchored somehow in their candy boxes.

When Trout caught sight of Billy's exhibitionists, he forgot completely about Maryjane, Kelly, his ranch, and politics. Drunkenly, he reached for one of the girls, trying to catch her by the bare boobs. She slapped him smartly on the hand, then across the face. C.T. tipped over, falling to one knee. Kelly helped him up.

"Holy Jumpin' Jehoshaphat! Jesus H. Jumpin' Christ, J.K., what is this place I'm invited to?" His drink shook in his hand and he stared. It was several minutes before he returned his attention to Kelly. "Meant to say you never amounted to more'n a stale buffalo flop. That trick you played on Washburn in the air-o-plane really took the cow's ass for a prize. You let me down and also the newspaper by which you were employed."

Kelly smiled distractedly. "Fuck it, C.T. It was a fake job anyway."

Trout shook his head spiritedly, finished his drink, and dropped the empty glass on the floor. "Bullshee-et, J.K. It was up and up. And when AmFreight takes this place over, you're out on your ass from here too."

"Listen, you fucking Texas crackpot . . ."

"Listen, nothin'," Trout interrupted. "Where's Perex? That goddamn greaseball is goin' to make my little girl an honest woman."

"Yeah, the sap," Kelly said crudely. "M.J. was knocked up by the Mangrovian foreign minister, Cinnabar Macoo, and you know it. Why are you dragging poor Perex into this? He never even banged her." He still wasn't sure that Perex actually had, even though Perex's words had seemed like an admission of it. "All on orders of your pal Washburn. That's why M.J., the dumb ass, took on Macoo in the first place."

It was one hell of an accusation and Trout's face duly blanched. "Don't you screw with Claud 'C.T.' Trout, Kelly, you sneak. I'll break your ass in so many pieces it'll take ten hound dogs a week to find your asshole."

Kelly traded him one for one. There was no reason not to: he was not related to Trout anymore, not even by marriage. "I'd like to take that hat of yours and shove it up your wrinkled old—"

"My Apache ass you would, you little snake dick." Trout pulled back his hand. Kelly was getting ready to dodge the punch and flee.

"Monsieur Jack, it is I, Victor. . . ."

Saved by the *belle,* he thought quickly. Beside Victor was the rosy-cheeked and magnificently bosomed Magda Starbright. She was in a full-cut black and pink crinoline dress which hung loosely from her protruding super-structure, cleverly concealed the enormity of her blowsy middle and behind. The dress was certainly one of Victor's triumphs: it accentuated while at the same time deemphasizing.

"Ah, ha!" Magda trilled. "It is the Monsieur Kelly of journalistic fame indeed and a pleasure for Magda's eyes, which have come to Paris for celebrations yet to be merrily consummated of the old year saying hello to the new, as in old Budapest."

Trout's fist dropped like a stone as he gazed with amazement at Magda. She draped him in a dazzling smile, blinding C.T. so thoroughly that she might have thrown a blanket over his head. Claud instinctively thrust a hand out for the bosom. Magda seized it and shook it vigorously.

"Name's Claud Trout, ma'am," C.T. yelled, throwing oil into his Texas accent. "Cowboy from down Texas way."

Magda knocked Victor to the side with one swing of her ass and exclaimed throatily, "Good heavens, little me!" She was seeing, Kelly realized, the spread, all one thousand square miles of it, the cattle, the gushers, all of the Trout treasury. "It is a Texas cowbody, tried and true?" C.T. nodded proudly. "A valiant conqueror of the desert and the red Indians, a man of bravery so rough and ready? Ruggedly bronzed from days beneath the sun so blazing as to melt such as Magda Starbright to a mere shadow of marzipan. But lusty and well hung too like a bull of the Hungarian *puztas.* . . ."

"None other, ma'am," Trout exclaimed so enthusiastically that his hat dropped on the floor. "Pick it up, J.K. I've got to say, pretty lady, that you sure are a pretty lady. I never seen jugs like them. And hung, you ask, ma'am. C.T. Trout is hung like a blue-ribbon stud."

Magda did not even glance at Victor. "*Cher* Victor, to

the bar, if you please. A glass of Tokay for Magda, dearest, and perhaps for said cowboy a drink in addition."

"A bourbon and water, little man," Trout said, his eyes only for Magda.

Victor knew then that he had lost her. His hope of retirement to lush Lancashire was blasted. He smiled dismally at Kelly. Kelly took the opportunity to slip away. He called Beatrice from the little room that had been his office. The maison was a madhouse but Beatrice sounded excited now. She said that she and Perex would arrive just before midnight.

Downstairs, it was worse than before. The guests were raping the buffet tables, like scavengers or locusts, laying them bare and then lurking until the waiters replenished them. God, the expense, and for what? The *fête de Zouzou* was a ritual now, that was the reason. If Zouzou dropped it now, they would all say she was finished.

A voice at his elbow said, "Monsieur Jacques, Madame is waiting."

So she had finally come downstairs. Crossing toward the archway, Kelly bumped a girl in a see-through top, surely not one of their models. She was pouring champagne down the bare chest of one of the slaves, licking it off with her tongue and, in the process, smearing her face with black and white body stain. And there was his old pal Simone. She was standing near the head of the stairs, holding fast to a disreputable Dutchman, one of their regulars, with a police record as long as your arm. In her *Erogenalia* number, Simone was a startling sight: a divided skirt, or pantaloons, with a braided slit that started at the small of the back, swept under her crotch and ended in a tassel at the navel. At rest, nothing was revealed but when she moved, as she did to shift her arm on the Dutchman, one saw her buttock cleavage and, in front, her shaven pube, a gash as clean as a surgical cut in a peach. There was no doubt this was an inspiring peek and if that was what *Erogenalia* was all about, then they had hit it squarely on the head. She saw his look and moved her legs again. It seemed to wink at him.

Zouzou was drinking champagne from a big goblet, offering her hand to a newcomer for a bone-dry greeting, muttering for all to hear her repertoire of obscenities, flashing rude and defiant grins at all who came within range. Yes, she was saying, Zouzou Mordaunt was still in control. One by one, the heads of the other maisons approached to kiss her hand and thus acknowledge for another year her supremacy.

He had seen Simone. Now here was petite Pauline, dressed in a rigidly constructed silk dress with a diamond-shaped cutout at each breast, the nipples glossed scarlet, and a third diamond-shaped hole at the loins. But this outfit was more modest than Simone's, for a ribboned replica of what was underneath covered what was underneath.

The crowd was barking now. The baying would come after midnight and then with the passing hours it would grow quiet as the drunks expired and were dumped in the street and the faint hearts went home. The *fête* received its second wind long after midnight when the jet set and the Beautiful People untied what was left of their inhibitions. This penultimate part of the event was what Zouzou enjoyed most, for she loved to watch them disgrace themselves. The terrible dénouement descended between 4:00 and 6:00 A.M. and then, bright-eyed and full of energy, Zouzou made the rounds, catching them at it behind the stairs or under chairs and tables, in the little rooms or, not unusually, in the middle of the salon. When it was over, Zouzou would proceed to her penthouse to laugh away what was left of the early morning. By then, naturally, it was New Year's Day. That was what the great event was all about: the expiation and renewal of the aged Parisian queen.

"You are late, Monsieur Kelly," Zouzou told him coldly.

"No, I've been here the whole time. It's the mob, and what a mob it is."

Pettishly, she cried, "So ugly this year. This is the last,

I swear it. Never another *fête de Zouzou*." She said the same thing every year.

"Madame, all the maisons are here."

"Yes, even Cuir. Such a horrid maison. Emil Cuir, none other than the diseased drippings off a camel's tool. But," she said bravely, "at least we are here, together again, I, you, and Monsieur Hercule. Does he not look lovely in his velvet?"

Hercule smiled in embarrassment. Zouzou herself was wearing a sagging black jersey dress and her most ancient, veiled page-boy hat. There was a gravy stain on the bodice of the dress and when she bent forward to stamp out her cigarette, Kelly could see all the way down protruding ribs to a gnarled navel. Her collarbones protruded grotesquely. Yes, she was thinner and certainly much more unkempt than before. A dribble of champagne slid down her cheek, smearing her sloppy makeup.

"Are the duke and duchess here yet?" she asked.

"Which ones?"

Zouzou barked an appreciative laugh, for of course, all the dukes and all the duchesses would be there. "You know the ones," she said. "And the princes and princesses? There are hundreds of them, *n'est-ce pas?* I do not give a damn for princes. *Merde!*"

Gently, Hercule handed her a plate of caviar and lemon wedges. She wolfed it down, while Hercule shook his head despairingly at Kelly. Although she continued to look around the room, Zouzou had descended into an opaque revery. The approach of Magda Starbright, with the rambunctious cowboy in tow, served to summon her back to alertness.

"Zouzou," Magda sang, "dear Madame Zouzou, it is an honor and a pleasure so distinct to see you on the eve of the newborn year."

Zouzou gasped with laughter. "Ah, it is our Hungarian noodle, is it not?" She mocked Magda unmercifully, even to the chirping voice. "And wearing, is it not, the dress made all those years ago, so many indeed as not to be mentioned."

Magda held up her hand, protesting. "Madame, most unfair . . ."

"And who, pray tell," Zouzou said, "is that odd-looking person standing at your side?"

Magda clutched one breast with both hands. "Sweet lady, this is my friend, from Texas so far, a cowboy. . . ."

"This cowboy," Zouzou snapped insolently, "he looks as though he was kicked in the face by his horse."

Trout was not at all put out. It was perhaps the mildest of insults that might have been directed at him. He honked a mild laugh. "Claud Trout, at your service, ma'am."

"Ah, yes, yes!" Zouzou cried. "You are the cowboy. We will have words, monsieur. In the meantime, do me the service of taking this late-grape out of my sight."

"Oh my, my oh," Magda squealed.

Zouzou smiled cruelly and when Trout had pulled Magda away, she turned venomously on Kelly. "And where is the so-delicate Countess de Beaupeau? Ironic, is it not, that at the very moment you leave Maison Mordaunt I will be going into partnership with your former father-in-law, perhaps your former wife and her doctor?"

"You saw Ehrlitz then?"

"Yes," she said slowly. "I feel I have known him for many years. The fool wishes to design intimate garments for Maison Mordaunt."

Kelly glanced at Hercule, who rolled his eyes. "As I told Monsieur Hercule," Kelly said, "much of the future depends on Aristide de Bis. I'm not exactly his favorite person."

"And with good reason," she said fiercely. "Le pauvre Aristide. He is in such disfavor now at the Élysee Palace. Aristide is very depressed. He is not pleased with you, no, although by now I hope he is reconciled to the course of—merde!—true love." Zouzou chuckled wearily. "What of Grovival, monsieur?"

"Bad stuff, madame. I told you."

"Bah! So you say. But I have been using Grovival for some months and I am a veritable picture of health. Am I not?" She retreated into herself momentarily, considering another matter. "You are aware of my discussions with Amalgamated Freight? Yes? This becomes necessary since our plans have been blown to shit. Partly your fault too, I may say."

She lowered her voice, casting a suspicious look toward the center of the room, thinking perhaps that Givenchy or Cardin or the others were listening. But this was not possible. There was an intense and drunken debate in progress between the Houses of the Left and the Right. A Molotoviste had just ripped the medals off one of the Versaillistes. Security people were anxiously hovering.

"Still . . ."

"Still, *quoi*? What?" she cried angrily. "At least Aristide has been successful in thwarting American imperialism in Mangrovia. But, a pity, in so doing he has endangered his political life. So now I must think of myself. *Voilà!* Amalgamated Freight. Hercule, I am right, am I not?"

Hercule nodded sagely. He knew now was not the time to talk reason or logic. Kelly saw his excuse to get away—a hobbling Maurice Moody was just coming into the salon with Olga and Count Boris.

"Madame, the *RAG* has arrived. And Count Blastorov. Shall I bring them to say hello to you?"

Her eyes sharpened. "Ach, Blastorov. Such a hero . . . Such a fool of a Russian. He may come over if he wishes. I have no reason to hate him now."

Two of the uniformed *commissionaires* were helping Moody across the room. He swung his telltale gray cast under a table and sat down. A mistake: he had chosen to sit with the House of Billy, the degenerates. Cardin and the others would be angered at that. All wanted the *RAG* to themselves.

Olga trailed Moody diffidently. She was wearing a long, plum-colored evening dress, her hair piled atop her head, and her grandmother's pearls. He had to admit that she was the epitome of grace. She held herself erectly and there was just enough haughtiness about her expression to set her aside from the mob. For a second, he yearned for the body under the dress, then thought of Beatrice.

"Hello there," he said.

"Monsieur Jack," Olga replied, without emotion.

But Count Boris caught his hand and shook it eagerly. "A treat to see you again, Monsieur Jack."

Moody was at his most disagreeable. "Hello, Kelly. I see you've collected the mangiest of the mangy." Moody was one to talk. His evening suit was unpressed and dusty, a strange white scum circled the collar of the jacket, there was black beard shadow on his chin, and his fingernails were dirty.

"Zouzou's sitting over there, Count Boris. She's asked for you," Kelly said.

Blastorov sputtered, "That is most unlikely." When Kelly assured him it was true, Blastorov hesitated. "Perhaps later."

Kelly asked Moody how his leg was and Moody said, "You see me. It's going pretty good, no thanks to you guys. I only came tonight to spite you. Every time I try to move I feel like getting this whole goddamn maison arrested for assault and battery. If I didn't work for your old man, I'd sue you."

"Don't let that stop you."

Boris Blastorov had begun to edge away, drawn by Zouzou's invitation.

"Hey, baby," Moody said to Olga, "come here, will you?"

Obediently, she moved closer and Moody dropped his arm familiarly across her buttocks. He grinned at Kelly and Olga looked uncertain. Clearly, some funny things had been going on at the RAG office.

"Olga and I have gotten to be very close. Ain't that so, baby?" Moody winked at him. "I've proposed to her, Kelly, but she won't say yea or nay. See old Boris with us tonight? He's watching us like a hawk. He doesn't trust me."

This pleased Moody and he smiled complacently, patting Olga's rear. Hell, Kelly thought morosely, if Moody had been there, it'd be a long time before he *cinq-à-septed* with Olga.

"I don't blame him for not trusting you," he said.

"I don't need your permission, do I?" Moody asked sarcastically, "if I try to make out with this little bimbo?"

"No, but I'd be very careful if I were you," Kelly said icily.

"Hear that? Hear that?" Moody yelped. "Another threat . . ."

Curtly, Olga said, "He has been drinking again, Monsieur Jack."

"The hell I have! That's a fucking lie, Olga and you better take it back."

Several of the Maison Billy gang returned from the bar. They were carrying soft drinks to go with their marijuana joints. A girl, one of them, collapsed into a chair next to Moody. Her eyes were glassy, as if a blind had been drawn across her consciousness.

But she was awake enough to see the gray plaster cast on Moody's leg. "It is a mummy," she observed dreamily.

"No," Moody snarled, "it is a leg. Did you ever see such putrid tits as on this one?" he asked rhetorically.

"Con," the girl murmured.

"Hear that, Kelly? I haven't been in France very long but I know that word."

From across the table, Billy Bostwick yelled, "Shut up, Moody. You *are* a cunt. And the *RAG* is a shitty paper."

"And you're a Frenchified faggot, Bostwick," Moody squealed.

Limonade splashed across the table, soiling Moody's coat that much more. "Goddamn you, Bostwick. You'll never get another mention!"

One of the many high emotional points of the evening came as Marlene, a Mordaunt model hailing originally from Hamburg, led a tranquilized donkey onto and around the dance floor. The animal was laden with baskets stuffed with party trinkets and long torpedoes of

French bread. Later in the evening, a second animal act was scheduled: a piglet would be carried in and everyone would get a chance to kiss its ass for good luck in the new year, another age-old European custom. . . .

Marlene was wearing one of the less shocking of the new *Erogenalia* numbers: a dirndl with a large heart-shaped cutout in the rear. The crease between her cheeks glistened with sweat, for it was now becoming mightily hot. Marlene's Teutonic features were chalky white, making her red lipstick all the more vivid. She led the donkey among the tables. It followed without demur until they reached the Chanelistes, then halted, seemingly fascinated by one of their number, a woman with a tiny face, uplifted nose, and mascaraed eyes. The two, donkey and woman, stared at each other. Then the donkey charged. He knocked the small Chaneliste off her chair and Kelly, transfixed, watched with horror as a long donkey tool unfurled. The animal dropped to his fetlocks, braying. The Chaneliste uttered a piercing scream.

"Holy shit!" Moody shouted, "the goddamn donkey is going to ball that little broad."

Kelly aroused himself and dashed across the dance floor. He seized the halter out of Marlene's hand and yanked it as hard as he could, at the same time leveling a kick at the donkey's hindquarters, trying to catch it in the balls. The donkey brayed again and kicked back, narrowly missing Kelly's leg. Fortunately, two security guards were nearby. The three of them succeeded in dragging the animal away, belting it around the ears with their fists.

"Jesus Christ, Marlene," Kelly panted, "have a care."

"Herr Jacques, it vent vild, dat stupide fucking animale . . ."

Kelly looked toward Zouzou. The old lady was shaking, shrieking with laughter. At the Maison Billy table, two stalwarts were choking over their limonade and Moody was whacking his cast with his hand. "Kelly, wait'll I write that up. . . ."

"You crippled prick," Kelly yelled.

But now, someone was pulling at his sleeve. He turned

to see a redhead. "You're supposed to be Jack Kelly," this woman said. "Zouzou told me to look you up. You're going to be working on this sex-juice project?"

"I am?"

"Who's this?" Moody demanded, not to be left out. "Introduce—"

"I'm a lady known as Madeleine. I work for . . ." She named one of the largest of the international conglomerates.

"And I work for the *RAG*," Moody said. "I'd ask you to dance but, as you see, I have this large cast on my leg."

"Pipe down," Madeleine said. She patted the cast. "I'm staying at the Meurice. Say, what do you have to do to get a drink around here?" She waved at a waiter, but he didn't stop. "Sure takes them a long time coming. . . ."

"It's so crowded," Kelly said. "I'll go to the bar. . . ."

"No, don't bother," Madeleine said. "I don't care, for it takes me a long time coming too. That's why I like guys with short cocks. They work harder at it."

Olga's face paled at the remark but Moody simply roared. Kelly turned away and Olga followed. They heard Madeleine's next remark. "Listen, honey, I marry Englishmen and I'm looking for a new one. But you're not English."

"I have a stiff upper lip," Moody spouted.

Sternly, Olga ignored him and said to Kelly, "I am not much impressed with the guests at *fête de Zouzou*, Jack."

He nodded. "Moody doesn't add much tone. But nothing to do with me, Olga. I'm just about out of this place now."

"What?" she said hopefully, "you are returning to the *RAG*?"

"Well . . . probably. But not in Paris. I'll be back in New York."

"Leaving me with Maurice Moody?" she said bitterly. "He importunes me and I am so very lonely. In the office, he plays obscene games with me. He is very wicked and Count Boris is suspicious."

"Olga, for God's sake, what's he done now?"

"Jack, I am hot-blooded. I become excited. I cannot answer. . . ."

"Olga!" Christ, that was disgusting. He put his hand on her arm, nudging the arc of her breast. There was an instant quivering of her nostril. "But you haven't . . ."

Sorrowfully, she said, "I become crazy, Jack. You have seen that."

Of all the women he had known, Kelly would have least suspected Olga Blastorov of nymphomania. Now he had a veiled acknowledgement that this was so. It excited him strangely. To know that a woman was not only ready, not only willing, but eager for it at any moment was thrilling. "What you mean is that—"

She wouldn't allow him to finish the sentence. "Jack," she said hotly, "I become possessed, a lost soul of a Dostoyevsky novel. I am not responsible for what can happen."

But the disgusting Moody? He had to know. "Olga, Christ, he's so filthy."

Noise swirled around them, people, waiters, but all that was forgotten as she said in a low voice, "Filth is no deterrent, Jack. In my fantasies, I have made love to swinish goatherds in the high Himalayas, to lepers, gangs of drunken pirates. . . ."

Gang bangs? Surely that was not a very romantic sort of dream. "Olga, goddamn . . . Gosh."

There was a tenseness about her body even now, he realized, as if she were headed toward spontaneous combustion, an undiscovered fire in the attic—basement would be more like it.

"Whatever happens," she said fatalistically, "I will still be your mistress."

But hell, didn't she understand a man could not take as a mistress one so promiscuous. "Olga, you've got to learn to control yourself. Last summer, when you went away . . ."

She moved her head uneasily, even the majestic crown

of hair, the be-pearled *poitrine* somehow degraded. She did not want to answer. She pressed his arm. "Jack, you have a moment now. Could we go upstairs, somewhere, *now*?"

Was there time? She moved her body close to him, dropping a hand to touch his thigh. Ah, the old trick: *mano morte*, they called it in Italy, the dead hand, next to his *équipage*. Up against one of the pillars, out of view of the archway, Olga slipped fingers into his pocket. But, was there time? The thought of Moody put him off. And Beatrice would be arriving soon.

He did not have to make the momentous decision. Olga was staring over his shoulder, goggle-eyed.

"*Dieu*," she whispered, "it is the monster himself, Aristide de Bis!"

Treachery! That was Kelly's first thought. He had been lured here by Hercule's assurance that Aristide de Bis was in the countryside.

Aristide stopped at the head of the stairs and surveyed the room with a supercilious stare. His entrance, as the various maisons became aware of it, put a definite damper on the festivities, reducing the salon to a moment of terror. For in the last few months Aristide had achieved a menacing and morbid eminence, not least, as far as many of these people were concerned, because of a new tack in his policy: war against homosexuals. For himself and his adherents, sex deviates could never be synonymous with the glory of France. He seemed to have forgotten, along with his Fascist friends, Kelly thought, that the fiercest fighters in Hitler's SS divisions were fags. But, for whatever reason Aristide's person and the immediate vicinity exuded vibrations of violence, intrigue, accidental death, and all things dark and vicious, like killing rays off a decaying planet.

"The woman?" Olga asked, in a deadened voice.

"Madame de Winter."

Aristide was so overwhelmingly evil in person that Olga's lust was dissipated. She stared fixedly at Aristide and Madame de Winter. Now, obviously having concluded that there was little to warrant any great notice, Aristide began to move slowly across the room, making his way toward the archway.

When he saw Kelly he stopped in his tracks and a look of pure hatred jumped the space between them. Kelly shuddered. The homicidal look faded and was replaced by one of scorn. Aristide slid toward them.

"Monsieur Kelly," he muttered, "you know Madame de Winter."

De Winter's eyes thickened with recognition. *"Bonsoir."* Her voice was guttural, like a man's.

Stammering, Kelly said, "I'd like you to meet Miss Olga Blastorov."

Aristide exchanged a look with Madame de Winter. "Olga Blastorov," he said softly. "Olga Blastorov." He smirked. "It was such a bad thing about your friend Maggi Mont."

Kelly hesitated. "No body was found," he said, but de Bis merely hooked a sneer to the corner of his mouth. For a second, Kelly was seized by a desire to announce to the assembled *beau monde* that Monsieur le Ministre, Aristide de Bis, was a sadist and murderer.

"Such a tragic thing for such a beautiful woman to be struck down so early in life," de Bis said, watching Kelly's face.

"We have no proof that she's actually dead," Kelly reminded him again.

Aristide scowled and nodded. There: he was not sure either. And he could be sweating out her reappearance. Aristide turned swiftly to his other great concern. "May I inquire after the health of my dear friend, Countess Beatrice de Beaupeau?"

"She is in very good health."

"Ah, *bon.*" Aristide's smile was guttering by now, like a burned-out candle. "You hear that, Madame de Winter? She is in good health."

"Oui," Madame de Winter said, her lips pursed bulbously. *"Bon . . ."*

De Winter was wearing a floor-length shocking crimson dress. It swelled at the hips and bosom, the latter much like an uplifted platform on which was displayed a heavy gold chain and a diamond-bordered black onyx cross, like those worn to the Crusades by the Knights of St. John. Her lips were heavily painted, her short blond hair neatly curled—long ringlets dropping over each side of her forehead in the style of the empire. But there was something false, or fakely feminine about Madame de Winter. Her chest was strong and firm but there was no hint of softness about it. The breasts seemed more pneumatic than real, just as the blond hair might have been some carefully implanted synthetic. It occurred to Kelly that de Winter could easily be a man in exquisite drag. Indeed, there was a hint of blond fuzz on her upper lip—but, of course, many women had hair on their faces. Madame de Winter was carrying a large pocketbook—he thought at first the leather was crocodile but on second look the grain was unusually fine and smooth, like pigskin but perhaps of more parchment thinness. He wondered what in the way of deadly weapons she had concealed in there.

"*Eh bien,* Monsieur Kelly," Aristide drawled spitefully, "we have at last solved our problems with Mangrovia, have we not?" He belched behind his hand.

"Have we? I'm not so sure of that, Monsieur le Ministre."

Aristide laughed forcefully. "You will remember our little list of options? Option one was fulfilled, thanks no little bit to your help. . . ." That would have been to warn Washburn away from Africa. "You received your reward in London. But now, I must tell you, I will pay no more."

Olga must be wondering what the hell he was talking about. Kelly realized he had to plough along. "There was no bargain, no pay."

Coldly, de Bis ignored the remark. "I am told that Rafael Trujillo Perex, international swindler, has returned to Paris." Kelly shrugged. He was not going to confirm it. "Only a tiny cog in the machine, but nonetheless culpable under French law. Madame de Winter, you see, is an expert on French jurisprudence, particularly as she is a functionary in the Ministry of the Interior."

"Vraiment?" Kelly said indifferently. Knowing what he knew about her, he was not about to be impressed by her cover story.

"Yes," Aristide responded hotly, "and there is no man without sin. Is that not so, Madame de Winter?" She nodded and wet her thick lips. Then, in an unexpected show of frailty, he passed the back of his hand across his forehead. He was totally exhausted, Kelly could see, but he managed another distorted laugh. "But, let us say, 'Let bygones be bygones. . . .'" Was this some sort of password? Ehrlitz had used the same expression. "What is past is past," de Bis added. "It is water . . . yes, under the bridge." He chuckled coarsely. "And there are big fish and little fish in the water. It is always easy to catch the little ones. But the big ones, they try to escape by ripping the net or jumping over it. But with the bare hands. . . . Is that not so, Madame de Winter?"

"Absolument," she agreed.

Kelly could feel Olga's body trembling. She was frightened out of her wits. Little dots of perspiration appeared on Aristide's forehead; the neck band of his stiff evening shirt was wet. He was obviously a man in great difficulty. His eyes wavered and far back inside them there was a wash of anxiety. Madame de Winter whispered something in his ear.

"Ah, Madame de Winter sees our friends from the House of Versailles. We will join them. Madame de Winter's gown, you see, was designed by the House of Versailles."

Nastily, Kelly asked himself where she might be wearing her decorations. "Madame Mordaunt will be surprised to see you," he said. "She thought you were in the countryside for the holiday."

"Yes . . ." De Bis snorted breathlessly. "There she is." He was tall enough to see over much of the crowd. "She sits there in the stinking smell of her cigarette, like one of the oracles of Delphi."

Solemnly, Madame de Winter said, "We are here because of vital affairs of state."

"Yes . . ." Kelly was struck by a sudden, stunning thought. Was it possible that the forces of the right wing would use the time of holiday, when the legitimate authority was sleeping it off, to mount their *coup d'état*? It would not be the first time such an occasion as a New Year's celebration had masked an evil plot. This was particularly so in France, where such family and national holidays as Christmas, New Year's, Easter, and Bastille Day were favored by revolutionaries for their machinations. Right-wing revolutionaries especially liked to put their endeavors in motion at times when they believed God's blessing would be with them.

"Well, Monsieur Kelly." Aristide sighed, winding up their conversation, "I would be grateful for a chance to talk to you privately. Perhaps after midnight—is there a quiet place in this madhouse where we and my charming companion could chat?"

Kelly did not have to reply. The Cuiristes, having recovered from their initial fright at the sight of Aristide, had begun to wave mockingly at the minister and Madame de Winter.

Madame de Winter sneered, "*Cochons,* unprincipled animals."

Kelly's first intention was to call Villa Peau and warn Beatrice to stay away. But it would be too late; she and Perex were en route by now, for it was getting close to midnight. Perspiration ran from under his armpits. What would happen was clear. Madame de Winter would arrest him and Perex—or worse. It seemed as though she was smiling at him in anticipation; her tongue treated her lips to a lascivious caress.

When they had drifted away, making first for the Versaillistes and then Madame Mordaunt, Olga whispered urgently, "Jack, what does this mean?"

"I don't know," he said worriedly, "but if I'm missing tomorrow, I want you to call my father. This is all such

horseshit, Olga, but I have an idea that de Winter creature might arrest me."

"Jack, she is too awful! And the minister—I think he is
insane."

"Olga, best that you go sit with Moody."

He was on his way downstairs in search of a telephone, hoping he might still catch them at the villa,
when he bumped into a man in a Lone Ranger mask. In
his confusion, he took the man for Perex. "Rafe, for
Christ's sake . . ."

"I beg your pardon," said the man in the mask.

The accent was terribly British. The woman, in a
matching black mask, said, "Who is the funny man,
ducky?"

"I haven't the faintest, my dear."

"I work here. I thought you were somebody else,"
Kelly said.

"I am not somebody else," the man said haughtily.
"If you work here, then point us to our good friend,
Monsieur Aristide de Bis."

"You are a friend of Aristide de Bis?" Kelly asked
slowly.

"I have just said so."

"You're with his party tonight?"

"Please stop asking stupid questions. . . .You're a
Yank, aren't you?"

"Yes." His mind was working. "May I ask your name?"

Churlishly, the man said, "If it's any concern of yours,
my name is Scarpa."

"The Earl of . . ."

"Yes, and this is Lady Scarpa."

"All right," Kelly said grimly, "Aristide de Bis is over
there . . ." He pointed toward the archway. "With
Madame Mordaunt."

"And, may I ask, my dear American fellow, is he per-
chance with his beautiful friend, Countess de Beaupeau?"

Ah, Scarpa, you rat catcher, Kelly told himself, now I
have you. The Man in the Black Mask. Kelly studied the
face. It was a pity he could not see all of it. His look was
so intent that Scarpa flinched.

"May I ask what you find so intriguing, my dear fellow?"

"I don't know. . . ." He tried it. "I sort of suspect you're a pair of gate-crashers."

"Good God! You are an impudent young man." Insulted by Kelly's doubt, Scarpa pulled off his mask.

Yes, it was Scarpa and now Kelly recalled pictures in the British magazine *Tatler*. Scarpa's face was cold, as much a rigid mask as the mask itself. The eyes were black points in a thin, white face, no doubt of it, the face of a ruined débauché. Lady Scarpa was his twin, so pallid one suspected she had never seen the sunshine, not to speak of the light of day. Her eyes were pits of smoldering refuse, the residue of a hundred disgusting orgies. Kelly trembled, despite himself, at the sight of them. They were two devils, on leave from the Inferno.

"I see, indeed," he said weakly, "that you are Lord and Lady Scarpa."

Throwing him two matching looks of withering intensity, they passed him, two thin figures, their limbs and joints loose from God knows what horrible practices.

Downstairs Beatrice was checking her sable. Perex stood waiting, a glass of champagne in his hand.

"Goddamn it, Rafe! Beatrice!" Kelly cried. "Get the coat back and leave. He's here. He's with that awful de Winter woman, or whatever she is," Kelly exclaimed.

Beatrice's face turned white and Perex downed his champagne in one gulp. "We're on our way, my dear. . . ."

"No!" Beatrice recovered first. "*Tant pis . . .* too bad," she said. "We are here and here we stay. I do not fear . . . *him*."

"The Man in the Black Mask," Kelly told her, hoping this would scare her off, "he's here too."

She faltered a second. "He is with Aristide de Bis?" There, she had said the forbidden name again.

"Bloody hell, Jack, what is this all about?" Perex demanded nervously.

"Scarpa is an old enemy of Beatrice's."

"Scarpa?" Beatrice asked.

"That's his name."

Attaching a name to the Man in the Black Mask was enough to put her fear to flight. Beatrice drew herself up. Her expression turned to stone, her lips curled angrily, and her eyes caught fire. Kelly was proud of her. This was class.

"I would wish to see this man called Scarpa."

"He's an English earl, Beatrice."

"All right, Jackelly, Rafe. Let us go upstairs."

Kelly made a last try. "Look, we could get out of here and run like hell for the château. Madame de Winter is after me. I think she's going to arrest the lot of us."

"Bah!" Beatrice cried. "She cannot arrest. Madame de Winter is not an official. She is an assassin, a woman who kills men in the midst of embrace. Jackelly, you are an innocent! You are not familiar with the highest form of perversion in the countries of the *Marché Commun,* the Common Market? Men such as Aristide de Bis and this Englishman called Scarpa—it is said their greatest enjoyment in life is observing as Madame de Winter, or others like her, strangle a man at the moment of climax. . . ."

Perex let out a strangled cry of fear. "Holy Mother of God, that's 'snuff murders.' There's been an epidemic lately. Oh, bloody son of a bitch." He clapped his hands to his cheeks, his eyes limpid, desolated at the mere mention of this sick form of entertainment. "I heard a lot about that while I was in jail. Now do you see what we're fighting against?"

"Do you think . . ." Kelly did not complete the question. Was this what Aristide de Bis had in mind for him? To be throttled at the extreme moment of pleasure by the blond superwoman? No way—de Winter was too ugly. "Beatrice . . ."

Laconically, she said, "The sport has become popular in Berlin. And surely you understand that when the Germans revert to such decadence the world should take care? For the French police, it would be an enormous accomplishment to try to convict Madame de Winter. So far, all reliable witnesses . . . have perished."

It was Beatrice who led them to the staircase. The whole room turned when they appeared. Beatrice paused for a moment, her hand on Kelly's arm, and looked around with a faint smile. Even the anarchic Cuiristes were impressed by her royal blue satin dress and the jewels that swarmed across her bosom. The Chevauxistes rose to applaud and the Cardinistes and Givenchistes blew her kisses. The royalist couturiers, the Versaillistes, rubbed stiff fingers against their palms. The Molotovistes grinned, for even these purveyors of tacky rags recognized a good thing when they saw it. The Chanelistes continued to chatter among themselves; they were an introverted, self-centered bunch.

Kelly, trying to be as brave as she was, led Beatrice across the salon to Madame Mordaunt. Gathered there now before the high priestess was a disparate group, all evidently in a state of extreme tension. Count Boris and Hercule stood a little to the back. Hercule, then Boris, smiled winningly when they saw Beatrice, for there was no man worth his salt who would not appreciate her beauty. To Zouzou's right, Aristide de Bis, Madame de Winter, and the revolting Scarpas were huddled together, now and then casting hateful looks toward Hercule and Count Boris. Olga was sitting beside Zouzou on the couch, bemused, as Zouzou stroked her bare arms.

Emil Cuir, Billy Bostwick, and Marco Chevaux, this trio of wasted beings, were now, as one, kneeling on the floor at Zouzou's feet. She ignored them, having given all her attention to Olga Blastorov.

"*Mais* madame," Marco pleaded.

"Madame Zouzou, *la reine* . . ." This, from Emil Cuir.

"A word, doll face, a word of wisdom," Billy whined.

Zouzou kicked at them and exploded, "Ah, *merde,* the adoration of these three is vomit steaming in the snow."

"*Madame!*" they protested in unison. Billy burst into tears as Zouzou caught him in the stomach with the toe of her shoe.

Aristide had ceased talking to Scarpa. He looked at Zouzou, fascinated, and then he saw Beatrice. His face twitched and his eyes became hungry. Scarpa gasped very audibly and Lady Scarpa drew in a rasping breath of air. Kelly was sure he saw drool trail through her heavily powdered face.

Without a word, not so much as a blink to acknowledge their presence, Beatrice went to Zouzou. She knocked over Emil, Billy, and Marco. They sprawled on the floor, their legs kicking like babies.

"Madame Mordaunt," Beatrice announced, "I am here. Beatrice!"

Zouzou's eyes squinted up at her with a frightened expression. She glanced at Aristide, then at Kelly. Kelly moved toward Hercule and Boris.

"*Quel assemblé,*" Hercule muttered in a low voice.

But Count Boris was chuckling with pleasure. "You see, Monsieur Jack, collected here, all the scum. Collected for us, possibly for extermination, vermin that they are. And I have the great good fortune of seeing again, after some years, my old comrade, Monsieur Hercule."

Boris bent from his rusty height to kiss Hercule on the cheek.

Madame Mordaunt took Beatrice's hand, Olga forgotten for the moment. The static tableau was jarred by the Earl of Scarpa. He positioned himself at Beatrice's elbow.

"Countess de Beaupeau," he purred, "it is a pleasure to see you again. You are looking most lovely." His eyes leered at her pale, white shoulders, now so unscarred.

Beatrice made a slight movement. "You are the Earl of Scarpa, I believe. We have never met."

This was one of the ultimate insults. Scarpa ducked as if she had slapped him. By saying they had never met, Beatrice was telling him she did not know of his existence and had no wish to know of it.

"Beatrice!" Aristide barked furiously.

Coolly, Beatrice turned her eyes on him. "Monsieur Aristide de Bis," she said, her words cutting like a whip, "kindly do not address me."

So saying, she left Aristide gasping and furious, but humiliated, to join Kelly. He introduced her to Hercule and Count Boris.

The lines were drawn, the camps established. Even Zouzou, in her strung-out state, realized that. She jumped to her feet and, cackling, demanded, "Silence! Silence!" Her voice, unsteady and crackling, sliced through the noise. She placed herself in the archway, between the anteroom and the main salon, again calling for silence. The orchestra stopped playing and those on the dance floor came to an abrupt stop. People stood on chairs in the back of the room to see what was happening. Zouzou waved her hand for total quiet, spilling cigarette ashes down the front of her dress.

"Silence!" she coughed rackingly, then went on. "All are commanded to stop their bickering, flirting, lovemaking! All are ordered to hold their glasses for the New Year's toast! For it is two minutes to midnight!"

Across the salon, arms lifted high. Within the immediate circle, glasses rose less jovially. Glances were passed of suspicion, hate, certainly of contempt and disrespect. Hercule and Boris glared at Aristide; and Aristide, his eyes half-closed, projected visual slaughter. Madame de Winter reserved her look for Kelly alone. It was one that promised violence of indescribable intensity. The two Scarpas, bewildered, watched Zouzou, sneers disfiguring their thin mouths.

Zouzou paused for a breath and freed an undertone of muttering in the main room. She stopped it again with a shout of: "Shut up! Have the courtesy!"

When the room was again silent, she snapped her fingers at one of her women. The latter ducked back into the passageway behind the anteroom and returned with a long, rectangular package wrapped in brown paper and tied loosely with a red ribbon. The woman placed the *objet* behind Zouzou on her throne.

It was midnight! Zouzou announced the new year with a great, hoarsely thundering cry, teetering back and forth. Cheers broke out, the crashing of glassware, yells off "Happy New Year" and "Hooray." . . . Kisses, hugs and grabs were exchanged, couples grappled and shrieked. Why? Kelly wondered. It was only the beginning of another year, another day on the calendar. There would be nothing especially good about the new year.

"Now, now!" Zouzou bellowed, her voice breaking against the wall of merriment. "We will take time for this!"

She pulled the ribbon off the package, then ripped away the paper.

"Voilà!"

Good God! Kelly was appalled. He came close to crying out his amazement.

Revealed to them was a larger-than-life-size portrait of Hercule.

He had been rendered in Napoleonic guise, in a high-buttoned jacket with short lapels, a foulard, and narrow trousers. A small curl twisted over his left forehead, and yes, comically, his right hand was thrust between buttons just over his heart. He looked like he was about to belch.

Hercule reeled back and clapped his hand over his eyes. His face, usually so unflappably calm, turned bright red. His mouth fell open and he uttered a rude exclamation.

Zouzou paid no attention. *"Voilà!"* she screamed a second time.

Then it happened, the most terrible reaction. From those who could see clearly, there arose a titter of laughter, a chorus of guffaws, a cascade of giggles from the right, like cannon fire from the flank, as deadly as grapeshot or shell fragments.

But worst yet was Aristide's loud and crude laugh. It was wicked, then wild, then out of control, exceeding all others.

"Aristide!" Zouzou was mortified. She could not believe it. "Aristide!" she stormed.

Hercule's face came apart with anger. "Monsieur!" he bellowed, his voice echoing through the room, overtaking even Aristide's tide of hysteria.

The Scarpas tittered behind their hands.

Aristide de Bis choked and finally crowed, "*Mon Dieu,* what is this! What is *this, chère madame,* that we see before us? *Chère* Madame Zouzou Mordaunt, do tell us from what part of the world this *freak* originates? *Regardez! Regardez!*" Aristide howled, turning so all would be sure to hear him.

"*Fasciste!*" Hercule shouted.

"*Oui, oui!*" Aristide screamed, by now quite unhinged and not to be stopped. "Is this from Corsica? Is this the descendant of the Bonaparte? *Non!* This is no Bonaparte. This is an impure crossbreed of midget and pigmy!"

His words were license for all the sycophants to begin screaming their derision. Cuir, Bostwick, and Chevaux pointed at the portrait, then at Hercule, making *phui* noises. People in the back jostled closer, their jeers filling whatever noise space was left in the room. The dense crowd began to rock. They were on the edge of riot, Kelly realized. He pushed Beatrice toward the back passage.

All hell broke loose. Hercule made for Aristide. Christ, was he reaching for his gun?

"*Petit monstre!*" Aristide pointed at Hercule. But when Hercule reached him, it was another story. He hammered Aristide with his tiny fists, his first punch catching him well below the belt, doubling him over in pain. Aristide tried to scoot out of the way but he was hemmed in by bodies. "Monsieur," he screeched, "I have immunity."

Kelly saw Hercule's lips forming the word but he could not hear it. His face was a study of murderous energy; the eyes had blanked out. Aristide tried to push him back to arm's length but Hercule went under his arms with stinging blows, leveled with the precision of a black belt. Aristide yelped repeatedly but he could not avoid Hercule. Madame de Winter, her face burning, attempted to intervene, bumping her heavy body against Hercule. But the little man was not to be deterred. His hands moved so fast Kelly could not see what he had done. Madame de Winter's protruding eyes widened with pain. Gripping her crotch with both hands, she hobbled backward and collapsed on Zouzou's sofa. She burst through Hercule's portrait, shredding the canvas irreparably.

The Scarpas were then attacked by a squad of the Cuiristes, borne away bodily, their legs kicking, a mixture of delight and fear on their ravaged faces.

The *commissionaires* and security men tried to stop it, finally succeeding in pulling Hercule off Aristide de Bis. Aristide staggered into the back corridor. Billy Bostwick was sobbing pitifully, huddled on the floor. His sheath had been ripped away and there was blood on his pathetic foreskin. Before anyone could stop them, the Cuiristes upturned tables in one corner of the salon. It was behind these that they violated the Scarpas. Kelly made no attempt to send a rescue mission. He could see their clothes being torn away and hear their cries. Tonight, they would get their fill. The *commissionaires* dragged Madame de Winter off the couch, leaving Zouzou standing alone in the midst of the chaos, quaking, her eyes unfocused. She stared at Kelly but did not recognize him.

Madame de Winter lay on the floor in the back corridor, moaning and trying to explain what Hercule had done to her. Aristide was a goner now, quite mad. His facial muscles were out of control. His shirt was torn and he had lost his tie.

"I am a minister of the government," he gasped. "There will be an inquiry. Madame de Winter has been injured."

If Zouzou did not know anyone else, she did know Aristide. "Foul pig," she shrieked, "foul pig! After all these years and what have you done! You!" She aimed a shaking finger at de Winter. "You have destroyed my picture!"

"Dommage," Madame de Winter groaned.

Victor appeared and behind him C.T. Trout and Magda Starbright. "Madame, Madame, are you all right?"

"I? I?" Her dark face was crazy. "Of course. It is this

. . . foul pig, this rat *merde* from the bowels of the Bastille who has perpetrated this . . ."

"Stampede, ma'am, stampede is what it is," Trout observed gleefully.

Perex jumped from the side to face Aristide de Bis. The Cuban's face was wet with tears.

"Mr. de Bis, you sir are no bloody gentleman." Aristide took no note of him. "You sir," Perex screamed, "are nothing but a no-good bloody mother-fucker." His hand flashed out and smacked across Aristide's face. "You were responsible for having me arrested on a trumped-up charge!"

Aristide's eyes blazed. "Perex! Latin degenerate . . ."

Trout pushed Perex out of the way. "Make room," he bawled, "only one way to stop a stampede like this." He opened his jacket, put a hand to the rear of his trousers and dragged out his pearl-handled revolver. Quite calmly, he stepped around the corner into the salon and loosed all six shots into the ceiling, taking pieces off the crystal chandelier.

The sound of the shots and the smell of gunpowder achieved its result: instant quiet, broken only by the screams from behind the Cuiriste barricade and the musical clatter of pieces of crystal hitting the floor.

"There we are, ma'am," Trout said smugly, tucking the revolver back in his belt, "that's the way we do it down Texas way."

Kelly felt hot breath on the back of his neck. "Oh, bravo, bravo." It was Magda Starbright. "Such a cowboy, brave and true. My own C.T. Trout."

The explosions also restored Zouzou to calm. "Thank you, monsieur," she told Trout. "Now, Jacques, tell the orchestra to resume playing and let the festivities continue until dawn. We will not be distracted by the cruel antics of Monsieur le Ministre, Aristide de Bis, foul *cochon.*" It was over between her and Aristide now. "Where is Hercule?"

He was standing just inside the corridor. His face was bruised, his velvet suit ripped. But he had saved the two Scarpas. They were wrapped in tablecloths. Lady

Scarpa's makeup was smeared and she was sobbing. The Earl of Scarpa had been beaten. Both his eyes were closed and his mouth was bleeding.

"*Les Cuiristes,*" Hercule said succinctly, explaining everything.

Lady Scarpa cried, "Aristide, those men tortured us unmercifully."

"They will answer for it," Aristide said.

"Peregrine was buggered five times," she reported.

"They will answer. They will answer," Aristide repeated.

"Where are the Cuiristes?" Zouzou demanded. "Arrest them!"

"They have left the building, madame," Hercule said. "They have all escaped." He smiled gently.

Aristide de Bis cried, "You! *Monstre!* You have hurt Madame de Winter very badly." The big blond was slouched on the floor, her back to the wall, holding her belly.

Hercule was not impressed. "Madame de Winter is a sadist."

Boris Blastorov, who had been quietly holding Olga until now, said, "And you, Monsieur de Bis, are a dishonored *collaborateur.*"

Aristide peered curiously at him. "Ah, Blastorov, I have heard you survived. The outlaw. The bandit Russian."

"Yes, monsieur."

Claud Trout turned irritably. "J.K., what the fuck is this all about?"

Kelly merely shook his head.

Outside, the waiters put the Cuiriste tables right again, swept away broken glass, relit candles, and served fresh drinks. The orchestra was playing, although in rather hushed tempo, and slowly, as they regained their composure, some of the guests took to the floor to dance. Several couples had started necking and feeling each other up. Nothing had happened to worry about. Such flare-ups were not unusual in Paris these days.

But Zouzou was not finished. She turned to Aristide.

"From you, monsieur, I demand an apology to my friend Hercule."

"Never!"

"I insist."

From his height, Aristide de Bis stared down at Hercule. "I am so sorry I have insulted you, little man. But you are not a Bonaparte. I have checked the birth records."

Hercule's face did not change. "And you, de Bis, are no de Bis. You are an imposter. You are a *Boche* from Lower Bavaria. Your name is Otto Pishl. We have known this all along."

De Bis sneered. "Nonsense, dwarf! You are suffering from the delusions of your inferior blood."

For all to see, Hercule jumped high and smashed a glove across Aristide's face. A glove? It was a leather glove, which Hercule then threw on the floor. Obviously, one of the Cuiristes had left it behind.

"That is a challenge, Herr Otto Pishl," Hercule announced.

Aristide's face was fearful. Whether he was Pishl or de Bis, he was trapped. He had no choice but to brazen it through. To do otherwise would have meant a complete loss of credibility.

"Hercule!" Zouzou exclaimed.

Hercule smiled. "Have no fear, madame." To Aristide, or Otto, he said, "Choose your second, monsieur, for we will settle this in the Bois this morning."

Aristide's head jerked proudly. "Very well . . . the Earl of Scarpa."

But there was a question. Was Scarpa well enough to go with them to the Bois? His lips were swollen but he was able to nod.

Perex whispered in Kelly's ear, "Bloody shit, my dear, this is where I came in."

Hercule said, "For my second, Count Boris Blastorov."

From her place on the floor, Madame de Winter whimpered, "Aristide, kill him. The dwarf has pulled out my guts."

Zouzou kicked her in the haunch. "Whore! Disgusting

whore! Monsieur de Bis, kindly tell us—are you Otto Pishl or Aristide de Bis?"

Aristide glared at her disbelievingly. "Madame—you know quite well who I am?"

Gently, Hercule broke in. "It does not matter, madame, who he is."

But Madame de Winter, Kelly knew, was more than a simple whore. She was a murderess. However, having been ministered to by Hercule's strong fingers, these wiry from his equestrian days, it would be some time before she lured more unsuspecting fools to the final embrace.

De Winter pushed herself painfully to a sitting position. She aimed her disordered face at Zouzou. "Me a whore? You perfidious hag! You were happy enough as whore-mistress to Colonel-General Ulrich von Unterstutzen by whom you bore a misformed cretin of a child. Ha! Perhaps that is our dwarf here!"

Zouzou lurched. Jesus! As numbed as he was by this turn of events, Kelly could not believe it. Hercule was too old to have been born during the war; he had been a prisoner in Germany. A child? Even Boris Blastorov's knowledge of the past was not as extensive as that. His monocle fell out of his right eye.

Zouzou screamed, "Hercule! This woman must die!"

"Yes, Madame." One knew it would be done.

Lady Scarpa had begun to pant again, forgetting her covering of tablecloth. It fell to the floor, exposing her emaciated and brutalized body: tiny breasts, chewed and bleeding around the nipples. There were slash marks on her back where the Cuiristes had whipped her with their leather belts. She was bowlegged and the nub of a white Mordaunt candle seemed to be sticking out of her ass. "They buggered me too," she screamed, then fainted.

"All will pay for this," Aristide raged. He banged his temples with his knuckles, a sure sign of approaching breakdown. "There will be massive retaliation."

"Cochon," Zouzou said softly, "yes, but first you must settle your accounts with Hercule, Monsieur whoever-you-are."

"De Bis is my name," Aristide said loftily.

A moment before, Madame Mordaunt would gladly have called off this new confrontation in the Bois. What had spun the coin for her were the words of Madame Marceline de Winter, loathsome enchantress.

CHAPTER

THIRTY-FOUR

Four carloads of them, witnesses to the challenge and those with a stake in the proceedings, either from present slur or past injustice, made for the Bois de Boulogne at 6:00 A.M. that New Year's morning.

When they left the Maison Mordaunt, the *fête de Zouzou* was still in progress, although beginning finally to run down. Faintly, first light glimmered over the road, across the fields and then in the forest when they arrived. It was bitterly cold but, rounding out the festivities, Zouzou had ordered blankets from her penthouse and thermos jugs of hot coffee. Kelly and Perex, quite taken with the adventure, particularly since they were not participating, and by now more than a little drunk, thought it provident to bring brandy and several bottles of Mordaunt No. 10 champagne.

Beatrice and Kelly huddled in one corner of the backseat, warm together under a blanket, she with one hand snuggled between his legs and in the other a glass of champagne. Beatrice was a little pie-eyed from the excitement of it all. Perex occupied the other corner, and ironically, it was Victor who faced them from one of the jump seats of the limousine. Up in front with the chauffeur, Magda Starbright and C.T. Trout were enveloped in each other, Trout's face buried in the expanse of Hungarian bosom. He grunted, from time to time, Texas words of endearment. Magda pitter-pattered Hungarian dialect. Perex was at the moment singing in a monotone, something Cuban, and weeping intermittently into a brandy glass.

Zouzou, close to nervous collapse, rode with the doctor and Hercule in the second car. In the third, Count Boris and Olga. The last of the caravan contained Aristide de Bis, Madame De Winter and the Scarpas. Madame de Winter, much the worse for wear and bleeding a bit internally, had insisted on coming although the others had recommended a trip to a doctor. But, as she hatefully put it, she wished to see the end of the tiny man who had done her in.

"Remember the last time we were out here, Victor?" Kelly asked.

Victor nodded humbly. "I will never forget it, Jacques. It was a shameful incident. Are you prepared now to tell me that you forgive me? For it was a foul piece of bad luck."

"But you've never said that you were sorry," Kelly pointed out.

"Jacques, I am very sorry."

"Then I forgive you."

"Ah, *bon.*" Victor smiled widely and with relief, as if this were the message he had been waiting for to make his happy day.

Perex mumbled cheerfully, "Look at it this way, my dear. If it hadn't happened, where would you be now? Working for the *RAG*. And you wouldn't be sitting there so gloriously happy with bloody Beatrice."

Beatrice nodded and kissed Kelly's cheek. Her grip tightened on the personage under the blanket. It was a toss-up, Kelly thought, whether he'd prefer to be here or in bed. "Rafael," Beatrice said, "I hope you will be happy too."

Her words reminded him of his next duty. Perex

frowned and, overhearing, Trout put his chin over the seat to growl, "This little pecker is going to be very happy, ain't you, Rafe?"

"Gloriously happy, gloriously bloody happy, yes."

"Good," Trout said. "Don't bother me no more." The next sound from the front seat was the slavering of lips.

The chauffeur slowed and looked inquiringly into the rearview mirror for instructions.

"Anywhere in here," Kelly said. "This is about the spot, isn't it, Victor?"

"Yes," Victor said. As they were getting out of the car, he murmured, "Messieurs, have you remarked the handbag of Madame de Winter?"

"Like a bloody suitcase," Perex said dismally.

"But are you aware of what leather that is?"

"Looks like pigskin," Kelly muttered.

"No." Victor's face became very solemn with the import of his revelation. "It is of human skin, cured and tanned."

"What's that you say, what's that you say?" Trout bellowed. Again, he had overheard. "Human skin? Froggie, that's some accusation. Holy Jumpin' Jesus Skydiver, that's macabre, *ain't* it, J.K.?" Trout's eyes fixed on the last car and narrowed as Madame de Winter dragged herself out. "The fuckin' woman has got to be a veritable . . . veritable what, J.K.? A veritable goddamn nut, that's what."

Kelly felt sick. "Yes, at least," he said.

The effect on Perex of the information was much more telling. "Holy Mother of Bloody Hell," he cried, "and I have a nervous stomach." He dragged himself to the other side of the car and bent over, retching.

"Victor, did you have to tell us that?" Kelly said.

Hercule and the doctor helped Zouzou out of the second car. She held her black leather box of dueling pistols in her arms, but she was suddenly very frail. Her face was pale, cadaverously thin and drawn. She stooped and her feet caught in her long black coat. She was still wearing her pillbox hat, the veil now in disarray. Kelly remembered the last time they had been here, less than six months ago. She had definitely faded since then.

As they had done that morning in August, the various groups huddled under the protective trees, Zouzou and her doctor alone in the center, waiting for the others to prepare themselves. Count Boris and Scarpa saw to the loading of the pistols. It was an incongruous scene, the men in dinner jackets, although much disheveled, the women in long dresses. But it was Scarpa who looked the most odd. He had lost his clothes to the Cuiristes and had been outfitted for the expedition in the only things in the salon they could find to fit him: a wool dress, a pair of large-size women's boots and one of the Mordaunt mink-lined city-slicker raincoats.

"Maintenant," Zouzou demanded, her voice barely strong enough to carry the distance between them in the silent forest, "are we ready to begin?"

A nod from the left, a nod from the right. Hercule and Count Boris, Aristide and the Earl of Scarpa approached her. Count Boris was in his element; he, unlike Zouzou, looked twenty years younger. His monocle shone in the tough morning light and he rubbed his hands together, not against the cold but in anticipation. Hercule, as Kelly had expected he would be, was deadly calm. Aristide's face was working, as if he were trying to control either fear or hysterical laughter. Alone, the other member of the de Bis camp stood ten yards away, her back to a tree, gripping her disgusting pocketbook.

It had rained slightly during the night and then frozen, turning the heavy grass under their feet into crackling sheaves of glass.

Perex joined them. "Champagne," he said.

"Are you all right now?" Kelly filled a glass. "Here's to Hercule!"

Zouzou commenced her recital of the by-now well-rehearsed Honorable Dueling Form. The adversaries acknowledge understanding and agreement. Then she offered them the leather box. Aristide, not speaking, chose one pistol and sighted it at the sky. Hercule took the other. Neither man showed any sign of the fear and nothing, evidently, of the panic Kelly had felt on that morning of his.

"*Alors*," Zouzou said harshly, slightly revived by the tenseness of the situation, "now I command you to take up your positions."

Hercule and Aristide marched into the center of the clearing and stood back to back. Hercule barely came to Aristide's waist. One thing about it, Kelly thought, he would not make a big target. Zouzou went on with her bit about counting to twenty, when they could turn and fire. Hercule's little body was straight and one felt the bigness of his heart and his determination. For a second, he looked twice as tall as his opponent, like a giant of courage.

"Well," Perex whispered loudly, "this is where that big asshole gets his."

On this side of the clearing, all were rooting for Hercule.

"Shaddup!" Trout said. "Let 'em concentrate, grease-ball."

"One . . ." Zouzou began counting and the two men moved apart, feet crunching in the frozen grass. Kelly glanced at Beatrice; after all, the man had been her lover. She had stopped breathing, tip of her tongue in her teeth. "Two . . ."

Then, goddamn if it didn't happen again.

Somewhere between the count of Five and Six, a shattering flatulent detonation rattled the treetops. A black, scrambling object plummeted from a branch over Aristide's head, its long tail stiff with fright.

A squirrel, in its observation of the unlikely scene, had been so surprised by the cannonlike fart, it had lost its footing.

It thumped on Aristide's head. For a second, he stood absolutely still, a disturbed expression on his face. His gun went off into the ground and he toppled over, unconscious. The squirrel was already long gone.

Hercule, at the sound of Aristide's fart, then the pistol shot, had begun to spin. When he completed his turn, Aristide was on the ground.

Fate had intervened once again.

But Madame de Winter was not prepared to leave it at that. Ferociously, she snatched open her pocketbook and dragged out what looked like a large caliber automatic, a .45 Magnum or something of the kind. She got off one shot in Hercule's direction—too late, for the fast little man had already dropped to the ground and was sighting the unreliable dueling pistol at her. She spun toward the neutrals. Kelly saw the muzzle, a big black hole, pointed straight at his heart.

Then there was another hole, right between Madame de Winter's astonished eyes. She dropped like a sack in the grass.

Beatrice stifled a scream and began to pant. Lady Scarpa swooned again. Olga Blastorov emitted a sensual groan, and a few yards away, Count Boris began cursing in Russian. Zouzou swayed and the doctor caught her. She thought Hercule had been shot.

Perex screamed, "Bloody shit!"

Hissing through his damaged mouth, the Earl of Scarpa exclaimed, "S'foul . . . S'foul . . ."

Kelly realized what had happened. Behind him, C.T. Trout was holding his smoking revolver in his right hand and smiling craftily. "Self-defense!" he hacked. "You saw her! The no-good despot was going to shoot me, crazy fuckin' bitch!"

"C.T., C.T., she was aiming at me," Kelly stammered. "I didn't even see you reload."

"I only had a couple of hours to do it, J.K.," Trout said sarcastically. "This folks, I've got to tell you, is what we from down Texas way call *deus ex machina* which, roughly translated from the German, means the gods has turned off their motor. . . . Well, any objections to *not* being shot in the ass, J.K.?"

"No, no."

"Hercule!" Zouzou recovered enough to scream.

Slowly, stunned, the pint-sized hero pulled himself out of the grass. "*C'est ça,*" he said, "it is done." But he had not fired at Marceline de Winter. Had he?

Perex's face was streaming with tears. Little icicles

grew on his eyelids. "C.T.," he blubbered, "you killed that goddamn cow."

"Listen, greaser," Trout said smugly, enjoying every moment of it, "I can take a wart off a flea's ass at a hundred yards. Just *you* remember that, boy!"

Count Boris had commenced to jump up and down. "Hercule, *mon cher,* the deed is done. Aristide de Bis has been dishonored."

Hearing his name, Aristide sat up in the grass, holding his head in his hands. Seeing de Winter's stiff figure, he began to wail.

"Looky that big Froggie mother-fucker," Trout said wonderingly. "Boy-oh-boy, I heard about duels. Never seen one except in Texas. But, J.K., J.K.," he said disbelievingly, "I never heard a man fart like that in my life. . . . All the bears must be to the French border by now."

"Grovival."

Trout's eyes popped. "Grovival! What you saying, J.K.?"

Now, if ever, Trout would understand the power of the Mangrovian vegetable root. "C.T., it's what I've been telling you all along. That was a dyed-in-the-wool Grovival fart."

Trout shook his head slowly from side to side. "He must've blown a hole in his pants, letting go a fart of that dimension." His eyes widened with concern. "M.J.?"

Kelly shrugged. "I don't know. Only time will tell."

Trout snickered wickedly. "Serve her right, Miss Thunder Pussy. She won't have to write home anymore, not that she ever did. She can send messages from the Mangrovia place like that—in Morse code." Again, he cackled and fell into Magda Starbright's arms.

Perex groaned pathetically but he recognized a way of sliding out of his predicament. "C.T. . . . . under the circumstances . . ."

"Shaddup, greaser," Trout snarled. "You get her whether you like or not, gasbag and all."

Zouzou Mordaunt faltered under Hercule's protective

arm. "Oh, Hercule," she moaned thankfully, "*mon petit cher . . .*"

Lady Scarpa had regained consciousness, reminding them of her presence by the loud chattering of her teeth. "Help me, Scarpa, you fool. I am freezing."

"Help yourself, love." Scarpa sneered.

"Someone help *me*," Aristide de Bis called plaintively.

Zouzou removed her head from Hercule's shoulder. Cruelly, she said, "Leave this dishonored creature with one of the cars and a chauffeur. Monsieur le Ministre, Aristide de Bis—Otto Pishl—has been unmanned. His career is finished. The opposition will hear of this and this very day. . . . You"—she pointed to a driver—"load that dead beast into the car. Aristide de Bis can deal with his friend Madame de Winter."

Scarpa whined, "And what of us, myself and Lady Scarpa?"

"Take a second car, sir," Zouzou said irately. "I would advise you and your putrid lady to return to your turd-shaped island and never darken the door of France again."

Scarpa cringed, then threatened, "Be assured, we shall never return to this country of scoundrels and misfits. We have been physically molested and psychologically intimidated. I shall take it up with the Foreign Office."

Trout had never liked Englishmen, even the best behaved. "Look here, sonny, get your scrawny little ass out of here before I pull up that dress of yours and kick it from here to the English Channel, snotty little limey. And take that titless excuse for a woman with you."

The Scarpas would have been a comical sight in any circumstances. And they were particularly comical now as they quickly made for a car.

Hercule helped Zouzou to her Rolls, where he and the doctor stretched her out on the backseat. She had commenced to babble. "To think that this horrid experience could happen to a monument of France, Zouzou Mordaunt, leading exponent of French realism. . . ."

Magda Starbright was something else. She ran on too,

in her own way. "Oh my, my oh! Oh, cowperson, C.T., with heart of gold, it has been so exciting. Just as in old Budapest. Will the tall man and the large woman be rising soon so we may return to the city? Magda Starbright feels herself hungering for a *petit déjeuner.*"

Trout looked at her closely. "Cookie," he said, "that woman is dead as a big door mouse and the tall man is going to fart himself to death before too long."

Magda gagged slightly. "Then is Magda Starbright, of thespian fame, not so hungry as formerly."

Trout chuckled moistly. "But still in heat, I hope."

Perex stopped the loose talk. "Let's get the bloody hell out of here, shall we?"

It was well and truly the morning after now. Kelly felt the force of letdown and anticlimax. The dull throbbing of a headache began. He closed his eyes. He had no feeling about the abrupt end of Madame de Winter, except relief. She had not been a human being; thus death in her case was merely academic.

As they crossed the city, its streets frozen in silence, fuming cold slowing its heart and lifeblood, Trout spoke. "J.K., you polecat, just let me and Magda off at the Crillon."

"Oh, my cowman . . ."

"Cowboy."

"Cowboy, sweet C.T., my garments of high quality and fashion are waiting at another hotel."

"Never mind about that, cookie, whatever you need, we'll send out for. I have in mind for us to stop in my hotel room for the next week or ten days."

It was about eight in the morning when they reached the Crillon. Trout and Magda went into the hotel arm in arm, wedded together like a two-assed beast of odd proportions, and disappeared. This, Kelly hoped, would be the last he'd ever see of Claud Trout.

An exhausted *commissionaire* let them into the Maison Mordaunt. Broken glass, shattered plates, destroyed bits of festive décor, squashed flowers, articles of underwear, even coats and ties and broken spears littered the floor of the downstairs boutiques, and upstairs in the salon it was worse. Tattered and burned tablecloths tumbled across the room, empty bottles were everywhere, broken stemware crackled under their shoes, chairs and tables were tipped over, and people had been sick in every corner. It was a disgusting sight, as if a rampaging army had marched through the night. There had been several fires, the *commissionaire* reported, his head hanging, several more rapes after the ruin of the Scarpas, two people had been taken to hospital with knife wounds, and an elderly man had died of heart attack while chasing one of the Mordaunt models up the glass staircase.

"*Merde!*" Zouzou's voice, however, was weak. She was past caring. "All we lack is a bombing raid."

The place was cold. During the night, the heating and air conditioning had broken down. The stench was of corruption.

Marco Chevaux was unconscious under the rented piano. Other, unknown celebrants were passed out behind drapes and under the catering tables—which had been plucked clean of every last morsel of food. A Cuiriste straggler was curled on Zouzou's throne, snoring, leather jacket draped over his head. A colorful *Croix de Guerre,* medal and ribbon, dangled from the wrecked chandelier.

"Monsieur," Zouzou muttered to the *commissionaire,* "I can see the *fête* was a success."

From above, as in a dream, came the sound of drunken voices.

Zouzou's voice was failing. "It is surely the last, Hercule. Never another *fête de Zouzou.* We are entering the age of death and damnation. I knew the end would begin this year." Her voice trailed away, leaving them all uneasy. Perhaps she was right. It did seem at moments like this that the end of the world was approaching.

A piercing scream, then honking laughter came from behind the tattered drapes at the archway. A redheaded woman, full-breasted and blowsy, staggered toward them. Kelly recognized her. It was the woman from the night before: Madeleine, of the cosmetic conglomerate. Another figure appeared behind her, all too recognizable. It was

Maurice Moody. Both were naked except for the cast that covered Moody from foot to knee.

"Hey, Hey!" Madeleine shouted boisterously. "Have you had yours today? I had mine yesterday. . . ." She chanted the suggestive song.

"Mon Dieu," Zouzou whispered.

"Ah, Kelly!" Moody spun on his cast, goggling at them shortsightedly, for he was without his glasses.

"Get dressed and get the hell out of here, Moody."

"I can't find my goddamn clothes and neither can she. Somebody stripped us naked and stole our clothes!"

Boris Blastorov fixed his monocle in his eye. "Sir! You are a disgusting spectacle. Cover yourself at once!"

"Go! Go!" Zouzou screeched thinly. "I can stand no more of this."

Hercule had not forgotten Moody, or forgiven. "Monsieur, *va t'en.*" It was the expression one used when ordering animals around.

"Ah, you," Moody said, "you're the little shit that busted my leg."

"And monsieur, I will break the other if you do not leave."

Olga stepped forward, a look of distaste on her face. But she had exaggerated, Kelly realized—Moody was not at all well hung. "I will take care of them," she said.

"Olga, I forbid," Count Boris cried.

"It is for the *RAG,*" she said simply.

Kelly felt Beatrice's body shake. Looking at her anxiously, he realized she was laughing. Count Boris looked perplexed; then he joined in. It was not a serious moment.

"What's so goddamn funny?" Moody demanded.

"You are, Moody." Kelly looked around for Victor. Victor was about to slide away. "Hey, Vic, you better call a cab."

"Yes," Victor said. "I will arrange for a garment for this lady and escort her to her hotel."

"Are *you* British?" the redhead called Madeleine demanded drunkenly of Victor. She stumbled to a chair and sat down, beavering them hugely.

Victor smiled ingratiatingly. "In my maternal line," he murmured.

"Then call us a cab, Cecil." Madeleine sighed.

Zouzou Mordaunt emitted a thin screech. "Liar! His name is not Cecil!" She sagged against Hercule, her head lolling back. Alarmed, Hercule picked her up and carried her silently toward the elevator.

"Mais," Beatrice said softly, "Madame Mordaunt is a heroine, Jackelly. Do you suppose that Hercule *is* her son?"

He nodded hesitantly. "It's possible, but he wouldn't be the one de Winter was talking about, not with the Nazi. Hercule is too old." But could it be that Hercule was the offspring of Zouzou and her greatest love, the Scotsman Angus?

CHAPTER

THIRTY-FIVE

That night, the first of the new year, they banqueted in the manorial hall of the Château Beaupeau: Beatrice and Kelly, Rafe Perex, and Olga and Boris Blastorov. It would be another night to remember. They drank ice-cold vodka in honor of Count Boris, then Beaupeau Brut champagne; ate smoked salmon from the local river and a huge Beaupeau goose Beatrice had ordered to be prepared before their departure from the Villa Peau; and finally consumed Beaupeau Napoleonic-era brandy with their coffee. The feast left them exhausted— and they had been weary enough before.

Kelly made the first toast, to them all, and then specifically to Beatrice, his love, so beautifully with child, unless, he thought, it was a false alarm. When she understood what he was saying, Olga became sullen.

"And here's to our enemies," Kelly added. "Madame Marceline de Winter, God rest her soul. . . ."

"If He can," Perex muttered viciously.

"And Aristide de Bis or Otto Pishl, whichever. Count Boris, were you aware of that?"

"No, *vraiment,*" Boris said, shaking his head. "But Madame Mordaunt must know if it is true."

"Now we know why Hercule joined the Maison Mordaunt," Kelly said.

"Because he is the son of Zouzou Mordaunt." Olga sniffed.

"No, no. Because he was on the trail of Aristide de Bis."

"Ah *merde,*" Beatrice cried impatiently. "What do we care about that now, Jackelly?"

He was surprised. He had never heard her use such a word before.

Count Boris stood up next, holding fast to the heavy table, for he had consumed considerable vodka. *"Mes amis,"* he began, "let me say, Monsieur Jack, that you are a noble person to be so forgiving. I find it difficult for myself." Boris's eyes were red-rimmed and sorrowful, but they, and his monocle shone vividly in the candle-light. He turned to Beatrice. "Madame Countess, I am aware of the past, and the past is dead. For my part, I may say that Aristide de Bis, or Otto Pishl, while in the service of the Vichy régime, and indirectly in the service of the Nazi occupiers, performed exactly the same poisonous service whatever his name. He held me in prison—I could show you scars. But I was released by my comrades. . . ." Oh no, Kelly groaned to himself, Boris was going to tell the Washburn story. "Monsieur Hercule, a man of Gargantuan strength, was one of my comrades, and George Washburn, your president, and at that time a hero of the *Maquis* was another." Boris was sliding past the story. Had Olga been lying to him? No, he was back to the story. "Together," Boris went on, his inflamed eyes filling with tears, "we burned de Bis's prison to the ground. But there was retaliation. My own wife was a victim, only weeks after the birth of our . . . the birth of Olga."

Oh, oh! Olga began to look perturbed.

"Thus," Boris went on breathlessly, "my own hatred for de Bis knew no bounds. My hope has always been to see my dead wife and my comrades revenged and today was that day. In a manner, Aristide's humiliation served the cause of revenge better than death. For he will live with his humiliation every day of his life."

Beatrice had become tearful. Boris's story was bound to move one so emotional as she.

"The wonder of it is, Count Boris," Kelly interrupted, "that you Europeans can be forgiving at all. A few years after the war and German tourists are welcomed back to every country they raped."

"Money!" Boris said scornfully. "Europeans forgive when it is profitable." He changed the position of his feet as if preparing to go on until midnight. "But, since today was such a special time of revenge, I have something more to say. . . ."

"Count Boris!" Olga cried.

"No, my child, I *must* unburden myself. You see," he said excitedly, rubbing his monocle on his napkin, priming himself, "Olga is not my daughter."

Christ, Kelly thought, there it was, splashed out on the table.

"Oh, Count Boris!" Olga groaned.

"No, no!" Boris thundered. Perhaps he was even more pissed than Kelly had suspected. "No, no, I must tell you that while I was in the defamed Aristide de Bis's jail, your mother fell in love with another and you are *his* daughter."

"Bloody hell," Perex shouted excitedly, "who's that?"

"Olga's father is . . . *Hercule!*"

Olga dropped her napkin and cried out. She had expected Washburn and had received Hercule. "You told me my father was George Washburn!" she screeched.

"True, my little one," Boris said sadly. "I told you that you were the daughter of George Washburn because I wanted you to be proud. Now I know that you can be far prouder of Hercule. I admit I have harbored a distinct dislike of Hercule through the years, but yesterday I forgave him. Now, I tell you that this brave, albeit small, man is your true father!"

Olga broke down. She wept without restraint, her shoulders slumped forward, head drooping and body shaking. Boris sat down, glaring straight ahead.

"God," Kelly said, "Boris—is this true?" Yes, it was, he could see that. "Does Hercule know?"

"No," Boris said shamefully, scouring his monocle. "He thought it was Washburn. My sainted wife slept with both men."

"Bloody shit!" Perex cried.

That was the proper comment, Kelly thought, his head abuzz with the reshuffling of the players and their parts. Like mother, like daughter, that was one way to summarize it. Additionally, therefore, he had not screwed the second daughter of the president, since Olga was not, after all, Washburn's daughter, was not a Russo-American child, but now a Franco-Russian. On top of that, it now turned out it was Olga's real father who had surprised them that day in his apartment. Thank God Hercule had not known of the relationship.

"I don't see any reason why we should tell Hercule about this," Kelly said.

Olga must have been thinking the same thing. "No, no," she cried, raising her head, her eyes wild.

Gently, Beatrice reached across the table for Olga's hand. "Olga, Count Boris is very brave to tell you this. You can be very proud of having Hercule as a father."

Well, in a way, it was good to know that Olga was not Westerley Washburn's half sister; on the other hand, there was as little resemblance between Hercule and Olga as between Washburn and Olga. In fact, Olga looked more like Boris, if the truth be known. For one thing, she was at least a head taller than Hercule. Her face was lean, Hercule's broad. Perhaps there might be a similarity in the dark coloration of the hair, the moist depth of the skin. It might have been logical to think that Olga's sexuality was inherited from Washburn but it seemed that this trait actually came from Hercule, now devoted lover of the ancient couturière. But that was an expression of sexuality too, sleeping so readily with history. Or *had* Hercule really slept with Zouzou, who was possibly, if one believed half the speculation, his mother? Most troubling of all, Kelly supposed, was consideration of Olga's offspring. Would they be as small as Hercule?

Beatrice, as hostess, put an end to the drama with wise words.

"Fathers are important," she said, "but we are drinking to ourselves, not our fathers. My father was very handsome but he was cruel and selfish. Would that I had had a generous man like Hercule for a father. Hercule is small, yes, but he is not a dwarf and in bravery he is a colossus. . . . So I drink to us, we who are here living and to Boris, a rare man and a hero too, a credit to all the Russians."

"Hear, hear!" Perex roared, nipping generously of his brandy.

Boris danced down the table to bend over Beatrice and kiss her emotionally on both cheeks. He began to sing a Cossack marching song, his voice, unexpectedly deep and musical, resounding against the high ceiling.

In a moment, the large, oaken door at the end of the long hall opened and a slim, middle-aged woman stepped into the room. She stared curiously at the singer. Boris hit several more high notes, then stopped, his eyes pulled to the woman. She was handsome, her gray hair pulled severely back.

"Crochet!" Boris bellowed.

"Blastorov," she said quietly, smiling.

Boris clattered across the stone floor. Crochet met him halfway.

"It *is* you, Crochet!"

"*Oui, et c'est toi,* Blastorov. I heard your wild singing."

Count Boris put a bear hug on the woman and led

her back to the table. "Incredible," he cried. "Another of the old comrades. It is Crochet of the *Maquis*."

"My business manager," Beatrice said.

Later, during the night, deeply secured in their down mattress after several hours of nearly motionless love-making on what Maggi had called Mount Sublime, now fulfilled, empty of desire and full of sleep, Kelly asked Beatrice, "Did you know about Crochet and Boris?"

He felt her smile crease the fine cotton of the pillow where their heads rested side by side. "No," she said, "my knight of the rippling sword. I did not know. But I have heard Crochet speak of her lost love. Now we learn it is this baroque figure of a man."

Boris and Crochet, she relieved of her duties in order to celebrate their happy reunion, spent the days riding the Beaupeau stallions, for both were fine horsepeople. They went off at dawn, galloping through the russet winter vineyards, across the fields and into the woods on the other side of the estate. It was beautiful to watch, this love in late bloom. Crochet joined them at dinner now, and altogether they made a jolly some. Even Olga, dispirited briefly by Boris's momentous moment of truth was in a good mood, probably, Kelly thought, because she had already begun her dalliance with Rafe Perex. Perex, for now, seemed to have put aside his foreboding about his mission to Mangrovia. His eyes were bright, and clearly he was receiving his required daily dosage of sex.

Beatrice and Kelly began to make plans for their wedding, and the date had been set for a week to the day. Harry Kelly, contacted by crackling telephone in the *RAG* office in New York, would be at the château for the event.

It was Crochet and Count Boris who surprised them. They would not marry but merely live in sin. Crochet, it seemed, had a husband but she did not know whether he was alive or dead. He had run off to America.

Toward the end of the week, following glorious New

Year's Day, Kelly received a phone call from Maurice Moody. "I don't know what you did to me at that party, Kelly, you and that goddamn Maison Mordaunt, but I've been hung over all week. A Mickey Finn? I want to know where the hell is my secretary Olga Blastorov?"

"Here."

"Well, when the hell's she coming back? The holiday is over."

"I don't know. I don't know if she'll ever be back."

Moody breathed balefully. "You've sold her into white slavery, you son of a bitch. . . . And where're my goddamn clothes?"

Kelly found Olga alone in the garden. He told her Moody had called. "Olga, that morning, before we came up here. Did you have it off with him?"

She shrugged insolently. "Is it so hateful, Jack? You did not tell me you were having it off with Beatrice de Beaupeau."

"There's a difference, Olga," he said stiffly. "You were talking about being my mistress. What kind of behavior is that?"

"I will still be your mistress even if I marry Maurice Moody."

"You wouldn't marry him! Jesus . . ." He took her arm and led her deeper into the garden. Beatrice was in her office with Crochet and Boris. Perex apparently was still asleep. "Take Perex," he suggested.

She tossed her head defiantly. "Who I marry is my business, if I cannot marry you, the only man who has ever thrilled me so much."

"Faint praise, Olga, faint praise."

At the end of the garden, they reached an evergreen cul-de-sac hidden from the house by row upon row of topiaried bushes and silent fountains.

"You can jazz me right now, if you want to, Jack."

"Olga, stop using those expressions. Listen, what about Rafe?"

"What about him?" she demanded indifferently.

"Do you like him, for Christ's sake?"

"Yes." She laughed derisively. "But he is not as good as you."

"What! I suppose you've had him, here in the château."

"Of course." She pushed close to him. Her fingers went for him.

"Remember, Olga, he's one of my best friends."

"Then you should be pleased for him, since I give better than I get," she said forcefully. "And I will tell you something else. If you return to New York, with *her,* I will follow you there. You won't get away from me."

"Hell, come on, Olga, be sensible."

"Kiss me." He put his mouth to her warm lips, feeling them part. Her hot breath burned across his cheek, cold in the near-zero weather. She pressed against him, her hand still gripping his personage. "Come into the forest, Jack," she pleaded.

"Olga, you have to learn to control yourself."

Her nostrils drew in passionately. "I am a woman, Jack, as you well know. I am desperate."

"You had Rafe."

"That was last night. Today is now."

This explained why Perex was still sleeping it off. She had worn him out. "Olga . . ."

"Yes," she said bitterly, "and how do you think I feel to learn that Hercule is my father? Do you not see that is a *little bit* disappointing, a cruel trick of Fate?"

"Now, Olga, we've already been over that. Hercule is one hell of a guy, and you should be very pleased to have him for a father. He isn't really all that short, you know. And isn't it pleasing to know that you might be Madame Mordaunt's granddaughter?"

Olga frowned fiercely and vented a dirty chuckle. "If so, then there is incest in my family."

"Olga," Kelly protested. "I don't think Hercule has ever slept with her. We don't *know* that."

"So," she said crudely, "I know *I* have." She noted his sudden collapse—of heart, nerves, hope. "Well? I did not know she might be my grandmother, Jack. I am so impatient with you all! She asked me to visit her. You know very well she is *bisexuée.*" She threw the French pronunciation at him; was that supposed to make it all right?

"Olga. Olga . . ." He stared at her. God, where was her salvation?

"She was very kind to me, Jack," Olga said.

She had backed him cleverly into a small enclosure within a stack of fir trees. Now, in his weakness and disillusionment, before he could get away, she expertly unzipped his trousers, reached inside, and dragged him out into the cold. God, it was freezing. Swiftly, she dropped to her knees in the pine needles and put her lips to him, warm, cold, then warm again. Frantically, as if *he* could save her, she tongued him, her cheeks making a vacuum of her mouth. In a thrice, she completed the job. Hating himself, he came with an urgency that was compounded by the sordidness of the act. Blissfully, she swallowed.

"Ah," she said, grinning with accomplishment. "You see!"

"Olga, we shouldn't have done that."

She stood up, smiling coquettishly. "There! It can be done even though you are to be married. If so simple during your engagement, then much easier after the marriage. I have proven this. Now, will you meet me in the wine cellar in an hour or so, for my reward? If you do not, then I will have Villars."

"Olga, Olga." How could he make her see reason? "Olga, you know you can't screw around with the help, particularly here. It's very bad form. Go back up to Perex. He's probably waiting right now."

She shook her head. "He is . . . I don't know. Not so good."

"Premature?"

"Yes, premature ejaculation," she agreed quickly.

Hell, he thought, just as Westerley Washburn had said. They walked separately back to the house.

In the afternoon, after lunch, Perex received a cablegram. He held it worriedly in his hand, then slowly opened it. As he read, his eyes lit up. He pulled Kelly to the side.

"Bloody, hell, my dear, I am saved!" he exclaimed happily. "The deal is off. I don't have to go to La Minge or anywhere in Mangrovia. Maryjane insists she likes it there, although it is very warm and cultural life is threadbare at the elbows. Caramba, Jack, she likes being one of the wives of that foreign minister!"

Sardonically, Kelly said, "Madame Cinnabar Macoo the third. Well, what the hell, she'll be a good hostess for him. That's what I told Ehrlitz. To hell with her."

"Christ, I am home free!" Perex raved. "What a relief, Jack." There were wet patches on his cheeks. He realized Kelly was chuckling. "You think it was humorous, bloody hell, Jack. It was not. And I will tell you. Whatever you assumed, I did not . . . well, to be honest, I did, once. She chased me around my house like a wild woman and finally caught me." He grinned shamefacedly. "But that is past."

"Same as me and Westerley," Kelly murmured.

"Ha! Yes, my friend. Tell me," Perex said, looking surreptitiously into the drawing room, "this Olga. She is an interesting girl."

Harry Kelly arrived with Hercule the following Wednesday. Beatrice, out of respect for Hercule and as a courtesy, had invited Madame Mordaunt to the château for the wedding. But, fortunately, she was too poorly to make the trip. Kelly had briefly considered inviting Victor too, but thought better of it. They would not be needing his woeful presence, and anyway Hercule had insisted that Victor remain in Paris to hold the fort at Maison Mordaunt.

Harry was in better shape, more relaxed and happier, it seemed, than he had been at their last meeting at Charles de Gaulle Airport. When the car pulled up in the drive, Harry and Hercule got out in a jovial state. They had been drinking a little from the bar in the back of the Rolls.

"Jack!"

"Hi."

They embraced on the wide stone steps. For Jack, it was a touching moment. Harry held him by the shoulders and looked at his face. "You're looking pretty good, kiddo."

"And so are you, Dad."

"Feeling a lot better. You know—no, you wouldn't know—I had a slight heart attack just after I got back from Paris. I'm okay now but I've got to take it easy."

Gripping Hercule's hand, his arm around his father, Kelly walked them up the steps. Beatrice was inside the front door with Perex and Olga, and Boris and Celeste Crochet.

"Beatrice, this is my father. Dad, this is Beatrice."

Beatrice smiled graciously and rose on tiptoes to kiss Harry Kelly's cheeks, first right, then left. "Welcome to Château Beaupeau, Mr. Harry Kelly."

"My . . ." Harry stuttered shyly. "I'm . . . pleased to be here. But I want you to call me Harry."

"And I am Beatrice."

Beatrice greeted Hercule next. Hercule performed a half bow and raised her hand the short distance to his lips. Beatrice was not having any of that. She bent to kiss him energetically on both cheeks. He blushed and turned quickly to shake hands with Count Boris.

"And Madame Mordaunt?" Beatrice asked. "She is not well?"

Hercule shook his head, then smiled a little. "She is as well as can be expected under the circumstances," he said slowly.

Harry had evidently heard the whole story in the car. "I understand that was quite a day. Mr. Hercule has been telling me about it—but I didn't see anything in the newspapers."

"Hushed up," Kelly said.

"Naturellement," Hercule said, as if anything else was unthinkable. "However, I can report a morsel of news of which you cannot be aware. Madame has been deep in conversation with the government of Premier Fernand Cachet. It is only through her efforts that Cachet's

coalition has not fallen due to *L'Affaire Aristide de Bis.* Monsieur Cachet is . . . an ancient . . . friend of Madame."

"*Quoi!*" Boris Blastorov exclaimed disgustedly. "Cachet?"

Hercule stared at him severely. "*Mais, oui, Boris, un ami.* Cachet was one of us."

"One of us?" Boris roared. He glanced at Olga. "*Oui. Merde!* One of us, yes, in the forest. Hell!"

Hercule frowned. "Yes, Boris, in the forest, so many years ago. It is time for you to forgive, Boris."

"How could I forgive?" Boris exclaimed.

Hercule shrugged. "The man was young, Boris—many men were enamored of your wife in those trying years."

Tears came to Boris's eyes, but the moment was really Olga's. She shrieked once and fell in Madame Crochet's arms. "Oh, Crochet, *sauvez-moi.*"

"Yes, little one," Crochet murmured, patting Olga's head.

"What ails . . ." Hercule started to say, then his eyes leaped. "Crochet? Crochet!" A smile burst across his face. "*Mon Dieu,* so many years!" He bounced toward her and Crochet gathered the little man in her other arm.

Harry Kelly looked very perplexed. "What gives, Jack?"

Kelly said, "All old friends."

Shamefacedly, Count Boris mumbled, "Many years ago, Hercule saved Celeste's life."

Madame Crochet's expression was happy, yet sorrowful. She hugged both Hercule and Olga to her riding habit.

Harry looked uncomfortable. He did not like emotional displays. "Beatrice," he said awkwardly, turning away from the three former members of the *Maquis,* "this is really a beautiful house. I have a feeling I've been here before. Is that possible?"

"Anything is possible," Beatrice said beatifically. She was still watching the threesome.

"You know," Harry went on, "toward the end of the war, I was attached to the First Division as a correspondent. I think maybe I came through this part of France. This house, yes!'' His eyes clicked delightedly. ''It was used for a few weeks as a command headquarters. I remember a tiny little baby. . . .'' Harry looked closely at Beatrice and slapped his Borsalino against his hand. ''You!''

His exclamation caused Hercule to turn away from Madame Crochet.

''My father was not here in those days,'' Beatrice said. ''He was a prisoner of war in Germany.''

Now Kelly was puzzled. It didn't seem that the chronology fit. According to her memoirs, Beatrice had learned philosophy from her father . . . yet she was a tiny baby at war's end? Had she been so precocious?

Hercule again took Beatrice's hand. ''Yes,'' he said, ''your father was in a prisoner-of-war camp near Munich. For a time, I was there with him.''

''Non!'' Beatrice cried. ''You knew my father! I did not. He died a prisoner in that camp.''

Dieu! Kelly muttered to himself.

''Countess,'' Hercule said with great dignity. ''Your father was a hero. He did not die—he was killed while trying to escape.''

''Oh, my!'' she cried softly, clutching her bosom.

Harry was still gazing at her fondly. ''Beatrice, when I was in this house, I remember a tall and beautiful woman.''

''Oui, ma mère.''

''She was beautiful,'' Harry repeated. ''I believe she was a poetess.''

''She died fifteen years ago.''

''God . . .'' Harry's eyes filmed, ''I'm so sorry to hear that.''

Beatrice dabbed her handkerchief at her face, then pulled herself up bravely. ''Well . . . such are the coincidences. But we are in the present, not the past. Monsieur Hercule, tell us more of Madame Mordaunt.''

Hercule paused thoughtfully, then said, ''In some months, when she is feeling better spiritually and the unfortunate affair de Bis has died away, she will be introduced into the French Academy."

Kelly nodded at Harry. "That's what she wanted. Good news, Hercule! But . . . you say *spiritually?*"

Hercule moved his head bravely. "Yes, she has been seeing a priest." He paused significantly. "Madame has a great new ambition—aside from becoming an *acade-micien,* this is to be prioress of an abbey."

"A nunnery?" Kelly asked incredulously.

Hercule nodded, not noticing Olga's grimace. "Yes, she feels it is time."

"But you? The maison?"

"The Maison Mordaunt will go on, as always," Hercule said simply, "no doubt supplied in the future with creations of the nunnery."

Emotionally, Beatrice cried, "Madame is truly one of the French *greats.*"

Amen, Kelly echoed to himself.

"And the verminous Aristide de Bis?" Boris demanded. "What of him?"

"Disappeared," Hercule said. "And there is no trace of the corpse of Madame de Winter."

At that, Boris recovered most of his good humor. He put his arm around Madame Crochet's slim shoulders. "We will drink to the happiness of our friends and the confusion of our enemies! But, we have no more enemies. Only the Bolshevik swine are left to subdue."

Harry said slowly, "I'll drink to the health of Zouzou Mordaunt. But you know, little friend, I can't picture her in a nunnery. Once they've seen *Paree* . . ."

Hercule smiled faintly. "What you say has merit, Monsieur Harry. And, as you know, Madame is a very whimsical woman. We all, Victor and I and our faithful seamstresses will be loyally waiting. . . ."

Later, when the others had dispersed and Beatrice had diplomatically left them alone, Kelly and his father settled in the library for a quiet drink.

Harry sat squarely, almost a stranger without his

Borsalino tipped back on his head, nursing a scotch and water, not his usual gin martini. He gazed into the fire, shaking his head philosophically, then glanced at his son.

"Good luck, Jack." He held up his drink. "She's beautiful. She looks just like her mother. I have to be honest with you, Jack. For about two months back there in 1945, I was madly in love with her mother."

"I know."

"What do you mean you know? How could you know?"

"It just couldn't have been otherwise."

Harry didn't get the point. "That's what I call one hell of a coincidence," he said, bemused. He shook himself and took a long pull on his drink. "I had lunch, by the way, with a pal of yours—Westerley Washburn."

"How is she?" Jack asked carefully. He was wearied of so many coincidences.

"Seems fine. She's well rid of Topovsky, I'd say. And she's very realistic about that old man of hers, definitely a mark in her favor. She's a good kid. Naturally, she's worried about Washburn—she thinks he's on the edge of a breakdown. I've *always* thought so." Harry chuckled. "She's not going to be so thrilled, though, when she hears about this marriage. Sounded to me like you and her hit it off pretty well."

"She's the ex-Mrs. Perex, you know," Kelly told him.

Harry whistled. "That too? Anyway, Jack, you're lucky to have such a bunch of good friends. . . . Hercule told me about Trout, that little moron. But a hell of a shot, I guess. No problems there?"

"Not that we've heard of. They'd cover it up. Trout got much taken by a Hungarian, an ex-actress named Magda Starbright."

Harry thumped his knee delightedly. "Ain't that a hell of a name? I used to know her a little in the old days."

"Of course," Kelly said.

Again, Harry didn't catch his meaning. "Hercule didn't say so but I hear he might be in for a big job when the new government takes over."

"Hercule? Is he going to run for parliament?"

Harry shrugged. "Maybe. I had a talk with our ambassador, Capone, and he says Hercule is being talked about for minister of defense. . . . If he goes for it, he'll run for the Longchamps seat in the National Assembly. I guess they figure they owe him something—after all, he's responsible for knocking that whole Aristide de Bis plot in the head."

Kelly slowly said, "Some day Hercule will be premier. I know it." Of course he would. He changed the subject. "My ex-wife is in Mangrovia. She's marrying the foreign minister, Cinnabar Macoo. She's having a kid."

"Well," Harry said heavily, "better him than you. You know that Grovival stuff? There's a hell of a stink about it in Washington. The Food and Drug people won't hear about it. It's nothing more than goddamn poison. Nevertheless, the Russians and Chinese are still interested."

"Side effects . . ."

"Yeah, terrific side effects. But my friends at the CIA tell me the Chinese don't care. They've offered to send over an army to build roads in Mangrovia. Hell, they're bigger capitalists than we are."

"Hercule tell you what happened in the Bois?"

Harry laughed heartily. "The fart knocking that squirrel out of the tree? Jack, that's hard to believe."

"Strange things happen."

"None stranger, for sure." Harry smiled to himself. "It appears the Chinese think they can refine Grovival for rocket fuel."

"Well . . . more power to them then."

Harry subsided thoughtfully, staring at the fire. He yawned. "You know, you're going to have to come back to New York. Doctor's orders. I might as well tell you. I'm going to have to have a couple of bypasses." He contemplated the room, then the fire. "You're marrying into all this. I could have myself, maybe, a long time ago, although I was already married, maybe not so happily. Anyway, Jack, I've got to ask you to come back and take over. I figure you're ready now. You've been through the mill here for the last few months and I guess you learned the diff between bullshit and french fries. You passed with pretty much flying colors. How would Beatrice feel about moving to New York?"

Kelly shifted uncomfortably. "She'll come with me. I've got something to tell you, Dad. She's pregnant." Harry's face dropped—that a baby could be conceived out of wedlock disturbed him—then he recovered as the prospect of a grandchild overcame religious doubts. "Dad, don't say anything. She's a little touchy about it. She's religious as hell and she'd just as soon . . ."

"I get you," Harry said. "I won't say a word. Listen, there's nothing wrong with having a religious wife. My mother was very religious and she was the best. She sat around all day playing with her rosary. I won't mention it. I won't even print it in the *RAG*." He laughed heartily and leaned forward. "Congratulations! I'm happy for you, happy for me too." He squeezed Jack's hand. "Don't forget, it keeps the line going. That's very important to the Irish."

"It'll be Franco-Irish."

"Nothing wrong with that," Harry said.

Later that night, when all the guests had been tucked in, Kelly and Beatrice locked themselves in their chambers, again facing each other on the love seat before the fire, hands entwined. They talked softly about going back to New York.

"First thing I'm going to do," Kelly said, "is fire that bastard Frank Court."

"Jackelly, please do not talk like that. Be gentle and forgiving."

"Some things are hard to forgive, Beatrice," he said irritably. "And Moody too."

"That shit," she said.

The prospect of a move to New York did not frighten her now. She had, for one thing, decided to put the château and the vineyards in the charge of Count Boris and Celeste Crochet. "And Olga?" she asked, "what about her?"

"I don't know. She's very thick with Rafe. Do you think Hercule has any suspicion he's her father?"

"If he does"—Beatrice glowered—"then he should speak to her in a fatherly fashion."

. What had she seen? Kelly's heart skipped a beat. But not to worry.

Beatrice continued, "Villars reported to me that Olga Blastorov approached him in the cellars." Ah, Kelly thought, clever Villars to deny all that had happened by reporting the half of it. "Villars told me that Olga Blastorov offered him her body, or failing that, then something else of a sexual nature with which I am not acquainted. . . ."

"What could that be?"

Beatrice was really annoyed by the impudence of Olga to importune one of her servants. "It was called a blow job, Jackelly. What is that, a blow job?"

Kelly winced. Just like Olga. "Oh, that," he said lightly, dissembling, "probably something to do with helping him blow out the candles. Villars must have gotten it wrong." He was going to have to speak to Olga about this.

"You think?" Beatrice asked. "That is not what it sounded to be. *Mais,* you are right, I must be generous. I should not think badly of her."

"No, she's had a big shock."

"Yes, *vraiment,*" Beatrice said. She was a woman of infinite intuition and she had proven it once again. But she did not know everything, he told himself comfortably. He finished his brandy and stood up.

"Let's go to bed, cookie. . . ." They laughed at this reminder of C.T. Trout. Hand in hand in the down-deep bed, curled to each other like spoons and engaging their splendid parts at the crossroads of creation, Kelly felt her muscles lock him into place. Caramba, as Rafe would have said, she had taken him in the grip of the mighty, the lost grip of the Chinese.

*   *   *

Rusty bells, tinny bells tolled in the Château Beaupeau Chapel of the Vine at noon of the appointed day. They were married beneath a gray sky shot through by hazy sun. And it seemed, yes, that all would be very happy. *Vraiment.* That is, truly.

A Novel Without Scruples

a novel by
Barney Leason

☐ 41-596-6   448 pages $3.50

With consummate insight and shameless candor, Barney Leason, author of *The New York Times* bestseller, *Rodeo Drive*, weaves yet another shocking, sensuous tale of money, power, greed and lust in a glamorous milieu rife with

From the seductive shores of the Isle of Capri to the hopscotch bedrooms of Beverly Hills, London and New York, Leason lays bare the lives and loves of the rich and depraved, their sins and shame, their secrets and